THE
LANGUAGE
OF
SPARROWS

THE LANGUAGE OF SPARROWS

OF

a novel

RACHEL PHIFER

David C Cook®

transforming lives together

THE LANGUAGE OF SPARROWS
Published by David C Cook
4050 Lee Vance View
Colorado Springs, CO 80918 U.S.A.

David C Cook Distribution Canada
55 Woodslee Avenue, Paris, Ontario, Canada N3L 3E5

David C Cook U.K., Kingsway Communications
Eastbourne, East Sussex BN23 6NT, England

The graphic circle C logo is a registered trademark of David C Cook.

This story is a work of fiction. Characters and events are the product of the author's
imagination. Any resemblance to any person, living or dead, is coincidental.

All Scripture quotations are taken from THE HOLY BIBLE, NEW
INTERNATIONAL VERSION®, NIV® Copyright © 1973, 1978, 1984,
2011 by Biblica, Inc.™ Used by permission. All rights reserved worldwide.

ISBN 978-0-7814-1048-9
eISBN 978-0-7814-1047-2

The author is represented by and this book is published in association with the
literary agency of WordServe Literary Group, Ltd., www.wordserveliterary.com.

The Team: Nick Lee, Tonya Osterhouse, Karen Athen
Cover Design: Nick Lee
Cover Photos: Shutterstock

Printed in the United States of America

First Edition 2013

1 2 3 4 5 6 7 8 9 10

061813

ACKNOWLEDGEMENTS

Somehow my jumble of notes and roughed-out scenes morphed into a book. I'm well aware that this wouldn't have happened if it weren't for the many friends, family, and experts who worked with me, cheered me on, and prayed for me. Thank you all for offering me your time and skill.

Christine Lindsay, my first-class critique partner and dearest friend, helped shape the story with her keen sense of plot and character, and prayed me through the writing.

Rebecca Middleton, my mother, always believed I'd publish a novel someday. She read through more than one draft with me, and I'm ever grateful for her honest feedback.

My sister, Melanie Miller, read and cheered on my book, as well as double-checked my photography details.

My family endured a few burned dinners and more than a few dust bunnies while I talked to my "imaginary friends." Their patience means the world to me. And as my youngest daughter has enthusiastically waited for the day she could find the book in the library, I've found a new reason to keep writing.

Alice Crider and the WordServe Literary Agency took me on as an unpublished author and supported my book from submission to publication.

The David C Cook team made the publishing process a breeze, and I particularly want to thank editors Tonya Osterhouse and Jean Bloom. Their eye for detail blew me away.

American Christian Fiction Writers mentored me and gave me the tools to write a novel.

My relatives Joyce Bell, Jean Carwile, Elizabeth and Jill Myers, and Kristen Phifer will probably never know how much their encouragement meant to me.

Patricia Abraham kindly acted as a first reader and corrected my Spanish.

Lidiana Burca read an early draft and provided me with a wealth of information on all things Romanian.

Dr. Matt Koepplinger provided me with information on catastrophic hand injuries.

Fr. Cassian Sibley of the Russian Orthodox Church Outside of Russia brainstormed with me on the kinds of things a Romanian Orthodox priest in prison might say (or might not say) and directed me to resources on persecution in communist Romania.

Debbie and Jerry Staton worked with me on flood rescues.

My apologies to all if I still got it wrong.

In addition to those who helped with the book's details, I'd like to thank those who helped me work out its themes. Chris and Karla Carroll and Charles and Leslie Smith of Sienna Family Fellowship influenced my thinking about loving our neighbors as Jesus does. Also, as I wrote *The Language of Sparrows*, I read and reread Pete Greig's *God on Mute: Engaging the Silence of Unanswered Prayer* and Ann Voskamp's *One Thousand Gifts* for their visions of the unexpected ways God brings us healing. These beautiful books influenced both my story and my life.

CHAPTER ONE

April knew she'd find her daughter close to home. That's why she didn't search the streets of Houston when the school called this time. And as expected, she found Sierra sitting in the apartment courtyard with her back against the willow tree. Oblivious to the cars speeding by and the crowded apartments surrounding her, she wrote in a notebook with utter concentration.

It wasn't until Sierra noticed her blocking the light that she glanced up. They looked at each other for what seemed like a long minute before Sierra spoke. "I couldn't stay there, Mom."

As she lifted her face to the sun, it took on a quality that didn't belong on a fifteen-year-old. April lowered herself to Sierra's level, taking a moment to balance on her pumps. "You couldn't stay in school because …?"

Sierra sent her a pleading look.

"Sierra," April insisted.

"It's not like my old school. There aren't any windows in most of my classrooms. It's so dark."

There it was—the best explanation her daughter could offer for skipping school. Again. Sierra, with her knowledge of languages. But she never could seem to find the words she needed most.

As they talked, Sierra's hand kept moving across the notebook in her lap. Writing by touch and not by sight, she guided the pen right and then left, then down. Every now and then she'd stop to hem a section of her strange script in black boxes.

"Baby, you've got to talk to me eventually."

"I *am* talking to you." But Sierra looked into the distance, tracking the movements of a cat, a blur of white that leaped from balcony to balcony. And her pen still moved.

April tried not to hate the symbols on Sierra's page—Hebrew, Greek, an occasional column of hieroglyphs. Pages of archaic languages were absorbing more and more of her time. The girl had filled reams of paper with ancient words since they'd moved.

April sighed. Only on the news did people disappear in an instant. One minute a girl was walking to her bus stop. The next she was gone. Cable stations broadcast the missing child's photo nationwide. Crews searched the woods. Everyone mourned when a child disappeared in a flash.

Not so the slow disappearances. No one called a press conference when Sierra's grades began plummeting, when she dropped each of her friends one by one or refused to make new friends when they moved to Houston. The alarms on the school doors didn't go off when she left in the middle of the day. The policeman at the front entrance didn't even notice her leaving.

Only a computerized phone call alerted April to Sierra's skipping classes at all.

There was no need to make threats or offer encouraging words. April had tried them all since they moved here last January. And Sierra was smart enough to understand the risks of skipping school—the danger of the streets where they lived, the potential failure to graduate, trouble with the police.

Instead of the old standbys, April looked through Sierra's letters until she found a familiar one—a hieroglyph in the shape of an eye. "I see you, baby."

That caught Sierra's attention. She looked directly at April and blinked.

The school might not notice Sierra's disappearing act. Maybe friends were nonexistent. Sometimes it seemed that God Himself had found someone more newsworthy to save. But it was impossible to disappear with a witness.

April underlined the hieroglyph with her index finger. "You are not invisible. I would have seen you walking past me if I'd been at the school. I see you, Sierra. Okay?"

CHAPTER TWO

As soon as she got home from school the next day, Sierra pulled on a pair of capris and a T-shirt and left the apartment. Her feet, following a map all their own, carried her to the bridge.

Rap music throbbed from a nearby car. Behind her lay a ramble of buildings and billboards. She hesitated. If Mom knew she was walking out here alone, she'd be upset. But Mom didn't have to sit in the classrooms with the walls closing in on her.

As soon as she crossed over the bayou into the neighborhood beyond, Sierra began breathing easier. There were little box houses and rows of old oaks screening out the sun. It was just the way a neighborhood should be. But most of all, it was *his* neighborhood.

Five houses down the street, she stopped. Today, the old man crouched by the front porch with a spade in hand. Sierra chewed on her lip, waiting, but he continued moving dirt around with his spade as if she weren't there. Sparrows pecked at scattered birdseed until a squirrel sent them into the trees with a rush of flapping wings.

She eased onto the front walk in his yard, moving closer to the porch, and still he didn't turn.

Her hands grew sweaty. "Hello," she finally managed. Brilliant! She'd had her opening line all picked out, and *hello* had definitely not been part of it.

He looked up then, with a shake of his head. "Hello? Is that all you have to say?" he said in his thick accent. Italian, she'd thought when they'd first spoken, but that wasn't quite right. There was something Slavic in his accent too.

She shook her head and tried again. "This city now doth, like a garment, wear the beauty of the afternoon."

"'This city now doth, like a garment, wear the beauty of the *morning.*' Do you propose to rewrite Wordsworth?"

She stepped onto his lawn, moving close to him now. "It's afternoon now. I don't think Wordsworth would have minded."

Every day, they exchanged quotes as she walked past his house. Once she'd tried to stump him. She'd searched the library to come up with an obscure poem from the Ming Dynasty. It hadn't work. He'd nailed the country and the time period.

He shot a glance at her feet. "Your ankle is bleeding. I have had an infestation of thorns. They are quite sharp."

She looked down, feeling the sting of the scratch for the first time. He went back to digging. Her cue to leave, apparently. They never spoke beyond their quote exchange, but she couldn't leave, not yet. Finally, he patted the soil around a group of flowers arranged by color order and stood with his back to her, slipping off his gardening gloves. He nodded and went inside, leaving the door open. Did he want her to follow him? Nobody left their doors open here, especially in September. They liked to keep the air-conditioning trapped inside.

She could imagine what Mom would say if she found out she'd gone into a stranger's house. But he didn't feel like a stranger. Sierra stepped through the doorway, but he was nowhere in sight. The living room held two chairs on heart-pine floors and one side table.

That was it. There was no TV, no clutter. There were no paintings on the walls. There was a curio cabinet, but unlike her mother's, there were no photos there either. The main thing that stood out about the room was what *wasn't* in it.

He bent his head out of the hallway in the back. Sierra raised her shoulders and acted as if she didn't mind wondering what to do as she crossed the room.

"We were never formally introduced." She imitated what her mother would say and reached out her hand. "Sierra Wright."

He nodded curtly. "Yes, Sierra. Come then." He turned without reaching for her hand and searched through the medicine cabinet in the bathroom. "Ah, there."

He drenched a cotton ball with alcohol and slid out a Band-Aid but didn't hand them to her. Instead he left the room, and she hurried to the sink where he left them, disinfecting the scratch and slapping on the bandage as quickly as she could.

"You know my name now," Sierra insisted, as she followed him back to the front, "but I don't know who you are."

He turned and gave her a long, hard look causing heat to rush into her face.

"I am not my name," he said at last, "but if it is this you ask for, it is Luca Prodan."

She could see his library through a pair of French doors.

That was how they met. She'd seen the books through the window and peeked in. She'd thought the room was empty, but he'd been there, sitting in the armchair, reading a book. He'd looked up at her with eyes as blue as Antarctic ice caps, and she was sure he could see right through her. After that, he was always in his garden when she passed by on her walks. He'd started the quote game.

The library was smaller than it looked from the outside. The whole house probably wasn't any bigger than Sierra's apartment. Still, it was the kind of place that made her want to curl up with a book in hand.

He caught her curious stare and started walking toward the library doors.

"Do you often look into the windows of people whom you do not know?" When she didn't answer, he said, "You do, yes?"

He waited. Sierra shifted.

Speak, she told herself. *You have to speak.*

"I-I have a thing about books. That day I was just walking by, but when I saw your library and then I saw you sitting there reading … I just sort of …"

"You sort of …?"

"I was … I don't know … enchanted." Enchanted. How uncool was that?

The old man gave her a half smile.

"I'm always curious about people and their books, I guess."

"You guess," the old man said. "Or are you sure you are always curious?" His English was as crisp as new paper.

She couldn't believe she was actually carrying on a conversation with him, but she had a desperate hunch that if she kept talking, he would invite her into the library and she could see what he had on his shelves.

"I'm always curious about people, but especially if they have a book. The one I saw you reading was big and looked like a classic. So I thought maybe *David Copperfield* or *Anna Karenina.* But you don't look like a Dickens kind of man."

That smile again. "No? What kind of man do I seem? A Tolstoy one?"

Sierra shook her head. He looked like a grandpa who should be picking tomatoes for salad. But the way he spoke. So demanding and clear. "*The Inferno?*" she tried.

He raised an eyebrow, but at last, he led her into the library and she quickly scanned the room. Books in English, German, and Spanish lined the shelves. Not translations. And then there were two shelves of books in a language she didn't recognize. The letters were accented by tails and loops.

He handed her one of the books—the thick, leather-bound book he'd been reading that day.

She ran her finger along the gold letters on the spine. She'd seen the marks before, but where? "It's not Greek. Or Italian."

"It is Romanian."

"You're from there?"

He studied her before answering, as if analyzing whether she could be trusted with the answer. "Yes, that is where I am from."

A new book. One she knew nothing about. A man with a story. Two stories in one.

"*Inchide Uşa, Într-o Ladă.*" She sounded out the words on the spine. She liked saying them. The sounds rolled and dipped on her tongue.

"You are familiar with Romanian?"

She shook her head.

"But you know that the *S* with a comma below it makes a *sh* sound. Where did you learn this?"

Sierra shrugged. He obviously loved books. He read several languages. But no one ever understood her fascination with alphabets. "I guess I just read it somewhere." She tried to say it casually, as if she'd stumbled upon the information in passing. "What do the words mean?"

"*Behind the Door, Inside a Chest.* It is a book of fairy tales."

When she started to put the book back on the shelf, he gave her a bruising glance. "You do not like fairy tales?"

She shoved a hand into one of her back pockets. Not that it was any of his business, but she wanted something more, something really deep.

"I like stories. The grown-up kind."

"Ah. But to live without the wonder of childhood is distressing. You must believe me, it is not the sort of life one wants to live." He paused. "Take the book. It is a gift."

Sierra looked at the floor. "Thank you."

He placed his hands over hers, pressing the book between her palms. Four scars circled the back of each of his hands, disappeared over the other side and back again, like rough, pink ribbons wrapped around a present. She couldn't keep from staring. She felt odd, hot, as she looked from his wrists down to his fingers.

Sierra pulled away. She wanted to ask, but she didn't want to ask. What had caused those scars? Something more than kitchen burns or shears that had slipped. But he had pity in his eyes, as if he felt sorry for her.

CHAPTER THREE

April parked in front of the string of walk-in shops. If the heavy mahogany doors to the gallery didn't tip her off, the BMWs and Volvos along the street certainly did. This wasn't where the middle class came to shop. She sat in the car, rifling her fingers through her short hair, feathering it, and checked her lipstick in the mirror for the third time.

When she entered the art gallery, a bamboo chime over the door clattered in a vaguely tropical tune. The place was as heavenly as she'd imagined. Angled columns divided the wood floors into geometric sections. Sculptures graced cabinets. Paintings hung on the walls—oils and acrylics on one wall; local landscapes in watercolor on another. And the smell ... wood and cloves and something else.

Money—it was the smell of money.

When her sister had called last week about the store manager job, April almost dropped the phone and her apartment grew a touch brighter. Hillary had found the job through her husband's network of influential friends. But it wasn't just a job. It meant being around art.

If it was one of Wes's friends, it meant a decent wage, too. She tried not to think what a job like this might mean for Sierra. If she thought about it, her desperation would show.

The store seemed empty, so April wandered through the works of art for sale, taking in the ones that caught her eye. A lomg drape of crimson silk drew her to one corner. Chinese characters ran down one side in black stitching, reminding her of Sierra's notebooks filled with foreign scripts.

A cough over her shoulder made her jump. An older woman with iron-gray curls towered over her. Her tailored suit made April doubt her own choice of clothing. True, her blouse was cashmere, but the cuffs of her standby interview outfit had grown slightly frayed over the years.

April tucked her portfolio under her arm and offered the woman her hand. "Ms. Baines? I'm April Wright." When the woman didn't seem to register the name, she added, "Here for the interview?"

The woman glanced at a mahogany clock. April resisted the urge to look. She was on time, a few minutes early even.

April followed Ms. Baines to a back office, where they sat at a cluttered desk, and flashed her brightest smile.

Ms. Baines didn't seem to notice. She inspected April's résumé, her mouth puckered as if she were chewing on something sour. "No college degree, I see."

April's heart dipped. Hadn't Wes told the owner about her background? "I finished my junior year at Rice University, but no degree."

Ms. Baines tapped the résumé. "And except for a couple of clerical jobs over the last two years, you don't have any work experience."

"I'm currently an executive assistant to the company VP." It was a small company, but she had some measure of skill. Surely the woman could see that.

"And no knowledge of art." It wasn't a question.

"No formal study, but it *is* my passion." Her blouse began to cling damply to her back.

Ms. Baines's dark eyes didn't relent. There was no point in prolonging this torture.

She stood. "I'm sorry, Ms. Baines. I thought you knew my background. You have a beautiful gallery. I would love to work here, but it's obvious I'm not what you're looking for."

Ms. Baines rested her chin on her fist and settled into her chair. "Perhaps I wasn't clear enough with your brother-in-law, Mrs. Wright. I told him the job is yours."

"I'm sorry?" April sat back down. She smoothed her skirt. It wasn't Ms. Baines who had been unclear. As her sister well knew, April wouldn't have come for a hand-out job.

A faint smile crept to the woman's lips. "I'll admit I'm not happy about your lack of experience, but Wes assures me you've got the personality for the job. And let me tell you, this job is all personality."

April stared blankly.

As if speaking to someone not quite bright enough to understand, Ms. Baines slowed her words. "The job is yours, Mrs. Wright. Saturday is your first day."

———◆◆◆———

April gripped the steering wheel as she drove home. Wes had told Ms. Baines she had personality. Well, she'd show her personality and then some. The woman wouldn't be sorry she'd hired her.

She exited the freeway toward her apartment, tuning out the weathered apartment complexes and stores with signs in a half dozen languages. When she'd thought about bringing Sierra home to Houston, hoping for life to come back to her daughter's face, she'd latched on to the things she missed most about her hometown: the spindly crepe myrtles bursting into fuchsia and white blossoms during the summer, the bayous crisscrossing under bridges all through the city, and the warm days that stretched far into the fall and began again before spring arrived anywhere else.

Of course, April had idealized it all. She'd needed the bright memories after Gary died. So she hadn't thought about how the air hangs so hot and humid it seemed it needed to be drunk rather than breathed, even into October. The crowded streets of the neighborhood where they now lived hadn't occurred to her either. The Houston of her childhood was spacious and green.

She passed a teenage boy pressed against a squad car. A policeman frisked him. For what? Weapons? Drugs? She pushed the gas pedal a little harder.

Inside the apartment, April checked the answering machine. There was no message from the school today, so she exhaled. Thank goodness for small mercies. She peeked into Sierra's room. It held so little color. Only the lavender quilt and plush kangaroo from Sierra's girlhood gave the room any life.

April had tried to get Sierra involved in a decoration project. They could afford a can of paint and a few knickknacks, but Sierra showed less than zero interest.

God had His eye on the falling sparrow. He carried the lamb in His arms. Hadn't April repeated those words to herself often? But if He saw, why didn't He scoop the little bird into His hand? Didn't it concern Him to see the little bird spiraling toward the ground?

She filled a glass with water, letting her thoughts return to the job at the gallery. Getting the job out of pity irked but to be among fragile, beautiful things again …

And if commission paid as much as she thought it would, it would only be a matter of time before she could afford an apartment in the suburbs, maybe even a small house. With a different environment, Sierra just might return to her.

Sierra's notepad lay on the table and April picked it up. She couldn't help but compare Sierra's notebook with the Chinese silk at the gallery. Someone would pay good money for that silk and decorate their home with it.

On a whim April carried the notepad to the balcony outside and looked at it in the natural light. She'd never thought of the writing as anything but Sierra's way of grieving for her father. It was Gary who'd taught her these languages.

She took a fresh look at the page in front of her. The different symbols—Greek, Hebrew, and several April didn't recognize—were formed in strokes so dark and fluid they danced off the page. Alternating rows flowed left or right depending on the language. Two blocks of pictograms ran top to bottom. The spacing was perfect.

April was no expert on ancient languages, but the page felt like calligraphy.

She tucked a strand of hair behind her ear, looking away and then back at the pad in her hand. Sometimes God allowed the sparrow to fall, but sometimes He gathered the winds under its wings and the little bird flew.

Sierra created this page with only a felt pen and notebook paper. What might she do with the right materials?

CHAPTER FOUR

Sierra found an empty table in the crowded cafeteria. But as soon as she sat down with her tray, Carlos and his friends swooped down next to her. She scooted the other way but couldn't blot out Carlos's wink.

"You don't have to sit so far away, Brown Eyes. We'll make room for you."

Carlos's friends chimed in. "Come on, baby. Move a little closer."

Sierra hid a shiver. They always called her *sweetheart* and whistled as she walked by. But Sierra wasn't pretty or popular. She kept her eyes on her lunch, building an invisible wall around her. She could feel people looking at her and laughing, even from other tables. Of course they were laughing. Everyone liked Carlos's jokes.

He only gave her a minute before he slid through her invisible wall, bringing his tray with him. He hopped sideways on the bench. "Hey, Sierra."

She kept her eyes on her tray and chewed on the rubbery chicken tenders.

The boys whistled and flicked their hands.

Emilio shot her a wolfish grin. "You're cold, *mamá*."

The bell rang and Sierra took a last swallow of juice. She waited for the table to empty so she could leave without Carlos's friends laughing at her. Everyone left but Carlos.

"Leave me alone." She threw the words out in a whisper and wished immediately she could call them back. She'd said something, and he'd repeat it to his friends now. Wherever she went now, they'd be circling her, needling her, seeing if they could get her to say something else.

"Sure, Sierra." Carlos gathered up his tray. He said it quietly, as if he meant it, but his trouble-making smile told her that wasn't the end of it.

She stood to pick up her notebook, but it was gone. There was no sign of it on the table or the floor or anywhere in the almost-empty cafeteria.

As Sierra dumped her tray, a girl named Jazzy breezed by her, looking ahead at Carlos. "You show him, Sierra. That's right, girl. Carlos is too big for his britches anyway."

As the crowds flooded out of the school for the day, Sierra plodded up the stairs to the second floor. She looked into a classroom, wondering why this teacher she didn't even know wanted to speak with her. He had his back turned to her as he flipped through a stack of papers on a shelf.

She coughed. "Mr. Foster? You wanted to see me?"

"Sierra. Come in." He picked up a notebook off his desk. Her notebook. "I found this on Emilio's desk. It's yours?"

He didn't hand it to her when she nodded. Instead, he turned one of the student desks around and, after sitting, pointed her to the desk across from him. When she sat down, he handed her the notebook but slid one piece of paper out, keeping it on his desk.

He leaned back. "Sierra Wright, you've been holding back on us."

She looked at the haikus she'd written for English.

"Is that how you were supposed to do the assignment?" he asked.

"I did it right." Her voice came out too mousy. She lifted her chin. "Ten haikus. Five syllables, seven syllables, five syllables."

He leaned in a little closer as if he didn't believe her. "Are you sure?"

She nodded and cast him a quick glance.

"You may be quiet, but you're sure of yourself. I like that."

She looked away.

"I'll be honest with you. These poems are terrific. It's a good bet Mrs. Velasco didn't get another set as good. Only one thing kept you from getting an A on them."

She chained her gaze to the desk.

"Right, Sierra?"

Why was he doing this? Just because he'd found her notebook? He wasn't her teacher.

"What was your grade for this?"

Sierra looked at the wall, imagining a window and a sky outside, imagining she could fly away.

"Look at me, Sierra."

She didn't. The silence lasted so long it seemed alive. She opened her palm, as if the quiet might settle in her hand.

Finally, in a soft voice, he said, "You can't get an A for work you don't turn in. I'm sorry if I'm getting personal. But C's and D's, Sierra? A quick glance through that notebook told me you're capable of making A's in the advanced classes. At the very least."

She closed her palm.

"Look at me."

He waited until she had to look up.

"I've seen you in the halls and crossing the street on your way home. I know you were new here last semester, but I haven't seen you speak to anyone yet. Now I can see you're angry with me. What I'm wondering is whether you'll tell me off."

She started to stand up. She didn't have to put up with this. But he began to read her first haiku aloud.

"White egrets rising, from still waters at sunrise, stretching wings for flight."

Her words sounded strange in his bass voice, fluid. She could hear the rustle of wings and the splash of the creek. She looked at her backpack but didn't pick it up.

"That was good," he said. "But I think you can do even better. Write ten more haikus. Write your heart out, Sierra, and you'll have an A. If you turn them in."

"You're not my teacher." She hated that her voice shook.

"Mrs. V. and I are friends. You have my word. She'll give you an A."

When she didn't answer, he went on. "You have a choice, Sierra," he said. "One choice will build your life up; another will tear it down. You're a smart girl, and I think you're going to make the right choice."

What right did he have to talk to her like that? She grabbed her paper and walked out.

Sierra sat on the stairs outside her apartment, crumpled in a heap, balling up the poems in her fist. She didn't want to write her heart out. She didn't want anyone even looking at the first poems, much less another set. But she knew deep-down solid in her bones if she didn't do it, he'd be looking at her all over again, calling her name and demanding to know why. Maybe even in front of other students.

She pulled the paper onto her knee and smoothed it flat. The poems made pictures. They were nice. That's what haikus were: nice. No one wrote their heart out in seventeen syllables.

A neighbor walked by the rusted playground. *"Buenas tardes,"* he called out.

"¿Es un día caluroso para dar un paseo, no crees?" Sierra smiled across the way at him.

The man waved in the air, answering in rapid Spanish as he passed.

A voice below interrupted the conversation. "The old guy says you should see the heat where he's from. This is nothing. But hey, you probably already knew that. Your Spanish is good."

Sierra froze. Carlos stood at the security gate of the apartment complex. What was he doing here? When he punched in the code and walked through the gate as if he lived here, Sierra stood and hurried back into her apartment, shutting the door behind her. She closed the curtains and slid down against the wall, her eyes shut tight. She could hear him talking. She couldn't hear what he said, only the rumble of his voice as he laughed with someone in the courtyard.

———◆◆◆◆◆———

She didn't turn new haikus in to Ms. Velasco. She was still look-ing for heart to put into the poems, she supposed. She slunk through the halls and tried to look invisible until the weekend. It didn't work. She saw Mr. Foster everywhere—on the second floor, on the stairs, at the crossing after school. He always called out a greeting to her, but he didn't ask about the haikus. Not yet, but he would.

Saturday she picked up the beaten page of haikus and walked to Mr. Prodan's.

He wasn't outside this time, and she didn't see him through the library window. She gave a hesitant knock. She would have taken him for a morning person, but when he answered the door, his clothes were rumpled and his hair looked like he'd been sleeping.

He blinked at her as if he didn't recognize her at first. "Ah, Miss Wright," he finally said. "Come in."

"I haven't come at a bad time?"

"No, no," he mumbled, leading her into the library. But there were circles beneath his eyes, and Sierra felt stupid for coming. As he slumped into one of the chairs, she noticed how European he looked—the frizzy, mussed hair; the heavy-lidded eyes and pursed lips.

"You are reading the book I gave you?"

She looked down. "Um, I read a few of the pages. I could make out some of the words."

He slapped himself on the forehead. "Ah. I gave you the book in Romanian!"

Sierra grinned. He was an absent-minded professor. "I like it though," she insisted. "I like looking at all the accents and loops. I wish I knew what the words meant."

"But you must read it in English, of course." He raised himself to pull a paperback from the shelf. The cover had gold lettering and had a picture of a wood trunk, viewed through a window. "You must keep them both." He gave the book to her and flexed his hands as he returned to his chair.

"And you have brought something for me this time?" He nodded at her page of haikus.

She handed it over, and he sat down with it, smoothing it in his lap, taking his time. Sierra rubbed her hands along the arms of the chair. Mr. Foster had said the poems were good, but as Mr. Prodan scanned the ten haikus, she knew they weren't.

"A teacher at school said I didn't put my heart into them."

He sighed. "You are fortunate to have such a teacher." He gazed at her in silence, the paper poised in his hands. "Your teacher is right. I suspect these poems are not worthy of you."

His words fell like heavy weights, and Sierra slouched in her chair. Somehow his opinion mattered, and she had foolishly hoped he would tell her they were good.

"This will not do." He gestured wildly at her. "You hide yourself. You make yourself small and cover your face with your hair, yes? But if you have any heart to give, it is yourself. And you have not shown Sierra Wright in these poems."

Her face grew hot. "How is a haiku supposed to show myself? Haikus are supposed to be about nature, not me."

He stood and paced in front of her. "You do not need to imitate Basho, the great Japanese poet. What does Sierra Wright notice on the street that I do not? What brings her joy? What brings her sorrow? That will be a haiku of your heart."

Sierra slumped more. The scene with the egrets *had* been important to her.

"You are angry with me, no?" Mr. Prodan said.

Sierra shook her head. She felt sudden, crazy tears about to fall, and that made her angry.

"It is good to be angry. There is passion in anger." He waved the page at her. "There is no passion in this. No self."

"I saw those egrets with my father!" Sierra heard the rise in her own voice and stopped.

"This time with your father was important?"

"One spring, he took me for walks along the creek by our house, just after sunrise. In the summer he went to Italy for a conference and he—he didn't come home. He died over there. He was just—just gone." Her tears began to fall, and Sierra furiously swiped at them.

He bowed his head, quiet. She was glad he didn't speak. There wasn't anything to say.

Finally, he clucked his tongue and said, "That would be a poem with heart, but it is not here." He tapped the page. "I do not see a father and daughter. I do not see grief. I see only nameless egrets."

"I'm supposed to write all of that in seventeen syllables?" Sierra sniffed.

"In seventeen syllables if you like, yes." Mr. Prodan stood. "I have not had my breakfast. Do you wish for a true Romanian breakfast?"

He led her to his backyard, where they sat in patio chairs. They drank black-as-night Turkish coffee and ate jam-filled crepes that tasted like butter and homegrown strawberries.

"Were you a professor in Romania, Mr. Prodan?"

He looked out at the trees. "When I was a young man, I taught mathematics at a gymnasium. What you in America call high school. But for many years, the only people I spoke with were my colleagues in prison, and it was not maths we talked of. When I returned to society, my desire for teaching had vanished, and I worked in a bakery in Bucharest." He moved his fingers away from him in a cutting motion.

Prison? But he didn't give her the chance to ask any more questions. He stood, dumping the coffee grounds onto the vegetable garden that sloped away from the back door.

What she really wanted to know was if it was in prison his hands had been scarred. She wanted to know because she could see the memory—whatever it was—in the iciness of his eyes. But here he was standing in the sunlight with her.

They looked away from each other. She couldn't ask about his story yet. She knew it was a story she would have to earn the right to hear. If she became his friend, if she came for more visits like this one, in time he might trust her enough to tell her how his hands had been damaged and how he had come to live in this house only a few blocks from her apartment.

CHAPTER FIVE

As the days passed, April fell into the routine of her new position. One Monday, she found the gallery's clean light shining down on a man in an Armani shirt and Italian shoes. With his arms crossed, he considered a floor-to-ceiling arrangement of African masks in polished ebony. April had seen similar work, but never anything this size.

He turned to her. "It's dramatic. I'll give it that."

She gave him her most winsome smile. "It *is* bold, isn't it?"

A subtle exchange of words was all it was. Boldness for drama, but the difference would mean something to this man whose demeanor spoke of money and position. She took him on a tour of the boutique, all the while asking him about himself. By the time they were done, he was imagining parties at his house with people gathered around the piece hanging in his two-story entryway, admiring his genius.

He held his hands out in surrender. "You've sold me. Where do I sign?"

After he left, April paced the boutique, the idea forming itself in her mind. There was so much space in the gallery, and so many of the items on display were big. Boldness sold well. The glazed vase that reached her waist, the Irish drum that took up its own wall, the life-sized painting of a woman sprawled in her sleep—they all said, "Notice me."

April made one stop on the way home. She arrived at the apartment with sacks of supplies and a plan. Inside, she practically skipped to Sierra's door but found only an empty room. Standing at the door, she stared at the perfectly made bed. She'd counted on getting started this afternoon. Sierra knew all too well that she couldn't wander around this neighborhood, but it was early yet. April wouldn't start worrying.

In the dining area she pushed the table into a corner and laid ceramic tiles across the floor. Putting them in order, she imagined them on the wall in a staggered arrangement of creams and Mexican reds and oranges.

When Sierra came in, she was rosy-faced with exertion. She looked bright and active, so like an ordinary teenager that April didn't have the heart to criticize her for not coming straight home from school.

"Hi, beautiful." April waved at the ceramics on the floor. "I've got a project for us." Sierra held back, eyeing the tiles.

April relayed how the Chinese silk had given her the idea. "If you can decorate your house with Chinese characters, why not Greek and Hebrew? You've got the know-how."

Sierra leaned against the door. "I don't know anything about painting."

April held up one of the blocks. "But you know how to form the letters. Think of it as an experiment."

Sierra's eyes narrowed. "Sure."

She passed April and went into her room. She'd be back. The project was too good for her to ignore.

In a minute, Sierra came and sat on the couch. She slung her arm over the back and inspected the squares.

April placed one of them against the wall. "I was thinking maybe a Bible verse. Rather than the running down feel of the Chinese characters, we'd have the Greek script running right and the Hebrew script running left. It would give the wall a feel of motion."

Sierra's eyes flickered with interest.

"What verse would you pick if you were going to do it?" April wanted Sierra to envision herself doing this.

Sierra closed her eyes. It only took a second. "'Deep calls to deep in the roar of your waterfalls; all your waves and breakers have swept over me.'" She looked so peaceful as she quoted the words. "Psalm 42," she said, opening her eyes.

April held her breath a few seconds too long. She'd thought "The Lord is my Shepherd" or even "God said 'Let there be light.'" Of course it would be something more original with Sierra. April didn't remember hearing that verse before. It sounded too much like the words of a drowning man, maybe even a man who *wanted* to drown. She gazed at the blank wall, imagining it covered in calligraphy. If those verses got Sierra into the project, she'd cover every wall in Sierra's psalm.

"All right," April said, a little too brightly. "Let's get to work then."

All evening, April mixed paints and cleaned brushes as Sierra hunched over the tiles, moving brushes in meticulous strokes. The rounded strokes of Hebrew and the angular strokes of Greek filled the arrangement. When Sierra finished each square, April added a decorative flourish as a border.

"You're a natural."

Sierra didn't respond, but her eyes shone all the same. Writing columns of Hebrew and Greek on a notepad was one thing, but seeing her words painted across the tiles must be another. This was art.

April brought in the toolbox. "Here, you want to help me with a hammer and the nails?"

When they were done pounding in the nails, Sierra stretched her back, obviously stiff. April picked up the first tile. "You can relax, honey. I'll hang them up."

She hung the tiles, leaving only one gap in the center where she planned on painting a centerpiece on the largest tile. Something with loose modern lines to accentuate the theme of the verse. That would have to wait until another day, though. It was late.

When she was done hanging the pieces, she looked back at Sierra, whose face had gone too still. April pulled back to the couch to see the wall through Sierra's eyes. The letters slanted so that the Greek flowed right and the Hebrew flowed left in a stream. The lines floated away from each other, which gave the wall a modern-art look. The trim added an effect. She didn't understand why Sierra was looking at the tiles that way. Once April added in the centerpiece, it would be gorgeous.

"Sweetie?"

"I can't look at that." And with no explanation, Sierra left and locked herself in her room.

April sank onto the couch, looking at the letters like a code she could break, a code to her daughter's heart. As she leaned back, taking in the wall, her newfound hope withered. Gary loomed out of the letters. Hebrew and Greek, art and poetry, love of God and a psalm of despair—his legacy filled the room.

She had a sudden urge to tear the thing down. Instead, April went into the hall, touching her fingers to Sierra's closed door. April prayed a meek little blessing through the white wood, something quiet enough for only God to hear. *Bless my little girl, heart and soul and mind.*

———◆◆◆◆◆———

Friday afternoon, April stood, taking in their masterpiece. The thing April liked least about her job was the varied hours. The commissions were too promising to turn down, but it bothered her leaving Sierra alone on Saturdays and, too often, past supper on weekdays, especially in this neighborhood.

She wondered what to do about the tiles. Should she take them down before Sierra got home from school? They added color and life to the apartment in a way she hadn't thought possible. She couldn't tear them down. It wasn't just Gary's legacy on the wall; it was Sierra's. April wanted her daughter to see her own passion and skill, large and beautiful, staring out at her every day.

The truth was, the tiles brought out something long forgotten in April, too. A sudden yearning took April to her boxes, packed away in the closet. Gary had given her a camera the year before he died. It was a peace offering, an apology, many things, but never a real invitation to use the thing, and so the camera had ended up in the box.

She found the Nikon buried under a package of unopened art pencils and scrapbook pages still in their plastic sheaths. It was a box of might-have-beens. She sat up straight, pulling the box into her lap, refusing the dark thought. It could be a box of yet-to-bes.

After slipping new batteries in, she carried the camera outside. The sun was too bright to capture anything today. Everything would look yellow and washed out even with massive photoshopping. Still, she zoomed around, focusing on this and that. The weeping willow poured its branches into the center of the courtyard. A napping cat lay under the steps. The old April came to life, a flutter of excitement making itself known in her hands.

She switched angles. Ricky Salinas, the owner of their complex, lifted his eyes as he strode to the office and waved at her. Behind him, a little boy swung on the swing set. Her camera froze on the boy in the screen, on his grubby little face.

The boy couldn't be older than five, but already he had a hard set to his mouth. His eyes were wide, not in wonder, but with wariness. His mother pushed the swing, but her face was guarded, too, as if she were waiting for the next blow. It was images like these that had caused her to pack her camera away.

April lowered the camera, looking at its black lines.

She'd first met Gary with a camera in her hands. Her camera had met his gray eyes, deep as the sea, and she'd thought, *As if everywhere he looks there's a mystery to be plumbed.*

She'd kept shooting a record of their life—Gary working at his desk, Gary holding their baby daughter, Gary asleep. She recorded him, because it's who she was and what she did. The camera didn't miss a thing. Not the hollows under his eyes or the growing hollowness within them.

In real life you could tune things out. The lens, though, found the true story, like it or not.

One day she'd knelt to capture his hand scribbling notes madly on a writing pad—an artistic image, she'd thought at the time. It had been the last straw. Gary knocked the camera out of her hands. Then he stared at the camera lying on the floor, his eyes big and remorseful.

With his eyes still on the camera, he said, "Just how much of my pitiful life do you need for your albums?"

The lens had been cracked, but he was right. It was about that time the same hollows appeared under Sierra's eyes. She was a few months shy of twelve then. So April gave the camera away and never looked back, not even when Gary replaced it with a camera that cost a month's salary.

April pointed the camera up, capturing a white-hot sky. She pointed it down and found the weeping willow. Despite its sad name, it was a beautiful tree, providing shade with its long drooping branches. She focused, clicked, and went back inside.

Pausing at the box, she considered, but finally tucked the camera back inside. A tightness coiled itself in her chest and she took a deep breath. The last few days had been entirely too bleak since her art project had gone awry. It was possible for a little bit of disappointment to build into despair and then into something too big to fight. April was an expert on the process, and because of Gary, also an expert in living positively. The first rule of living in the light was to spend time in the light. And the next was that if you wanted to be a person with energy, you had to act as if you already had it.

In minutes she was dressed for a run and driving to the park. But even on the verge of October, it was still too hot for anything but a lazy jog. The shade from the huge oaks gave cool, green light though.

Pace by pace, her chest lightened and the day moved back into the good column. There was a whole life full of yet-to-bes. She was already thinking of new ways to live large and bright. For Sierra and for herself.

Chapter Six

On the way home from school, Carlos pulled into step beside her. "Hey Sierra with the brown eyes."

Why was he always calling her that? Brown eyes were nothing special.

"I've got some things to do at your place today. Maybe we could walk there together."

Sierra nodded and kept moving.

"You're gonna say something to me one of these days." He flashed her a smile that said he was used to getting what he wanted.

She sped up her steps, but he matched her stride easily.

"No, really," he said. "You'll talk to me. And hey, maybe you'll even smile at me like you smiled for that old guy."

They crossed the street and Sierra headed down the sidewalk. She wouldn't blurt something out this time. Anything she said would only double his effort.

When they entered the courtyard, she made a straight line to her apartment, but he kept pace with her. She clung to the railing, and he started up the steps with her.

She stopped. "Bye, Carlos."

"I'm a gentleman, you know. I always walk a lady to her door."

"Not necessary."

"Sure it is." He kept by her side until they were at her door.

"Bye," Sierra said again, with more force this time.

"I could come in for a while."

"I don't think so. My mom's at work." She studied her fingernails. He winced. He actually looked hurt for a few seconds. Who knew? Maybe he was. It couldn't be easy taking rejection from a bottom-feeder like her, even for a bet with his friends.

"Some other time then."

All afternoon, Sierra sat in her room with a pen raised over her paper. *"Write your heart out,"* Mr. Foster said. *"Put Sierra Wright into these poems,"* Mr. Prodan said. There were no words that could live up to the requirement they'd given her. She shoved the paper aside.

When the afternoon began to dim, she couldn't stand it anymore and began walking down the steps, out the gate. Once Sierra turned into his neighborhood, with its quiet houses and clean sidewalks, it seemed safer than ever, much safer than her run-down street covered in gang graffiti. The trees took the edge off the heat of the day. She knew Mom wouldn't like her walking past their street, and she knew what she would say about visiting a man who'd spent time in prison, but Mr. Prodan wasn't a criminal.

Romanian prisons hadn't been like American prisons. Sierra knew a thing or two about Eastern Europe from her books. Secret police spied on regular people. The communists didn't arrest people for murdering and stealing but for being brave enough to speak about their ideas. And Mr. Prodan had lots of ideas.

As she turned the corner onto the street, Sierra came to a halt. A pickup truck sat in Mr. Prodan's driveway, and a man stood at his door.

She stood still, debating with herself. Under the shade of the old oaks, Mr. Prodan's grass was trim and neat. The man was probably only selling something. She began walking again, taking steps slow as creek mud. Mr. Prodan came to the door, his hands folded in front of him. The man handed Mr. Prodan a small package. They nodded, and then the younger one turned back to his truck.

Mr. Foster? What was he doing at Mr. Prodan's? It was odd, really odd. Mr. Foster backed out of the drive and drove by her. He slowed his truck and looked straight at her as he passed, then kept his truck idling at the stop sign. Sierra took a long steadying breath and shoved her hands into her pockets.

Mr. Prodan was about to step back into his house, but when he saw her, he came out to meet her. "My student has been writing haikus?"

She shook her head.

"Mr. Prodan," she said, trailing behind as he turned back into the house. "Why was that man at your door?" She nodded her head in the direction of the street outside.

He stopped with his back to her, just outside the library. "It is not important."

"Well, I guess it's none of my business."

"That is correct."

"It's only I know Mr. Foster, and I wondered. It was kind of weird, both of you helping me with the haikus. That's all."

Mr. Prodan turned to face her. "Haikus? What has the man you saw to do with your haikus?"

"Mr. Foster's the teacher who told me I needed to put my heart into the poems."

"Ah," he said. He blinked. He balled up his hands and then turned pale. She could actually see the color fade from his face.

She sat down next to the bookshelf and waited. The silence echoed. Finally, she said, "Is there something wrong, Mr. Prodan?"

"I'm sure he is a fine teacher. He is my son." His voice was way too quiet.

Sierra went cold. She didn't know why. Mr. Prodan was *her* special friend. There was nothing so terrible about Mr. Prodan having a son, but she didn't like her two worlds colliding. Maybe that was all.

She looked at Mr. Prodan, who would not meet her eyes. She rubbed her hands on her jeans.

No, it was more than her two worlds meeting. His skin going all white, his glance turning away from her—it was just bizarre.

She waited for an explanation, but he said nothing else. At last Sierra said a quiet good-bye. "I'll see you soon, Mr. Prodan."

He waved her out the door, as if he were shooing her out. What else was there to do but go home?

Days passed. Mr. Foster didn't ask Sierra about her poems. Not only that, but when she saw him in the hall, he turned back into his classroom. Sierra trudged down the stairs outside his classroom, feeling the emptiness inside her widen into a gulf.

Thursday night she had just drifted to sleep when she woke with a start. She should have thought of it long before. She sat up and rubbed her eyes, looking at the yellow light that seeped through the curtains. The room seemed all wrong in the jaundiced light. Everything seemed wrong. How could Mr. Foster be Luca Prodan's son? He didn't have Mr. Prodan's name. He wasn't even Romanian.

She hardly slept that night. She had crazy dreams about Mr. Foster being a KGB agent and Mr. Prodan being marched through a frozen wilderness with a group of prisoners. She would wake up and nod off, only to have a new thought charge through her. Why wouldn't a son use his father's name? And what kind of father didn't want to talk about his own son?

CHAPTER SEVEN

April's sister cajoled until April agreed to come over on her day off. She did owe Hillary a thank-you, after all. The job at the gallery was entirely her sister's doing.

Hill insisted it was a mom's day out. *A day out from what?* April wondered. Hillary's sons went to a private school; she had maid service and only worked two days a week as a counselor. Wes kept her sister in style deep in the wooded suburbs north of Houston.

They sat on the patio, eating Cobb salad and drinking iced tea. The steady rhythm of her sister's waterfall cascading into a rock pool made for nice background music, but as the conversation drifted, April couldn't escape a sinking feeling that her sister had invited her here for a life-fix from Dr. Hillary.

"About that apartment, April …"

The old Dupree stubbornness crept up April's spine.

"Sierra needs a better environment. Wes and I agree on that," Hill said.

Of course Wes agreed. Twenty years of marriage had taught him nothing if not to agree with everything Hill said.

April took a sip of tea. "It's not forever. Sierra needs to know that when life doesn't go as planned, you keep going. You keep going on your own two feet, and life gets better."

"Look, I've found a little house for rent a few miles from here. We'll foot the bill until you can manage. And with Sierra's IQ, she could get a scholarship to any private school in the area. I've already got a place reserved at the school my boys attend."

The offer was oh-so-tempting. A house, a yard, good schools. But Hillary was an expert at arranging other people's lives. April was grateful for the job, but she wouldn't be any more beholden to Hill. Not to mention that moving close meant Hill would pop in anytime she felt like it, trying to tweak every detail in Sierra's day.

April shoved her salad aside. "Hill, it's going to take more than a change in economic status to get Sierra back on track."

Her sister gave her the Hillary stare. "Sierra can't get better in that ghetto. Let us help."

April looked at Hillary, silent, then away at the waterfall as comprehension lit her sister's face.

"Oh my." Hillary drew the words to a breathless length and widened her eyes in exaggerated horror. "April Dupree Wright! You still haven't told her about Gary."

April had lived several states away until Gary died. Her sister had only caught glimpses of the happy, inquisitive girl Sierra used to be. She had no idea what it was like to watch the life drain from her own child's face.

Her sister leaned forward. "What did you tell her? 'Honey, Daddy went to Italy and the conference went a little long?'" She began counting on her fingers. "Let's see, it's lasted over two years now, right?"

Sometimes April wondered how her sister could conduct therapy with such a blistering personality. As Hillary was only too aware, Sierra knew her father had passed away. She just didn't have the whole story.

Hillary gave a dramatic sigh. "She's going to find out, and if you're not the one to tell her, it isn't going to be pretty. Trust me and my professional experience on this."

April cocked her head. "What I hear you saying is you're uncomfortable with my parenting style."

April's therapist jokes never amused Hillary. She flashed pity April's way as she stood to refill their glasses. "Well, April, you might as well cover your ears so you don't hear the time bomb ticking."

"Hill, the bomb's already gone off. Sierra can't cope now. If I tell her—"

"If you tell her Gary committed suicide, you think she'll follow him," Hillary finished for her.

Suicide. The word sliced through her. April didn't think she would ever get used to hearing it thrown around in a sentence.

Hillary softened her voice. "You tell her you're going to pull through together. She'll believe you. No one can motivate people the way you do."

April coughed on a bitter laugh.

If only she had talked to Sierra when Gary died. But after the first few words about Gary getting run over, Sierra fell into such a cataclysm of grief—hysterical sobs, closing herself in her room, refusing to talk to anyone. It had felt best to wait a few days, maybe even a few weeks, until she was stronger, to explain that he'd intentionally walked into oncoming traffic. But Sierra never did grow stronger.

Hillary answered the unspoken words. "Sierra's not her dad. She's bewildered and scared, but she's strong."

But that's what terrified April. Sierra *was* so much like Gary. Was she strong too?

As April let herself into her apartment, Ricky Salinas called up to her. "Hey, pretty lady."

He supervised a couple of teenage boys in the parking lot as they carted bags of lawn fertilizer from a truck. She waved and smiled.

"Hold up," he called. "I've got something to tell you." He left the boys and jogged up the stairs to meet her. "It's not good. I live in the neighborhood." He waved his hand in the direction of the bayou. "And I have friends a few streets over. One of them saw Sierra going into an old guy's house. She doesn't have a grandpa over there, does she?"

The hair on April's arms stood on end. "In someone's house? You're sure?"

April found it hard to believe Sierra would be brave enough to *speak* to a stranger, let alone go into his house.

He nodded. "Yeah, not a guy many of the neighbors like either. Mrs. Cisneros, she's got two teenage girls. So she said she didn't like girls entering a stranger's house, especially a weird old man like this guy. She walked right over there and told him he ought to send her away. And he said to her, 'I don't believe this is your concern.'" Ricky put on his best la-di-da accent for the man's words.

April stared bleakly into the sky. Sierra knew better. So much better.

Ricky leaned his hand against the brick wall. "I thought you should know. Especially since Mrs. Cisneros is talking about maybe calling Child Services."

April swung her head up. The air was suddenly suffocating.

"You all right?"

"Yes," she said weakly. "Thanks for telling me, Ricky. I needed to know that."

Only the hum of the air conditioner greeted her inside. She checked in Sierra's room.

It was empty. Again. She went back outside to ask Ricky where this man's house was, but he was nowhere in sight. She started to ask one of the boys where he'd gone but then saw Ricky's truck pulling out of the complex.

She paced and waited, waited and paced. Sierra didn't come home. April's skin crawled at the thought of Sierra in a strange man's house. Surely it was all a mistake.

She was about to pick up the phone to page Ricky when the front door opened.

Her daughter had color in her cheeks and a glint in her eyes. April held on to the back of the couch, taking in her little girl's appearance. With Sierra's dark eyes and ivory skin, she was stunning, at least when she didn't hide behind that veil of hair.

"Been for a walk?" April tried to say it without accusation.

The light faded from Sierra's face. "Mom," she started, but didn't say anything else.

"And a visit?" April asked quietly.

Sierra cringed but didn't deny it.

April smoothed Sierra's hair behind her ear. "A stranger's house, baby?"

Sierra's eyes glazed, and she found a spot on the sofa to stare at.

Ricky was right. Her daughter had gone into a stranger's house. April would like to believe the man wasn't dangerous. But he'd done nothing to earn her trust. Nor his neighbors', apparently.

April's mouth went dry at the thought of what might have happened. "Don't go to his house again. I love you too much. Okay?"

Sierra shook her head, backing away. "He's not like that."

"Maybe not." Despite herself, her voice rose a notch. "But we have no way of knowing. He's a stranger. Promise me, Sierra."

Sierra looked at her in disbelief. "Mom!"

When April didn't give in, Sierra stormed to her room. April sank onto the couch, resting her face in her hands. The distance between them was growing into a yawning gap. Letting Wes foot the bill was starting to sound like a life buoy. Even if it did mean putting herself and Sierra under Hill's iron will.

Sunday afternoon, April looked out her bedroom window. Sierra casually walked down the stairs. April made it outside before Sierra could take another step.

"Where are you off to, sweetheart?" She said it with all the nonchalance she could muster.

Sierra turned a pinched face up to her. "I have to see him, Mom."

"Why?" April walked down the steps to meet her, searching for her best listening voice. "What is it about this man?"

Sierra shook her head, her hands outstretched in front of her. "I just do."

"I need more, Sierra. I don't know him."

"He's real, Mom. And deep."

April looked off at the drooping branches of the willow tree. "He sounds intriguing. Maybe we can arrange a meeting. But you can't go into his house alone. I will not allow it!" A shiver ran down her back. She sounded like her own mother.

Sierra drew back as if she'd been slapped, but in an instant, her face cleared of all emotion. She stood so placid, so regal, she might have been Queen Nefertiti. Sierra turned back up the steps, closing the apartment door behind her with far more gentleness than required.

Just like that, she was gone before the conversation had even started. There was no mother-daughter talk. Not even a teenage storm.

Things were stiff and stilted between them the rest of the day, and when she went to bed that night, April slept restlessly in thirty-minute snatches, her mind whirling the whole time. Her alarm clock seemed to mock her—12:37 a.m., 1:05 a.m., 1:24 a.m. Finally, she fell into a sleep of wild dreams.

When she woke, it was to the echo of a scream. She sat up, burying her face in the tangled sheets. She looked around for a few seconds, afraid the scream had been real. But it was only him. His scream, threading around her and choking her.

Slowing her breathing, she looked around, through the dark, hoping she hadn't cried out. Gary was always there, in her dreams, in her unspoken thoughts, chiding her, as he never had in life. If she'd kept trying, kept believing, he might have made it one more day and then another, until they found help.

It was a pervasive thought—what she could have done, might have done, for Gary. Major depressive disorder, the doctors labeled his condition. But even they admitted that the severity of his depression left them bewildered.

April believed in him for a long time. She stayed by Gary's side during all the therapists and clinics and prescriptions. She created a positive environment for him. The one thing she never did was admit the truth, not once in fourteen years. It seemed too harsh to suggest that he might not ever get better. She wondered now if keeping a picture of a recovered and fully functional Gary alive had only been one more impossible burden for him to bear.

In the emptiness, April's Bible called out to her. Stress used to send her flying to the book. She'd prayed. Oh, how she had prayed and sought the God of mercy through its pages.

She rested her head on her knees. Now she worried one more prayer, one more scripture, one more broken dream would crush her completely.

"When God feels farthest away, that's when He's closest." Gary's friend, Joe, had told her that after Gary had his first breakdown. She'd considered his counsel words of wisdom at the time, and over the years she repeated them to herself, an unchanging refrain.

But tonight, looking at the Bible on her bedside table, she felt a lightning bolt was surely contained in its pages, that if she were brazen enough to open it, God would strike out at her as He had at the children of Israel when they spurned Him in some idol-worshipping way.

She reached out to the Bible, smoothing its leather cover, but she didn't open its pages. Instead she sat in the chair near the window until the sky lightened to pink.

In the morning, Sierra ate her cereal in grim silence. April opened her mouth to speak several times, but what could she say? The answer was still no. So she only opened the kitchen curtains to let the morning light in and turned on some quiet music.

Sierra slung on her backpack. April wanted to run to her, hug her, give her a smile for her to hold on to for the rest of the day. But she could see a hug would be rebuffed, so she only called, "I love you."

She might as well have said it to an empty room.

An hour later, as she was getting ready for work, the phone rang.

An authoritative-sounding woman's voice came over the line. "Ms. Wright, this is the tenth-grade counselor at Armstrong High School. We have a situation at the school with Sierra, and I was wondering if you could come by."

Chapter Eight

The long hall and the artificial lighting against the gray floors and red lockers made April feel as if she'd fallen down Alice's rabbit hole. Was this how Sierra felt at school every day? After treading acres of tile, she finally found the glassed-in office. The secretary directed her to a plastic chair before she was called into a conference room.

Inside the room two men sat at a table. A police officer sipping coffee out of a Styrofoam cup and, next to him, a man with close-cropped hair and glasses. At the end of the table, a woman in a suit sat next to a younger woman with an open file before her.

Sierra sat on one side of the table, all alone, staring at a loose thread in the burgundy carpet. Four adults and one child. Were they trying to terrify her?

April took the seat beside her. "I'm here, Sierra," she said softly.

"Mrs. Wright? I'm Liza Grambling, the principal." The older woman extended her hand to April and rattled on. "Apparently, one of our students' parents has noticed your daughter spending a lot of time at an old gentleman's house." She looked up to be sure it wasn't a surprise to April and went on. "There's no reason we have to get involved, of course. A lot of schools wouldn't."

"I understand." April's understood all right. The school barely noticed when Sierra left campus, but they were all ears when she walked into a stranger's house long after school was over.

The woman smiled at her as if they were old friends. The principal waved toward the men at the table. "This is one of our campus policemen, Officer Wilkins. Mr. Foster is a teacher at our school, who is here at Sierra's request. We've also asked a representative from Child Services, Ms. Barnes, to be here."

Ms. Barnes nodded at April.

The introductions complete, Ms. Barnes closed her file folder. "Sierra, now that your mother is here, we'll get started."

April's stomach had an iron ball in it. Her daughter traced designs into her jeans with a thumbnail.

"Sierra?" Ms. Barnes said in a velveted voice.

Sierra nodded but didn't look up.

"Do you want to tell us what happened?"

Sierra shook her head, her eyes wide.

"Sierra, I know your conversation with the gentleman seems perfectly innocent," Ms. Barnes said. "And maybe it is. Maybe the gentleman you've visited is entirely above suspicion. But we don't want you to get hurt."

Sierra fixed her gaze on Mr. Foster, some kind of challenge in her eyes. The teacher held eye contact, and April had the odd sense that an unspoken conversation was being carried out. She placed her hands in her lap and studied the man. He had a face that meant business. If it weren't for his starched shirt, he might even pass for the policeman. The only incongruous part of his looks was the pair of rimless glasses that softened his appearance.

THE LANGUAGE OF SPARROWS   57

The policeman cleared his throat. "Sierra, I know it feels unfair. But when you've seen what I've seen ..."

April waited for Sierra's response, but her daughter turned to Mr. Foster as if the policeman hadn't even spoken. "Have you talked to him?"

The teacher opened his mouth to speak, but it was the policeman who answered. "I have. And he understands he is not to spend any more time with you."

The teacher held up his hand to halt the conversation.

"Sierra." He bent his head toward her daughter. He waited for a painfully long time. Sierra didn't look away, not once, but she began to tremble. The man's unwavering gaze made April think of one word: *power*. It probably gave him quite an edge in the classroom.

"There's nothing to be frightened of. I just want you to know something." He reached out an open hand toward the window. "Going into a stranger's house is life and death sometimes."

Sierra's face crumpled. She started to speak, halted, and began again. "A stranger?" she croaked.

Something in the teacher's face changed. Muscles tensed. But his words were still soft. "He's a stranger to *you*, Sierra."

April looked from Sierra to the teacher. A line of electricity flowed between them, but she couldn't work it out. What was it that smoldered between their words? But then whatever it was fizzled out, and Sierra turned to stare at a bland watercolor on the wall.

"What if I go anyway?" Sierra said. "You don't understand anything about him."

Mr. Foster's chest heaved, but he didn't answer. The officer spoke up in the silence. "I spoke with Mr. Prodan, Sierra. He agreed to send you home if you come to his house again."

Finally, Sierra turned toward April, a look of silent pleading written on her face. A small whimper escaped her. April's eyes burned in sympathy.

April stood. "I thank you for your concern." She sent a firm nod to the four adults. "I think we can take care of things from here."

Sierra raced out of the room. April watched her go, tapping her feet, until she heard the outer glass door open and swing shut. When Sierra was gone, April turned to the adults in the room, speaking in a low voice. "If one of you, just one of you, had taken Sierra aside and spoken to her like a friend, she might have heard the sense in what you'd said. All you've done here is make her feel she's under attack."

Ms. Barnes opened her mouth, but April stepped out of the room and into the hallway. If the woman dealt with children in crisis every day, surely she should see the problem with a conference like this.

Sierra was all the way down the hall and entering a classroom, so April leaned against the wall, willing the tension to leave her.

Mr. Foster walked out but stopped upon seeing her. He looked back at the glass wall.

April straightened. "Something went on in that room between you and my daughter. I'd like to know what it was." She regretted the accusation in her voice. He had a way about him. He was probably good at his job. But she was at a loss.

The bell rang and a rush of kids flooded into the hall. The noise level was overpowering as kids called out to one another and hooted with laughter. They had to step aside as a couple of boys shoved into each other on purpose, jibing each other with insults.

Mr. Foster moved in closer to be heard. "You have every right to understand what took place in there, Mrs. Wright, but I have to get to class right now. Can I call you?"

———◆◆◆◆———

April and Mr. Foster spoke by phone the next day. He said he didn't believe in having conferences by phone if it could be avoided. April wasn't surprised. That piercing blue look he gave was something else, and he probably knew just what he had and how to use it—with students and with parents.

"I'd be happy to meet you during my conference period or after school, even up to six," Mr. Foster said over the phone. "What time is good for you?"

"I'm afraid it would have to be next week. I'll be working afternoons and evenings all week."

"What about Saturday?"

Saturday? Was he some kind of superteacher? "That's so generous, but I'm afraid I'm working Saturday, too. Really, a phone conference might be best."

"What time is your lunch break Saturday?"

"Uh, noon," she mumbled. "No, look, Mr. Foster, you're a busy man."

"Not too busy for this. And it's fine. I owe a buddy of mine a visit. He just happens to live in West University. That's just a few minutes away from your gallery, right? We'll talk, and then I'll drop by his house."

———◆◆◆◆———

When the bamboo chimes clacked in tune and the gallery doors opened, April was busy with a customer. She nodded to Mr. Foster and checked her watch. He was ten minutes early.

He nodded as he entered the store and then moved off to a side alcove. With his hands behind his back, he inspected a piece of melted jewelry and coins. April couldn't help but think the work of art looked like child's play in front of him.

She turned to the woman at the register. "I'm slipping in a care guide with your receipt. And of course, you can call us with any questions." But the whole time she spoke, she studied the teacher.

As her customer left, April came up beside him. "I don't think that's exactly your style, Mr. Foster."

A glimmer of a smile crossed his face. "Not exactly. And it's Nick. I don't think we had a good introduction Monday." He reached out a hand to her. He looked across the street to the café. "When's your lunch break?"

She looked at her watch as if she didn't already know the time. "In ten minutes." Then she looked across the street to the café.

Without looking back at her, he said, "I'll reserve a table."

She watched him cross the street from the window. There was something about him, some undercurrent, and April was more anxious than ever about his exchange with Sierra. What was between them? And how was he involved in her visits to this stranger's house? The fact that Sierra wouldn't discuss the teacher or the old man only put her that more on edge.

The store remained quiet for ten minutes, except for the chattering in her head. The minute hand moved as slowly as a turtle. When it finally hit twelve, she called to the back. "I'm at lunch, Ellen. Be back in thirty."

"Righto," came the reply.

She strolled into the café and sifted through the Saturday lunch crowd. A hum of voices in conversation filled the restaurant, settling the rising disquiet inside her. Passing polished tables and gleaming wood floors, she found the teacher around a corner.

He was tapping his fork against his napkin and looking out a narrow window. He stood when he saw her and pulled out a chair. This wasn't like any teacher conference she remembered. But then, in the not-so-distant past, teacher conferences had been easy. *"She's a pleasure to have in class,"* her teachers used to say. *"She excels."* Never had April thought she'd be having a conversation like this one with Nick Foster.

A waiter came for their order. "Just an iced tea for me," April said. Lunch could wait.

Nick nodded. "I'll have a Coke."

The waiter left, and April took a deep breath. "My daughter won't talk to me. She's spitting mad at me because she thinks that man is a friend. I understand why she's mad. What I don't get is why she was furious with you."

"That man is my father."

April shook her head to clear it. At the conference, they'd spoken of the man as if he were a danger to society, a criminal even. And Nick Foster hadn't once spoken in his defense. "Your dad?"

She caught the flash in his eyes.

A shiver went up her back. "Your father's dangerous?"

He didn't answer right away. "Not the five o'clock news kind of dangerous."

"But?"

The noise of the lunch customers grew distant as he searched for words. "I know what Sierra sees in him. He's read enough to fill libraries. On his good days he's got laser insight. But, man, he's a tough guy." Nick shook his head. "He'll be your friend one day, and the next, he uses words like jackhammers. He wouldn't think about how he could scar a fragile girl like your daughter."

April softened. This man wasn't even Sierra's teacher, but he recognized her for what she was.

"I've watched the way she takes it at school," he went on. "She lets those boys intimidate her. Honestly, I'm afraid for her. Even if my father didn't hurt her, what was she thinking? Whose house is she going to let herself be talked into next?"

April raised her chin. "Boys intimidate her at school?"

"If she'd just tell them to get lost, the game would be over. It's her distress that keeps them circling."

Her voice shook. "The game?"

"Bad choice of words. It's a game to them."

When had Sierra stopped talking to her? Did she think April wouldn't understand? Or did she simply want to save her mother from any more anxiety?

April looked up. The smells of garlic and tomatoes and fresh bread drifted over from the next table. But something edged in on her attention. His name. She looked up at him. "Wait. You're Nick Foster, right?"

He looked straight at her. "And my father's name is Prodan."

April tipped her head, curious now. "And?"

"We came from Romania."

April's mind whirled. Nick Foster had no trace of an accent. The way he spoke wasn't particularly Texan, but his words held no hint of a European background either. He could be from anywhere in America.

"I came here with my mother when I was four," he continued. "My father wasn't able to come with us at first. And then when the Romanian government offered him an exit visa, he chose not to accept it. He finally joined us when I was sixteen."

"And you changed your name?"

He hunched a shoulder. It wasn't a subject he was comfortable with, clearly. "Yes, when I got my citizenship. From Nicolae Prodan to Nicholas Foster. It's a translation."

He spread his hands, European in style, but quickly put them down as if they'd betrayed him.

She hesitated, unsure how to respond. "I appreciate your honesty, Mr. Foster. I'll be sure Sierra stays away from your father."

"Nick," he insisted.

She gathered up her purse.

"I realize I'm not Sierra's teacher. But we're here. Would you like to talk it out?"

She held her purse in her lap. What was there to talk about?

He leaned across the table. "April, I teach the kids everyone else has given up on. The ones who sleep through class and fail the state test. The ones who are going to drop out as soon as it's legal, maybe before."

"What you do for a living is admirable, but I'm not sure what it has to do with Sierra."

"I know Sierra is in a different category altogether. She's smart. She's got an involved mother. But in a way, she's right there with them."

She knew what he was saying. Sierra wasn't living up to her potential. But April didn't want to hear her child grouped in with failing kids. Sierra wasn't like them.

She reached to take a sip of her tea but only knocked the glass nearly over. He had the glass upright and still full in less than a second. He began tapping his fork again, looking right at her, making her agitated.

"Don't do that," she snapped. And then in a softer voice, "Just say what you're thinking. Please."

He laid the fork down, and regret unveiled itself on his face. "I'm saying I deal with at-risk kids all the time. And I think your daughter is at risk. Dangerously so."

April looked away.

"Have you considered therapy?"

April stifled a sigh. It must seem downright negligent to anyone who knew Sierra that April didn't have her in counseling. How could she explain the years of counseling, psychiatrists, and hospitals, and Gary growing steadily worse with each treatment? How could she explain that counseling had driven Sierra deeper into depression until the counselor recommended checking Sierra into a psych hospital? She wasn't having that conversation with a man she barely knew.

"Sierra saw a couple of therapists when we first moved here. It didn't work out well." She glanced at her watch. "Look, I have to get back to work. I appreciate your coming here on your day off. But I think this is something Sierra and I are going to have to deal with on our own."

He wrote his number on a paper napkin. "If you want to talk about it."

She shoved the napkin in her purse. The last thing she needed was someone else telling her Sierra was in danger. She could tell he knew she wouldn't call. Just as well.

"Thank you for coming all the way out here, Mr. Foster. Nick."

April walked across the street and back to work. Fifteen minutes later, as she looked over receipts in the back office of the gallery, Ellen popped her head in, holding out a takeout box. She winked. "You've got an admirer."

April shrugged and took the box. An admirer? Hardly. Inside were rosemary chicken, wild rice, and a chocolate chip cookie. Square cursive spilled across the napkin: *Couldn't let you go back to work hungry. Nick.*

What kind of teacher came all the way across town for a parent conference and then delivered lunch? He made her think of Sierra's words about the old man—deep and real.

She'd take Nick's word that his father wasn't safe for Sierra to be around but wondered precisely why. She peeled a strip off the chicken and put it in her mouth. Of course she wasn't about to let Sierra spend time alone with a man she knew nothing about. But "words like a jackhammer"? That was a rather vague threat.

CHAPTER NINE

Mom called for dinner. Sierra stayed by her bedroom window, mesmerized by the outdoors. When she came into the room, Sierra pretended she didn't notice.

Mom didn't leave, but Sierra kept her attention on the window. "I'm not hungry."

"You have to eat, Sierra."

She didn't answer. Mom put her hand on her shoulder. "We'll get through this, I promise."

Sierra breathed a sigh of relief when Mom finally went back to the kitchen. October had come, and the stifling heat had given way to the first cool front of the year. People opened their windows. Kids came outside to play on the playground. Adults hung flower boxes on their balconies.

Mr. Krishnamurthy and his wife paced around the parking lot. It was their afternoon ritual. It didn't matter what the weather was like. Across the way, a woman had a tub of soapy water on the porch. She stood on her tiptoes, washing her windows, the railing, the door, the porch, everything. Her little girl sat on the porch, cooing at a terrier in her arms. How was it that life went on as if nothing had happened?

On the playground, a boy pushed his brother on the swings. Their mother looked away, so she didn't see her older son hit the younger one hard in the middle of his back or the way the little one refused to cry.

Sierra stared over the fence.

Later, Mom brought in a plate of sliced apples and mozzarella. Sierra pretended to be busy doing homework, but the blank notebook paper gave her away.

She pulled up her legs and curled up on the chair in front of the window. She remembered a big red sketchbook her father had given her. He told her to record everything while he was away at his conference in Italy. A nature book, he said, to show him what he missed during her summer walks. She had sketched the dogwoods losing their blooms and the creeks receding from their banks, the hot July sky and Argie, their Labrador, sleeping under a tree. But when Dad didn't come home, she'd put the sketchbook away. And they'd had to leave Argie with neighbors when they'd moved.

She kneeled at her dresser, looking through the book without taking it from the bottom drawer. She flipped through the pages. It was still three-quarters empty. Finally, she carried it to her desk, tore out the sketches, and put her pen to the paper.

A haiku came to her whole and already formed. She mouthed the words. "Standing on tiptoes / brown arms slick with soap-water / she scrubs the door clean." There were a dozen more tumbling behind it. All she had to do was scroll her pen across the paper. There would be no egrets. She would tell about the Krishnamurthys taking their walk and about the little boy holding back his tears and his mom, though she pretended like she didn't see what was going on, growing mottled with worry. She would tell about the wind swallowing the sounds of traffic and playing children and the crisp light outlining her neighbors outdoors.

"Standing on tiptoes," Sierra wrote. But she couldn't make herself finish the haiku. Who wanted to know about the things she saw around her in the October world anyway? Only one, and she couldn't take her poems to him.

What she really wanted to tell him was about the day they told her she was no longer allowed to visit him. She wouldn't be able to write about the horrible things they'd implied about him, of course. But maybe he would understand how the world had turned into a strange faraway place and how she felt she was drifting away from everyone. She would write and write to him until her fingers cramped and the pen bled dry.

She flipped through the empty pages one by one as if she might find one that was so clean and inviting that she would be able to write on it. It was when she got to the last page that the idea occurred to her.

She found her drawing pencils, also shoved into the bottom drawer, and drew a portrait of him, sitting in his armchair, his hair mussed, his eyes penetrating, his head tilted, the way she remembered him. Using a heavy pencil, she shaded his eyelids to show their heaviness, and then she used a softer pencil to hint at the lightness of his eyes. With the edge of her graphite, she showed the sunlight pouring in on his bookshelves. She was no Rembrandt, but anyone could look at it and say, "Yes, this is Mr. Prodan, inside and out." And he was not the kind of man they thought he was.

She tied the book up with a piece of Christmas ribbon and shoved it in her backpack. Without taking a shower, she turned out the lights and curled up in bed, dry-eyed.

———◆◈◆———

The sun finally rose, and somehow Sierra got dressed and to school. She meandered from class to class, not quite remembering how she got to each room. After school, she passed a bunch of guys leaning against the lockers.

"Hey, hot thang," one of them yelled out.

Emilio made a circle around her, looking her up and down and shaking a hand in front of his face. "Mmmm, mmm."

Sierra froze and tried not to see him. There was laughter behind her, then it suddenly got quiet. She turned. Carlos had his hand on Emilio's shoulder. Emilio reached up to remove his hand, but Carlos, with a face hard enough to be carved in rock, didn't let go.

"You want her, she's all yours, man," Emilio said.

Emilio and his friends headed down a side hall, but Carlos was still there. "You need to tell them to back off, Sierra. Let them know they can't talk to you that way."

She shifted her backpack to her other shoulder. Hadn't he been the one teasing her just a few weeks ago? She thought back and wasn't sure anymore. She wasn't sure what to say. *Thank you.* That would be good, but she didn't say it.

Carlos closed the distance between them. "Hey, I'm going over to your place again." His bright smile startled her. "Maybe I could walk you home?" He spoke so quietly and bent his head to her, as if he asked a special favor. A strand of his hair fell into his eyes, and he pushed it back.

She closed her eyes. She couldn't breathe. "I have to talk to a teacher. You go ahead."

"I'll wait."

She shook her head.

"Later then."

He shrugged like it didn't matter. She moved into the stairwell but turned to look after him walking down the hall. He walked like he couldn't get to the door soon enough.

She trudged up to Mr. Foster's room. At first she thought he'd already left for the weekend—the classroom looked empty—and she went hollow inside. Waiting for this moment was what had gotten her through the day.

She turned to leave, but then she heard a movement. Mr. Foster rose from behind his desk. He had been kneeling beside a box of books.

"Sierra." He said it in a pleasant voice, as if he'd been waiting for her to stop by.

She closed the door behind her, but he said, "Leave it open, please."

No, he wouldn't want anyone to accuse *him* of being a molester, would he?

She laid the sketchbook on his desk and dropped into a student desk.

Mr. Foster picked up the sketchbook, but he didn't untie the ribbon. He looked at her, a question in his eyes. He looked American, but she wondered now how she could have missed it. He had Mr. Prodan's light eyes, his mouth. It would be easier if he looked like a stranger.

She gathered her courage. "I—" Her breath came in a short burst. "It's for him."

"You want me to give this to my father?"

"He's not what they accused him of."

There was no argument in his eyes, just sadness.

"He's not dangerous." Her voice cracked. "How can you not know your own dad?"

Sierra could swear he flinched.

"He's not dangerous," she repeated.

He tapped her sketchbook. He didn't look sorry or mad. He just slid her sketchbook into his satchel. "You have my promise. I'll give it to him."

"It's none of my business. Your dad told me it wasn't. But I still think it's strange that you don't have his name."

"None of your business? Is that what he said to you?"

Sierra wanted to shake her head and say it hadn't been like that, but she couldn't remember what it had been like now. Mr. Prodan hadn't been unkind though.

"I'll tell you." Mr. Foster came around the desk, leaned against it, and lifted up his hands to her. "If you want to know."

She wanted to hear Mr. Foster explain why his dad got all quiet at the sound of his own son's name. But instead she shook her head. "I'd rather hear what your dad has to say about it."

He placed his hand on the satchel. "Fair enough, Sierra. I'll give your book to him this weekend."

Chapter Ten

Sunday night, Nick drove to his father's house. He killed the engine and stared at the house before getting out. Nick had just stepped onto the clean-swept porch when his old man came out. He had aged since last week. His shoulders sagged. The skin on his face hung slack.

"I've brought you something from Sierra Wright," Nick said.

His father looked at the sketchbook without expression but put out his hands.

"May I come inside?" Nick kept the sketchbook against his side.

His father took his time to answer, as he so often did. "Of course," he answered at last. "Come."

There were only two chairs. The couch had given way years ago and had never been replaced. Nick didn't like to come in here. The address might be the same, but it was a different house from the one he had grown up in. All of Mom's feminine touches were gone now.

His father took a seat. Nick took the other chair.

Before he could tell the old man about Sierra's book, his father stood and began pacing. He swung around to face Nick and let out a raspy breath. "They came to my house, Nicu. The police came inside and questioned me. Did you know of it?"

"They were being cautious, Dad. You see the crazy stories in the news. They were just trying to protect Sierra."

"They came inside and questioned me," his father repeated. "As if I were a criminal, they asked me what I did with her." His voice cracked, and he stopped to calm himself. "I said I gave her a book to read and I read the poems she wrote for school. They laughed at me and told me that was not the sort of thing a man does with a pretty girl. They claimed I had done things to her."

His father came close, way too close. He put his nose in Nick's face and shoved a finger into Nick's chest. "They threatened me with lies, your American police!"

Nick tried not to feel pushed into a corner, tried not to feel seventeen and castigated by his father yet again. He removed his father's hand from his chest.

Dad turned away and made a noise that sounded too much like a sob. "They made me say I would not welcome her in my home. By using a packet of lies they made me do this. They are no better than the secret police. No better!"

Dad pounded a fist into the kitchen cabinet, and then did it again so hard Nick thought the Formica would splinter.

"No better, Nicu."

He began shouting, striding back toward Nick. "Secret police! American police! What is the difference? Tell me! If the truth does not matter, they are all the same."

Nick looked out the window, away from his old man's tirade. The authorities would never have hurt his father. This was America, and however cold his father's manner was, he was innocent. But he couldn't push away the thought pinching his conscience. He should have known that the police, Child Services, or some authority might speak to his father. And he might have prevented it.

Nick looked at the scars on his father's hands, a permanent record of what authorities meant to his father.

"I told them I would not see her again," Dad said, breathless. "I told them what they wanted me to say to them. But it makes me ill. The girl believes I have turned her away?"

"She blames the school. Me." Nick handed him the sketchbook. "I don't think she blames you."

His father held the book as if unsure he should open it. At last, he sat down, pulling the ribbon away. He turned page after page without stopping. He didn't say anything, but his fingers slowed as he went on without finding anything. Nick himself felt a growing sense of alarm. What kind of message was a blank sketchbook?

But at last his old man turned to a portrait that was more eloquent than a journal full of writing. Dad studied it for a moment and closed the book, his face haunted. "Oh, Sierra," he whispered. "My child."

Nick looked up, startled. Never had his father said his name with such feeling. Sure, there were good reasons why he wasn't a whole man. But just once, couldn't he say, "Nicu, my son" with any degree of feeling, anything besides weariness or contempt?

⸙

Monday morning, Nick woke in the early quiet. The gray light of dawn tempted him to go back to sleep. The day would be merciless. Every hour in the classroom was a battle, one he'd come to look forward to, if he were honest. But the only way to make it through was to spend these few minutes not in bed, as his body craved, but sitting on the deep windowsill of his study, praying. He stumbled across the hall, leaving the covers behind.

Too tired to pull out words of his own, he leaned back against the window and began with the words he knew by rote. "Our Father which art in heaven, Hallowed be thy name."

He rubbed his eyes several minutes later, realizing his mind was drifting. To Sierra and his old man. He glanced at the clock, at the bookshelves, at the bars of sunlight shining between the slats of the blinds onto the carpet.

"Our Father which art in heaven," he began again.

His mother had taught him that prayer before he could read. He'd learned it by heart in both Romanian and English.

In the most brutal years of his life—when Mom died; during Desert Storm; when Caroline drove off, stone-drunk, to her death; during his first year of teaching—he'd lost the words to pray. His world became an empty void. Words became meaningless, and belief a shaky thing he couldn't count on anymore.

But that prayer, the one he'd learned so early, stayed with him, and when he prayed it, he had the sense that at least God was present and listening, until at last, he found God filling the empty spaces again.

The fourth sentence always tripped him up though. "And forgive us our debts, as we forgive our debtors." How could he pray that? He hoped God had more mercy than he did.

"Help me to forgive." It was the only honest prayer he could say.

But no matter how often he prayed *Help me to forgive*, it didn't get any easier to speak with his old man. What need did a forty-year-old man have for his father's approval anyway? Prison had broken Luca Prodan and left Nick fatherless for all intents. He needed to accept that and move on. He forgave his old man. He always did. But sooner or later, Dad would say something offensive, and the anger washed back in, galling him.

Nick closed his eyes, tuning out his study, and went through the words of the prayer one more time, forcing his mind to focus on the words and to mean them.

After he said amen, he went downstairs to the kitchen for a cup of coffee and then stood on the deck in back. He leaned on the wood railing and drank down the hot, bitter stuff. A cool breeze rippled over him. The sun crested over the pine trees, lighting up the hill that sloped down toward the stream below.

Maybe his relationship with his father couldn't be salvaged. But at least he could save Sierra Wright some heartache. Her mother had enough spirit to set the girl onto another track. Sierra would forget his old man soon enough.

He smiled, thinking of April Wright, with her artsy, short hair, standing up to tell off the school for interfering. She had enough spirit all right. He wondered how a capable, stylish woman like her ended up in his school's neighborhood. And what had happened to give Sierra eyes that held her whole battered soul within them?

No mention of a father or husband had come up either time he'd spoken with Sierra's mother. Somehow he suspected their problems were connected to the missing Mr. Wright. Surely there had once been a Mr. Wright.

CHAPTER ELEVEN

April stopped in the middle of scrubbing the kitchen sink to watch Sierra sitting in front of the TV. She'd been flipping an international news station on and off all evening as if she were searching for something. Apparently, she found what she was looking for because she put down the remote and leaned forward to watch the woman broadcaster. What was it she found so captivating?

April thought the broadcaster was speaking Italian at first, or maybe Portuguese. Then she caught the ribbon of text trailing at the bottom of the screen—Bucuresti. Bucharest, the capital of Romania.

April almost had the sense Sierra understood what the woman was saying, the way her eyes blinked in sync with the rise and fall of the broadcaster's voice. Her daughter already spoke French and Spanish. Who knew? With Sierra's abilities, she might be picking out some of the words. Romanian belonged to the same family of languages.

She put down her sponge. A simple warning wouldn't turn her daughter from this man. Like her father before her, when something captured her attention, nothing would distract her. Food and rest, not to mention companionship, would take far, far distant seconds and thirds until she mastered her subject. And clearly, the one and only subject on her mind right now was this old man from Romania.

79

She sat on the couch beside Sierra. Her daughter's ever-present notebook lay by her side, but instead of writing alphabets of the ancient world, Sierra used the familiar letters April knew. Boxed-in words with loops and accent marks filled the page. It didn't take a genius to know what she was doing.

"Picked up much Romanian yet?" April refused to let Sierra see the wave of hysteria coursing inside.

Sierra gave her a shy smile. "A little."

When the news program switched to Bulgaria, Sierra put the notebook away and got ready for bed.

But at one in the morning, April found her sitting in the corner of the living room next to the tiles, reading with the aid of her book light.

April sat down beside her. "What are you reading?"

Sierra looked up at her, blue smudges under her eyes. Without a word, she lifted the book, a thick leather volume. April strained to see it in the dim light. It wasn't in English. Romanian? Where could she have possibly found a book in Romanian?

April sent her to bed, but it was almost two before the sounds of Sierra tossing and turning in her bed quieted, and April could fall asleep herself. When Sierra came out of her bedroom in the morning, she moved like a zombie. Her oatmeal sat untouched on the kitchen bar.

When she trudged off to school, April sank onto the couch, looking at the tiles. Sierra never mentioned them. April saw her glancing at them from time to time, but she couldn't fathom what was in her daughter's head.

It was time to do something about the empty middle. She would take care of it before she went to work. Dragging the large center tile from the coat closet, April took it outside. She laid the cream ceramic on the balcony and kneeled beside it.

Dipping her paintbrush in ebony acrylic, she hovered just above the tile. She wanted loose lines to match the feel of the running letters that would surround it. Black and bold, yet abstract. With her thickest brush, she painted the outline of a woman and child and then a symbol of water on both sides. She didn't fill them, leaving the impression of a large hieroglyph.

When it was dry, April hung it and stood back from the completed project. Sierra could make of it what she wanted. April had conveyed her message, not in empty words, but in images. Her daughter would see it every day when she came into the apartment.

They were in this together. The waters might rise high, but they would surge over them together or not at all.

———————◆◆✕◆◆———————

On April's afternoon off, she went for a run. Back at home, she took out her camera, but she couldn't bring herself to take one picture. She found herself pacing around the apartment. Her daughter needed light, and April couldn't give it to her. Somehow this man, Luca Prodan, had provided something Sierra needed though.

On a whim, April logged on to the Internet. There was no phone number for Luca Prodan, but with a little digging, she found his address.

Unable to keep herself from snooping, she looked up the house records. The title and property taxes were in Nick Foster's name. Something wasn't right. Why wasn't there anything in this man's name except his address?

She looked up directions and picked up her car keys. What would she say when she found this Luca Prodan? She wasn't sure yet, but she had to get a sense of who he was. What sort of grown man wanted to spend time alone with a teenage girl he had no relation to?

She passed apartment complexes and stores with bars in the windows and crossed over the bayou. When she found the street and the house number, she parked at the curb, inspecting the house.

She saw what brought Sierra here. It was a simple home. It wasn't even half a mile from urban decay. And yet, under the shade of the huge oak trees and decorated by bright gardens, the street breathed. April's heart tightened at the thought of her daughter feeling trapped in their concrete world when this green refuge was calling to her.

April knocked on the front door. There didn't seem to be a doorbell. She was at the point of knocking again, when she heard shuffling steps and the door opened. This couldn't be the man. He was stooped and frail. Why had no one told her?

"Mr. Prodan?"

"Yes." He had his son's piercing gaze. And for all his frailness, his single syllable spoke volumes. His gaze turned into a knowing smile. "You are Sierra's mother, I think."

"I'm April Wright."

"Your eyes are very alike."

April looked up in surprise. People were always saying Sierra looked like Gary. But then, this man had never seen Gary.

He didn't invite her in, and it seemed he held to the door frame for support.

"I …" April fumbled, shook her head, and tried again. "I hope you don't mind my coming. I don't know what the police said, but they said some things to you, I think."

"Untrue things."

"Sierra has missed you." April tucked a strand of hair behind her ear. "I hope you understand. It's impossible for a mother to let her daughter go into the home of a man she knows nothing about." She closed her eyes. She was bumbling it.

"Perhaps. But I did nothing to hurt Sierra, and it was wrong, what the authorities said to me."

I'm sorry, April wanted to say. But she couldn't say that. She wanted him to know she would not back down in protecting her daughter. "I wanted to meet you for myself. I can't send Sierra here to spend time with you without supervision," she said. "But I don't know how I can tell her not to speak with you either. I thought if I came here and spoke with you, we might find a solution."

Mr. Prodan inclined his head and stepped into the house. April followed. She took in the immaculate, bare house. He led her through to the kitchen, and they sat at a table beside a large window.

The window looked out on his backyard. Rows of herbs sloped away from the house, and a cluster of giant pine trees stood in the center of the yard. Soft breezes wafted in the branches, sending pine needles spiraling to the ground.

Mr. Prodan busied himself in the kitchen. He didn't ask her if she wanted anything. He simply served her strong coffee and a pastry with some kind of herb sprinkled on top.

"Langoş, it is called." He said as he handed her the pastry.

April looked away from his hands, not wanting to be rude. But she was curious. The scars were so uniform and unlike anything she'd ever seen.

He sat down next to her at the scarred table. "You should know there is no miracle to make you trust me. To trust is to believe. And to believe in what has not happened yet ..." He lifted one shoulder in a very European gesture.

She swallowed. "Yes, well, it's fair enough to trust for myself. But it's reckless to make that decision for my daughter. She's the one who would have to live with the consequences if I were wrong." She looked up. "You have a son."

He sent her a quizzical glance.

"He was once Sierra's age. I'm sure you were careful about who you let him associate with."

"I believe our circumstances are quite different."

She studied her pastry. How were their circumstances so different? Mr. Prodan and his son had been separated for some years according to Nick, but he'd only been a year older than Sierra when Mr. Prodan arrived in Houston.

"I do not think Sierra wishes to come here with her mother," Mr. Prodan said. "My years of fatherhood have not been as they should be, but they have taught me this much. Children have a different type of honesty with their parents than they have with friends. Otherwise, I would invite you to come and visit me with Sierra."

April had been so sure she would see more options when she spoke to this man, but instead she found only more questions. "So what should we do?"

He shook his head. "I would very much like to see Sierra again, but it is more important for her to have peace with her mother first."

Faith. That is what he was telling her. Her only way forward was to have faith in him. April looked into his eyes. This was a man worth knowing, as Sierra found out for herself.

It was hard to imagine a man less likely to hurt her daughter in the perverted way she had imagined. Even less in the way Nick Foster suggested. How could this gentle man use words like jackhammers?

But then she'd only known him a few minutes. He was still a stranger. She had to know more.

April inched forward in her chair. "What did you do in Romania, Mr. Prodan? Where did you live?"

"I was a secondary math teacher. In Bucharest."

His eyes were all-knowing, and she had the feeling he knew she was investigating him, but that didn't stop her. She inclined her head toward the library. "You've got a lovely collection of books."

On that subject he opened up to her like a beloved friend. He leaned back and almost began to chat.

He liked to read theology and philosophy but was content to read a good children's story or a classic romance. He gave a small laugh. "I learned English by reading children's books by Enid Blyton, and eventually I moved on to Henry James. I got quite a few odd stares my first years here in America. It took me some time to realize that the language has changed since those writers put pen to paper."

Outside, the afternoon light softened. She took a last sip of coffee, cold now and thick as molasses, and stood to go. "I haven't found any answers. But I'm glad we met." She let out a nervous laugh. "You're not the man I imagined."

He gave her a quiet nod and led her to the front door.

As she stepped onto the porch, she inhaled the sharp scent of marigolds and dead leaves. Her gaze traveled along the oaks and stopped when she realized a truck was parked in the driveway. Nick

Foster, his sleeves rolled up to his elbows, carried several bags of groceries. She'd understood from their conversation that he wasn't on close terms with his father.

April stole a glance at her watch. They met on the walk, and she stopped to look up at Nick, who seared her with his icy blue eyes.

"I had to see for myself," she said. "I needed to know what kind of man he is."

He shifted the grocery bags to one hand and used the other hand to push his glasses up. "Was it a good day or a bad one?"

April wasn't sure how to answer that. "He wasn't what I expected. He seems … wise."

"It was a good day then. You were lucky."

Mr. Prodan, still on his porch, bent over his flowers, studying them. He made no move to meet his son on the walk, and his face remained blank, as if he didn't realize Nick stood in his yard. Nick didn't look his father's way either. What was that all about?

Why did she feel the need to apologize for coming here and for liking his father? "It bothers you that I came to see him, doesn't it?"

He shot her a sardonic smile. "I wouldn't want him to ruin your day. He can be tough to deal with."

"But you care enough to buy his groceries?" *And pay his property taxes?* But she wasn't about to admit to snooping.

He shifted some bags back to his other hand, inspecting her for a moment. "Sure, he's my father." He stared off at the dim November sky. "It's complicated. It's just better if I do it."

Complicated? Luca Prodan was elderly; maybe he needed the help. But what had caused the rift between the two men? The gentleman she'd spent the afternoon with was pleasant and courteous, and she couldn't imagine his offending anyone. Well, their family complications weren't her business.

"Look," he said. "I don't own my old man. If you want to visit him, you're more than welcome. Just take care."

"Okay, I will," she said. "Have a good afternoon, Nick."

He still stood in the yard looking after her when she turned the street corner.

CHAPTER TWELVE

Sierra didn't go straight home after school. *It's only a walk,* she told herself. She needed to see the green lawns and oak trees. That was all. She wouldn't go to his house. But somehow, she found herself on the corner, a few houses away.

Mr. Prodan stood on his porch, sweeping the dead leaves. The heaviness drained from her. It wasn't a walk she needed after all. Not lawns and trees. She needed him.

He stopped sweeping and looked straight at her. How could people tell her she couldn't talk to him? They didn't know him like she did.

She started walking again, her feet as unsure as the first day she'd met him. She walked into his yard, but he didn't move. He stayed on the porch.

"Hi, Mr. Prodan," she said softly.

"Your mother does not know you are here?"

She shook her head.

He nodded at her, but then he looked off. "Because of your visits, the police came to my house. They asked me questions. They accused me of things I did not do."

She sucked in a deep breath. "I'm sorry," she whispered.

"*You* do not need to be sorry!" His voice rose suddenly, and a boy riding his scooter slowed to look. "Do not be sorry, Sierra, for what you have no need to be sorry for. But you cannot know what it is like to be questioned by the police. For me! For a man like me!"

He leaned the broom against the house and shuffled to the door. "Go, Sierra. You must go. Do not come here again."

He waved her away, as if he could make her disappear with a flick of his hand, and then he went inside, closing the door behind him.

Sierra began walking back to the bayou, her steps quick now. Mr. Prodan didn't want to see her. She'd brought him only pain. Head down, she quickened her steps until she was practically running.

———◆◆◆◆◆———

Sierra pulled her headphones from her drawer at home. She sat on her bed with her laptop and, within minutes, found the site she needed on the library page. It was exactly what she wanted. The tutorial said it was best to take it one lesson at a time, but Sierra couldn't help herself. She gulped a week's worth of lessons in one evening.

Her heart sped up when Mom peeked in and gave a worried glance toward the computer, but then she left. It was midnight when Sierra finally put the headphones away. In her sleep, Romanian phrases murmured through her dreams, along with the spiraling script she was only just learning. When she woke, a Romanian greeting hovered on her tongue.

At school, she doodled in Biology as the teacher went over the human genome, and she'd soon filled a page with bits of the Romanian alphabet. It wasn't so different from English. Only a few letters came with added loops and tails. But she wrote some sideways, some right side up, some in boxes, all in her heaviest, neatest handwriting, and she liked the look of the page.

As they crowded out the door after class, Carlos lifted the notebook from her hands. "Is that some kind of code?"

Sierra shrugged. "Just an alphabet."

He put his finger on a block of letters. "*An* alphabet?"

"The Romanian alphabet," she conceded.

"Cool." He cast her a curious glance.

Sierra retrieved and closed her notebook, feeling protective of her new words. "I've got to get to my next class."

"Sure. See you at lunch." He lowered his head, giving her a smile, his head close enough that only she could see.

Sierra couldn't breathe. *No,* she wanted to say. *Don't look at me like that.* But he was already outpacing her as he hurried to class. He glanced back at her one last time before he turned into the stairwell.

———— ◆◆◆◆◆ ————

The next day, Miss Lee frowned when she picked up Sierra's geometry homework, a worksheet only half filled in. Mrs. Velasco didn't say anything when she didn't turn in her English homework, but she noticed. Sierra could see by the brief look she gave her.

In the hallway, Jazzy breezed by. "Hey, girl, there's a party tomorrow at Shawna's."

Sierra looked up. "What?"

"Don't look so shocked. Carlos thinks you're cool. You can come."

"Yeah, whatever." But Jazzy was already passing her by.

———— ◆◆◆◆◆ ————

Jazzy left a message on the answering machine and Mom's face lit up when she heard it. How could her mom not see that a man like Mr. Prodan was twice as safe as a party like this? What would Sierra do? Stand on the edges of the room like a wallflower twice over? She didn't have the heart to tell Mom it would just be a bunch of drunk kids. Maybe she could drop in and get right back out.

At the party, Sierra sidled through the solid wall of kids unnoticed. The music blasted, and her whole body vibrated with the sound. Someone handed her a drink. It was an amber drink, and she was sure it wasn't anything she wanted. But she held on to it. It gave her hands something to do.

Jazzy waved wildly from the second floor but went on flirting with a football player, and Sierra pulled close to the wall. Too late, she noticed Emilio laughing with a bunch of guys, and he'd already seen her.

Even with his slow saunter across the room, he cornered her before she could find a path out of the crowded room. Sierra slunk back, looking for a way out. But there were walls and clusters of people on all sides. Everyone talked and laughed. No one looked her way.

Emilio took her arm and led her to an empty sofa under the stairs. "There's nothing to be afraid of. See? We're just talking."

He winked at his friends.

He was only holding her hand, and loosely at that, so why did she feel cornered?

"You are sweet, aren't you, *mamá*?"

Sierra searched the room, but everyone clustered in their own little packs, laughing and screeching. Emilio's arm was warm and foreign against hers. He smelled like smoke and something else, some kind of musky incense. Of course. Emilio was a pothead.

She closed her eyes, trying to shush the scream building inside of her.

"You're shy, hey? That's all right. I can do the talking."

He didn't look like he had talking on his mind. He put his arm around her and began to knead her neck. The whole room seemed to rock with the music, and she wished she could disappear. She was staring at the glass in her hand when it was suddenly lifted away from her.

"What are you doing here, Sierra?" Carlos took her glass in his hand.

She leaned her head back. "What are *you* doing here?"

"Weirdest thing. I kept asking myself why I would come to a party like this, but I felt like I should. I guess I know why I'm here now."

A long look passed between Carlos and Emilio before Emilio got up with a heavy sigh and walked into the crowd. Sierra let out a long breath.

Carlos put her glass on a coffee table and pulled her up by the hand. "Come on."

Like a mindless drone, she followed him out of the house, just glad to breathe clean air. When he opened the door to an ancient Mustang, she halted, long enough to shoot him a doubtful glare, but not long enough to walk away. She didn't care anymore. She just didn't care.

Once in the driver's seat, he rolled down the window. "No air-conditioning. Sorry."

She rolled down her window without a word.

He took off, and within minutes they were on the freeway, speeding past lit billboards and glass buildings, her hair ruffling around her. The air was cool and dry and smelled like diesel. But then he turned onto a dark road and the air turned humid, heavy with the smell of trees and grass.

Within minutes he'd left the crowded streets of Houston, and they were in the countryside, a secluded place right in the middle of the city. How did he do that? In the dark night, all she could see were the shapes of trees and the narrow road before them. She looked at Carlos, but he had his eyes on the unlit road.

"How far were you going to let him go, Brown Eyes?"

Emilio had held her hand. That's all.

"'Cause if you don't tell him no, he's going to think you want to be with him. At a party like that, who knows?"

Her pulse did a little beat in her throat.

"You didn't want to be with Emilio, did you?"

She gave a slight shake of her head.

He pulled off on a side road, and the gravel kicked beneath the tires. When he stopped, she stared out at a glistening pond of dark water. There was no moon in the sky, but the stars out here filled the sky, pinpoints of light against endless black.

Carlos walked to the pond, but she sat in the car, frozen. Why did he bring her here? He didn't seem to be making a move on her. Tonight he was acting like the big brother she didn't have, and one with a bad attitude. But what if she were wrong? She shivered in the soft breeze as she looked at his back.

He stood at the edge of the pond, his hands crossed behind his back, while she mindlessly rotated the radio dial back and forth to give her hands something to do. He stood there for long minutes, until she finally got out and joined him. Still, he didn't turn around. He didn't look at her, and she was forced at last to say something.

"What are you looking at?"

He turned to her and gave her a victory smile. He'd made her speak first, but she didn't care.

"It's nice, isn't it? You can even smell the leaves and wood."

"I'd like to go home now."

His smile fled. "Sure. It was stupid. I thought maybe I'd bring you out here. You'd see the stars and the water." He swallowed and lifted a shoulder to the pond. "I thought maybe away from the school and those apartments ... I thought maybe you'd see me. And you'd talk to me."

She gave him a sideways glance.

He gave a disgruntled sigh. "Emilio and me, we're not the same, Sierra. Don't go thinking we are."

She nodded miserably.

"I'll take you home, but hear me out." He sat on the grass at the edge of the pond. Sierra sat down beside him, leaving a large gap between them.

He gazed at the stretch of grass between them. "I'm not going to hurt you, Sierra. I saw you that first day in Biology. The second I saw you, I knew the floor was cracking underneath you. But you didn't try to act all cool or brave. You're playing it honest."

He turned to her and waited. "You know how I knew?"

Sierra shook her head.

"Because I know what it's like when the floor's not where it's supposed to be ... right under your feet."

Sierra looked at him, trying to see some sign he'd been through something hard, but she didn't see it. His face was clear.

"My parents died in a car accident my freshman year. I went to live with my brother, but it was too much. Even when he lived at home, we never got along. And he had this wife who was always telling me what to eat and when to go to bed, like I was the same as her little boy. At my new school ... I don't know. It was like they were speaking Klingon or one of those weird languages from *Star Trek*. I tried to be one of them, but it was just an act."

Something lightened in Sierra's chest at those words. They were real. Only someone who had been there knew how to describe it. "I know," she said softly.

"I know you do."

"So what happened?"

"I finished tenth grade. I was sixteen. I told my brother it wasn't working for me. He and his wife, they tried to persuade me to stay. Oh man, there was some yelling when I told him I was leaving. But in the end they let me go."

Sierra stared at him. "They let you go where?"

Carlos gave a short laugh. "Stupidest thing. During the summer, I hung out by this gas station with the illegal guys from Mexico waiting for someone to come by looking for workers. I was tall enough I could blend in. I got jobs mowing lawns, cleaning out warehouses, laying concrete, and at night I slept under a bridge." Carlos shot her an embarrassed grin.

"I got a landscaping job from a tip, and this guy, Enrique Salinas, found me. He owns several apartment complexes. Told me if I could carry my weight, I could work for him and stay with his family. It didn't take me long to see I needed an education. So I went back to school." Carlos spread his hands. "Ricky, he pays me for the work I do, but he and his wife, they take care of me."

Sierra looked at him, feeling a new shape come into focus for the guy she'd thought she'd known.

"Don't look at me like that." He laughed a little nervous laugh. "Look, I know I'm crazy. I'm not going to hurt you though. That's all." He stood and looked down at her. "I just thought maybe I'd walk you home from school sometimes, and we'd have something to say to each other."

Desperately, she searched her empty word banks for something to say to him, anything to let him know she'd heard him. *Sorry about your parents?* No, a story like that needed some kind of deep response. And she couldn't even string *hello-how-are-you* together on a good day.

The only sound was of the water lapping against the edge of the pond. She opened her mouth, as if the words would magically take flight if she just gave them an opportunity. But there was nothing, just nothing to say.

Carlos waited for her to speak. Finally he looked off at the stars. "Okay, Sierra. I'll take you home now."

Chapter Thirteen

It wasn't a good day for a visit from the principal. That morning, Nick had dropped off Dad's prescriptions, and they'd had words. In third period, one of his students almost hit him, and Nick lost an entire period to a dialogue on the power of self-control. By the last class of the day, he was not in a peacemaking frame of mind.

The principal's familiar high-heeled step clicked down the empty hall, and Nick knew before she stopped at his door that she was coming to see him. It surprised him she hadn't visited his classroom sooner. She asked probing questions after staff meetings, but so far she'd left him alone. She was new this year, and new principals usually didn't take to Nick. They liked things done by the book.

But his kids had years of failure behind them. The book had never worked for them. It always took new principals some time to believe in his methods.

To the naked eye, his classroom would seem like chaos. Some of his kids clustered in groups. Some worked alone.

Teresa held court with three of her friends, putting chapter twelve of *Ender's Game* into street language. "So the dude in charge is saying, 'This guy wants to kill our boy, right? The one the whole world's been waiting for, and you ain't gonna do anything about it?'

And the battle-school dude says, 'You got that right. Our boy, Ender, he can take care of hisself.'"

Juan-Luis, unable to keep still, stacked books on the bookshelf. He didn't appear to be on-task, but he was. He absorbed everything Teresa said as he sorted. Keep him at a desk, though, and his energy would explode.

Farideh sat still as a hawk, listening to *Ender's Game* on an MP3 player. When she'd come to him in August, she'd been reading at a fourth-grade level. Her reading level had jumped two grades since she joined his class.

Jackson sat alone. He'd finished the book ahead of schedule and sat drawing impossibly small pictures of *Ender's Game* for a comic book. He hadn't turned in one assignment until Nick discovered a page of gang art under his binder and began giving him assignments that involved art.

Liza Grambling came into the room and looked for a chair. Principals liked to sit in the back and observe, but his classroom didn't have a back. Students sat facing different directions in scattered chairs. She found an empty desk close to the door and began writing notes. The pursed set of her mouth spelled trouble.

Nick circled through the students, stopping to join in their conversations. He'd put up large posters in his classroom that lined up with the required lesson plan. A computer spit out work sheets for the entire tenth-grade English team, but while he made sure his classes were familiar with the lingo for the state test, they needed more than those cookie-cutter work sheets.

The bell rang and the kids trailed out of the room. Liza closed her notebook with a thump. "Interesting lesson, Mr. Foster," she said.

She strutted to the whiteboard, stopping to stare at today's

objective: *Deciphering unfamiliar vocabulary through context clues.*
Nick crossed his arms and leaned against his desk. The school must
have scored low on that part of the test last year. He had no issue
with teaching context clues, but it was the fourth time this year the
assignment had come up, and it wasn't even Thanksgiving.

After a long inspection of the board, she swiveled to Nick. "How
did they manage on your assignment today?"

"Great," Nick said. "My kids can knock vocabulary out of the park."

"May I see some of the worksheets they turned in?"

"They didn't do any worksheets, Liza. We did speak about great
words like *translucent* and *percolate* though. *Null gravitation*, too. We
also read chapter twelve of *Ender's Game.*"

The pained look she gave him was almost comical. "I don't
believe that's on the literature list this year."

"That's the beauty of skipping worksheets. You get to add in a
few extra novels."

She stepped close to Nick's desk, peering at him in a way she
obviously meant to be threatening.

Nick would have to give it to her straight. "No one fails in the
same way. And none of my students can be turned on to school in
the same way. If I use the worksheets everyone else is using, these
kids will get the same result they've been getting: failure."

She crossed her arms. "I appreciate your concern, Mr. Foster.
But there's a reason for the system. It's been researched by experts."

Experts? Did she even believe that?

Liza's eyes grew harder by the minute.

"Look," he tried. "Take a look at my test scores last year. A 70
percent passing rate, and that's from one hundred and eighty plus
kids. Each one was expected to fail."

She sent him a frosty stare. "Your zeal is admirable, but I'm putting you on warning. I'll be stepping into your class next week, and I expect to see the standard English II lesson taking place." She flicked a glance at the objective on his board. "Being taught, Mr. Foster. Understood?"

She marched out of the classroom. He might have saved his breath. She hadn't come to listen.

He'd like to crow over the kids who changed course while in his class. But he couldn't forget the ones who slipped through his classes without tuning in, the ones who joined gangs or quit school instead. He refused to waste an entire week on worksheets.

The door to the stairwell clanged closed, and the sound of Liza's heels tapping down the stairs carried up in a faint echo. He rapped his knuckles against the desk. He needed fresh air.

———◆◈◆———

Nick went to the park a mile from school instead of going home. He pulled his truck into a space, slammed the door, and trekked down the dirt trail but came to a halt when he saw her.

April Wright sat on a bench, her camera pointed at a group of Chinese men performing Tai Chi by the pond. She didn't have the camera in front of her eyes, but held it beneath her chin. Maybe she was testing the light. She sat so still, not just focused, but like something she saw had wounded her or thrilled her or both. He followed the angle of the camera to an old gray head. The man flowed in his movements, his expression serene.

April jumped a little when he sat beside her.

"Fancy meeting you here," he said.

"Mr. Foster." She flashed him a smile, the joy and sorrow both gone from her face. A pity.

"Nick," he reminded her. "Can I see?" He pointed at the camera. She handed it to him. "There's not much."

There were no Chinese men on the screen. The first shot showed a weeping willow. It was good as far as landscapes went. He had a sense of the weight of the branches as they arched toward the ground. He clicked back and found an image of a little boy sitting in a swing, the expression on his face haggard. Two pictures, that was it.

He handed it back. "You're good. I bet you have albums full at home."

A look of yearning came into her eyes and disappeared as quickly. She laughed and flashed him a smile. Her eyes crinkled. It was a look of pure sunshine as she shook her head. "No, I haven't taken pictures for years."

He glanced at the camera. Nick had thought of getting a high-quality digital but had changed his mind when he saw the prices. The one she held in her hands cost a good five thousand dollars, a steep price for a woman in this neighborhood. There was a story there.

Nick had a weakness for stories, but he'd learned the hard way. Women with stories were a handful. So the words surprised him as they left his mouth. "If you like pictures, there's a place I know you'd love. Are you busy?"

Her mouth opened and closed. She leaned back and gave him a once-over. "No," she said. "Sierra is at a church youth club. I'm wasting time until I pick her up."

He spread his hands in a question. "I bet you haven't seen this part of your neighborhood."

She smiled again. That spunky smile got him. He found he didn't want to leave her just yet. *Just an afternoon looking at pictures, Nick,* he told himself. *That's all.*

They strolled back to his truck. He opened the door for her and she lifted herself in. They drove around the corner and parked in a shopping center blocks from school. Not a sign in the place was in English. There was a sari shop, a Vietnamese noodle house, a Spanish bookshop, a pawnshop that had signs in Spanish and Chinese, and an Ethiopian mini-mart.

That's what he loved about this part of town. It was as if the entire globe had poured itself into a few blocks. Though most of the immigrants who lived here came from Central America, they were from hundreds of other places too.

He led her into the glassed-in shop at the end. The smell of wool greeted them. Persian rugs hung from the wall and lay in stacks all the way to the back of the store. Almost before the door swung closed behind them, Ali came rushing to meet them.

"Nicholas, my friend."

He kissed both of Nick's cheeks and grabbed April's hand. "You are a friend of Nicholas? Ah, he is a good man."

April looked back at him, her head tilted. "So I've gathered."

"You are searching for a carpet to buy?" he asked April.

"No, Ali, April is a photographer." Nick pointed to the camera still hanging around her neck. "Do you mind if she looks at a few of your photos?"

His face lit up. "Photos? Come, come." He yelled something in rapid-fire Arabic to the young man in the back of the showroom and led them to a curtained doorway.

Nick lifted the curtain for April, who sidled by him, and then they were in the back room he'd brought her to see. She made a little gasp as she looked around. The office/kitchenette had three walls of photos, hundreds of them cascading from ceiling to floor.

She went to the first wall and began browsing. Nick stood back, happy to watch. He'd been right to bring her here.

Ali came to stand beside him, a grin on his face. "I think your friend likes them, eh?"

She stopped next to a photo of a refugee child whose dark eyes appeared to look directly into the viewer's, asking a single question: *why?*

"You were a journalist?" she asked, turning to Ali.

"I took photographs for a newspaper. In Libya."

She let that sink in. "But you couldn't continue?"

Ali shook his head. "I did not wish to photograph propaganda. I thought perhaps in America I could photograph the truth. But I am a foreigner. Sometimes I take photos for a small Arabic newspaper, but for a career, I sell carpets." He waved as if to dismiss his failed dreams.

"Look. Spend all the afternoon looking if you wish." He turned to the telephone, dialed, and began speaking in a barrage of Arabic again. After he hung up, he strode back into the front of the store.

Nick stood behind her. "I only got to see two of your pictures. But I could tell you would like a place like this."

She nodded, as if it would be too much to speak, and moved down the wall. He moved with her. She put her finger under another photo, this one of two sheiks embracing. It was a picture of peacemaking and diplomacy, yet their cold eyes told another story.

"When I was a kid, I saw myself behind the camera," she said, "getting pictures like these. I thought I was going to work for *Time*, be some kind of big-shot photographer."

"What happened?"

She laughed. "It's not a dramatic story. I got married."

"He didn't want you to be photographer?"

"We were idealistic. We thought he could be a professor, holding down the homestead. I'd jet-set around the world taking pictures, coming home to my sweetheart when I could. But life doesn't work that way." Her brown eyes grew dark. "He passed away a couple of years ago,"

Nick put his hands behind his back. She looked up at him, and he caught the scent of her shampoo. Sun from the skylight above sparked red and gold lights in her hair, and he had a sudden crazy desire to trace the white line of her neck. She made eye contact, and he felt a flash of guilt, as if she'd read his thoughts.

He stepped back, shaking his head to clear it. He knew better. Teaching had taken the place of his wife a long time ago. It was best to keep it that way.

The awkward silence grew until Ali came rushing in with bags. Scents of saffron and steamed meat wafted through the room.

"Ali," Nick chided. "What have I told you about feeding me every time I visit?"

The man chuckled. "The men and women who teach our children must be well fed. That is what *I* have told *you*!"

His wife bustled in with a teapot and poured out milky tea for them. She set the table for two, unpacked the boxes of lamb and yellow rice, and then she and Ali left. If Nick guessed right, Ali was up to a little matchmaking.

April looked at the table with a glint in her eye. "Mmm. I do like lamb." She looked at the pictures. "Thank you, Nick. This is a treat."

They sat at the table and ate quietly at first until she put down her fork. "Tell me about your job, Nick."

He talked about his kids for a while. It didn't take much to get him talking about them.

"How do you arrange your classroom when you've got them on all these different assignments at once?" she asked. She kept asking about his students, what their expressions were as they tuned in for the first time. Her questions were those of an artist visualizing a scene.

He leaned forward. "Enough about me. Tell me about your photography. What do you like to take pictures of most?"

"Faces." Her own face lit up. "Ordinary life in all its glory. I was quite the pest growing up. Invading neighborhood barbeques, following my sister and her boyfriend on their walks, capturing my dad grumbling as he balanced the checkbook."

He took a forkful of saffron rice. She didn't mention her husband or her daughter. "Why did you stop?"

She shook her head. "It's a long story."

When he sat back to wait for the story, she laughed, the sound reminiscent of warm caramel. "It's time for me to pick up Sierra."

"Okay, okay. But take a picture before you leave. You've got the camera. Go ahead. I'd like to see what you can do here."

"A picture of what?" She gestured around the room. There wasn't much photo-worthy in the office.

"I guess I'm the only face," he laughed. "Take one of me."

She looked down at her lap, color rising to her cheeks.

Ali's wife came in and began to clear away the dishes.

"May I?" April asked, lifting the camera from her neck.

The woman inclined her head in agreement, and April clicked twice.

Nick came behind her and looked at the screen. It was a good shot. He could sense the older woman's shyness, her precision as she wiped away crumbs. Her personality shone through the image. But then he realized—April was willing to take a picture of Ali's wife, but not of him.

She had a way of capturing people through her lens. The few photos he'd seen spoke deeply about the people in the picture and gave him a sense of the woman behind the camera. She was a professional, an artist, but when she'd refused to take his picture, she'd had all the shyness of a blushing sophomore.

Chapter Fourteen

April's hope fell as she pulled up to the church portico that evening. Sierra slumped against a brick column, ignoring the other girls clustered together.

"Did you meet anyone nice?" April tried. The words sounded ineffective even as they left her lips. But it was church for goodness' sake. Someone must have reached out to her.

Sierra slouched in her seat. "I'm not going back."

April clutched the steering wheel as she turned out of the parking lot, then glanced at Sierra.

"You only went once. Give it another tr—"

Sierra gave her that stare. Okay, so she wasn't going back to the youth group. It had taken enough pleading to get her to try the youth group in the first place. April's last desperate hope that Sierra would find a friend at church or school wilted away. And where else would she connect with someone?

At home, Sierra went into her room, closing the door behind her with a definitive click. April didn't have to look in on her to know what she would be doing—sitting on her bed, looking up Romanian sites. Obviously, keeping her away from Mr. Prodan was only fueling the obsession.

At least when Sierra had fallen in love with Spanish, she'd

overcome her shyness to practice the language with a couple of neighbors and watched Spanish television shows. But with no one to speak Romanian with, her new words only drove her to endless Internet surfing alone in her room.

April didn't feel right about letting Sierra spend time alone with Luca Prodan though. As much as she liked him, she didn't truly know him. And how many likeable neighbors and uncles ended up on the news after some girl went missing? Even Nick didn't think the relationship was a good idea.

She swallowed a couple of Advil to stave off a creeping headache and pulled on her sweats. Curling up on the sofa, she glanced at Sierra's closed door. Would another visit to the elderly man resolve anything?

It couldn't hurt.

On her next day off, April made up her mind. She drove over the bayou, marveling once again at the sudden change from gray to green, and parked in his driveway. He stood on the porch, washing his front windows. It looked like too strenuous a task. He strained to reach the top of the window, ran down the window with his sponge, and then wrung it out over a bucket, flexing his hand afterward, only to begin again.

April rested her head on the palm of her hand. Washing windows at his age? Impressive, to say the least. He had also recently planted pansies for the cooler weather, and his shutters appeared to have a fresh coat of black paint. He got around for one so frail.

She waved as she got out of the car.

He gave her a formal nod. He had seen her, but as was his way, he took his time to acknowledge her presence. There was something she liked about that. Everyone was always in such a rush. It was nice to see someone who wasn't.

She met him on the porch. "Do you have plans? I was hoping you'd go to lunch with me."

He gave her an unblinking stare as he wrung out his sponge over a bucket. "I have made a soup and fresh rolls. There is enough for two."

April wanted to see this man out in public. Who was he? She wanted to get a feel for him, and the best way was to see him among people.

"I still remember those pastries you gave me last time I was here. You're an excellent cook." She flashed him a bright smile to encourage him. "But I have a coupon for Blue Ziti's. It would be fun."

He gave her a bemused glance. "Another time perhaps."

He started back into the house.

She reached for his arm. "Please. It's my treat."

He turned back to her. "Why does a beautiful young woman want to spend her day with an irritable old man, I must ask myself."

She let her hand drop and studied the pansies, then looked up at him seriously. "Would you believe me if I said the well-being of my family rests upon it?"

He stood still, inspecting her, and finally nodded. "Yes, I think I might."

It took him several minutes to get himself into the passenger seat and to buckle his seat belt. All the way to the restaurant, he kept touching the window and looking up and down the street.

Once sitting at the booth in the restaurant, April studied Mr. Prodan as she flipped through the menu. In the restaurant's muted light, he seemed more like the confident man she remembered. The restaurant was full, as always, but his eyes stayed on their table.

He ordered the baked fish and only ate a few bites. April ordered her favorite—baked ziti with mushrooms and an unseemly amount of melted cheese. She cleaned her plate.

As they ate, they talked about Sierra. He explained that he'd read her poems and shared books with her.

"Your daughter has a sharp mind," he said. "But she needs permission to use it."

If only he knew. A sharp mind didn't come close to describing Sierra's brilliance.

They talked about the book he was reading, written by an obscure Israeli author she'd never heard of. He asked her what she was reading.

"You wouldn't find it interesting."

He took a sip of water. "I enjoy all things in print. You must tell me."

She wound a bit of left-behind melted cheese around her fork, embarrassed. "It's a romance. Medieval."

"Ah. And where would the world be without romance? What keeps the lovers apart?"

She should have picked up the Pulitzer she'd been meaning to read. But she'd wanted something light, and light it was.

"Well,"—she rolled her eyes—"there's a duke's daughter. But she's in danger, so she's hiding in an abbey. A wounded knight is under her care. He thinks she's a nun, though, and being the honorable man he is, wouldn't dream of interfering with her vows."

"And yet," Mr. Prodan broke in, "he cannot help but lose his heart to her. What of the woman? Does she return his love?"

"The knight has a seal in his belongings, which seems to implicate him in her father's murder. She hopes desperately he's innocent, because she's never met another man like him." She flushed. "Silly, isn't it?"

"No, no." He straightened his fork and knife next to his plate. "There is nothing silly about true love. It is good to escape from the harsher realities."

An escape from harsh realities indeed. Knights and duchesses and true love that healed all wrongs. Oh, if only.

They moved on to talk about the weather and his garden. Mr. Prodan chatted, drawing her into the conversation. He was kind, intelligent, articulate. An old-fashioned gentleman. He could hurt no one. She could see no reason not to allow Sierra to visit with him. If the two spent their time in a public place like this restaurant, say, or the library, what was the possible harm?

While she paid the bill at the register, Mr. Prodan inspected a sales display of soup standing in a pyramid. She signed the bill and turned around to see him turn a jar of tomato soup.

"I wonder what ingredients they have used," Mr. Prodan said.

Two policemen carrying takeout bags went by—beefy men with hard faces. But one stopped to steady the pyramid of jars, and his words were polite. "Careful, sir. They're about to fall."

"Yes, yes." Mr. Prodan raised his voice, as if the man might be losing his hearing. He stared at the policeman wild-eyed, his hand still touching the soup jar. The officers shot him puzzled glances and went out the door. April laid the pen on the register. Luca mouthed something—quick, silent words. Not to her. He seemed to be speaking to himself.

He let go of the soup, and the entire pyramid went toppling to the floor with a crash. Glass and soup littered the space around him.

The cashier turned to someone behind her. "Get a mop out here, okay?"

April rushed to him. "Mr. Prodan ..."

He stood in the middle of the puddle, looking impossibly boyish and helpless. "Take me home. Please."

Poor man. She walked carefully through the broken glass. "What were they thinking, putting glass bottles in such a fragile display, right?" She forced a laugh.

He pronounced his words slowly as if she, too, were deaf. "Take. Me. Home. That is what I said, Mrs. Wright. I did not wish to come here with you. And I now wish very much to go home."

She let the stinging words roll away and reached a hand to help him step over the mess. He refused her hand and did not meet her eyes.

"Careful with your shirt. There's glass."

April pulled aside the cashier, offering to pay for the ruined soup, but she waived her off with a bright smile. "No harm done. You go on and take care of him."

Mr. Prodan refused to bother with the shards of glass lodged in his shirt. He refused to speak all the way home and sat without moving.

At his house, she intended to help him to his door, but he stopped her with a freezing glare. "I do not wish for your help, Mrs. Wright."

He walked stiffly to the door. She sat in the driveway, taking out her cell phone and then putting it back into her purse. She couldn't just leave him, not like this. Nick would still be in school, but he'd be out soon.

She swung home to look up Nick's address. Today was one of the few days she could be at home to greet Sierra after school, but she couldn't let Mr. Prodan suffer alone at home, and she couldn't talk about him to Nick with Sierra by her side.

He lived in a clean, manicured part of town. As she drove into his complex, she found slate-blue townhouses perched around a curved drive. Slender pine trees shaded the complex.

She sat on his steps. The half-hour wait was no hardship in a place like this. And it gave her time to organize her thoughts. How could she convey to him what had happened to his father in the restaurant?

He didn't see her when he pulled up or as he strolled up the sidewalk, rolling up his shirtsleeves. Then he looked up and his face broke into a smile.

"Hey, Nick." The soft, blue sky overhead and the smell of pines and wood smoke made her wish she had something better to say. "I spent some time with your dad today."

His smile faded.

"Why don't you come inside?"

He unlocked the front door and led her into a modern, well-furnished home. The opposite of his father's house, she'd say. Modern couches and plush carpets made her think of a model home. A fireplace with ceramic tiles and built-in bookshelves re-enforced the image.

But happily, he had stacks of essays on the coffee table, an open book on the sofa, and a soda can on the mantel. While he opened the blinds, she stepped into the open kitchen. Despite the art deco flour jar and all the modern appliances, it was a good bet he didn't cook much in here. His kitchen made her feel like an intruder, as if she might leave a smudge. She pulled a hand towel to make it a tad crooked. There, that was better.

She went back into the living room and sank onto the sofa.

He sat on a leather ottoman, facing her. "What happened?" Somehow he seemed to know she wouldn't be there without a story to tell.

She pulled her arms around her knees. "There were two policemen."

Nick closed his eyes. This wasn't new territory for him then.

"Your dad kind of lost it. I took him out to lunch, and he accidentally toppled a soup display. He got very upset, hardly said a word to me after."

"He'll be fine." Nick looked down. "He doesn't get out much. For good reason."

April melted against the suede cushion. "You'll look in on him then?"

He nodded. "You wanted to know why I buy his groceries? That's why." Nick took off his glasses and massaged the bridge of his nose. He pushed on the ottoman with his hands like he would get up, but he didn't. He stayed there near her, their knees almost touching. "He gives me mostly grief for my trouble, but he's my father. Someone's got to look out for him."

"You're a good son then, Nick." How could Luca Prodan intentionally irritate his son or give him grief? It didn't fit with the intelligent, well-spoken man she had spent time with. Falling apart, sure. But being outright mean?

Nick's eyes right then made her think of choppy, cold waters. She felt an unaccountable desire to take his hands in hers, to tell him she understood the pain of loving someone who couldn't give you the kind of love you needed back.

Instead she picked up a black-and-white photo in a gilded frame off the corner table. A dark-headed couple with a little boy smiled in front of an outdoor café. Luca Prodan was so young and fit in the picture it gave her chills. His pride for his beautiful wife and their son shone out of the picture. Nick, a boisterous toddler, stood on a chair between them.

He stood and walked behind her to look at the picture. Something bothered her as she looked at the idyllic family. It was the young Luca Prodan.

"When was this taken?" She lowered her voice.

"1974."

That was it. The man in the picture looked young, possibly in his early twenties, possibly even in his late teens. She would have guessed Mr. Prodan to be about eighty. "My math isn't what it should be, but it doesn't add up."

"What?"

"His age. He looks so young here."

"Ah. My father is fifty-nine. He'll be sixty next month."

She shook her head, trying to make sense of the twenty-year gap. There was no way the man she had lunch with today was fifty-nine. The white hair, the stooped shoulders, the graveled voice—they belonged to a much older man. She opened her mouth, trying to find the right question. "Fifty-nine?"

Nick's jaw visibly tightened. "Wait here."

Nick ran up the stairs. She could hear him open a drawer before running back down.

When Nick came into the room with another photo in his hand, she stood and stepped in close to look. This was of Mr. Prodan, too, but he was old, older than he had been when she'd left him this afternoon. His white hair was badly cropped, his cheeks sunken, some teeth missing from his attempted smile. His eyes were huge in proportion to his narrow face.

He looked like a ninety-five-year-old man, but there was more to it—the way his clothes hung slack on his frame, as if no one could find clothes small enough for someone so emaciated. He could have been a survivor from a Nazi concentration camp.

"He was twenty-nine in this picture," Nick said.

She swung her head up to look at Nick. It took her a few minutes to find any words at all. "What … what happened to him?"

"My father spent five years in a communist prison. This was taken just days after he was freed." Nick looked out the window. "He won't speak of why he went to prison or what happened to him there. Not even what he did in the years after he got out, before he joined us in the States. This picture—and his inability to cope in public—are the only clues he's offered about his missing years."

"Oh, Nick," April breathed. Luca had spent five years in a gulag? What had they done to him there? Starved him, clearly. Tortured him? It explained his reaction to the men in uniform today. Luca Prodan needed a friend.

But could Sierra be that friend? Men who had suffered trauma deserved mercy, but they weren't always safe. She remembered a Vietnam vet in their previous neighborhood who almost killed his wife one night. For a few minutes, he'd believed she was the Vietcong. At the very least, Luca Prodan was prone to meltdowns. She couldn't put Sierra in that position.

CHAPTER FIFTEEN

"Hey, Brown Eyes."

Sierra stopped in the middle of the hall and waited for Carlos to catch up. It took him only two long strides.

"What are you doing this weekend?" he asked.

"Nothing special."

"Yeah? Me, too."

Sierra didn't know what to say to that, so she started walking again. It didn't seem to bother Carlos. He smiled and walked beside her as if she'd given him the answer he wanted.

On Saturday morning, she saw Carlos through her bedroom window. He was kneeling in the apartment courtyard with Ricky, laying stones for a new path. So that was the man who'd taken him in after his year on the streets. Ricky owned their apartment complex.

She knew she should get breakfast, but she stayed at the window. Even as he hefted stones into place, Carlos had a sly smile, like he knew a private joke.

He moved about his work with slowness, but he wasn't lazy. He made her think of an animal in the wild, taking its time but poised to leap. That was it—he had a lion's grace. She told herself again that she ought to go have breakfast, but she still didn't leave.

In the early hours, it must have been cold, but later Carlos pulled off his sweater, working in only a T-shirt. Then, without warning, he looked up at her window. Sierra dodged behind the curtain quickly, but she saw him laughing. He knew she was watching him. He'd known the whole time. And somehow Sierra wasn't sure she minded.

❖

Thanksgiving passed by with the necessary dinner at Aunt Hillary's. In the first week of December a cold front blew in from Canada. The skies turned thick and gray, and storefronts turned on their lights in the middle of the day. At school, the hallways seemed more packed than ever with everyone in their winter coats. There was talk of sleet on the forecast.

Sierra zipped up her jacket. How would Mr. Prodan handle the cold? Would he be used to it after living in Romania for so many years? But he looked so frail.

After school, Sierra knocked on Mr. Foster's classroom door.

He met her halfway.

"I wanted to make sure your dad's okay."

He didn't answer right away. "My father's in the hospital. I checked him in yesterday."

She had known somehow he couldn't withstand the weather. "What's wrong with him?"

"It's just pneumonia."

"*Just* pneumonia?"

He leaned back against his desk. "No, not just pneumonia. He's asthmatic and has low immunity to … well, just about everything. It complicates things. He's getting special treatment at the medical center though. He'll pull through."

She stood hovering in the doorway, putting her hand against the frame to steady herself. She looked at Mr. Foster, willing him to offer something. "I need to see him."

He opened his hands. "I'm sure he'd love to see you. Why don't you ask your mother to bring you by?"

Sierra swiveled away and began walking home. It was drizzling and cold, and her coat and jeans were wet by the time she got there. She didn't stop to change. She pulled off her coat and looked up METRO to get the bus schedule to the medical center. She grimaced when she saw it. It would take almost two hours and three buses to get there.

As she paced, she saw Carlos working in the courtyard. He wore a sweater and a ski cap but kept at his work, chucking blocks of broken concrete into a wheelbarrow. Sierra curled and uncurled her fingers. Two hours by bus or half an hour by car.

———◆◆◆◆◆———

She waited by the Dumpster where Carlos brought the full wheelbarrow. Her breath came out in puffs of steam.

Carlos hefted a load into the bin. "You'll get a cold standing out here. You ought to be inside."

"I need your help."

He stopped. "Okay."

"Give me a ride to the medical center?"

He wiped his forehead with his shirtsleeve. "You know, people usually smile and say please when they ask a favor."

"Please, Carlos. I have a friend in the hospital."

He looked up at her empty apartment. "Sure. I'll take you. Your mom knows, right?"

"Does it matter?"

"Go call her, Sierra."

She rubbed her arms to warm them. "Never mind. I'll take the bus."

He grabbed her wrist. "I'll take you to see the old guy. Just tell her."

She narrowed her eyes. "I never said who I was going to see."

He looked down. "Yeah, you're right. I guess I don't know all your friends. Who is it you're going to see?"

"Never mind," she bit out again. He had it all figured out, didn't he? And when he laughed, it just made her angrier than ever.

"It's no big deal, Sierra. Ricky knows the neighborhood, and he told me he was in the hospital. Give her a call. She'll understand he's too sick to hurt you."

She went back to her apartment, wandering by the phone, picking it up and putting it back in the cradle. Mom never saw reason when it came to Mr. Prodan.

She looked at the schedule she'd written down and stuffed it into her pocket. She only had three minutes.

She grabbed her spare change and rushed through the front door to the bus stop. She was lucky. Right as she got to the stop, the bus pulled in with a squeal of brakes and a gust of carbon monoxide. She found a seat halfway down the aisle and shivered. She'd forgotten her coat.

An hour and fifty minutes and two buses later, she arrived at the medical center. It was late, almost dark. She tried not to gawk from the bus window. The hospitals were stacked one after another. It was as big as downtown.

She'd gone to the medical center in their old town for some of Dad's appointments. It had been one big hospital with some doctors' offices, a children's clinic, and a psychiatric center. What could one city need with so many hospitals together in one place? Mr. Foster hadn't even told her which one his father was in. She'd assumed there would be only a few. She stepped off the bus at its second stop.

The lawns in front looked frozen, each blade of grass standing stiff and separate. Nurses and med students, catching the bus at the end of their shifts, thronged the wet sidewalks. Fast-moving cars made her hair fly into her face as a full commuter train zinged by, setting off an electronic bell on the tracks.

She wrapped her arms around herself. Where would she even begin? She looked up at the heart institute. That was one hospital she could cross off her list at least.

She went into the next hospital. Crowds of people scurried through the huge lobby. A twenty-foot Christmas tree and matching nutcrackers towered over her.

"I need Luca Prodan's room number," she told a girl not much older than her who sat behind a desk.

"I can only give patient information to authorized family members."

Sierra took two seconds too long. "I'm his granddaughter."

The woman gave her a wary look but began typing. "Spell the last name."

Sierra spelled it for her.

"I'm sorry. I don't find him listed here."

She visited a second and a third hospital, but the clerks there refused to give her any information. She made a loop. Crowds of pedestrians waited at a light as policemen waved cars into parking garages. Sounds of Arabic and German crossed between two women in burkas and a couple pushing a baby stroller.

So many people, and they all looked like they knew exactly where they were going. She was the only one wandering around the medical center aimlessly. She felt suddenly as lost as she had the time she'd been separated from her mom in the mall when she was six. But she was not six. She held her head a little higher and kept pace with the rushing people around her.

She passed a sprawling cancer center and a gold-towered children's hospital. The buildings were enormous. The next building she went into looked like a hospital, but once inside she could see it was just a private office building closing for the night.

She walked down another street, and another, shivering inside her sweater. The streetlights flickered on and soon the sky was black. Finally, she slumped down on a bench. The sidewalks were empty now. Traffic thinned to a trickle. A policeman watched her from a doorway.

She looked back at him, trying to appear like she had a good reason for being out late at night by herself.

She craned her neck to watch a Life Flight helicopter lowering onto a roof several blocks away. If she boarded that, maybe she could tell from the air where all the hospitals were in this layout.

Freezing in the wind, she glanced at the skyline behind her. Where was Mr. Prodan? Was he in pain? Visiting hours were probably over, but she couldn't go home. She just couldn't. But eventually, she couldn't stand the cold anymore.

THE LANGUAGE OF SPARROWS   125

The bus back home was almost empty. It was nearly midnight by the time the bus roared into her neighborhood. She exited before she got to her apartments. The rain had evaporated into a dry cold now.

She didn't know where she was going, only that she wasn't going home. She wasn't about to face Mom with that hopeful look on her face—as if she could make Sierra be an ordinary teenager and force everything to fit into a picture-perfect life if she just smiled enough.

Sierra's face stung in the frigid air. Her lips were numb. She didn't look up because she knew it would only frighten her. This wasn't a street to be on after dark. It was cold enough, though, that she hoped everyone would be inside.

She thought of Carlos, who had lived on the streets, but she shoved the thought away. He'd have a thing or two to say about her being out here.

"Hey, honey." Across the street, a woman in pumps and a slinky dress with a fur shawl called out to her. "Come on over. I'll keep you warm." A man's laughter echoed farther down the street.

Sierra walked faster. She walked and walked until she came to the bridge. Then she knew where she'd go. It wasn't exactly an inspired hiding place, but the tension melted away as soon as she crossed the bayou and saw Mr. Prodan's street outlined in the dark.

She glanced around furtively. There wasn't even a kitchen light on along the street. A dog barked far away, but otherwise it was quiet. It was easy enough to pull the metal bar up on the gate and let herself into the backyard.

She stood on the back patio, the icy air cutting into her skin. She felt stiff and frozen. But she didn't mind somehow. Thoughts of

strawberry crepes and Turkish coffee and summer afternoons with
Mr. Prodan warmed her.

She imagined a nurse waking him in a few hours and giving him
a breakfast of rubbery eggs and weak coffee.

This was the place she wanted to be. Though it froze her back-
side, she lowered herself next to the doorway, trying to stay invisible.

When the sky began to soften and lights began to turn on in
neighbor's houses, she heard the gate squeal open.

Soon warm hands touched her face. "Hey, *Ojos Café*. I looked all
over the medical center for you."

Carlos. Still calling her Brown Eyes, in Spanish now.

She was too numb to move her lips. Too numb to do anything
but shiver uncontrollably. She refused to look at him, but he crouched
before her at eye level.

Sierra shook her head, as if he'd asked a question. Maybe he had.
Wasn't that why he was here? To say, *Come home, Sierra?* But there was
no talk of home. He just stared at her with a clenched jaw and black eyes.

He put his jacket around her shoulders, unraveled a scarf from
inside a pocket and wrapped it around her neck, and then took her
hands in his and began to chafe them into warmness. She was too
cold to resist and fell into his arms of warmth.

Neither of them spoke. If only it could stay that way. She didn't
want to hear him say it was time to go home. She didn't want to tell
him she was never going back. But eventually, one of them would
have to break the silence. It would have to be her.

Sierra pulled back. "I-I wanted to make sure he was okay." That
was all she could say before her teeth began chattering.

Carlos nodded, stood, and pulled her up with him. "I know."
His voice was low and sad.

He wrapped his arm around her. Too tired and frozen to ask where they were going, she let him lead her to the car and drive her wherever he wanted to take her. He stopped by a drive-through and got two hot ciders. Thawed by the warm drink, she knew what had to come next. But he didn't talk about what came next.

"So what is it about this old man, Brown Eyes?"

She shrugged. "I don't know."

Carlos didn't accept that answer. He waited for her to say more.

"I can be who I am when I'm with him. I'm not too smart or too uncool. And I don't need to be saved from myself. We talk, that's all."

Carlos blew on his cider and turned a corner with one hand on the wheel. "Sounds like a nice guy."

"The thing is, I think he liked me being there too. I don't think anyone pays attention to him either."

"You're friends."

She nodded, pleased. That's what Mr. Prodan was: her friend.

The conversation trailed off, and Sierra looked out the window. Headlights filled the road as people hurried to work. They stopped at a red light a block from home.

"I don't want to go home."

He looked at her hard. "Don't turn your back on your mom, Sierra. Family's not something you want to give up."

She knew why he said it. He wished he had his family back. Well, that was fine for Carlos. He had warm memories of his parents.

He drove her home, as she'd known he would. It was sunrise when they walked up the steps to her apartment. Sierra slid out of the jacket and handed it back to Carlos before she opened the door.

Chapter Sixteen

April leaped off the couch with a strangled cry. She threw her arms around her little girl. "Where *were* you?"

Sierra stood like a statue in April's embrace, then broke away and ran into her room. April was alone again in only a matter of seconds. She buried her face in her hands. After a long night speaking with the police, calling everyone, anyone who might have seen her daughter, and then sitting tight as they told her to do, she felt like splintered glass.

"Give me wisdom," she whispered, looking up to the ceiling. "Give me light." It was a prayer of habit, more than anything. April was accustomed to unanswered prayers, but she couldn't stop praying altogether. She wasn't ready to admit that kind of defeat.

She marched to Sierra's bedroom and raised her hand to knock on the door, but stopped to take a deep breath first. She didn't want to storm in on the offense. She had to win this battle with love, not force.

She tapped on the door, and when she got no answer, opened it with a gentleness she didn't feel. Sierra lay huddled in the rumpled bed. April sat on the corner of the bed, waiting for the storm, stroking her daughter's back. The tears never came, but still, Sierra kept her face buried in the pillow.

"Sierra," April said in her softest voice. "I'm not here to accuse you. I'm here to help you."

Sierra looked up from her pillow. "He's got pneumonia."

"Who?" But who else? "Don't answer that, sweetie. I know who you mean." April smoothed the blankets, searching for the information Sierra wasn't sharing. "Where were you? At the hospital?"

Sierra's mouth quivered, and her face crumpled. She shook her head.

"Where did you go?"

"Mr. Foster said he was in the medical center. But there were so many hospitals. I couldn't find him."

All of April's anger melted at the thought of Sierra wandering through the blocks of unending hospitals, all alone in the cold, wet night.

"I went back to his house and sat on the patio in his backyard."

"Sweetheart, I am not your enemy. Did it occur to you to tell me he was sick?"

Sierra shook her head violently. "You wouldn't have let me visit him, Mom. You and Mr. Foster think he's dangerous, but he's not."

April pulled Sierra into her arms. She rocked her daughter as if she were three again and a hug could make everything better. She smelled of apples and ginger, reminding April of the days of applesauce and bath times.

Finally she stood to go. "Rest, baby. I'll take you to see him after you've had some sleep."

Alone in the living room, she looked up at the center tile on the wall—mother and child in outline. They were in this together. How could Sierra not see that?

———◆◆◆◆———

That evening they walked through miles of corridor before they reached the hospital's main elevator bank. On the ninth floor, another long corridor brought them to a set of double doors. April guided Sierra through them.

The nurses at the station waved them in. But when April opened the door, Luca was asleep. With only the fluorescent recess lights on, the room was left in a dim glow. His breathing rattled. His color was a shade lighter than skim milk. Sierra looked back at her, and April gave her an encouraging nod.

Nick sat in a window seat, grading papers on his knee. Keeping the quiet, he stood and motioned for them to sit on the padded bench next to him.

A newspaper lay on the bench and April picked it up, preparing to fold it and put it in the corner. She stopped when she saw it was probably in Romanian and handed it to Sierra, who began poring over it.

She felt Nick's eyes on them before he whispered to Sierra, "So what's happening in Bucharest?"

Sierra looked up at the wall, at the TV. "The government is meeting to make their budget stronger. And they're preparing for the anniversary of the December Revolution." Sierra looked down then. This was the part where she'd downplay what she'd said. It's what she always did when she got caught being brilliant. "At least I think that's what it says. I can't make out all the words."

Nick looked directly at Sierra. "It sounds like you made out the words just fine."

There was no doubt in April's mind what he was thinking. Sierra had a way of throwing people off when they realized what she could do. She wasn't just bright.

They dropped back into quietness. April watched Mr. Prodan, only vaguely aware of Nick and Sierra on either side of her. Luca was a shrunken, pale version of the man he'd been only a few weeks ago, and he hadn't seemed strong then.

He stirred and opened his eyes, but didn't appear to see them.

Sierra drew close to his bed and leaned over to take his hand. "Mr. Prodan," she whispered. "It's me, Sierra. I'm here. Is it all right?"

"Sierra Wright," he said with wonder in his voice. He struggled to sit, and April could tell even that small effort cost him. He looked at the window where April and Nick sat. "If I knew this is all I should have to do to earn your visit, I should have gone swimming in the bayou with the first chill in November."

"I won't stay long," Sierra whispered.

Her daughter was at ease with Luca Prodan, and the man appeared to relax with her by his side. It all seemed so right.

Luca smiled at Sierra. His face appeared blue in the artificial light. The lighting made the scars stand out across his hands. April winced, recalling the picture taken after Luca's release from prison. She didn't want to consider what might have made the scars on his hand or how vicious his life must have been during those years.

But the thought that really plagued her was the suspicion that what made the relationship between this man and her daughter work was an unnatural bond of pain. Sierra had suffered. Gary's illness, and then his death, had left a scar. But was a man who had lived through a gulag the only one who could understand her?

Mr. Prodan caught April's gaze. He had such gratitude in his glance. She wanted to give him something of worth. And there was only one thing April had to give him—time with her daughter.

She motioned to Nick, and they stood. "We'll leave you two to talk. We'll be in the lobby if you need us."

———◆◆◆◆◆———

With winter coming on, it grew dark early. The lights from the other buildings in the medical center shone outside the ninth-floor lobby, but the hospital had turned the inside lights down for the evening. The smell of waxed floors mixed with coffee from a nearby kitchenette. Nick stood beside her, looking into the darkness.

April turned from the window and leaned against the windowsill to face Nick. It was clear what she had to do. "I'm going to allow Sierra to visit with your dad again."

She waited for some kind of response but only got wary silence. Nick had such natural goodness when he was with her, with Sierra. He was at ease. But when the subject turned to his father, he always took on such tension.

"She ran away last night," April went on, needing to make him understand.

Nick shot her a worried glance.

"She was trying to find Luca, but didn't know the hospital name. Spent the night in his backyard. She's teaching herself Romanian. Studying Romanian history. Luca is all she can think about."

April shook her head, her voice rising a notch. "She's so like her dad. It doesn't matter how high the stakes are, what the cost is to herself or her mental health. She'll grieve for your father until I allow her to see him. I know you've said he can be mean-spirited. And I've seen firsthand he can't always cope."

April's voice grew hoarse. "Sometimes faith is all that's left. And I'm going to have faith that your father will be good to my daughter."

Nick stopped her with a raised hand. "April, you don't owe me an explanation."

She didn't. But she wanted him to approve. She wanted him to say something encouraging, to remove the doubt that she was endangering her daughter.

"You know her best," he said. "Trust your mother's intuition. I do. "

It would have been nice if he'd said, "You can trust him with your sensitive daughter," but he'd given her the most optimistic answer he could.

She stole a glance at him, imagining what she would see if she aimed a camera his way. She'd been afraid to take his photo at Ali's shop. Pictures were intimate things. But today, she felt she needed to know. He was Luca's son. He held a key of sorts to her daughter's future. What kind of man was Nick?

He held his shoulders straight and kept an unwavering gaze. He had a certainty about him. A sense of being in charge. He was a leader, she thought, able to lead others under fire. That was the kind of man he was. Who were his troops? His students?

But there was something else. It wasn't in his eyes or the way he held himself. A camera might not even capture it. It reverberated off him—a rugged loneliness, a sense that if anything had to be done, it would be up to him and him alone to do it.

How much did Luca have to do with that loneliness? And if Nick could reach out to others—to his students, to Sierra, to her—why couldn't he reach out to his own father?

He stretched his hands on the sill next to her. "Don't forget one thing, April." His voice startled her, as if he'd caught her aiming her invisible camera. He waited for her full attention. "Sierra is your daughter."

April shook her head, not following.

"You're modeling strength for her. And compassion. You're showing her a dozen other traits that will serve her. Whatever road she's got to go down, my guess is she'll find the way with you showing her the route."

April fiddled with a strand of hair at her neck, looking into Nick's eyes, holding on to the words for all they were worth. He suddenly seemed nearer than he'd been, though neither of them had moved.

Nick *was* Luca Prodan's son. As far as April was concerned, that was a good thing. Her daughter would profit from the old man's wisdom and directness. Those were traits he had given his son, whether or not Nick realized it.

Chapter Seventeen

Hillary assumed April and Sierra would join the rest of the family for Christmas Eve. She was already rattling off orders to April on the phone about what to bring for hors d'oeuvres before April could tell her it wasn't a definite thing. She wasn't sure taking Sierra to Hillary's was a good idea. Sierra was spending time with Luca, quite a bit of it, but April had yet to see the improvement she was hoping for in her daughter.

With Luca, she lit up, but otherwise, she kept to herself, averted her eyes, hid herself in oversize jackets and dark colors. And Hillary had a way of dictating every detail of a get-together that was only likely to make Sierra retreat further. April couldn't tell Hill that though.

"Let me talk to Sierra, and I'll call you once we've ironed out our plans."

"Okay," Hillary drew out the word. "We're family, April. And it *is* Christmas."

April tapped the counter. They *were* family. So maybe they hadn't bonded like sisters in a movie, but Hillary was all she had left.

Nick called soon after and invited them for Christmas lunch at Luca's. That was the encouragement April needed. Sierra could put up with Christmas Eve at Hillary's if she knew they would spend the next day with Luca.

The candlelight service at Hillary's church was serene with an extrav-
agant choir that could have performed on any professional stage.
The lights in Hillary's gated neighborhood glistened, and April began
humming "God Bless Ye Merry Gentlemen" the last few blocks to
the house.

At Hillary's, the foyer and winding stairs were decked in tinsel,
and a huge Christmas tree graced the living room.

"Sierra! I've missed you, girl," Hillary squealed as she wrapped
her in a fierce hug.

Sierra looked at April with a plea in her eyes. Hill might have
figured out by now Sierra wasn't a touchy-feely type.

"Come on, sweetie." April loosened Sierra from Hillary's grip.
"Let's put these presents under the tree."

In the kitchen, April and Hillary dished dressing and cranberry
sauce into Christmas bowls. Wes's parents sat in the living room,
enjoying the lights and their grandsons. April was pleased to see Wes
had enlisted Sierra to hang mistletoe. There was something almost
like a smile on her face.

"April," Hillary said in a loud whisper. "Have you told her?"

April rolled her eyes. Surely her sister wasn't bringing up suicide
on Christmas Eve.

"No," she said through clenched teeth. "I haven't."

Hillary stirred the mashed potatoes with a vengeance. "That girl
is in serious trouble. Look at her. Her hair's in her face. Her eyes are
glazed. You've got to get professional help."

April huffed out a laugh. If only Hillary could see Sierra on
one of her bad days. It wasn't as if April sat on her hands while her

daughter grew worse. They'd tried a couple of antidepressant prescriptions when they'd first moved back to Houston, but they had caused Sierra to spiral into an even more frightening depression, and April had quickly ended the treatment.

During Gary's worst times, April toyed with a theory that experimenting with cocktails of antidepressants and antianxiety medications initiated his more serious depressive cycles. She wasn't about to begin that nightmare with Sierra.

Hillary moved closer to her. "Look, April," she said in a sandpaper whisper. "Kids have a way of knowing things. It's a good bet she knows deep down how Gary died. Until you start talking about it, it's going to eat her up inside."

April braced her hands on the granite countertop. Did Sierra sense that her father's death hadn't been an accident? Sierra knew what her dad had been dealing with. It was possible that on some unconscious level she knew. But Sierra was not in any frame of mind to take another blow. And for goodness' sake, it was Christmas! April let out a deep breath.

———◆✦◆———

After dinner, the family sat in the living room. The floor lay cluttered with gift wrap and boxes, and everyone admired their presents. Christmas carols played in the background. People laughed. It was all exactly the way Christmas should be.

But after Sierra shoved a half-eaten piece of pecan pie away, April ended the evening with a sigh of relief.

———◆✦◆———

The next day they drove to Luca's, a strawberry cheesecake in Sierra's lap and fresh rolls in the backseat. They needn't have bothered. The dining room table was overflowing with platters of sausage, bowls of sauces, pastries dotted with nuts, soup, cabbage rolls, and a braided loaf of bread glazed with honey. Scents of paprika and vinegar drifted across the kitchen.

Sierra's eyes were alight.

Now *this* was Christmas.

The four of them sat down to eat.

"You're quite the cook, Luca," April said.

He gave a slight nod. "It is a hobby."

Luca ate a few forkfuls of food but seemed to take all his pleasure in the company rather than the food. In the middle of a pleasant conversation, he gave a biting glance to Nick, who must have seemed too preoccupied with Luca's plate. "You do not need to look after my eating habits, Nicolae. You have my oath. I will not waste away before the new year."

Despite the father-son tension, the meal went well.

April insisted on filling everyone's glasses, as her mom and grandmother had done every holiday meal. Everyone talked lightly. There was laughter.

At the end of the meal, Luca raised his glass in a toast. "To celebrate the birth of our Savior."

Glasses clinked.

After lunch, Nick and April began to clear the table and ran soapy water in the sink. Luca and Sierra moved into the library. April watched them out of the corner of her eye as she moved back and forth between the dining room and kitchen. They looked at one of his bookshelves, both animated, talking, even laughing. Sierra gave no half-smiles to Luca.

Nick came beside her at the sink, taking dishes as she put them in the drainer and drying them. His nearness made her feel a little unsteady. But that was pure silliness. He was Luca's son, a friend. That was all.

She looked up at him. "A man who helps with the dishes. I *am* impressed."

He laughed, lines crinkling around the corners of his eyes. "Don't get any big ideas. I'm just keeping you company."

They looked away from each other and turned back to the work at hand. They spoke quietly, both keeping attention on the scene behind them, listening for the words that reached them from the library.

"Correct me if I'm wrong," April said, "but I think Sierra might be as good for your father as he is for her."

"It does seem so."

When the clean-up was finished, April and Nick sat at the kitchen table discussing work, art, places they'd been. Though both were drowsy from the big lunch, time passed quickly. She looked up in surprise to find the afternoon light dimming as it came through the window and the crows beginning to caw. It bothered her how much she liked sitting across from Nick, close to him, chatting. The very air seemed sharper when she was around him. *Friend,* she reminded herself. Goodness knows, there was no room in her life for anything more.

When Nick took off his glasses and rubbed his eyes, she stood to give Sierra notice. "Five minutes, honey."

Nick walked them to the car. "Take care, April," he said, and with a nod to the other side of the car, "You have a good one, Sierra."

He held the door for her and closed it when she'd buckled her seat belt. After a sleepy wave, he turned back to the house. April started to pull out of the driveway, then stopped. She'd forgotten her bread basket.

"I'll be right back," she told Sierra.

The door still stood open. April started to knock but couldn't help but stop when she heard the men's voices inside.

Luca's muted voice, weary and rough as gravel, carried from another room. The library? "There is no need for you to stay now, Nicu. The women are gone, and I know you do not wish to be here. Go home to your own empty life."

April drew a breath. It wasn't exactly a jackhammer of a word, but the unkindness wasn't in keeping with the old man she knew.

"Merry Christmas to you too, Dad," Nick said.

She heard a rustle as someone stood, and then Nick was in her line of vision, picking up a half-filled water glass from a side table.

"I forgot my bread basket," she said quietly.

His face was drawn tight. "I'll get it for you." He went into the library and quickly returned. "Merry Christmas, April," he said, as he handed her the basket, but the merriness of the day already felt like a handful of dust. He watched from the doorway as she walked back to her car and pulled out of the driveway.

<hr />

At home, a lump sat under the welcome mat. April pulled out a wrapped gift and flicked on the light switch inside to read the label. *To Sierra. May your Christmas be bright. Feliz Navidad & all that. Carlos.*

April weighed the present in her hand. It felt like a book. That meant it must be from someone who understood Sierra reasonably well. It was so much more her style than the gaming system from Hill.

April handed the present to Sierra. "Who's Carlos?"

"Someone from school." Sierra carried it off to her room.

A boy from school. Probably every other parent with a teenage daughter dreaded those words. But to April, they were a ray of hope. She prayed for anything—well, almost anything—to bring life back to her daughter's face.

Before they went to bed, April and Sierra ate a bowl of granola together in their pajamas. April gave her a smile, trying to draw one from her daughter.

"Good night, beautiful," she said.

"Night." A fleeting smile crossed Sierra's face.

Not tired enough to sleep, April rummaged through her closet and pulled out a box of photos. She sat on her bed, sorting through them. Mostly they were of Gary and Sierra. The photos had once been her pride and joy. She lifted out one of Gary with Sierra in his lap. She was about six. He had circles under his eyes, as dark as war paint, and he leaned back in the recliner, his eyes closed. Sierra didn't seem to mind. She snuggled against his chest like a newborn.

Even in Gary's decline, he'd shown tenderness to Sierra. There were times April kept Sierra away from him, afraid the collapse of her father would be too frightening.

But usually, even when he was unable to function, he held Sierra in his lap. When his eyes were swollen and his tongue thick with the worst of depression and he was too far gone to speak, he crossed his fingers over his chest, a love letter in sign language to his little girl.

She gently traced a finger over the corner of the picture. *Oh, Gary.*

Their marriage had been turbulent and never, ever easy. But he was the only man she'd ever truly loved. What she wouldn't do to have a bit of his warmth now, his presence, his soul-deep understanding of Sierra.

April thought of Luca speaking to her over coffee with his slow, thoughtful words. Surely he loved his son. What would cause him to speak with such meanness to his only child, who bought his groceries and paid his bills? April put the photos back in the box. Nick and Luca were none of her business.

But she knew they were. They became her business the day Sierra walked into Luca's house.

Chapter Eighteen

Sierra sat, in a sweater, on the steps outside, soaking up the thin sunshine. It was mild for a January afternoon, but then Houston winters were unpredictable. Winds off the gulf battled with the ones blowing in from the Arctic. One day, it would be balmy enough to be spring. The next, the temperature dropped to freezing. Today, the winds must have signed a truce.

Her stomach growled. She'd forgotten to eat lunch. A familiar mewling came from beneath the stairs. Someone else apparently hadn't eaten either.

The white cat had been haunting the stairways and ledges for months. Sierra couldn't convince it to come within petting distance, but she could sometimes coax it close with a bowl of milk.

The cat didn't belong to anyone as far as Sierra could tell, so she named her Zana after a fairy tale in Mr. Prodan's book. Zana let out a plaintive meow. She was a demanding little thing for one who wouldn't let anyone so much as scratch her ears.

"I'm coming, your highness."

Sierra rushed back into her apartment and then back out with a paper bowl full of tuna.

Zana eyed the bowl greedily but wouldn't approach until Sierra drew back onto the landing. Then she stepped lithely to the bowl, reminding Sierra of an albino leopard from a wildlife show. As soon as Zana licked the bowl clean, she darted off across the courtyard, under the willow tree, and sprang up a fence to a balcony in the next apartment building.

Sierra ambled back into the apartment and lay on her bed looking out the curtained window. She missed Argie, their chocolate Lab. He had been friendly, often resting his weary old head in her lap for as long as she wanted him there.

She closed her eyes, trying to remember those days. She could remember their last house. She could remember the yard. She could remember Argie. But no matter how hard she focused, she couldn't think of a single memory that took place there.

Sierra sat up cross-legged. She just needed to think harder. She searched for birthdays and Christmases, vacations or meals at home in their different homes—Virginia, California, Colorado. But she couldn't find even one mental clip. A surge of panic flooded through her.

She looked past the solid walls, the clear windowpanes in front of her. She could remember what Dad looked like, basically. She remembered the walk by the creek she had written about in her haiku. She had remembered that one so easily when she wrote it. But there must be other memories. There had to be a whole file of others right next to it in her memory banks. No one forgot her father.

She imagined herself walking through their house. But all she saw were closed doors. The door to Mom and Dad's bedroom—closed. The door to the living room—closed. She could see a light coming from Dad's study, but she couldn't remember what was inside. How could she have forgotten everything?

The harder she tried to remember, the more a band of pain wrapped around her head. The bed seemed to move beneath her as if she drifted on the ocean. She gathered Ky, her stuffed kangaroo, to her and buried her head in a pillow as the pain pressed against her forehead.

———◆◆◆◆◆———

"Hey, sweet girl."

Mom opened the door, and Sierra blinked at the light from the hallway.

Mom walked into the room and sat on the side of the bed. "It's your big sixteen tomorrow. Have you thought any more about what you'd like to do?"

Mom didn't ask about what friends to invite. She knew there wasn't anyone.

Sierra sat up, toying with her socks, pulling them on and off her heels. "Mom, can you tell me about Dad?"

Her mother arched her back. She gave her a cool smile, and she looked at some imaginary spot in the distance, the way she always did when Sierra asked about him. "What about Dad?"

"I can't remember him. I tried to think of things we did together. Of even just being together."

"Your dad loved you so much, sweetie."

"But we did things together, right? Why can't I remember?"

Mom fluffed a pillow. "It's the heart's way of letting go. We have to let the memories fade a little or the grief would stay so fresh we could never move on."

Sierra closed her eyes. She didn't want to let go. "Can you tell me one thing we did?"

Mom grew quiet, her gaze drifting. She was searching. Why did she have to search so hard for a memory? There should have been lots of them, right?

Mom's gaze lit on a book sitting on her dresser, and her eyes went soft. "Your dad was a great storyteller. He never read you bedtime stories. He told them. You'd cuddle up in his lap, from the time you could talk. You grew out of the cuddles, but he was still telling you stories even when you were in middle school."

Mom brought her knees up to the bed and curled beside her. "He told you ancient folktales or something from the history books. He could paint a picture with words like no one else. When I listened in, I could feel the salty ocean air on my face or smell the hot swords smelting over a fire. You would look up at him, your eyes wide, and I could tell he'd carried you away. He threw in foreign words—Greek or Persian, Aramaic, Latin, wherever the story came from—and you seemed to pick up what he meant."

Mom looked into her face and seemed to see something. She frowned, putting her hand on Sierra's forehead. "Are you feeling okay, baby?"

"Just a headache."

"I'll get you an Advil."

Sierra reached out and touched Mom's arm. "Tell me more."

Mom smiled again, and this time it reached her eyes. "Why don't I brush your hair like I used to? And we'll talk."

Sierra sat on the floor in front of Mom. The strokes of the brush did seem to ease the band of pain. A nice feeling tingled down her neck as the brush massaged her scalp. But it wasn't Mom's words she heard, but Dad's, in her memory.

"Many years ago, before the age of towns or farms, when nomads moved from place to place looking for fresh berries and wild growing grain, a girl about your age, Talar, slept with her clan under an open sky. The stars glittered with a fierce light, because it was the night of the new moon...."

His voice had lilted up and down as he told the story to her. In the memory, she was lying on her bed in the house in Glendale, so she must have been about nine. Sierra could almost feel her father there with them. She closed her eyes, resting back against Mom's knees.

He would lower his voice. *"The camp was too quiet when Talar returned before dawn. The fire had died, and the night watch didn't call to ask who approached."*

Sierra remembered the way he stopped as if that were the end of the story. She refused to believe it, and he laughed, finally telling her the rest.

On one level, she listened to Mom's soft cadence as she told her about old birthday parties when Dad was still around, but on another level, she recalled Talar's story word by word. It was as if she were spending the evening with her family still together.

The next afternoon, a gray sky loomed and winds blew. Sierra pulled on a hoodie and went outside. She dribbled a long ribbon up and down the stairs. Zana looked at the ribbon with her sharp blue eyes, but it took a few minutes before she approached for a pounce. Sierra raised the ribbon higher, still swinging it.

"Come for it, Zana," she called softly. She'd get to pet the elusive cat yet.

Zana eyed the ribbon with a jealous eye but didn't move closer.

Sierra was so intent on Zana she didn't notice Carlos come through the gate. He strolled up the walk toward her and she moved to the bottom of the stairs. "Hey, you got yourself a fur ball."

The kitten sidled up next to his ankle.

Sierra stared, openmouthed. "How did you do that? How did you get her to come to you?" She couldn't take her eyes off the cat, making friends with him as if she did that with every stranger passing by.

Carlos shrugged. "Animals know who to trust. That's all."

"She won't get near me."

He picked the kitten up and placed her on his shoulder. "Girl kitties like men. That's just how they are."

Sierra sat down on the stairs. Carlos pried the cat's claws from his shirt and freed her into Sierra's lap. With him standing close by, Zana stayed, but she kept her eyes on him, ready to leap.

"Make friends with her. Somebody's probably scared her along the way. Show her she can trust you next time."

Sierra petted Zana's long silky body. "Hey, Zana," she whispered, feeling shy with Carlos watching.

He laughed. "Zana. Couldn't of named her better myself. Sounds like some exotic princess."

Sierra closed her eyes, letting the sound of Carlos's voice wash over her, deep and sure, his laugh like a roll of faraway summer thunder.

"I'm sixteen today," she said, her eyes still closed. She didn't know why she said it.

"Sweet sixteen, huh?"

Thank goodness he didn't say something stupid about never been kissed, even if it was true.

"What are you gonna do?"

She shrugged.

"No birthday party?"

"Dinner out with my mom, maybe."

As she listened to his voice, she watched the shifting light through her eyelids. A shadow blocked the light and the air stilled next to her. She opened her eyes to find Carlos beside her on the step. Zana leaped from her lap and watched them from the sidewalk.

He offered a self-conscious smile and a lift of his shoulder. *Oh no.* He was thinking that stupid sweet sixteen thing. She could tell. "Don't you dare say it, Carlos."

He laughed. "Say what?"

He knew what. She could tell by the goofy smile on his face.

She looked at her fingernails. "Sweet sixteen and never been kissed. Don't say it."

"I didn't say it."

But he kept looking at her. An intense quiet settled between them, making her all warm, and he leaned toward her.

"I can't," she whispered.

"Okay." He drew back, his jaw clenched.

"I'm sorry."

"Don't be." His words had sharp edges. "Look, I know I'm not good enough for you, Sierra. Never have been. I can't help it. I've always liked you anyway."

"Not good enough? What does that mean?"

"I'm the guy who lived on the streets, the one who takes care of your lawn, right? You're the girl who knows all these strange alphabets and languages. You said your dad was a professor, right? I get it. You need your own type."

His words seemed to swallow her. She looked straight at him so he'd believe her. "No," she said faintly. "That's not it at all."

"What then?"

She shook her head "It's not you."

He placed his hands on her knees, making her heart beat too fast. "If it's not me …?"

She didn't know what to say, and his gaze grew black.

"It's not you," she insisted.

He dropped his hands, but he stayed beside her. "Sierra, you look in the mirror, and what do you see? Because I have to wonder why this pretty girl I know is working so hard not to be seen or touched or even talked to."

"I don't know." Sierra felt herself rocking. "It's me. I'm all wrong."

He put his hand over hers, lacing his fingers through hers. Sierra went still. He kept her gaze. "You're not all wrong, Brown Eyes. I think you're all right."

Sierra wanted to believe him.

"You sure it's not me?" he said.

"I'm sure, Carlos."

After he left, Sierra felt the impression of his hand over hers, the air calm as if he were beside her still. Zana blinked at her curiously, as she lay on a rail all the way across the complex licking her snowy fur.

CHAPTER NINETEEN

Three weeks into January, Nick passed Cindy Velasco in the staff lounge. She carried a stack of first semester finals under her arm. Out of curiosity, he asked, "Have you looked at Sierra Wright's yet?"

Cindy's face told him she didn't have good news before she slid a paper from the stack of English II papers.

The multiple-choice section formed a window. Rows were bubbled in with multiple answers, and connected with lines to form the panes. In the bottom margin, a penciled cat napped on a ledge. The essay on the next page bordered on illegible. What was that in the middle? It looked like ancient Greek. The last paragraph was a poem—in Spanish. This paper wasn't a final. It was a cry for help.

Cindy held out her hand for the final. "I know this girl's smart, Nick, but I don't think she's going to pull through. Honestly, I think she belongs in your class."

Nick laughed. "Fat chance of that. Liza's on my case for 'departing from the scope and sequence' as it is. She's not about to let me have another kid to mess with."

Cindy gave him a playful punch to the shoulder. "You'll win Liza over by May. You win them all over eventually."

Nick held on to the final. "Do me a favor? Give Sierra an incomplete. I'll talk with her."

She pursed her mouth. "Only for you, Nick. But if she doesn't come to retake it by Friday, I'll have to give her the grade she earned."

He watched her as she left the lounge. There was still hope. The year was half over, but there was still hope for Sierra, and he would find out what it was.

That night, he stood on his back deck inhaling the crisp pine-scented air, still thinking of Sierra's final. April was doing everything she could for her daughter. His father was chipping in. When Sierra was with him, her face came to life. She talked to his old man and didn't try to hide who she was.

But at school she was the old Sierra, hiding her face behind a sheath of dark hair.

The girl put all her effort toward failure. There was a way to get her cooperation, but as Nick pounded his palms against the railing, he couldn't find the solution. He closed his eyes in silent prayer.

Ask her.

Nick looked out at the trees, which shivered in the cold wind. An answer to prayer? But Sierra Wright wasn't going to tell him what would make school turn around for her. He doubted she knew herself.

He remembered all too well being seventeen and his world coming apart at the seams—his mother fading to a skeletal version of herself in her fight against cancer; his father, a stranger who rejoined their family only because of Mom's impending death, insisting on a new set of rules for him. He hadn't been able to put his angst into words, much less tell anyone what he needed. The only language he knew was to stand outside in the rain, pummeling a tree until he fractured his fist.

What Sierra was doing was worse. All her anger, silent and scalding, was turned inward.

Did he have anything to lose by asking her? Not much, he had to admit. But getting her to speak to him at all would require a miracle. Nick looked up at the starry sky, his laugh winging out into the night air. He prayed to the Father of Miracles for one of his own and put his worries aside.

⸺◆✦◗◆●⸺

The next day, Nick watched Sierra leave the hall. He would have to connect with her outside of this place. The school itself was stifling her. Fraternizing with a female student, and after school too—one more thing to grate on Liza, but it was the only way.

He stepped up beside Sierra as she crossed the street on her way home after school. He handed her the final with Cindy's "Incomplete" written with a thick red marker at the top. Scrawled underneath were the words, "See me."

Sierra glanced at the English test, her eyes dark and miserable. "I'm not retaking it."

"Your choice."

They strode across the crosswalk and onto the concrete toward a cluster of apartment complexes. Afraid one of them would be hers and his chance would be gone, he jumped into his question. "How do you feel about Cuban?"

"What?" She stopped and gave him a slant-eyed inspection.

"There's a place down the street that sells great Cuban sandwiches."

"I'm not hungry."

"Me neither really," Nick plunged on. He wondered if her time with his father might be the thing. "How about Romanian pastries?"

"What do you want?" Her voice was raw.

"I want to talk to you, Sierra. Away from school."

She looked at his feet.

He sighed. "A conversation. That's all I want, Sierra."

"Where is it?"

"The Romanian place? A few miles. Give your mom a call. I'll drive you."

She swung her hair. He knew that look. He'd seen it in the mirror a couple of decades ago. She wasn't about to call her mother for permission.

Sierra walked back with him to the parking lot, and he let her in his truck. Before he got in, he made a call to April to give her a quick briefing. April sounded surprised, but quickly agreed.

The Romanian teashop was in a quieter part of town. It was slow this time of day. The small scattering of tables only had one other customer. Nick arranged his silverware on the tablecloth. "I'm not a subtle guy, Sierra, so I'm just going to say this straight out. You're barely getting by at school, and it's not because you can't handle the work. What would turn things around for you?"

Sierra sank down in her seat, her eyes boring a hole through her bread plate. Nick's confidence fell at her invisible act. But then she looked up at him, almost startled.

"I hate school. I hate it and nothing will make it turn around for me."

"What do you see yourself doing then? When you're finished with school."

"I don't."

"Come on, Sierra. Everyone has some kind of dream. You don't imagine yourself writing the great American novel, being an ambassador, or raising kids …?"

She shook her head slowly, her eyes clouded.

He leaned in toward her. "Okay. What kind of things do you like to do when you're not at school?"

He could almost see her squirm. "Words."

Nick nodded at her to continue, but Sierra just looked down at her plate. "I like words."

"Explain that to me, Sierra."

She bent her head. The waiter stepped up to their table. He knew Nick from past visits and asked Nick in Romanian what they would like. Sierra watched the conversation. Her eyes registered. She understood the waiter, just as she'd been able to read the Romanian newspaper at the hospital.

When the waiter walked away, Nick asked her in Romanian, "How long have you been studying the language?"

"Three months," she answered back in Romanian. "On the computer."

He asked a few more questions, and Sierra answered. Her pronunciation was good, not that Nick was the best judge. It had been the language he spoke at home, literally his mother tongue. But since his mother died, he rarely ran across someone to speak it with. It had been his own choice not to speak it with Dad—the twisted terms of an angry teenager first meeting his father after twelve years apart. Now English was their habit.

She wasn't fluent yet, but a little practice with his old man and she would be. She spoke as though she'd been studying the language for a year, not only a few months.

He switched back to English. "Those are the kinds of words you like?"

She nodded, and he could feel an energy vibrate off her in the silence.

"Tell me about the languages you know."

"Some Spanish. French."

"Some, Sierra?" he insisted.

"I can carry on a conversation in Spanish. I read a little in French."

"Which books?"

"*Le Comte de Monte-Cristo.*" She said it with the French pronunciation. And then, as an afterthought, "Camus, Baudelaire, Madame Guyon, Victor Hugo, Robbe-Grillet."

"And in Spanish?"

"Cervantes, Garcia Marquez, Neruda, Borges." And then quietly, "Teresa de Ávila."

Relief washed over her face, and her shoulders drooped as the blistering energy subsided from her. As if she'd been forced to hide all her life in case someone noticed how brilliant she was.

The waiter laid two plates of jam-filled tarts on the table, topped off their coffee cups, and glided away on the soft carpet.

Nick cut into a pastry. "You're taking French in school, I know. Did you study Spanish?"

"I watched it on TV." She waved a hand, as if it were obvious that anyone could pick up Spanish by watching *novelas* on Telemundo.

He began speaking to her in Spanish this time. Nick had learned to communicate with the parents of his Latino students with a tutor and years of hard practice. But Spanish words rolled off her tongue as effortlessly as if she were a native speaker, and to his ear, Sierra's accent was flawless. She even had the figures of speech down.

He switched back to English. "You're a good writer. Is there anything else you like to do with languages?"

"I just like to see them on the page. How they look on the page and how they feel in my mouth, what pictures they make me think of. Sometimes I look up the audio Bibles online and listen to a passage in different languages, even the ones I don't know. You know, so I could imagine how the Beatitudes would sound to me if I were Vietnamese or Polish."

She flushed and looked around, as if she couldn't find a spot to focus on.

Nick leaned back, rubbing his forehead. *Ask her.* And he'd asked. Why didn't April have her in a program for kids—for what kind of kids? For those brilliant in foreign languages? Nick laughed to himself. There had to be something better for her than a typical classroom. Even the advanced classes at Armstrong would be too slow for her.

Nick would get April's daughter help one way or another. "Sierra." He waited for her to look at him. "I think I know. But I want you to tell me: Why do you hate school?"

She shook her head.

He didn't want to put an answer in her mouth, but she wasn't volunteering, so he asked, "Are you bored?"

"A little."

"And?"

There was a long lull. "It's noisy. And dark. The kids are everywhere. Some days, just the sound of the markers squeaking on the whiteboard or someone flipping through their notebook makes me feel like my brain's going to explode. At home, there are windows, and it's quiet."

"You like working at home better?"

She nodded.

"But you're not doing your homework either."

She looked down, embarrassed.

"You're working on your words, aren't you?"

Silence.

"Look, we'll figure something out for you. I don't know what. But I don't want you to be miserable at school any more than you want to be miserable sitting through it." He stood.

"Mr. Foster," she said on a soft breath.

He waited.

"I was tired." She looked down, her eyes intent on the tablecloth. "I stayed up late the night before. Well … all night. Writing. I couldn't sleep. That's why I failed the English final. And Biology. I passed my others."

"Do you have trouble sleeping, Sierra?"

"Sometimes."

Sometimes? Nick had a hunch that that hungry mind of hers kept her awake too many nights.

"I'll take you home. But I want you to come tomorrow and retake those two finals. It's a teacher workday, but I'm sure your teachers will work with you."

He smiled and was rewarded with a flicker of a smile in return.

At home, he thought and prayed until he had knots in his shoulders. He couldn't solve this for her. She needed to solve it for herself, if the solution meant anything. But somehow he had to talk her through it.

He hadn't asked about her personal life. He knew she had some grief to overcome. But he also knew, he just *knew* if he could help her find a home for that mind of hers, the girl would take off. Maybe not socially. Maybe not emotionally. Not at first, but they would follow.

An idea began to beckon to him, but he didn't like it. There was one person who had welcomed Sierra. And Sierra felt understood by him. A ferocious lump grew in his chest at just thinking about talking with his old man about Sierra. He'd have ideas. But hand them over to Nick? Not a chance. Every constructive word with his father had to be fought for, while a dozen other words, said or not, waited in ambush, ready to undo every step of progress they made.

———•◦∞◦•———

Friday evening he found Dad in the back of his house painting a little picket fence for his garden. It was sunny enough. It had even been warm earlier, but with twilight hovering close, the temperature was dropping, and a cold wind blew through the nearby pine trees.

"You shouldn't be out of doors, Dad." He didn't mention his father's deep-chested cough that lingered after the pneumonia.

His old man shot him a look of disgust and kept painting.

"I came to talk about Sierra," Nick said.

That earned a response. His father swabbed the paintbrush on the sides of the can and laid it across the top. Rocking back on his heels, he looked up, silent. Why did it irritate Nick so much that his filial concern earned a glare, but the very name of Sierra grabbed his father's full attention?

Nick pulled up a patio chair. "She's brilliant."

His father nodded, as if this were old news to him.

"Not just smart. You've seen her writing and it's beyond what I'd expect out of a teenager. She taught herself Spanish from television. She's fluent enough to read *The Count of Monte Cristo* and *Les Misérables* in French from a couple of high school classes, and in three months of online courses, she can more or less converse in Romanian."

"Ah." His standard invitation to keep talking.

"But she's barely passing her classes." Nick waited, giving his old man a dose of his own silent treatment before continuing. "I think she's bored out of her mind. She's boxed in at school."

His father rose and took a chair next to Nick.

"Why do you come to me? I am not fit to speak with the girl, your friends at the school say."

"I wasn't the one to say it."

His father gave him a steely stare. He never accepted Nick's omissions or half-truths. They both knew Nick could have made the school understand. He could have intervened with April if he'd wanted to.

"She needs help, Dad, and you know her better than any of us."

After a long bout of silence, his old man turned to face him. "She needs to be set free. I knew this when I first met her."

"Set free?"

"You cannot expect such a mind to stay within the confines of a school, especially such a poor school as yours."

Nick ignored the criticism of his job. "How do I let her out of the confines?"

"Tell the girl to study literature. Any kind of literature she wishes, from the ancients to the moderns. Tell her she must write to you about what she is learning. It is all she needs."

Nick sat rigid. His father was right. She would gulp down novels and poetry and biographies. She'd overflow with essays and creative responses far beyond his expectations. She could probably read the whole western canon in the original languages. But it didn't solve anything.

Cindy Velasco couldn't get away with assigning Sierra different work from everyone else in her class. There wasn't a chance he would be able to convince anyone else to give her an individualized curriculum, even if her work soared above the rest of their students.

And even if they would tailor the assignments for her, she would still be required to sit, suffocating, through classes all day long.

He had the answer. It just wasn't a workable one.

Nick rubbed his chin. "I don't think so. The school would never let her manage her own education."

"I did not speak of what the school will or will not allow Sierra to do. I spoke of what she needs."

Nick looked evenly at his old man. It was obscure statements like these that made conversation impossible between them. Reality never influenced his father's words. Everything and everyone, including Nick, was judged against the perfect standard in his father's imagination.

"Thanks anyway, Dad."

But as he drove away, his father's words, *set her free*, sank their teeth into him and wouldn't let him go. There had to be a way to set her free.

CHAPTER TWENTY

Just before dawn, in bed and with a throw wrapped around her shoulders, April held her open Bible on her lap. She flipped through verses she'd highlighted in better days. "You will know the truth, and the truth will set you free."

She let the pages flutter close. She couldn't tell Sierra the truth. If Sierra knew Gary had taken his own life, what might she do? It just wasn't a truth her daughter needed. Not now. Maybe not ever.

The truth in that verse was about Jesus anyway, not Gary's death. April closed her eyes and leaned back against her pillows. She could try to convince herself the verse didn't apply to her situation. But if Jesus's truth meant anything, so did every bit of truth, including hers.

That morning, she scrubbed the house down. She vacuumed. She dusted. She cleared the kitchen counter of junk mail. "A clean house, a clean mind," her father used to say.

Her father knew about positive thinking. Her mom's spells were mild and infrequent compared to Gary's, but Dad was always there, pouring sunshine into their lives, keeping them active, and focusing their attention on the rainbows, not the mud puddles. He'd had the will to keep April and Hillary from following Mom into the darkness when she went into one of her moods.

Her parents were gone, but Dad's words still saved April's sanity often. A clean house, a clean mind indeed.

She carried a pile of papers to the trash can but stopped midway through the living room, spying Sierra outside talking to the boy who worked on the grounds. A good-looking kid. He stood with his feet planted firmly and his shoulders held high. As he talked to her, Sierra laughed. She laughed!

But a doubt sprouted. He looked a little cocky. And Sierra was so fragile.

April slid the curtains open wider, letting in the sunlight. "Be good to my little girl," she whispered. "Help her keep that smile."

<hr />

Mr. Prodan had been in the kitchen when April arrived at his house on Monday.

April stood in the doorway. "I hope you don't mind my stopping by. You seemed so pale at Christmas, and I just wanted to make sure you're getting on after the pneumonia."

"Yes, yes." His voice still held a tinge of hoarseness, but his color had returned.

He invited her in, and they made small talk as he rolled out dough. With his wounded hands, he held the roller at an awkward angle, as if he couldn't quite make his thumb rest on the handle. The man always seemed to be cooking, and yet never had a spare ounce on his frame. Did he even eat the meals he made?

"Call me prejudiced, Luca, but I had this idea that European men didn't cook."

He chuckled. "I did not even put a kettle on to boil until I was thirty. I was a scholar and much too important to cook. But after my time … my time apart from my family, I needed a simple occupation. A kind woman invited me to work in her bakery, and I found I enjoyed the simple pleasure of forming a piece of dough or of cooking a puree to just the right thickness."

She leaned against the counter and for a time they talked about his favorite subject: books. She told him about the gallery and the types of art she sold. He asked intelligent questions. They didn't speak of the day at Blue Ziti's. They didn't speak of Nick or Sierra. It was an unspoken pact to stay on safe topics.

As she looked around the room, she noticed something. Everything was practical—a clock, cooking utensils, a filing tray of unopened bills. There were no mementoes of Romania, no anniversary knickknacks, no pictures of his wife or of Nick in his youth.

Even with her mixed feelings about her memories of Gary, she kept pictures of him around the apartment.

Sunlight poured through the window over the sink, lighting Luca's frazzled curls and his skin. As he began to cut pastries out of the dough, she greased a pan for him.

Maybe Luca's decision to stay on safe ground had robbed him and Nick of too much already. She couldn't forget the hard look in Nick's eyes on Christmas Day. He didn't know the truth. His father wouldn't even discuss his past. It wasn't her business. And yet she found herself broaching the subject.

"Luca, don't you have any pictures?"

"Pictures?"

"You know—photos of your family."

"Yes, of course."

She looked around her as she washed her hands under the faucet. "Where?"

He smiled faintly. "In a drawer."

"I don't want to interfere."

"And yet you will." He was amused.

"I see your son's pain. I see yours." What right did she have to talk to anyone about erasing the past? She sighed. "I can't do anything about my own family's pain, but it doesn't keep me from wanting to do something about yours."

He put the pan of pastries on the counter and turned to face her. "Our situations are not so very different. There is nothing to be done. What time can heal, it will. What it can't must be endured." He pursed his lips and gave his European one-shouldered shrug, as if the matter were settled.

"I can't admit that kind of defeat." Her voice sounded hollow, even to her own ears. "I can't. I know Sierra will have her father's suicide—"

She stopped. Luca blinked. Her throat was suddenly parched. How did that slip out? But she'd started it. She needed to finish it.

"His suicide," she went on, "the one she doesn't know about but I suspect will be part of her life until the day she dies. I'm not willing to admit that my only prayer is for time to heal a little of her sorrow."

He didn't speak, but the compassion in his eyes reached out to her. April felt as if she'd been holding her breath and hadn't realized it. Since moving to Houston, she'd only spoken to Hill about Gary's suicide. And the crazy thing was, it never occurred to her she needed to say those words aloud.

"My husband … My husband ended his own life after years of fighting severe depression."

His face went soft, as if some invisible barrier had been let down. "I wish I could give you a better hope. Your daughter is young. Perhaps, perhaps. But my experience has only taught me this: God is not afraid of pain. He does not try to keep us from it. He does not avoid it for Himself. So I suppose we should not fear it either. If Sierra's pain is meant to be, she will live with it. She will carry it and live her life in spite of it. As will you."

Was that all that remained? Bear it and go on? She didn't think so. "There's got to be more. There's love. Given time, it will work its healing on Sierra. And me. Even you, Luca."

He only said, "I hope you are right."

Who did that sound like? She let out a dry laugh. "You reminded me of Nick just then. He's afraid to hope too."

She folded a hand towel and put it on the counter, not because it needed folding but because her hands needed something to do. "It occurred to me that you and I, we're playing the same role. We're both of us keeping our stories from our children. And I wonder if the bitterness we see in them is the result."

She felt a small shock in him, though he didn't move and his expression didn't change.

Softly, very softly she said, "It's difficult for you to remember those years. Only you can know how difficult."

"What good is remembering?" His voice sliced through the air. "I cannot undo the past. I was not there to raise my son, and now he is a man halfway through life himself."

"The past, no, but you could change the future. Tell him what happened. He's going to have a hard place inside him until he knows. Without your past, he's missing his own story."

He gave his head a vigorous shake.

"I won't press you." She came beside him and turned his hands over to the scars on the soft sides of his palms. "I can't imagine how frightening it would be to go back there, even in your memory. I don't blame you for not wanting to speak of it. I'm the last person to blame you."

How could she, of all people, blame him for shrouding his story in secrecy? Still, she didn't let the matter drop. Some sense that what she was doing was right—some still quiet voice? —kept her talking.

"I'd help you if you wanted. If you'd tell the story to me, if you couldn't tell it to Nick, I would transcribe it." She held on, hoping her touch would reassure him. "You know the saying 'A picture's worth a thousand words'? Art can convey things to the heart—maybe to Nick's heart—that your words might not. I'd arrange your photos for you and illustrate those things you don't have pictures for."

They stood, locked together by their hands, an awful quiet hovering in the space. He looked to the door, as if he could spring free by leaving her presence.

"I'm sorry," she said in her quietest mothering voice. "The last thing I'd want to do is hurt you. It's your past. You have to do what you want with it."

She let go of his hands and poured him a glass of water. She stayed as the morning wore on, not wanting to leave him wounded and frail. When she was sure he was okay, she said, "I'll leave you, Luca. Call me, if you need anything." She turned to go. "You're like family to me."

And it was true. She had no extended family to speak of. As much as she loved Hill, her sister wasn't someone she turned to for comfort, nor did Hill seem to need her.

He didn't say good-bye. He returned to his pastries, spooning goat cheese into them.

April stood outside the door listening to an eerie silence. She remembered him at Blue Ziti's, standing like a lost child in a pool of broken glass and tomato soup, all because he saw a policeman. What did she think she was doing, asking him to relive the jagged days of his past?

But she couldn't rid herself of the notion settling into her bones that he needed her interference. It might be hypocritical of her—the woman hiding her husband's suicide from her own daughter—to demand the truth from him. And oh, how she felt every ounce of that hypocrisy.

But there *were* important differences. Nick wasn't a sixteen-year-old on the knife's edge of depression. He was ready to hear his dad's story. And it had been over thirty years since Luca went to prison. Wasn't it time he faced his story?

CHAPTER TWENTY-ONE

Luca called April a few days later. His house was so bare she was almost surprised to learn he had a phone. After all, she had not been able to find a phone number when she looked up his address for their first meeting.

His voice carried over the line, old and faraway. "I will tell you my story." He drew in a long, shuddering breath. "I will tell it to you only. I do not think my son would listen if I told it to him in person."

●◆▶◀◆●

A few days later, April joined Luca in his library. Luca's home, simple as it was, enchanted her. It was a place of natural light and warm wood. Did he feel it too? Did his neat selection of books and armchairs give him charm and meaning where he would otherwise have nothing else?

She felt like a reporter with her minirecorder in hand. The strangeness of helping Luca tell his story struck her all over again. Yet, it felt so right.

She eased into a chair.

Luca, standing at the window, turned to her. "I will tell you the beginning and the end of the story. But the middle I cannot tell you. I do not think I can tell that."

"Okay."

"Nicolae needs to know why I went to prison. And he needs to understand why I did not join him in America when I was freed. But I cannot talk of prison."

"This is your story to tell as you want to tell it, Luca."

She was relieved to see the haunted look leave his eyes. He even had a lightness in his movements. April pressed the Record button.

Luca sat down, and only then did she see the black-and-white photo in his hand. He handed it to her. It was an image of a fresh-faced girl with braids. She was a Balkan beauty—dark hair, high cheekbones, and sleepy-lidded eyes. She was in a school uniform, but something about her seemed older than a schoolgirl. The jaunty angle of her scarf and her bold stare into the camera spelled trouble.

Luca's face brightened. He saw her studying the girl in the photo and gave a faint chuckle. "What is your freedom worth, eh? For me, it was worth her. I was sixteen when I first set my sights on her."

"What was her name?" April asked.

"Tatiana Călinescu."

Luca looked at the picture, and then away, his mind traveling far away from this place. He was a natural storyteller. His voice trailed off, soft and lilting, carrying April with him as he began his story.

"Freedom. There was little of it in Romania. The only freedom I knew had to be whispered. The communists had been in power since before I was born. At school, in unison, we shouted out slogans of devotion to the state until our throats ached. We sang folk songs to honor our leader. On television, there was only more of the same thing.

"In our apartment, my parents spoke in whispers so the neighbors would not hear. They listened to *Vocea Americii*—the Voice of

America—on the radio, but only at the lowest volume. They whispered about escaping to freedom in the west. They whispered their prayers.

"It was wisest not to have religion or politics. Success could only be achieved by conforming to the masses. My future appeared bright. I was a clever student preparing for a career in mathematics. It seemed very safe, as math was a language without religion or politics. This is what I thought.

"I only wanted one thing to make my future the brightest: the prettiest girl in the school. All the boys flirted with Tatia, but she would not acknowledge them. She would not even look their way. She was clever, too; second in marks only to me."

"Tatiana was your wife?" April asked, holding up the photo. "This is Nick's mother?"

"You are skipping ahead in the story." Luca wagged his finger at her.

It *was* his wife. The woman in the photo at Nick's had aged into sophistication and motherhood, her hair puffed up in a 70s do instead of braids, but it was the same woman. April had imagined the woman who linked Nick and Luca as a quiet saint of a woman, someone who waited patiently for her heroic husband during his imprisonment and dutifully raised her son alone. This vixen of a girl was something of a surprise.

Luca coughed and rested back in his chair, his eyes closed.

"I knew I could not win her by paying court to her. The other boys had tried all their romantic tricks. So I pretended she did not exist. If she even asked me to borrow a pencil, I acted as if I did not hear. I courted other girls. But of course, I worked hard in my schoolwork so she would be impressed. And on the soccer field, if she should be there, I was an acrobat.

"She did not seem the least interested. I knew I would have to find a new method. But what? My marks fell then. I did not sleep or eat properly.

"Finally, one winter day while we waited on the sidewalk for school to start, I decided I would do whatever it took to win her attention. I put on what I believed to be a very funny skit. Our leader was so lauded he was not allowed to be shown on television doing normal things, such as blinking or wiping his brow. There was also a list of words that could not be used in public. Not even the very powerful used these words.

"So I pretended to be Ceauşescu. I stood tall, giving a speech about the greatness of Romania and socialism, but I wiped my brow, shivered in my coat. I sneezed. And I coughed out sections of my speech where it was obvious I was talking about such things as informants. I did not say his name. My comedy was a great success. My friends laughed, but not too loudly.

"As we went in to the school, Tatia pulled my scarf to stop me from entering the doors. She looked at me and me alone. I would have gone to be burned at the stake to win such attention.

"'Are you such a great fool?' she hissed. 'What if someone reports you?'

"'I thought you were a lover of truth,' I retorted. I gave her my most careless smile.

"She said to me, 'Nothing is worth going to prison. Nothing!' She was very vehement.

"I promised to be good from then on, for her and her only. She shook her head and walked ahead of me into the school, but from then on, she did talk to me. I got into terrible trouble at school for the scene. They even threatened to report me to the authorities. But I was a favorite with my teachers.

"Tatia became my friend, and then after a warm kiss one summer evening, something more. We were in love.

"But when I returned to school that fall, my best friend, Andrei, said to me, 'Are you mad? You cannot be Tatiana's boyfriend!'

"All the boys were in love with Tatiana. They had all tried to win her. I stared at my friend, certain he was the mad one. But Andrei said it was only a contest to see who could get a response from Tatia. Comrade Snow Maiden, he called her. But no one would be seen with her. Her grandfather was an Orthodox priest who'd spent ten years in prison for his refusal to pollute the Bible and prayers of his church with communist rhetoric. Her father also had been interrogated for sheltering nonconformists. Somehow, I did not know this.

"The man who married her would already have a mark against him. But I loved her madly."

April handed Tatia's photo back to Luca. He took it and quietly put it back in the desk drawer.

"You were so young," she said.

"We were children. It is hard to think now of having such power to determine our lives at such an age."

April smiled. "How old were you when you married?"

"We were nineteen." He looked long at the library window. "We do not have photos of the wedding. We ran away to a small village and married in secret. I was allowed to attend a teacher's college, but I lost my place at the university. My star had burned out."

"A great loss."

"I never once regretted it. All of my plans blurred next to Tatia."

April felt a small pang. What must it have been to be Tatiana, to be loved like that? "You were fortunate then?"

"So I was. So I am still to have been loved by Tatia. But in Romania, we have a saying. Good fortune is made of glass."

"Luca," she said, "I was ready for a story of espionage or a mystery of some kind, and here you're telling me a love story."

"Yes. I suppose you are right. A love story."

He seemed pleased with the idea. April rather liked it herself. What a romantic thing to say. All of his plans blurred next to Tatia.

Communist Romania had been such a severe place. She wondered exactly what loving Tatia cost him in the long run.

CHAPTER TWENTY-TWO

Pale sunshine leaked into Sierra's bedroom, all citrus and morning dew. On her bed, her World History book lay open to a chapter on the Renaissance, but her mind wandered. She thought of what Mr. Foster had said. "Don't you see yourself doing something?"

Why was her future so blank?

She took out her journal and a black pen. Sierra wrote "There's a future with me in it" in dark letters across the top of one page. She underlined the words. She drew a box around them. It didn't feel any more real for having written it. She drew bars through the corner, then the middle, until the box was a checkerboard of crisscrosses, and the words were illegible.

At school she tried to focus but found herself translating the word future into every language she knew, writing it in every script. At the end of the day, she stopped at her locker and then headed toward her usual exit. Emilio and his friends stood just outside on the steps, throwing mock punches at each other.

Once Emilio saw her, he swung around to rest his hand high against the door frame. She'd have to slink close to him and under his arm to get out. She turned back inside to take another exit, but he, and all his friends followed her in. The halls were empty. Within seconds, he'd trapped her against a locker.

"Sweet Sierra," he crooned.

She looked around for someone, for a way out, but she was on her own this time.

"I guess I better act fast before that Doberman of yours gets here, eh?" Emilio said.

He smelled of good things—cologne and mints—but all she could think was that the close smells would suffocate her. She was going to throw up. His face moved too close to hers. Sierra squeezed her eyes shut and choked out a single word. "Stop."

"You don't mean that, baby." He massaged her neck, moving his hand slowly down to her shoulder. "Let me show you what feels good."

Her throat squeezed tight. She heard laughter around her. *Please, Emilio,* she tried to say. *Please stop.* But the words wouldn't form on her lips.

"Ever heard the saying 'No means no,' Emilio?"

Sierra opened her eyes. Mr. Foster stood in the hallway with his arms crossed. Emilio backed off. "Aw, man, Mr. F. I wasn't disrespecting her. I was just helping her know her own mind, you know."

Mr. Foster shot her an encouraging look. "Are you okay, Sierra?"

She nodded, afraid of what her voice would sound like if she spoke.

He looked over his shoulder to Emilio's friends. "It's time to leave the campus. School's over." He waited for them to leave and then walked with Emilio down the hall. "We're going to have a talk about what respect means, my friend."

Sierra hugged her arms to herself, waiting for the trembling to stop before she practically ran out of the school. The citrus sunshine the morning had offered was gone. Thick, gray clouds roamed in a windy sky instead.

Carlos leaned against his car in the apartment parking lot. He didn't say hello or anything. In fact, he looked kind of annoyed and she suspected one of his friends had already texted him about Emilio. Or worse, they'd recorded the whole thing and posted it for everyone to see.

"You got anything to do this afternoon, Sierra?"

She shook her head, still afraid if she spoke her voice would break.

"You want to spend the afternoon on the beach? It'll be quiet this time of year. I'll have you home before ten."

Sierra shrugged and went back inside to call her mom. She washed her face and put on lip balm. She took a few deep breaths before coming back out. "My mom checked you out with Ricky. He says you're all right."

Carlos surrendered a small smile at that, but he wasn't his normal cheerful self.

High winds battered the sides of the car as they drove the hour-long span of freeway. Sierra ignored the landscape as they sped by. It was all chain stores and McDonalds anyway, with the metal towers of oil refineries in the distance.

By the time they got to Galveston, the sky had descended low and wintry. They drove down a hilly road toward the water. Weather-beaten mansions spoke of another time, another class of people long gone. They passed a gothic castle and in a flash Sierra was nine again. They were visiting Grammy and Gramp in Houston and took a day trip to Galveston. Her father drove them, pointing out Bishop's Palace to her.

The name reminded him of a story, and he told her about the nuns of St. Mary's tying orphans to themselves with clothesline, hoping to save the children from the crashing tidal waves during the hurricane of 1900. She shivered. Another memory.

Carlos gave her a sideways glance but didn't say anything. He drove down to the seawall. Waves lashed the sand. The ice-cream vendors and little shops with flip-flops and sunglasses she remembered were closed today. The beaches and piers were empty, but there were a couple of surfers on the insane waves in the distance.

"You ever ride the ferry?" Carlos asked.

Sierra shook her head. "I haven't been here since I was a kid."

He drove past the restaurants, past the brightly painted beach houses on stilts, past everything, until they reached land's end and the ferry dock. At this time of day only a few cars lined the entrance, and in a few minutes the ferry docked, and Carlos drove the car on.

Sierra stole a look at Carlos as he stopped the car. He was really quiet, but it seemed like a quiet filled with squalling thoughts.

After the captain finished his safety speech and the ferry pulled out of the dock, Carlos inclined his head. "Come on."

"Are you okay, Carlos?"

He didn't answer. They got out and went to stand on the other side, where waves beat against the side of the ferry. They were all alone over here. Most of the passengers seemed to have stayed in their cars.

She didn't blame them. It wasn't much of a sight. The water was brown, and the narrow strip of water leading out to the gulf bobbed with tankers. It smelled like fumes.

But something about the lights on the tankers against the gray sky and the rolling waves beneath them made Sierra feel free. The wind blustered against her face. There was space and movement. And Carlos's silence didn't echo so much.

The ferry chugged to open water. With a swift movement, Carlos reached out and grabbed her wrists, turning her toward him. Sierra jerked back, but he had her wrists in a lock. She waited for the joke, but he didn't deliver any punch line. His grip was iron-tight.

She stared at him.

"Tell me to let you go, Sierra."

"What are you doing?" she said in a harsh whisper.

"Tell me to let you go."

She shook her head. She wasn't playing this sick game, whatever it was.

His voice grew more insistent. "Say it so I know you mean it."

The wind whipped her hair into her face, and she couldn't see. "Let me go."

"I don't believe you yet."

His hands tightened, and her wrists stung. "Stop, Carlos. You're hurting me." She gave a hard jerk of her wrists.

"I almost believed you that time." He dropped her wrists. "But you're going to have to do better."

Sierra flipped her hair back and stalked back toward Carlos's Mustang. She planned on getting inside and locking the doors, but he reached it first and blocked her. He leaned against it, his arms crossed. The ferry engines thrummed beneath her feet. She could feel fear flash into her face, like a burning flame. This wasn't like Carlos.

"Tell me you want in." His face grew stiff again.

"I thought I could trust you." She threw the hot words out. "So much for that."

Sierra searched for safety. She crossed to the back of the ferry in sight of a woman with her little boy. Holding on to the gate post, she leaned her face against the wonderful cold metal. The rigs disappeared in the gray, and only the lights of a ferry going the other direction winked under the darkening sky.

Water churned in streams behind them. She thought about calling her mom to come get her, but it would be better if she could get Carlos to take her home. Then she'd never speak to him again.

His hand touched her back, and she stiffened. "Don't touch me."

"I believed that. If you'd said that to Emilio, he might have believed you too." He dropped his hand and moved beside her.

She glared up at him.

He tipped his head to her and spoke just loud enough to be heard over the engines. "You can trust me, Brown Eyes."

"Is that what this was all about? Emilio?" Her voice broke.

"Yeah, Emilio." The rail vibrated as he wrapped his hands around it. "I know Emilio, Sierra. He won't understand if you whisper you'd rather not. You have to tell him to get lost. You have to show him you mean it all the way. Scream if you have to."

The sound of the waves, muffled by the low-lying clouds, slapped against the sides of the ferry. She tried to imagine herself telling Emilio to get lost or screaming at him.

"Hey." Carlos picked up her wrists, gently this time. Red cuffs circled them. He rubbed the marks with a calloused thumb, as if he could heal them with a touch. "I didn't mean to hurt you."

"It's okay."

"It's not okay if someone hurts you. Not even me. Tell me it's not okay."

She closed her eyes.

"Don't shut me out, Sierra. You've got to do this."

She opened her eyes, but she looked out at the water. Why wouldn't he leave her alone?

"And when you're done telling me it's not okay, there's more. You've got to push me away. You've got to tell me to get lost the first second I get in your space."

"Carlos." It was all she could think to say to make him stop. The grayness beat against the ferry. The fluttering flags on the pike above them seemed like they were battling the wind. But how could you battle the wind?

He took her chin in his palm and lifted it so she looked at him. "You're not trash people can just throw around any way they like. It's okay to let people know they need to treat you right."

She looked away.

He lowered his voice. "Look, Sierra, you're doing everyone a favor if you tell Emilio to treat you right. Every time he pushes you around, you lose a little bit of yourself, but so does he. Every time you make him stop, you get a little piece of yourself back and so does he. I've seen how it works on the street."

He was quiet for a minute. "You got something special, Brown Eyes, but you won't get to keep it if you don't stand up for yourself. You got that strength in you. I know you do."

She shook her head. She didn't have that kind of strength. She didn't have any strength at all.

Carlos gave a short laugh. "You do. You were pretty good all those months at letting me know you didn't want anything to do with me. You just need to take it further. Louder, you know. Let Emilio know you mean it and don't back down when he doesn't give up."

They docked at Bolivar Peninsula, and Carlos drove them off the ferry, past the convenience store and the beach houses, out to a grassy, deserted beach. They got out and walked down an incline and through the sand weeds to the water's edge. The waves were a little calmer on this side of the water. She picked up a few shells to put in her pocket and followed a crab. She dipped her finger in the surf, but it was too cold to wade. They walked side by side in silence as the sky turned from gray to black.

"It's time, Brown Eyes."

Time to go? She didn't want to go yet. Now that she knew what was going on in his head, she wanted to spend a little more time with Carlos. It was nice out here with the waves and wind, and she was getting used to hanging out with him.

But Carlos didn't head for the car. He backed up to the water's edge and made a running leap at her. She dodged his impact just in time.

"Good. That's a start," he said.

She stared at him, her teeth clenched. Talking back? Self-defense? She started to walk back to the car. She didn't need this.

He intersected her path. "You've got to learn, Sierra. If you won't do it for yourself, do it for the people who care about you."

It was no use arguing with Carlos, so she opened her hands in defeat. For a full hour he came at her and showed her how to block him with her arms. He got close to her and wouldn't get out of her face until she made him stop.

"Look me in the eyes, and say it again louder, Sierra," he said.

"I don't want to yell, Carlos," she sighed.

He held her shoulders. "Yell, Sierra. I'm Emilio. And I'm about to do something you don't want. You've got to make me get out of your face."

"You're not Emilio. You're not going to hurt me. And I want to go home."

He lifted her wrists. "Oh, yeah? I did hurt you. Tell me to stop before I do it again."

He grinned, and she submitted. "Get lost," she said.

Carlos laughed. "I didn't believe that for a second, Brown Eyes. Say it so loud it hurts your throat."

She didn't think she could yell. But one more time, as loud and clear as she could, she called, "Get lost!"

When she said it, he started it all over again. He showed her how to kick, and told her to think of places to go when she ran.

"You did good, *Ojos Café*," he finally said. "I think you could stand up to Emilio if you needed to." He paused. "And you will need to. Juan and Danny and Logan have all been watching; he's got something to prove now."

Sierra collapsed onto the sand, afraid she'd break into hysterical sobs or hysterical laughter. She didn't know which. She felt so weird. Carlos sat down beside her. "What do you say to some fried shrimp and hush puppies?"

She pulled her hair back when it blew around in a ruffling wind. The cold felt good against her warm skin. They watched as clouds drifted out to sea, leaving a clear patch of starry sky. Far away, they could see the lights of oil tankers come into focus.

Carlos drove back to the ferry, and when they got back to the other shore, they ate at a quiet restaurant across the street from the seawall. From her perch by the window, the waves looked calm, but Sierra knew their height was only hidden by the dark.

She took a sip from her Coke. "Thank you, Carlos."

He reached out, not quite touching her wrist. "I'm sorry I hurt you. I just don't want you to put up with Emilio again."

"I know. That's why I said thank you."

He smiled like it was the nicest thing anyone had ever said to him. She knew it wasn't. His parents must have been nice people. People like Carlos didn't appear out of nowhere.

"But next time you do something like that, don't spring it on me."

He popped a shrimp into his mouth. "Yeah. I thought if I said a day on the beach, you might come. If I said a course in self-defense, you probably wouldn't. I'm sorry if I scared you."

They lingered over their dinner until Carlos reminded her that she was supposed to be home by ten. She shivered as they walked to the car, now that she'd cooled down. Her jacket was in the car, but Carlos insisted on giving her his. She nestled into it, letting it engulf her. It smelled like him—skin and guy soap.

They drove back to Houston through a close layer of darkness, zooming across the long bridge to the mainland and then onto the freeway, sailing past the lights of refineries, past glowing buildings downtown, and then into her part of town.

At her door, he circled her wrists, loosely this time. "One more time. Make me let go," he said quietly.

His hands felt warm against her skin.

"Make me let go," he said, his voice firmer.

She looked up at him, trying to get out the words she wanted to say. Finally, she forced them out. "I don't want you to let go."

He looked at her with those warm eyes. He brought her hands up to his face and lightly kissed each wrist. "Good night, Brown Eyes."

Chapter Twenty-Three

Nick found his annual job evaluation in his in-box before the first bell. He opened it without leaving the mailroom, zeroing in on two short lines indicating he had failed to meet expectations. It came as no surprise, but that didn't make the low scores any less infuriating.

Poor classroom discipline? Poor teaching methods? He didn't think so. The dishonesty of the report swirled in the pit of his stomach. Reaching kids no one else could was the one thing he did well. Folding the paper into eighths, he shoved it into his pocket and strode to class.

As if the evaluation weren't enough, Liza sent for him after school. She had the blinds closed and the office dim. Sitting behind the huge mahogany desk, she flipped through a file without looking his way even after he sat directly across from her.

"Emilio Cantu," she said, without looking up.

"He's a student of mine."

She sent him a hostile glance. "It's come to my attention he assaulted a girl in the hallway. You witnessed it and didn't report it."

"I had a long hard talk with Emilio, Ms. Grambling. And the girl's mother happens to be a friend of mine. She *was* informed."

"We have a code for handling assault, Mr. Foster. This is a serious matter."

Nick sighed. "There's a fine line between assault and intimidation. Emilio didn't hurt the girl, though I'm sure he scared her."

He didn't mention Sierra's name. The last thing Sierra needed was to get pulled into one of Liza's interrogations.

"As I'm sure you're aware, we have a zero-tolerance policy at Armstrong."

"My mistake. I thought I handled it. It won't happen again."

Liza closed the file, clearly not satisfied. "It's not the first time you ignored violence on campus."

Nick cocked his head. "To my knowledge it is."

"What about the incident with Ryan Brannigan?"

"I was the only one Ryan threatened. And a classroom conversation helped not only Ryan but all of his classmates think of better ways to handle their stress."

She clicked her pen against the desk. "Zero tolerance, Mr. Foster."

"I understand. It won't happen again." He stood to go. How did she even find out about Ryan's threatening to hit him?

She slipped two pink notes into a folder. "I'm putting the notations into your file along with your refusal to follow the district-wide curriculum. You're walking a fine line, Mr. Foster. I would hate to see you subjected to disciplinary action."

Nick gripped the back of the chair. "Noted."

He ground his teeth as he left. The reprimands were only weapons in Liza's arsenal. They both knew what she was after. Fall in line. Drop everything else. Spend every second of class time prepping the kids for the state test for the next two months. Once he did that, the other complaints would disappear.

He started for his classroom, but changed his mind halfway down the hall. Today he was going home. On time.

———◆◆◆◆◆———

That evening, Nick sat in front of his TV watching talking heads discuss college basketball. But in a short while, he switched it off and went upstairs. He was lucky. His punishment for having his own standards in his classroom was a possible suspension, maybe a transfer. It wasn't prison.

The irony that he'd taken up his old man's career was not lost on him. Not that he knew exactly why his father had been sent to prison. But according to his mother, Dad's trouble with the secret police first began for speaking out in his classroom.

It had been a conscious decision for Nick to follow the same path. He wanted to be the man he'd believed his father to be in his idealistic youth. It didn't matter that his father had turned out to be someone different.

He'd even tried to express his passion for teaching to Dad once. He showed him a file full of letters from his kids and told him about the students, adults now, who had let Nick know he'd made a difference in their lives. He thought perhaps they could bond over a shared calling, but his father's only response had been to read the letters in silence and finish with a curt nod. He never brought the letters up again.

Nick went into his study, leafed through his files of letters from alumni students. Greedily, he drank in the letters from his kids, now grown and holding jobs as government officials, engineers, lawyers, ministers, even teachers.

They'd sent pictures of themselves with their husbands or wives and their children. There were even notes from kids who'd made mistakes, from teen pregnancies to crime. They still thanked him for helping them, though the truth of what they'd learned in his classes had dawned on them late.

How could he devote two months of school to work sheets and test prep? The kids who were assigned to him were at war with life.

He looked at the ceiling and swallowed a groan. He was not going to lose it. Fellow teachers had advised him to lay low for a while. "Play along," they said. "Liza will be gone soon."

Principals never did stay long, not at tough schools like Armstrong. But by the time Liza left, the Emilios and Ryans in his class would be gone too. There were no second chances. March, April, May—it was all the time he had left to feed their minds and hearts before they moved on to a different set of teachers or dropped out of school altogether.

He swallowed his anger and went downstairs for his tools before swinging out to the back deck. Dark was already falling, but it was time to do something with his hands, something that gave back more than it took.

———◆◆◆◆◆———

April dropped Sierra and Luca off at Barnes and Noble, their standard haunt now. A lady from her church worked at the coffee shop there, and April had given her instructions to call if anything went awry. But it had been a few months now, and with Sierra in tow, nothing in the public place had set Luca off.

She used the opportunity of being on her own to stop by Nick's. He needed to know what she was doing with his father. No one answered when she rang the doorbell, but a scraping sound came from the back. She peeked around the corner of the townhouse and found Nick sitting on the deck's railing, wearing jeans and a long sleeved T-shirt.

He held something—a block of wood and a knife. His face furrowed in deep concentration as he carved slowly, shaving strokes along the block with only the dimness of the deck light to see by.

She'd told herself she'd come about Luca. But when she saw Nick, she had to admit that Luca wasn't the only reason. The air came alive as Nick focused on the block of wood as though it were the only thing in the world. She liked being near him. It was as simple as that.

April coughed. "I'm sorry if I'm interrupting."

He looked up, startled, and then sent her a slow smile. "You're never an interruption, April."

Her heart did a little flip, and she sent it a quiet warning to behave itself.

He motioned her to a patio chair and joined her, setting the wood and knife on a table.

Trying to still her tapping feet, she sat on the edge of her chair and paused. "I've been visiting your father."

He pulled his chair to face her.

"You're going to think I'm interfering."

"And are you?"

It had been a few weeks since she'd seen Nick in person. She had forgotten that gaze, that deep voice. She'd forgotten what his nearness did to her. She sat up straight, trying to shake off this feeling.

She wasn't a seventeen-year-old kid anymore, and there was nothing she could do with the feelings Nick brought out in her.

She forced herself to speak. "I'm getting your dad's story about his time in Romania."

Nick let out a short laugh. "Good luck with that one. As far as I know, he's the only one who knows that story. And it's not one he tells."

"He *is* telling me. He didn't think he could tell it to you in person, but he wanted you to hear it."

His stared at her with a quizzical smile.

"He's *your* dad, Nick. It would mean a lot to me if I had your blessing."

He didn't miss a beat. "You've got it. For all the good it will do."

April looked at the stars, bright in the clean, cold sky. Neither of them said anything. The silence dropped around them like a soft quilt.

Finally, Nick rested a leg over one knee and cleared his throat. "Mind if I ask what you're up to? I know you want to make things nice, but my old man isn't going to make that easy for you."

Strength emanated from him. She could feel it, and it bothered her how much she liked it.

As if she were his echo, she cleared her throat. "Nick, I know what it's like to love someone who isn't as whole as you need them to be. I can only imagine what it's like to live a story where you don't know the first chapters driving the plot. I wanted you to have your dad's story, and I wanted him to have the chance to tell it." She pushed up the sleeves of her sweater. Her skin felt warm despite the cool air. With a weak laugh, she added, "Like I said, I'm interfering."

He gave her a long hard look. She'd let a few of her secrets drop and with his silence, Nick gave her an invitation to go on, but she couldn't do it. The truth had just slipped out with Luca, but for whatever reason, she couldn't get out the words *suicide* and *my husband* tonight.

"Don't be upset, Nick. It's a good thing, your dad talking."

"Tension is how my old man and I do things. I'm not upset. It's just been a hard day."

"Want to talk about it?" she asked.

"Not really. I'd rather talk about you."

"Me?"

He opened his mouth, closed it again, and then came to stand beside her, resting his hand on her shoulder. It was only a touch, but it made her feel boneless. How long had it been since a man had touched her? How much longer than that since a man had made her feel sheltered? She looked up at him but then quickly looked away.

Nick dropped his hand, and she felt unaccountably bereft. He went to the railing, his back to her. April willed herself to tell him good-bye. It would be the right thing to do.

Instead, she joined him.

He turned to her. "I haven't been able to stop thinking about you since Christmas, April." He shook his head. "No, that's not honest. I haven't been able to stop thinking about you since I saw you in that park with your camera and you looked like you were lost in some no-man's-land between heaven and earth."

There it was, said out loud—he shared her feelings. April stood mute in the silence.

A streak of uncertainty flashed behind his eyes when she didn't say anything.

She wanted to draw him to her. She wanted to tell him how she felt. But it wouldn't work. They both had too many demons. And Gary had taught her too well how those demons smother romance.

He was so strong, so generous. And he brought out a part of her that had been long forgotten. But she had nothing to offer Nick. Neither could she walk away. She was caught in the net of his nearness.

"April. Say something. Don't leave me hanging here."

"Nick, I—" What she wanted to say and what she should say battled it out, leaving her speechless. She tilted her face up to his, trying to find the words that refused to come to her. How could she tell him no? And how could she tell him anything else?

Nick bent to her, drawing her face close to his with his hand. He lingered close, giving her a chance to draw away.

His mouth covered hers, slow and questioning. She answered him with a returning kiss.

It was the wrong answer. It didn't matter. Her head could scream "Run fast and far!" all it wanted, but her heart knew what it wanted—this.

He drew back.

"Nick, I-I ..." she stuttered. *Hold me and don't let me go.* It was on the tip of her tongue, but she said what she had to. "Anything between us ... It wouldn't work."

His face grew tight. "I'm sorry. I thought ..."

"I'm sorry too."

She wanted to erase the hurt on his face. But if she let him know how she felt, it would only be a matter of time before loved bloomed ... and then died under the pressure of their families and past hurts. A broken heart would only add bitterness to his life, to Sierra's, maybe even to Luca's.

So she searched for words to soothe the rejection without offering hope. "You're an amazing man, Nick, and the best of friends.
Like a brother, really. I wish it were different."

The words only seemed to draw more hurt into his eyes. He slid
his hand behind her neck, as if he would pull her to him again, but
then he sighed and dropped his hands to his sides. "Okay. Good
night, April."

As she walked away, the sound of knife shaving wood started
again—a low, mournful sound.

She sat in her car with the window open far too long before she
switched on the ignition.

CHAPTER TWENTY-FOUR

April threw herself into work over the next few days, but no amount of arranging sculptures or designing sales flyers could keep her thoughts free from him—the sound of her name in Nick's deep baritone, the feel of Nick's hand on her shoulder, his kiss. She looked forward to seeing Luca on Monday, and not only for his sake. Somehow being close to Luca made her feel close to his son. Adolescent thinking perhaps, but there it was.

When she walked into Luca's home, she felt confident. The first bit of his story had gone well. There were no traumatic revelations. Luca himself even seemed to enjoy the memories. One point of anxiety needled at her confidence though. Eventually the story must turn toward prison.

Late February had brought in a hint of spring and lifted her spirits. Luca led her outside to the backyard where they sat next to his garden. Cool sunlight filtered through the pine trees, lending a soft edge to the day. Hummingbirds flew madly around a feeding glass.

As she settled into a patio chair, she searched for features of Nick hidden in Luca's face. Nick had similar eyes, but Luca didn't turn them on her like a force. Something about their faces was alike, but Luca had decidedly European mannerisms. The most striking similarity was difficult to define. The way they looked straight out, as if life were coming at them head-on and they'd need to be ready for the impact. Only, Nick appeared ready to charge into the fray, whereas Luca inched away as if he could miss the onslaught.

He glanced at the hummingbirds and closed his eyes. His lids were blue. His hands lay heavily on his knees. When he didn't start the story, April began to doubt herself.

"It's a more difficult part today?" she asked softly.

"My years with Tatia and Nicu were the happiest of my life. But it is these years I have questioned the most. If ..." He inhaled deeply. "*If.* It is a useless word, no? You cannot make different decisions than the ones you made. You cannot make other people be other than what they were."

He leaned back in his chair. His eyes grew dim as he went into his memories.

"Nicolae was born just one month after our first wedding anniversary, and Tatia and I were both filled with such joy. I held our son to my chest, and he liked it there. Tatia said he liked the rumble of my voice when I spoke to him.

"When I held him—so fragile, so small—I knew I must commit him to the care of God. But like my parents before me, I said my prayers over him in secret.

"I soon obtained a position teaching secondary students. We were happy, and I put my worries aside."

April thought of the little boy in the picture at Nick's home. "How old was Nick when you went to prison?"

"Four. I believe the only memories he had of me are the ones Tatia remembered for him. I do not think he recalls trailing at my heels like a small shadow. Tatia scolded us for laughing and running through the apartment, but of course, she was really glad to see us bound together as we were."

"Have you ever told him that?" April asked.

He shook his head.

"What happened?"

"One of my students made an elaborate algebra equation in class, but it was quite wrong. I said to the student, 'In mathematics, you do not invent the answer. If you add two apples and two apples, you discover you have four apples, but you do not invent the apples. An algebra equation is more complex than a sum, but you are still only searching for what is already a fact. It may seem that one method is as good as another one. But the truth cannot be invented or created. To find the solution, you need the correct method.'

"This must have impressed the boy, for he went home and told his father, who worked for the Securitate, the Romanian secret police. I cannot say why my lesson upset the authorities so, except that in Romania we were used to someone trying to tell us in some fashion that two plus two equals fifteen. Encouraging neighbors to spy on each other was meant to equal freedom, and uneducated fools were meant to be great scholars.

"At any rate, they took me to a room, a narrow concrete room with one bright light, and questioned me.

"'Why do you spew capitalist propaganda on our youth?' one man screamed at me. Another one spit on me and slapped me. They wanted me to say I was a foreign spy. Finally, they left me alone and another man came in. He was a great warrior of a man with a scar along his cheek. He sighed and stared at me until I trembled.

"'You can go home, but only teach maths from now on.' He did not lay a finger on me. He gave me only a mocking smile, and I thought then I might have liked him in different circumstances.

"The man drove me home. Tatia ran outside our apartment block to meet me. Her tears wet my face as she helped me inside.

"She put plasters on my cuts while Nicu asked, 'Why is Daddy hurt?' I could not answer my son. He was too young to understand which things must be whispered and which things might be spoken aloud.

"Tatia kissed me over and over. 'I am married to a hero. Your students know now that truth is real. It cannot be invented at the government's whim.'"

"So you did it again?" April leaned forward.

He shook his head. "Not for a long time. It was almost the end of the school year, but one day I mentioned Galileo and Copernicus and how they were threatened because they saw the equations no one else did. I was taken by the Securitate again.

"'Do you think you are like Galileo?' one said as he slapped me in the face. 'You are nothing!'

"They beat me severely. The man with the scar once again drove me home, but this time I returned with a broken arm and cracked ribs."

"Tatiana was right. You were a hero," April said softly.

"Pah! I wanted nothing more than to run away." Luca looked down. "We went into the forest and looked over the hills into Yugoslavia. Others had escaped before us, but we would have to get through the border unseen and then across another communist border to Austria or Switzerland. Nicu was small. He might be taken from us. Or killed."

The wind shuffled leaves around their feet, and April cringed at the hollowness in his expression.

"I returned to work after the summer, and Tatia came often to meet me after school, her hand clutching Nicolae's so tight. Life was very hard for the families of political prisoners. I determined I would never make trouble for her again. I taught only math formulas. I held my tongue. And our life was so quiet.

"But still there was something wrong.

"One day, many months after my last interrogation, I spoke to Tatia, but she looked just beyond me instead of meeting my eyes. Many times she would start to talk to me, but then she would shake her head and say nothing.

"Nicu grew fretful, and Tatia would hold him as if it were her last moment with him. He would pat her hand. One could not tell whether she was comforting him, or he was comforting her.

"She woke sometimes in the middle of the night and did not come back to bed. I would find her on her knees, praying. It seemed to me all of her passion had turned inward into a fire burning at her from the inside. I could not fathom what caused her distress. But sometimes it seemed a joy crossed her face. I could not make sense of it.

"'What is wrong, Tatia?' I would say.

"'Oh, you must not worry, Luca. I am so tired sometimes. That is all,' she would answer, and she would smile with such sweetness, I would think truly that was all.

"But one night, after Nicu was asleep, she stood at the window, alone in the dark, looking at nothing. I came from behind and put my arms about hers. She screamed as she pulled away, clutching her sides, and crumpled to the ground.

"She looked at me with eyes wide and horrified. 'Oh, Luca, what have I done?' she wailed.

"I went to her on my knees, but she covered her face with her hands and refused to look at me. 'Don't ask me, don't ask me,' she said. 'Don't ask me, Luca.'"

Luca's color washed away as he whispered Tatia's refrain. "'Don't ask me.' That is what she said to me."

"Luca?"

He looked up at her as if only now remembering that he wasn't alone with his story.

"Can I get you some water?"

"No," he said in a thin voice. Slowly, a pained smile came to his face, but the attempt did nothing to ease April's mind.

"Why don't we stop for today? You need to rest."

He waved a feeble hand at her. "It was you who wished to hear my story, Mrs. Wright."

April laced her fingers through his. "You're not well. I could hardly continue the story now, could I? I'll come back when you've rested."

Luca gave a wheezy laugh. "Am I so weak as that? Very well, next week then."

April stood to go. What had happened to Tatiana? What had happened to her to reduce her husband to pale angst even decades later?

Luca's eyes were closed. He seemed so impossibly old for a sixty-year-old man.

<hr />

The next morning, Nick came to April's door. It was Tuesday. He should be teaching. They looked at each other without speaking.

Memories of the moonlit kiss came flooding back, but she could tell by his military posture and unwavering gaze that that wasn't why he'd come.

She opened the door with a smile, but his earnestness put her on guard.

He threw a quick glance into the living room but didn't come inside. He shifted his feet. "My father is sick, April. He's in bed, too weak to get out."

"What's wrong?" She dreaded the answer.

Nick took a step back and folded his hands behind him. "April, you know my father is very frail."

"Do you think talking about his past caused him to get sick?"

"Look, his health has never been what it should be, not since prison. I don't know."

April looked at her feet, remembering how white and disturbed Luca had been as he talked about his wife. Maybe it was her own questions she needed to ask, not his. There was no maybe about it. It was so much easier to unravel someone else's hurt than your own.

"Can I see him?"

He gave her a curt nod. "Sure. But April, let his story die. He doesn't need this stress."

CHAPTER TWENTY-FIVE

Later, Nick led her to Luca's bedroom. It was furnished in the same naked style as the front of his house. A bed, a chest of drawers, a bedside table in a square formation—that was it. There were no pictures, no luxuries.

He sat up halfway in bed with pillows behind him, looking tired, but at least he had some color in his face.

Nick shot her a silent plea to be brief and went to the kitchen. She heard the sound of running water and soon smelled brewing coffee.

April sat down on the bed. "I'm sorry, Luca. I would never have done anything to make you sick."

In a reedy voice, he said, "Open the drawer." He nodded to the bedside table.

She pulled open the drawer. A neat stack of photos in frames lay to one side. She pulled them out, along with some papers underneath. On the top lay the same photo of his family that graced Nick's living room. The second showed young Luca in a swimsuit on the beach with Nick on his shoulders.

Below this, she found one of an older Tatiana and Luca, obviously taken after she had become sick. She wore a silk scarf, covering, April was sure, a head bald from chemotherapy. Though gaunt and wasted, she looked into the camera's face as if she had the last joke on life and not the other way around.

April touched Tatiana's face, a sudden sorrow cutting through her. She didn't even know the woman, yet she felt her loss.

She flipped through the stack of photos of Nick from childhood but found none of him as an adult. There was a pile of yellowing newspaper clippings underneath the frames. She smoothed them on her lap.

A neighborhood paper reported on the men returning from Desert Storm. April's hand stilled on a fifteen-year-old wedding announcement about Nick and a beautiful brunette. Stapled behind it was another clipping from not even two years later telling of a fatal car accident in which one Caroline Foster drove into a telephone pole. The article reported that she'd ingested a toxic amount of alcohol. April swallowed a lump in her throat. *Oh, Nick.*

She took a breath and flipped through newer clippings in the back that told of Nick's passion for his career. He had been named Teacher of the Year by his school district recently, and last summer he'd won a grant to take low-income kids on a tour of historic sites in New England.

April traced the headline of the last article, letting her index finger move down the column to quotes by Nick. She raised her head. "You must be very proud."

Luca gave a small nod.

"Does Nick know you've kept these?"

Luca shook his head.

A Bible lay on the bottom of the drawer, and beneath it, an image, painted on wood, of Jesus holding a jewel-encrusted book. Why were these things not decorating Luca's walls and shelves? The whole house cried out for color.

She looked up.

His eyes grew watery, and he knotted his hands together. "Even here in America, I cannot bear to bring out my Bible. Or my pride in my son. I speak in whispers as if the secret police will still find me."

"It was too much for you." April should have known. Of all people, she should have known how painful speaking about the past could be.

Luca covered April's hand. Even the small movement seemed to sap his energy. "If I had been the hero Tatiana believed, I would have told my son of what happened long ago."

April shook her head. Had she really counseled Luca on his relationship with Nick? What nerve! What arrogant-headed nerve!

"Come back in a few days," he said, leaning forward. "I will tell you why I went to prison. For Nicu. But I shall need your help."

As if even the plan of telling his story cost too much, he sank back on his pillows and closed his eyes.

April folded the top of the blanket over Luca's chest. As much as she longed to hear Tatiana's story, she doubted his plan. "Are you sure, Luca? Your health."

"I am sure." He didn't open his eyes.

April closed the blinds to dim the room. She glanced back from the doorway. His chest rose and fell as if he'd already fallen sleep.

She found Nick in the kitchen nursing a cup of coffee at one end of the counter.

"Your dad's sleeping now."

He nodded and took a sip.

April circled the kitchen, then rested her hands on the end of the scarred counter across from Nick. Afraid she was interfering again, she hesitated. "Nick, if you don't mind my asking, what's wrong with your father exactly?"

"What does he have? I don't know. He has asthma and chronic respiratory infections. Occasional pain no one can explain. Gastrointestinal issues. You name it. He never recovered from prison. When I came to see him last night, he was too weak to answer the door. I don't know what it is this time. Maybe just fatigue."

"He wants to continue telling me his story in a few days."

Nick gave her a hard stare, and she knew she'd earned that look.

"I was wrong," she admitted. "I shouldn't have pushed him to tell me about something so traumatic. But if he wants to tell what happened to him, don't you think I owe it to him to listen?"

Nick turned away from her. A bowl of something sat on the counter, some recipe Luca had started and hadn't finished. It looked crusty now, and April ran water in the bowl to clean it out. It was too hard to see Nick turning away from her, blaming her.

"I won't do it if you think it's best not to."

Nick heaved a sigh. "He has the right to do what he wants. Just keep a close eye on him."

She turned. "I'll look after him as if he were my own father."

"April ..." He leaned back against the counter but didn't continue.

She waited. The few feet between them felt too close. Or too far. Memories of the night on his deck drifted between them like a soft mist. She was thinking of it. He was thinking of it. But what could they say?

"About the other night, I wouldn't ... I don't ..." He stopped.

"It's okay." She searched for something to say, something to ease the moment. How was it that she, voted the sunniest girl in her senior class, could bring so little light to anyone in her life?

She took his hand. "The other night is forgotten as far as I'm concerned. You're so dear to me, Nick. As close as family."

Liar, liar, liar, a little voice inside cried. She had relived that night so many times it wasn't funny. She felt many things for Nick, but brotherly love didn't exactly top the list. She wasn't about to tell him the truth, though, because as soon as they both admitted how they felt, there would be no turning back.

She had courage enough for anything, but not that—not putting her heart into another man's hands. Especially not Nick's. She already felt too much for him.

He turned her hand, inspecting it, as if he couldn't understand how it had come to be linked in his.

"Family? A brother, April?" He gave her a dark smile and took his cup to the sink, emptying the dregs and rinsing it out. Turning back to her, he said, "What I wanted to say is I hope I didn't upset you the other night. I'm sorry if I did."

His face was strained, his shoulders taut, and April wished she could reach out to him and, with a touch, soothe away the losses that ate at him. It would be so easy, so natural.

"You didn't upset me, Nick," she said in a barely audible voice.

Chapter Twenty-Six

The shower was running, which meant Sierra had only a few minutes before Mom came in. She laid the pencil sketches on the dining table, trying to arrange them in order. Okay. She didn't have any business snooping in her mother's satchel, but one of the sketches had been sticking out and she hadn't been able to stop herself.

She straightened the first page. It was of Mr. Prodan, really young, sitting with a pretty girl. Underneath it was another sketch. It was Mr. Prodan, too, but he looked awful—old and skinny and badly dressed. What was that about? It gave Sierra a sick feeling deep inside. She wasn't sure if the feeling was from how terrible Mom had made him look or from the picture being in her mom's things.

Why was Mom drawing Mr. Prodan? He was Sierra's friend, not someone for Mom to spy on or whatever she was doing with these weird pencil sketches.

Tell her that. She heard the words in Carlos's tough, urging voice. But this wasn't like a boy getting too close. It wasn't a danger she could block with raised arms. It was just wrong.

Next, a picture showed a woman holding a little boy. The bones of her face were drawn in sharp angles, and she had shadows beneath her eyes. The woman seemed overcome by something too horrible for words.

In the following drawing, the same woman sat on the floor with her face in her hands and Mr. Prodan knelt by her side. He was young, maybe in his twenties, but he had the same unruly hair and light eyes.

Sierra stepped back. A bitter taste came to her tongue. The pictures told a story, like one of the thriller comic books the boys in school read. Only the text balloons were missing. Sierra began to tap her foot, working out her jitters. What kind of story was her mom drawing? And why?

Sierra left the pictures on the dining table so Mom would see them and would have to say something about them. The shower stopped, and Sierra went to the sofa to wait.

Mom swung into the living room, dressed in a sweatshirt and with her hair wet and messy. "Hey, I have this absolute craving for strawberry shortcake. What do you say?"

Sierra sat on her hands. "Sure."

Mom saw the pictures and bent over the table, looking at the sketches. She stood straight, taking her time, looking all concerned.

"Do you want to ask me something, Sierra?"

Sierra shook her head.

Mom could never hide her feelings. The brighter the smile, the blacker the worry. She sat on a chair across from Sierra and tucked her legs under her. "I guess you want to know what those pictures are about."

Sierra didn't say anything, and she went on.

"I'm helping Luca Prodan write down his story."

"His story? The one about prison?" She could hear the whine in her voice, the sound of a little girl about to stomp her feet, but she couldn't help it. Mr. Prodan's story was hers, not Mom's.

"Sierra?"

"He's *my* friend, Mom."

Mom's eyes widened. "I'm not stealing your friend, Sierra. You two have a special bond. No one's going to crowd in on that."

Mom's rational voice tore a hole in her confidence, but she went on. "It was my story! What happened to Mr. Prodan in Romania ..." She looked to the window, knowing she sounded crazy. "He couldn't tell me yet, but he was going to."

Mom furrowed her brow and got really quiet, giving Sierra a too-patient look. "Did he say he was going tell you his story?"

"No, he didn't say. But he would have told me when he was ready."

"Sweetie, he would have told you if he could. But he hasn't even been able to tell his own son. He needed help for that."

Sierra closed her eyes. The conversation was going nowhere.

"It's really hard for him," Mom said. "He's only doing it because his son needs to know."

"He could've told me. I'm a good writer. I could have written it for him."

"One day, I wouldn't be surprised if he told all of it to you. But there are some things you just don't tell to ..."

"To what? To a kid? I can write better than most adults. Even better than you, Mom. I could have done it."

"Oh, sweetie, you're a gifted writer. I have no doubt you could write Luca Prodan's story. But he cares too much about you to fill your mind with torture."

Torture. The word splashed through her veins like Siberian sea-water. She'd never thought of it like that, but it didn't change things. Mr. Prodan was her friend, and she would listen to as many terrible things as he wanted to tell her. "I could have done it," she whispered. "I could have helped him."

Mom leaned forward and massaged Sierra's knee. "You're helping him more than you know. You're his friend."

Mom leaned back. "I want you to know, I'm not getting the story out of idle curiosity. Nick Foster *needs* this story. He doesn't know what happened to his dad. And without that understanding, it's hard to make sense of so much else in his life."

Something gurgled into place in Sierra's thoughts. "You really know all about what Mr. Foster and his dad need, don't you? *Their* story. They need *their* story." The biting words left her mouth before she'd known what she intended to say, but Mom didn't respond. With a pat to her shoulder, Mom got up and strode toward the kitchen. She ran water in the sink and turned on the oven.

In the living room, Sierra doubled over, massaging her temples. "You never want to talk about him," she finally said.

Mom turned off the water and looked into the living room. "Did you say something?"

"I said you never want to talk about him."

Mom looked straight at her. At least she had the decency not to pretend like she didn't know who Sierra was talking about.

"Is there something you would like to speak about? Something specific you want to know about Dad?" Mom's voice didn't invite questions.

Sierra closed her eyes. No, there wasn't something *specific* she wanted to know. Anything and everything would do. The big nothing she knew about her father ate away at her. And so did Mom's distaste when she talked about him.

Sierra opened her eyes. "Is there something *specific* you'd like to tell me?"

Mom looked away and began chopping strawberries with a furious knife.

Apparently not.

Sierra got up and stalked to her room. What was the use?

———◆◆◆◆◆———

After school the next day, Sierra caught up to Carlos. He waited for her at the traffic light.

"Hey, Carlos. Do you ever have trouble remembering your parents?"

"I'm fine. Thanks for asking."

Sierra laughed. Thank goodness for Carlos. He never let her get away without proper hellos and good-byes.

"And you?" he went on.

"Fine."

Her internal clock ticked as she waited for him to return to her question. They crossed the street and walked on in silence. When they arrived at her apartments, he stopped. "A little bit. The memories fade more every year. I've visited my grandpa in El Salvador a couple of times just to hear him talk about old times. But I try not to think too hard about it, not about losing them anyway. They wouldn't have wanted that for me."

She walked beside him, studying the sidewalk.

"What's on your mind, Brown Eyes?"

She switched her backpack to her left shoulder. "I can hardly remember my dad. That's not normal, is it? I mean, I was thirteen when he died, but I don't remember anything. I sort of remember what he looked like. But I can't piece together more than two or three things we did together. And my mom won't talk about him."

"You're smart enough to scrounge up some memories if you want. There's photos, right? And friends and relatives. Places he went." He opened the gate for her. "You sure you really want to remember?"

Sierra stopped inside the security gate, looking back at the busy street. Not want to remember? Why wouldn't someone want to remember their own father? Maybe if their dad was a drunk or something. But Dad wasn't like that. Even without her memories, she knew that.

"What places did your dad go?"

"We lived in other places most of my life. Colorado, California, Virginia, New York. My mom and dad met here though. At Rice."

"So you got your brains legally. I've got to get to work, but tomorrow we'll take ourselves a university tour. We'll drive to Rice and you can see where your dad used to study."

❖◆❖

Sierra didn't sleep much that night. To walk the same paths her father had, to see the library where he'd researched. Why hadn't she thought of it before?

The next day they drove to Rice. It was just a few minutes beyond the hospital where Mr. Prodan had stayed when he had pneumonia. Carlos took the car down a long drive with trees on either side that were so full they met overhead, and then parked. Sierra got out of the car, taking in the scents of mingling flowers and the smell of French fries drifting across the commons.

Harvard probably looked like this. Carlos led her past the red brick buildings and down the cobbled paths. Ivy climbed brick walls. Packs of students laughed or argued over this or that. There were Greek columns and manicured hedges. She could almost dance for being here.

"Your kind of place, isn't it, Brown Eyes?"

She stretched out her arms and turned in a circle. It was.

He hefted his backpack next to a bench. "What's our plan?"

She looked up in surprise. "You don't have one?"

"This is your adventure. You feel any closer to your dad here?"

She nodded. She did. This was her dad's world. Without being able to put her finger on any specific memory, she knew he'd breathed easier here too.

"What did your dad study?"

"History."

Carlos waited on her to make the connection. "It was almost twenty years ago though. No one in the history department will remember him."

"You sure? I bet there's people he went to school with who stuck around."

Sierra gave a slow nod. "But how would I find them?"

"I know you can figure this one out, Sierra."

She laughed softly. "Yeah, I guess."

She glanced around. How would she even find out where the history department was? She could ask one of the groups of students, but she didn't like speaking to strangers. They walked until she found a security guard and asked him for directions.

Carlos let her lead. At the reception desk in the history department, she looked back at him, willing him to speak for her. He nodded encouragement but stayed in the background.

"Excuse me," she said quietly to the girl.

She held up a finger telling Sierra to wait, and Sierra saw she had earbuds in and was transcribing something. After a moment, the girl said perfunctorily, "May I help you?"

Sierra stood straight, trying not to fidget or look too young. "I was wondering if there was someone who was here about eighteen, nineteen years ago—either as a professor or a student. I'd like to speak with them, please."

The girl eyed her suspiciously. "May I say what this is regarding?"

"I need to find information about my father. He was a history student then."

The girl got up with a huff and meandered down a hall. In a few minutes she came back with a gray-bearded man with rolled-up shirtsleeves. He smiled pleasantly. "You're researching the good old days, eh? Eighteen years ago?"

Sierra nodded.

He pushed up his shirtsleeves even farther. "Sure, I was fresh out of grad school back then. Who was your father?"

"Garrison Wright."

"You're Gary Wright's daughter?" The light banter was gone. The air felt chillier somehow, and Sierra dug her hands into her pockets to warm them. Gary, he said. He knew something about her dad. She could tell he didn't want to talk by the way he took off his glasses and looked absently down the hall, but she forced herself to keep talking.

"Were you one of his professors?"

"Not exactly." He scratched his head. "What kind of information are you looking for?"

"My dad passed away a few years ago. I'd like to understand him better. General stuff. Memories. What he was like. Things he did."

The man screwed up his mouth, then took a pencil and notepad off the desk. "Why don't you give me your email address? I keep in contact with some guys who were friends with your dad. I'll send you their contact information."

She wrote down her name, email address, and phone number. It would have been nice if this professor told her more, but at least she was getting somewhere.

Back in the car, Carlos said, "So you're getting some contacts. You sure you want to know what they have to say?"

It was the second time he'd hinted that she might not want to know something. "Why wouldn't I?"

"You seem pretty torn up sometimes. I wonder if your memory's not trying to do you a favor by forgetting." He shrugged. "That prof looked like he might have a memory or two of your dad he'd rather forget."

Sierra held on to the door handle. "My dad was a good guy."

"Never said he wasn't."

When Carlos pulled up to the complex, Sierra's apartment windows were dark, the lights off. "Your mom working tonight?"

She nodded.

"Come have dinner with us then."

"Yeah, sure. Okay."

He drove past Mr. Prodan's neighborhood, a few streets farther down, and pulled up to a beige box house. It had great landscaping—azalea bushes and a pathway made of white pebbles.

The inside of the house lacked the charm of Mr. Prodan's house though. The beige carpet wasn't as pretty as Mr. Prodan's wood floors, but family pictures and ceramic ornaments filled every nook and cabi-net, making it homey.

Two boys lay in front of a TV watching cartoons. As soon as they saw Carlos, they leaped up and barreled into him. He lifted them each with a single arm and growled into their necks, swinging them around before dropping them to the floor. In an instant, they flung themselves back at his legs, and he laughed. "Later, guys. Later."

"That you, Carlos?" a woman called.

Carlos led Sierra into the kitchen, where he hugged a tall, bony woman.

She threw her buttered hands into the air. "Carlos! I've got greasy hands. You go on now."

He laughed, and she shoved his shoulder with an elbow.

"Hey, Ana. This is my friend, Sierra. I thought I'd bring her over for dinner. This is Ana, my guardian."

"Guardian nothing. You don't need guarding, boy." She smiled at Sierra. "Nice to meet you, Sierra."

Carlos led Sierra to the back of the house and stopped at a closed door.

"Leave the door open, Carlos," Ana called.

He smiled and turned to Sierra. "My place. But you can't go in yet."

Sierra waited, thinking maybe he wanted to clean it up first.

"First, you have to tell me what it looks like inside."

"I've never been inside. How would I know what it looks like?"

"Yeah, but you ever think about it? 'This Carlos dude's always around. I wonder what kind of place he lives in. What's he do with himself when he's not bothering me?'"

Sierra's face warmed. How often did she think of Carlos when he wasn't with her? A lot, but she wasn't going to admit that. She closed her eyes, concentrating. His room would be neat and well thought out but inviting and casual. Like him.

"Wrestling posters?" She teased.

"Nope."

"A daisy bedspread?"

"Nope."

"A disco light," she threw out.

"I'm disappointed in you, Brown Eyes. All those books you read, and you can't guess what's on the pages inside by looking at the cover."

"I'm opening the cover now." She pushed the door and it swung open.

It was nothing special at first glance—a bed covered by a Texas Longhorns comforter, a desk with a computer and a few library books on it, a laundry hamper in the corner.

Nothing really caught her attention until she found the huge sketch pinned to the wall. It was a superdetailed drawing of an old house—a Victorian with a wraparound porch and gingerbread latticework. A forest and a pond edged the corner. She went in to look closer. It had personality. She almost touched it, but quickly put her hand back by her side, as if it were a piece in a museum that had one of those gold plaques asking visitors kindly to refrain from touching.

She looked up at him. "Did you draw this?"

Carlos handed her a binder. "Here. This is the rest."

She flipped through the pages, one at a time. Drawings of the house from different angles and various rooms, landscaped gardens, and footbridges filled the book. Lines were penciled to the sides and underneath the drawings with arrows and dimensions noted. The notes looked like work from geometry class. Some of the drawings were done on blue paper like builders used. He'd even included a few magazine clippings of rooms with sticky notes listing dimensions and formulas for the columns and windows.

There was life in the drawings. It reminded her of her mom's wordless sketches. "I almost feel like you're telling a story. It's just missing the words."

"I guess. A story of my future, I hope."

"What is it?"

"There's this abandoned house out close to the pond I took you to. I used to think about what I could do to fix it up. Then I really thought about it. Not one house, lots of houses. I'm going to be an architect."

"You'll be good, Carlos. You're good at everything you do."

He beamed. "I thought when I made enough money to buy it, I'd turn it into something for kids who don't have anywhere to go. At least, that's what I thought of at first."

"Not anymore?"

"Later. But I think I'll make a house for my family first."

"What family?" Sierra asked, confused.

He looked out the window. "I'm not always going to be a yard guy, you know."

She laughed. "I never thought of you as a yard guy, Carlos. You're the only high school guy I know who's supporting himself. I knew you had a plan."

"Yeah, I got a plan." He coughed and took the binder, shelving it with a row of binders.

She put her finger on the binders. "Are these all architecture?"

He nodded and rested his hand against the wall. "Ever think, what if we ran into each other later on? You standing in front of a room of megabrains all day, wowing them with everything you know. And me a big-time architect. Maybe I'd take you out to see my house by the pond."

She looked up at him, trying to hear through the words to what he was trying to tell her. She didn't realize how close they were until she heard a man clear his throat at the door. Ricky boomed out, "None of that now. None of that."

"Just showing her my room, Ricky."

"Make sure that's all you show her, *mijo*." Ricky winked and put a hand on Carlos's shoulder. "Not used to having girls back here."

Ana called them to the kitchen and put them to work setting the table. Dinner was a loud, raucous meal with Ricky and Ana and their two little boys laughing and passing food around. Carlos joined in the fun. Sierra ate her lasagna slowly, watching, taking it all in. The laughter, the fun, the love—it made her go soft inside.

She thought of sitting at a table with Mom and Dad. What would they have joked about? Would they have joked?

After dinner, Ricky gave her a pat on the back. "Ana liked having a girl over here among all of us boys. You come on over anytime."

As Carlos drove her home, she said, "It must be really nice living in a place like that."

"Like what?"

"Everyone so happy and acting like you can do no wrong."

"Yeah. I'm lucky they took a chance on me." He looked straight at her. "That's the kind of family I want. Loud or quiet, it doesn't matter; just lots of love."

"Me too."

He pulled into a parking space and walked her to the apartment. At her door he tilted his head and paused. "The house on my wall. If you want it, it's for you and me, later on."

Sierra went all warm. She tried to speak, but the words wouldn't come.

"You don't have to say anything. It's years away. I know that."

She lowered her eyes. "Why me, Carlos?" What a terrible answer, but the words popped out of her mouth before she could pull them back.

He looked up at the night sky, like he had to think hard. "Why you, Brown Eyes? I don't know. You might be more trouble than you're worth." He laughed and smoothed away a strand of hair from his eyes. The laughter left his eyes then. "You know where I've been, Sierra. And another thing. You don't see what other people see when they look at you. You got a whole world in your eyes. One day, you'll be able to share it with some guy, maybe me."

"Oh, Carlos," she breathed. What else could she say?

He unlocked the door for her and flipped on the light. Like an old uncle, he kissed her on top of her head before jogging down the stairs. She stood at the window, watching him get into his car and drive away.

Her insides thrummed. She was sure everything in her glowed. Carlos Castellano. Who would have thought he would even look twice at her?

She imagined herself in the house in the picture. She imagined herself sitting on the porch, loving Carlos, being his wife, the mother of his children. Maybe she would be a professor, too, like he'd said earlier. Like Dad. She could almost see herself in that life. Almost.

Mom came home, and they shared a bowl of sherbet. Neither of them mentioned their earlier conversation, and Sierra didn't care. Before bed, she checked her email. There was a message from a Rice address already.

She stared at the unopened email, all the warmth of the evening gone. She stood up with a shiver and looked at her computer. Somehow, it had become an alien thing invading her space.

Leaving the inbox open, she got dressed in her pajamas and brushed her hair. The computer seemed to stare at her as she got ready for bed. Maybe Carlos was right. Did she want to know what Dad's friends remembered about him? Mom didn't want to talk about him. The professor hadn't wanted to talk about him. There had to be a reason.

She stood by the computer, her finger poised above the Enter key.

Why would you forget your own father? You wouldn't. Unless there was something too terrible to remember.

She took a deep breath and steeled herself. One way or another, she had to know. She hit the Enter key, and the message popped open.

Chapter Twenty-Seven

When April dropped by Luca's midmorning, no one answered the door. She never had seen a car in his driveway, so she doubted he'd gone far walking. After his last spell, it surprised her he could leave his house at all.

She sat on the porch, enjoying the crisp morning. A breeze wafted through the trees, leaving the air clean and tangy. It wasn't long before Luca walked up the street. He was carrying a single grocery bag.

She met him at the curb. "Maybe it's a bad day for your story. If you've already been out, maybe it's too much for you."

He had a twinkle in his eye. "Any day Mrs. Wright visits is a good day for me."

April laughed. Was the man actually bantering with her?

He let her into the house, which was tidy and bare, as usual. She could do something with the place, given half a chance. A few splashes of color on the walls, some artwork …

Luca coughed. "A man should always worry when a woman comes into his home with such a gleam in her eye."

He'd caught her in her designs. "I can't fool you, Luca. I was thinking what a treat it would be to turn this place into a home."

"A home? Is it not already a home?"

His voice was sharp, and she realized too late her words might offend. Maybe he didn't realize how bare his house was. "It's a house," she said softly. She waved at the empty walls. "Seriously, Luca, a monastery would have more decoration."

He smiled, clearly not irritated, so she went on. "A little paint to mirror the colors in your garden and some knickknacks could really give your house some life. It has such sweet lines already."

An answering glint came into his eye. "If you like. It has been a long time since I have had a woman's touch about, but do not spend much money. I do not care for luxury."

"I might have guessed that. I'll keep it simple."

April went into the kitchen and poured water into a kettle. He watched her turn off the heat under the kettle and put tea bags into cups, but he appeared lost in some faraway land of thought.

She inclined her head. "What is it, Luca?"

His gaze returned to the here and now. "There is more than friendship between Nicu and yourself, I think."

April couldn't help the startled laugh that escaped. "What gave you that idea?"

"Perhaps I am weak, but I am not blind. I have seen you together, and I saw something—some desire, some feeling. Was I mistaken?"

"Yes," she finally said. "And no."

"Ah." He retrieved a lemon and began to cut it into sections. "It is good to let time take its course. It is wise to tread cautiously with bruised hearts." He moved his hand through the air, as if erasing an imaginary blackboard. "But this old man must be careful not to imagine dreams that have no foundation."

He paused and his voice grew faint. "It is only that when I first saw Sierra, she brought my daughter to mind. And I could not help but hope."

April had begun to pour the water and almost dropped the kettle. Its sides sent a bracing heat through her hands as she steadied it on the heat pad. How many surprises did he mean to spring on her today?

"Your daughter?"

His mind had gone to that faraway place again. "I was not allowed to see her. But I imagined her to have Tatia's dark hair and fair skin. I imagined her to have the intelligence of one raised in the Prodan home. Someone much like Sierra."

April removed the tea bags and squeezed the lemon into the tea. Together, she and Luca moved to his library. He didn't come to sit across from her. He stood by the window, closing his eyes, as if convincing himself to return to Tatia crumpled on the floor.

She retrieved the recorder from her purse, switched it on, and sat down to wait. Half turned from her, Luca began to speak.

"I sat by Tatia's side. She would not speak to me of this thing that made her scream at her husband's touch. I raised her sleeve, a long sleeve, though it was warm outside. Her arms were bruised. Earlier she had cut her lip and sprained her wrist. A fall, she said, and I believed her. Why wouldn't I?

"At last she said, 'It is not what you are thinking, Luca.'

"'What then?' I said. Her words did not put me at ease.

"'Don't ask me, Luca. There are some things that are better not to know.'

"In Romania, we were great secret keepers, but it had not been so between us. We argued in harsh whispers that night so the neighbors would not hear us. I pleaded. But she would not tell me. How could it be best not to know what had left my wife battered and frightened?

"It was Nicu who told me at last. He had nightmares, and I went to his room late one night to comfort him. He shoved me away at first, as if I were the culprit who caused his mother's misery.

"Quietly, I began to ask him questions. Then he wrapped his little arms around me and told me the whole terrible story."

Luca came to sit across from April. "A mountain of a man with a scar down one cheek, Nicu said, had been visiting his mama. I knew right away who he meant. The Securitate man who drove me home. He slapped her. And threatened her. He beat her. It was because I was a bad man that he treated her so, Nicu said. I made her do bad things. My four-year-old son watched his mother be struck and berated in my name. It is no wonder he recoiled from me."

April closed her eyes. Did Nick remember? Or was it a black hole deep in his subconscious eating away at him?

"When I told Tatia I knew the Securitate had been questioning her because of me, I wept. I was so ashamed to have brought her harm.

"'No Luca,' she said. She put her finger against my lips to quiet me. 'You were so brave. So brave to speak to your students. Dear Luca, so many children do not have parents brave enough to tell them that there is truth. To them, the only god they know is Ceaşecescu. And the only act of bravery they know is to spy on each other for the state. So many children have never heard the story of the Good Samaritan. They have never heard of Jesus praying to forgive His murderers or of the Good Shepherd looking for His lost sheep. Luca, they do not know.'

"I was confused. 'I have not spoken to my students of the things of God,' I said.

"She did not look away. She did not answer me. A chill came down my arms. 'You have been evangelizing children.'

"She did not deny it.

"'The Securitate knows,' I said with certainty. 'They are interrogating you.' She was fortunate. Others who had taught religion to children had been sent to prison. Some had never been heard from again.

"'Luca,' she whispered. 'I didn't want you to know of it. You have enough worries, and if they asked, it would be clear you did not know what they were speaking of. But they are saying now you are the nonconformist, and you are making me do it.'

"The solution was clear to me. 'They will leave you alone if you stop,' I said to her. I suppose this also is why she did not tell me what she was doing. I drew the attention of the Secret Police by my carelessness, but I would never encourage her to do anything so bold.

"'What of Nicu? What of the baby?' I said to her."

April moved to the edge of her seat. "She was pregnant?"

He looked away. "Yes, she was pregnant. Perhaps over halfway through her time. It was a difficult time for Tatia. She did not eat well. She did not sleep well. She continued to be ill after the nausea should have passed. As her belly grew, Tatia covered it with her hands as if she would protect the child. But I had seen the same look in her grandfather's eyes. He also defied the state for God's sake. She knew the consequences."

April had no right to ask, but she could not help herself. "What happened to your baby girl, Luca?"

He did not answer her immediately, but when he did, he shut his eyes. "Tatia talked more of the Bible to our neighbors, and there was another interrogation. Our daughter was born the next day. Luciana weighed only a kilo. She died ... that same day."

He gripped the arms of the chair as he prepared to go on.

"I came to see Tatia in the hospital after the birth. It was the first time I saw her after the interrogation. Tatia sat in her bed in the hospital ward. 'Black and blue' you say in English. Yes, her skin was black and blue and green and red. One of her eyes was swollen half-shut. Her arm hung limp. This is how they questioned us in Romania. I leaned down to her so the other patients in the ward would not hear us. She choked out a whisper. 'Say I did the right thing, Luca. Our neighbors are God's children too.'

"I told her what she wanted me to say, of course, but I did not mean it.

"Tatia's tears pooled in her eyes, but she smiled at me with the radiance of a saint. I do not believe she knew that there were Securitate men outside waiting to take her away from her living child as well."

April swallowed. What pain for one man to bear.

Luca had turned waxy.

"Please rest now," April said, quietly. "Nick won't forgive me if you get sick."

"Do I look so terrible then?"

April offered him a watery grin. It felt strange, yet right, to smile after the dark memories they had relived, as if they were able to open the curtains to sunshine after a stormy night. She took his hand and led him to his bedroom. "Lie down, Luca. I know you'll probably give me a poor grade on my cooking skills—they're nothing like yours—but I'll make something for you to eat when you wake up."

April prepared a simple casserole from noodles she found in Luca's cupboard and leftover beef tips and tomatoes she found in his fridge. She mixed a fruit salad, covered it, and put it in the fridge. Hopefully, his stomach would be able to tolerate the meal.

She wiped the counters with a damp cloth, seeing not the Formica, but the streets of Bucharest as she imagined them.

As the casserole baked, she curled up in a chair with a notepad, jotting down ideas for Luca's house. It wouldn't take much—an accent wall, embroidered cushions, a few ornaments. Possibly, she could even convince him to put up a photo or two, maybe the one of Luca with little Nick on his shoulders.

April exhaled. She could make his house sparkle. She had the skill to bring a house to life, but not a home and certainly not a heart. Gary and Sierra gave evidence to that.

CHAPTER TWENTY-EIGHT

As Nick pulled up to the curb of his old man's house, he was surprised to find April's car parked in the driveway, and behind it, a work truck. Surprised, but not displeased. He had no call to spend time with April, and he knew she didn't want his company, but he still found her sunlit smile gave him a reason to smile. The fact that she didn't want him perversely made him want to be around her more.

At the door he heard voices and laughter. He let himself in and found a work party in progress. Plastic sheets wreathed the chairs and side table, and the smell of new paint permeated the air. Sierra and a boy Nick recognized from school sanded the paneling next to the floor. Dad sat at the table through the archway into the dining room, looking dazed, while April perched on a ladder next to the far living room wall, now a blazing red. Next to her stood a man Nick didn't know.

Everyone was laughing. Sierra and the boy were laughing. The man and April were laughing together. A lightning strike of jealousy flashed through Nick. She'd told him she didn't want him, and she was free to find someone she did want. Still, the thought of her with someone else soured his day.

April turned, her mouth forming an O of surprise. "Nick!" She climbed down the ladder with a hand from her friend. "Just in time. Your dad's agreed to a little update of his house."

His old man stood and gave a bewildered shake of his head. "A few cushions and something to hang on the wall, she said. And two days later she is painting my wall red and making a new house of it."

Nick could tell he wasn't really annoyed. The house was festive and his old man practically glowed.

With a nod to the stranger, April said, "Oh, Nick, please meet Enrique Salinas. Ricky, this is Luca's son, Nick. And that's Sierra's friend, Carlos."

Nick forced a polite smile toward Ricky and nodded at Carlos. "What can I do to help?"

She put him to work painting a second coat on the higher reaches of the accent wall while she laid out some pictures on the dining room table for his father to see. Before Nick started painting, he noticed the teens had stopped sanding and were working with a pencil.

He crouched next to them, inspecting the pencil marks. "What's that you're doing, Sierra?"

"We're stenciling in a design. I found it on a website about a Romanian castle. It's the etching on the wood gates. We'll paint it later."

Nick knew better than to admire the idea too much. But it was impressive. In addition to Sierra's brilliance with languages, she'd obviously picked up her mother's artistic talent.

"She's got the whole world in her mind, this one," the boy said. Nick liked him immediately, the more so because he'd found a compliment Sierra could take.

"That she does," Nick agreed.

The two turned back to their work. Nick began painting, and Enrique came over to paint from the other end of the wall. "She's a nice lady."

Nick gave a nod meant to choke off any conversation. He didn't intend to discuss April's merits with her new boyfriend.

"Just lights up a room, doesn't she?"

Nick kept painting.

Enrique chuckled. He angled his left hand for Nick to see his wedding band.

Nick pretended he hadn't noticed, but a slow grin worked its way to his mouth and wouldn't be quashed.

"You got it bad."

"Guess I do," he admitted. There was no point in hiding it. Nick brought the paintbrush against the wall in long, careful strokes.

Enrique didn't give up. "You should've seen her smile when she saw you. The lady needs someone. Ask her out."

Nick didn't answer, but Enrique kept at it. "Why not, man?"

Not that it was anyone's business, but to stop the train of conversation, he said, "April loves me like a brother. Her words."

Enrique squinted into the dining room where April still arranged pictures on the table, gave a shrug, and turned back to painting. "If you say so. I'd be a little weirded out if my sisters looked at me like that, though."

Nick turned the brush sideways to paint the corner. It was true. Her glances were just a few seconds too long or a few seconds too short. Her smiles were too golden for someone she viewed as a brother.

That didn't mean she wanted a relationship. So why didn't she tell him the truth? "I like you ..." but what? "Teachers aren't my type?" "I want a man who makes six figures?" Or more likely, "I'm not ready to move on after my husband's death."

He glanced at her standing with Dad and found her looking back. Like a schoolgirl, she looked away, pretending it hadn't happened. Her lie stung more than the rejection itself. If nothing else, he believed he was the kind of man she could be honest with. He turned back to the work at hand, swabbing crimson up to the top edge of the wall.

After they finished the second coat of paint, Enrique clapped Sierra's friend on the back. "We're going to get going. Nice to meet you, Nick."

"Hey, Mrs. Wright, do you mind if Sierra comes home with us for dinner?" Carlos said.

Sierra looked up at the kid with big, adoring eyes. Nick noticed Sierra hadn't once spoken to his old man, and her encounters with April had been cool. But she had her attention on a boy her age. That was a sign of progress, right? After April gave her approval, they were gone.

While the wall dried, Nick pulled the plastic sheets off the chairs. April brought framed pieces of ornate woodwork, the wood rich in red hues, and laid them on the floor. It would look good against the wall, and like Sierra's stencils, brought to mind the old gates you might see in castles or monasteries in Romania. Then she went to the side table, and placed two framed photos on it—one of Dad with Mom just before she died, the other of Dad with Nick on his shoulders back in Romania.

He looked for Dad to see what he thought about the photos, but he had busied himself in the kitchen, determined not to see, as usual.

He came to her side. "It's been a while since I saw those."

"I thought it was time you did."

She had a speck of red paint on her cheek. He used his thumb to rub it. She looked at him, away, and back again. It gave him a dark pleasure to see her squirm. She knew exactly how he felt about her. Would it be so hard to come clean with him?

"Guess it will take more than a finger to remove the spot. Dad's got turpentine in the shed, but I've heard margarine works as well."

She scooted by, walked to the fridge, and pulled out a tub of margarine.

He followed her. "Allow me." He reached for a paper towel, dabbed it in the margarine, and rubbed it against the smudge, letting his hand linger just a little too long against her skin. "There, all gone." And he held up the stained paper towel as proof.

"Thanks," she said weakly.

"My pleasure." He was probably laying it on thick now, but it was fun.

Dad rummaged in the kitchen drawer and pulled out a cutting board. "April and Nicu, go in the backyard, if you please. It is a fine evening, and I do not want help cooking."

April looked at her watch. "Oh, I should probably get home and fix dinner myself."

Laying out pickled tomatoes on the board, Dad said, "I heard your daughter say she would eat with Carlos and Enrique." By his suppressed grin, Nick gathered Dad was in on the game. A first, their siding together on something.

"Only fair to stay for dinner, April," Nick added. "Free labor has to be repaid some way. It's an old Romanian custom."

They'd hemmed her in, but she didn't complain. April sauntered next to him to the backyard. In this old part of town, yards stretched out, leaving room for kids to play or gardens to be planted. The scent of honeysuckle filled the air, sharp and sweet.

April stopped to give him one of her too-brief glances. "I never properly thanked you for getting Sierra to retake her finals. I can't tell you what it meant to me."

He laced his hands behind his back, shrugging off the disappointment. It was a safe subject, something he couldn't turn around to the subject he wanted to talk about. But he needed to talk to her about Sierra anyway.

"No thanks needed." He waited, seeking her gaze. "I wonder if you know just how bright Sierra is. I deal with a lot of kids, but I've never come across one who's got such a mind driving them."

A battle-ready look rose to her face, and she went tense. What had he said? He thought he'd complimented her daughter.

"I've talked to a couple of her teachers," he went on. "Every now and then she'll turn in something absolutely, wonderfully brilliant. It's college material, publishable even. But give her review questions or a work sheet to complete, and she won't even try."

"Nick, I know all this. Sierra … she's so brilliant it terrifies me."

Since when was God-given brilliance terrifying? "Have you thought of getting her into a school for gifted kids?"

"Oh sure, I've thought of it. From the beginning, I've thought of it. When I found her reading *A Little Princess* to herself in kindergarten. When she wrote a collection of fifty-something original stories with a made-up world of fantastical creatures in third grade. When she read a history of the Incas in Spanish without ever taking a language course. But now, I don't think she'd be able to pull it together, even if the school were tailored for her. Her mind is somewhere else."

"What about homeschooling? There's nothing more tailored than that."

April drew to a stop. He could tell he'd somehow said something else to offend her.

When April didn't answer, he went on. "Your daughter could give herself a far better education than she's getting at school. And with her abilities, she'd have no shortage of experts who would mentor her."

April pressed her hands together until her knuckles turned white. She lifted her chin. "Sierra needs structure. She doesn't need exceptions."

Why wasn't he getting through to her? April was too bright not to understand what he was saying. "I wasn't thinking of it as an exception. She would be doing more work than the other students, not less."

"You don't understand!" Her words came out as a cry.

Her distress sent a shudder through him, and he let a few seconds pass. "Okay, April. Why don't you help me understand?"

"I've seen the adult side of unfettered brilliance, and it's not pretty. What happens when she gets to college and gets assigned something she feels is beneath her, or gets a job and the work isn't challenging enough? She needs to learn how to get along with normal people and live a normal life."

"Give her some freedom first. She'll move inside the lines when she has to." Nick waved a hand in the air. "Or she won't. I was never a fan of the lines anyway."

She glared.

"Why does she have to adapt?" Nick said. "The library is filled with books by and about people who drew their own lines—inventors and poets and people who turned history on its head."

She didn't respond. He spoke quietly, hoping she'd hear him in the gentleness of his voice. "April, she won't pull through this way. Ignoring her genius won't make it go away. Sierra *isn't* normal. And she's starving—mentally starving—at school."

That hit home. He could see the shock register in April's eyes, but still, she shook her head.

April was more open-minded than this. "Speak to me, April. Please."

She let out a deep sigh and looked up at the sky. "Sierra is … Sierra's dad … I wish …" New energy filled her face, and her eyes blazed, even as she looked away from him. "I can't."

The refusal set off a fuse inside him. She didn't owe him anything. But he'd been her friend before he kissed her. According to her, he was still a brother to her. And all he was doing was trying to help her struggling daughter. A little honesty would be nice.

He rolled his shoulders. "Your secrets are yours to keep or tell. But I've yet to find silence solving much of anything."

She smiled. Always the dazzling smile, but it didn't fool him this time. Her dark eyes hinted at the story, even though her words wouldn't. She loved Sierra too much to refuse her the help she needed.

He reached for her hand, but she stepped back.

"Nick …" She stared hard at the roof behind him. "It's so complicated. I wish a simple conversation would solve everything, but it won't." She dropped her arms to her sides and didn't go on.

That was it. She wasn't going to explain, though Sierra's father seemed to be part of it. Something about unfettered brilliance.

He rubbed his temple. It hurt down to his bones. She didn't want his touch. She didn't want his counsel. She didn't want him.

Finally, he said, "Fair enough. Why don't I go see if dinner's ready?"

He swung toward the back door, his only thought to get away. In the living room, the red wall, the gold cushions, the photos brought him to a halt. What a difference an afternoon had made to the house. Color, art, even Dad's history decked the house. April had brought life to the empty shell.

A movement from the library door caught his attention. His old man sat in an armchair, his eyes reflecting Nick's own regret. Nick knew his frustration must be written on his face for anyone to read, if Dad, who'd been immune to the ups and downs of his life, found something there to sympathize with.

"If we could make everything better with only a paintbrush," Dad said.

Nick let out a bitter chuckle. "Not so easy with people, is it, Dad?"

CHAPTER TWENTY-NINE

The March sun warmed the air. April spent her days off at the park or taking Sierra to outdoor cafés rather than setting up another interview with Luca. She could almost see him growing frailer before her eyes. Unquestionably, it was the memories taking a toll on him. There didn't seem much more of the story to tell anyway since he wasn't willing to discuss prison.

Finally, Luca called her and asked when she was coming. She paused. There was no point in stalling. "Today," she said.

He led her into his backyard, where the grass had come to life, sparrows chirped, and the pear tree near the kitchen was beginning to flower. His yard gave her a taste of Eden. She could only hope the lovely weather would keep his mind from straying too long near the world of his Romanian prison.

"Are you sure?" she asked him one last time, as she took a patio chair across from him.

"I am sure." She turned on the recorder.

He cupped something in his hands—a piece of newsprint, she thought—as he began to speak, carrying her back to the Romania of 1976.

"It was a simple decision to make. Nicu was young, and he needed his mother. Tatia would never survive prison. I left the hospital and turned myself in to the authorities waiting outside. I told them, 'She did not want to speak of God to children. I made her do it. And because she loved me, she did so.'

"I cannot say if they believed me. I think they did not. But they agreed to let her return home to Nicu, and I was sentenced to five years of reeducation. That is what they called imprisonment. I did not even get to say good-bye to them."

Luca paused and began to talk again.

"My cell mates were priests and missionaries imprisoned for preaching illegal sermons and evangelizing Romanian youth, political dissenters, men who had kept secret printing presses and held revolutionary meetings. I had no place there. Who was I? Only a man who had tried to protect his wife and son."

April smoothed her skirt and started to switch off the recorder.

"Are you done so soon?" he said with a tinge of amusement in his voice.

"You said you would not talk of prison, Luca."

"I did say this, but we are telling the story for Nicolae. The story will mean nothing without this part."

"Luca? You've exhausted yourself already." It was true. His face was gray, and he hadn't even told her of the torture to come.

But he stood and trained his eyes on her. "I am too exhausted, am I? Exhausted?" He leaned on the back of his chair. "You are right. I *am* weary. Five years I spent in prison, and it has consumed the remaining years of my life! I am exhausted from turning my head from those memories. I will face them now."

She sank farther into the patio chair as he stood up and paced in a circle. She had never seen Luca so passionate.

The sky clouded over, and a chilly breeze raised the hair on her arms.

Luca looked at the sky with wry amusement. "I am going to tell what happened in prison," he said in a hoarse voice. "Will you listen?"

April nodded, her throat dry. "Of course, Luca."

He came back to his chair and turned the newsprint carefully over in his hands.

"You think at first there is some inner core no horror can touch. My body became ill from a diet of oily soups made from rotten vegetables. Bread was given only once a week. I had diarrhea. There was no privacy. My cell mates had seen it all before, but I tried to find some bit of self-respect.

"'It is no use,' a man in the corner of his cell said to me. He seemed very old, but they all did. It only takes a year, a few months of prison, to bring a young man to old age. 'If you will survive here,' he said, 'you will do it by accepting there is nothing left for you. No health. No wholeness as you know it.'

"I glared at him. If I was to survive for my family, I should have to be very strong. How dare this man discourage me before I began to try?

"'Our only strength here,' he said, 'is to be the broken body of Christ.' I learned later he was an Orthodox priest, Father Mihael.

"At night, men sobbed. They prayed aloud. They called out to their wives and mothers. But other men reached out. They held the sobbing men like babies. And when I was that man, when I came from being beaten, when I cried out in my sleep for Tatia, it was my turn to be held and prayed over.

"The guards forced us to stand with backpacks full of rocks all day long. They made us lie with four men on top of us. They beat us. In winter, they put us in cells with ice dripping from the walls. They commanded us to jog for ten hours, twenty hours. They would entice prisoners with the lure of freedom if they would beat other prisoners or urinate on them.

"They forced me to say that I and my friends were guilty of dozens of violent crimes by questioning and threatening for hours, days sometimes, until I began to believe it was possible I had done every terrible thing they said I had done. I lost my name and became only a number.

"They took pleasure in breaking us. Father Mihael was right. You could hold on to nothing worth having. I was angry I was not braver. I was humiliated for the men who cried out and for the men who held them.

"The first Sunday, the guards gave out bread. I was so hungry, I almost swallowed my piece whole. I did not even taste it. But most held on to their bread. This was to make it last, I thought. Then Father Mihael began to say a prayer, and each man brought his bread to him, and he blessed it. In this terrible place they were having the Eucharist!

"One man turned to me, tore off a chunk, and offered it. I looked at it greedily, wanting to fill my stomach with one more piece of bread, but I shook my head. This was idiocy.

"I listened to their prayers, but I felt I should go insane if I joined them. How could one think of God in a place He had abandoned to the devil?

"So I worked out difficult equations. I recited passages of poetry I recalled. Above all, I remembered Tatia and Nicu. My only prayer was for their safety.

"I had been in prison for some time. I cannot say for how long, because days were lost to me. One of the guards came to visit me.

"'Your family is dead,' he said. 'They are no more.' And he walked out.

"Tatia and Nicu ... They were all I had been holding on for. I had foolishly believed I could protect my family, and now they were dead. I was already broken. What was left to break? There had been a small part of me holding on, hoping I could survive for them until I was freed. This part of me was now gone. I was thankful. I could surrender to death now."

April kneaded her hands together. Luca's eyes faded. His shoulders slumped. She could see that living through the memory again had cost him.

"Luca, you can stop now. If you want."

He didn't seem to hear her. He seemed locked in his prison. But he must have decided that the only way to freedom was to find the other side of the memory.

He sighed and began speaking again.

"There were saints in my cell. When a broken man was called for a beating, a stronger man would pretend to be him. When one man went insane, others brought him back with their care. They even prayed for the guards who beat us. But I was not a saint. I wanted only to die. You think when you live in such a place all you must do is give up. Illness and death surrounded me. Torture was daily.

"I provoked the guards for extra beatings. I gave other men my soup. It would be soon. But I did not die. My body, young and still strong, refused to cooperate.

"In my sleep, I heard a boy crying. I woke thinking Nicu was in the other bedroom. I wanted to go to him, but I had no strength to get up. Then I realized it was not a boy crying. It was me.

"Father Mihael handed bread to me and made the sign of the cross. 'Confess your sins, Luca. You can find God's goodness in this

place, most especially in this place.' Thinking of the secret commu-
nion after my wedding, I confessed my sins and ate. He handed me
his water. 'We have no wine, but Christ is able to turn water into
wine, if He chooses.'

"If I was unable to die, I did not take to life either. *I am like the
hermits of old,* I thought. *I will give myself to prayer.* I thought of Tatia
teaching Nicu his prayers. And I found solace in the prayers, but I
was not a saint."

"You sacrificed yourself for your family!" April said. "You
endured that terrible place without turning against God. Isn't that
enough for sainthood?"

He let out a bleak laugh. "To be a saint, one must overcome the
world. I overcame nothing."

As if speaking to the trees, he turned away from her and went
on with his story.

"The guards mostly ignored the religious services. But there was
one who liked to provoke us. One day he came into our cell with …
it was sacrilege. Human waste.

"'Bless this, Father,' he said. 'Here is the holy Eucharist.' Father
Mihael did not move. His eyes, large in his thin face, were full of pity
for the guard. The priest stayed very still. Only his lips moved in a
quiet prayer.

"After some time of yelling and coercing, the guard saw Father
Mihael would not be threatened into blessing it, and he began to
beat him in front of us all. I sat by and allowed it. What choice did
we have in such a place? But I thought of Father Mihael's wife and
children—four sons and a daughter—whom he prayed for daily. At
the crack of splitting bone and the sound of his head hitting the
stone floor, I thought of them.

"The guard stood to wipe the sweat from his face, and something came alive in me. My arms and legs found strength. I moved quickly. When he looked back, I stood between him and Father Mihael.

"The guard laughed at my small act of bravery and tried to shove me away, but the harder he tried to reach Father Mihael, the more determined I became. The priest was forgotten. He turned his attention to me.

"'You want to be a martyr. Very well,' he said to me.

"The guards tied rope around my hands until they burned, and they secured me to the beams above, with my hands stretched out and my feet together. 'You are a martyr now,' they laughed. 'Just like your Jesus.'

"I felt the struggle to breathe, the bruising of my ribs, the stinging of my hands against the rope. *I will die now,* I thought, but my lungs refused to stop fighting for air.

"The men, the priests and the Christians, prayed under me and over Father Mihael lying wounded on the floor. They recited the Beatitudes and the Psalms and prayers recounting the passion of our Lord. They prayed through the afternoon and then the night and the next day without sleep. Even now, I wake sometimes hearing the sound of those prayers.

"The evening guards took me down, I tried to spread my arms, but they would not lift.

"'You have not killed me,' I wanted to say. 'Only God can take my life.' But my tongue was swollen, and the guards laughed at the croak that came out of my mouth."

April started to speak, but she could find nothing to say. She blinked away her tears. What could she possibly say? So she only reached out to him and covered his hand with her own.

He looked up at her blankly.

She opened his left hand, massaging the scars. "Luca. Oh, Luca."

With his other hand, he offered her the newsprint. It took her a few minutes to gather enough strength to look at it. It was in Romanian. "What does it say?"

He looked off into space, not at the paper. In a raspy voice, he said, "'Father Mihael Bălanescu died peacefully in his bed on the eighth of August, 2007.' His son, a priest also, sent it to me."

"You suffered for something so important, Luca. You gave him back to his family and to his church. When did the communist government fall? 1989? That's almost twenty years he had because the guards didn't kill him that night."

She closed her eyes briefly and opened them to find Luca inspecting her. "I believe you know something of what I experienced," he said.

She shook her head. It was an unworthy comparison. Coping with a depressed husband hardly ranked with five years of torture.

But he gave her a firm nod. "Sacrifice is sacrifice, however it is done."

Chapter Thirty

Sierra sat cross-legged on her bed. Mom was sleep, and the apartment was quiet. The only light came from her laptop. She rubbed her temples and took two gulping breaths. This was it.

The email from the professor she had met at the university contained two names, two addresses for Rice alumni who had known her father. Dr. Louis Bernard had a Johns Hopkins email and a Maryland address. There wasn't an email for Dr. Joseph Wheeler or a telephone number, only an address in Tonkawa Creek, Texas. She looked it up. It was in East Texas, population four hundred and thirty, just over a hundred miles north of Houston. But she couldn't find any other contact information for this man on the Internet.

Sierra stood and paced the carpet between her bed and the wall, her hands behind her. She wanted to talk to these men face-to-face. When they spoke about Dad, she wanted to see if they drew back like the Rice professor had, or if they smiled and began chatting the way old friends do. She didn't want them to have time to think about it if she sent letters. She leaned her head against the cool glass of her window. This man in Tonkawa Creek was her best option. She couldn't call him or email him to set up a time though, and how would she get there?

It was time to act grown-up. That meant not relying on Carlos to drive her there and not upsetting her mom about the whole thing.

She'd just go. This man wasn't an ax murderer. The Rice professor said Dr. Wheeler had been Dad's roommate at Rice, and they'd earned their PhDs at Cornell together. Sierra picked up her plush kangaroo and held it to her chest as she sat back on the bed.

She'd find a way to reach him.

———————

Saturday morning she left the apartment with a plan. Outside the apartment gate, she looked across the bayou to Mr. Prodan's neighborhood. It would be nice to speak to him about Dad and the professors, but he was Mom's friend now.

So she turned the opposite direction and caught a city bus to the Greyhound station, where she boarded another bus to Tonkawa Creek. She had a whole row to herself. Sierra pulled on her jacket and rested her head against the cushion, tuning out the beat from a nearby iPod.

In no time, they'd left the city behind. Freeway turned into interstate, and malls gave way to acres of pine. It was like a movie about the deep South as they sped by shacks and rusted cars and dirt roads. Old people sat on porches and cows grazed in meadows.

Shortly before noon, the driver pulled into a gas station and called out, "Tonkawa Creek!"

She was the only one who exited the bus.

Cars whizzed by on the road, but they all appeared to be going somewhere else, heading for towns where they had Walmarts and McDonalds.

Aside from the convenience store and post office, nothing even indicated this was a town. A white steeple poked out of the trees,

THE LANGUAGE OF SPARROWS

and down the road, a little brick building perched on the edge of the highway. She closed her eyes to the empty place. She could do this. She'd come all this way so she could.

The man at the post office shot an amused glance at her sandals when she showed him the address. "Yeah, I know it. You cross the interstate and follow it about a mile or two. You'll find Tiber Pines Road, just a dirt road. It's about two, maybe three miles down that road."

Sierra thanked him and began trudging up the road. When a gap in traffic left room, she sprinted across the interstate to the center turn lane, then waited again to dash to the other side. A truck honked at her as she hiked up a hill along the grassy shoulder. Finally, she found the turn off—a dirt track, lined on both sides by pine forest. She hiked up and then down its inclines.

Sierra didn't go far before she needed to remove her jacket and tie it around her waist. It was a mild March day, but the sun shone overhead now. She fanned her hands to keep gnats from swarming into her face. A woodpecker drilled in the distance.

What brought a history professor way out here? It would be a long drive to any college, and none of those of any reputation. She wiped her sweaty palms against her jeans. This man's life wasn't her concern. What mattered was that he would tell her about Dad's.

After what seemed ages, she found a rusted gate. Next to it, overgrown ferns almost hid a wood sign with the name Wheeler engraved into it. She unlatched the gate and tramped down a gravel trail.

Horses grazed on a hill in the distance. On this side of the meadow stood a neat farmhouse that had rockers on the porch. She didn't see a car. It was so quiet, Sierra grew nervous, wondering if she'd come all this way for nothing. The place looked empty.

She looked around as she approached the house. Tools were strewn about in the yard—a saw and some kind of cable.

Once on the porch, she cupped her hands around her eyes to see through a picture window. In the living room, books and periodicals lay piled on the furniture, but no one stirred.

Sierra knocked and waited, knocked again. No answer. She followed the wraparound porch to the back where a barn stood next to a pond before the property fell into more forestland.

A man came out of the barn. He looked about fifty and was as different from her dark, scholarly father as anyone could possibly be. His age showed in the wrinkles around his eyes, but he stood tall, probably six and a half feet, and fit with a full head of wheat-colored hair. He wore work clothes covered in sawdust. This couldn't be Dr. Wheeler, could it?

Standing at the barn door, wiping his forehead with a handkerchief, he watched her walk across the yard to meet him. She hadn't thought what she'd say when she met him. She could hardly throw out, "Hi, I'm Gary Wright's daughter and I need to know who he was." The way he glared at her, she didn't think he wanted company anyway.

The first words out of his mouth confirmed it. "You're on private property."

But as she drew close, he worked his jaw. "Well now, if you aren't the spitting image of your daddy."

Sierra hadn't expected that down-home accent. She didn't know what she'd expected, but not this man. He didn't appear as if he'd ever set foot in a university classroom.

She held out her hand. "I'm Sierra Wright."

"I know who you are, little girl. Didn't I just say that?" He ignored her hand and put his arm around her shoulder. "I've been praying hard for you and your mama. It's good to see you. Where's Miss April?"

"In Houston." A drawl slipped into her words, as if Dr. Wheeler's accent were contagious.

"You drove out here by yourself?" He glanced down the road for her car. "Guess you are driving age by now, aren't you?"

Sierra coughed. "I took the bus actually."

He gave her an even glance. "Is that right? Well, come on inside. I'll get you a drink."

Inside the old-fashioned kitchen, he poured a glass of iced tea for her and gulped down an entire glass himself before pouring a second glass. She studied him. He felt familiar. Had she known him once and forgotten him?

He shuffled papers and books off a sofa, but threw up his hands. "Oh, it's nice enough outside. Let's go on out."

They sat on the edge of the porch. Sierra's legs dangled over the side, and a golden retriever came sniffing at her ankles before coming to heel at her master's feet.

"So what brings you out here, munchkin?"

Sierra stared off into the trees and reached down to scratch the dog's ears. She cleared her throat. "Dr. Wheeler, it's been almost three years since my dad died."

He held up a hand. "Call me Joe."

"Joe," she said quietly. "I can hardly remember him—my dad. Someone told me you might be able to tell me something about him. I can't … I mean I don't seem to remember …"

"They do seem to slip away, don't they? The memories of our loved ones." He looked straight at her. "It hit me hard. Haven't been the same myself since. Can't imagine what it was like for y'all. I did try to check up on April, but I know how it is. When you lose some-one, writing back to well-meaning friends is just one more thing you'd rather not be responsible for."

He stood. "Let's walk over to the meadow."

The path was worn, and though it led uphill, it made for an easy stroll. "Your mama told you I was the last one he spoke to?"

A little jolt hit her chest. No, of course Mom hadn't said anything. She never talked about Dad at all. "My mother didn't mention it."

"We ran into each other at the conference in Rome. Had lunch, and I could tell he wasn't doing good. Lifting his fork seemed more than he could manage.

"Before we parted ways, he said, 'I'm doing it for them, Joe.'

"I said, 'Doing what? For who?'

"Your daddy smiled at me and said, 'You'll know.' I thought he was too tired to make sense. I told him he ought to sit the next session out. Get some rest. He looked at me and said, 'That's exactly what I intend to do.'"

Joe picked up a twig off the path and broke it in two. "I should've known. We'd been friends for over twenty years. If anyone knew how much he struggled, I did. I should've figured it out." Joe swallowed hard.

Sierra looked back at the path. He should have known what? They'd covered a lot of ground, and the house was in the distance, almost hidden by the cypresses on its eastern side.

"Believe me, I never would have let him go, if I'd had the slight-est inkling."

Inkling of what? Was he somehow supposed to have guessed a van would lose control as Dad crossed the street?

Joe's voice cracked. "I should have asked him what he meant. If I'd known, I'd have walked that mile with him. I'd have stepped in front of that van myself to stop him."

A buzzing rang in Sierra's ears. The grass turned a fuzzy green; the sky faded.

She knew what Joe was telling her.

But it couldn't be true. Mom would have told her if he'd ... if it hadn't been an accident.

"I'm sorry, little girl. I can't tell you how many times I wish I had that day to do over."

His words sounded like they came from a tin can, but she forced herself to respond through stiff lips. "It wasn't your fault."

She kept walking somehow. *Eu merg, tu mergi, el merge, noi mergem.* She desperately began conjugating verbs. It wasn't Joe's fault. It wasn't Dad's fault. It just was.

"Sierra-girl, are you okay?"

Sierra nodded. She even smiled. "I'm fine. I just ... what did he have for lunch that day?"

"I don't guess I recall."

She worked hard to keep the smile. "It's all right. I just wondered." She walked on, though her legs had turned to rubber and the ground felt too soft to hold her up. "I guess you wouldn't remember a thing like that."

Had she said those words? Or had she only thought them? Everything seemed so unreal that she couldn't say.

He stopped, dropping the twig, and looked hard at her. She tried to return the look, but his face was too hazy, and she stared off into whiteness. No one's fault; no one's fault. It's just how things were.

"You didn't know your daddy killed himself, did you?"

She tried to form the words, but the terrible buzzing swallowed her attention.

The world bleached itself of all color. She had a vague sensation of his hands around her shoulders—large, hard hands—and then the feel of grass beneath her, prickling her neck and arms. She closed her eyes to shut out the awful glare.

The ringing finally stopped, and she could put two thoughts together. She opened her eyes and saw the colors that should be there covered in shadows. She sat up.

"Easy now." Joe sat beside her, gripping her arms. "Let the blood work its way back into your head."

"I'm sorry," she whispered. "I'm so sorry." She didn't know what she was sorry for. The words just rolled off her tongue.

"Hey, now. I never would've told you. I thought you knew."

"My mom knows?" she asked.

He chewed his lip. "I gave her the news myself."

The dog nuzzled at her hand, and Sierra burrowed her head into its fur.

"I can't remember him," she said. "I tried, but no one would talk about him."

———————

Joe helped her up and insisted she lean on his arm as they walked back to the house. From a rocking chair on the porch, she looked out at the horses grazing while Joe went to get a glass of ice water for her. Too tired to drink, she put the glass against her face and let the coldness chill her flushed skin.

"Why did he do it?"

Joe sighed as he sat in the rocking chair next to her. "You ever met your grandparents?"

"Not my dad's parents. I think they died when I was little."

"Crazy as loons. I went home with him one summer to meet them up in Kansas when we were roommates in college. My sophomore year, it was. They were threatened by your dad's genius and didn't much take to me either."

"Threatened?"

"Gary's mind was like a sieve. He read every book in the town library before he finished junior high. He heard a fact, and it was burned into his mind forever. He picked up languages the way other boys picked up baseball stats. But were his folks proud? No, they called *him* proud and too good for the likes of them. He wanted to please them. But there was no way with a mind like that he could be content with anything but learning and lots and lots of it."

Joe leaned his head back. "I thought he'd be okay. He'd make peace with who he was. But they were always in his head, accusing him, telling him he was prideful, odd, wrong. The more he pretended they didn't exist, the harder it was for him. The more he was driven to work. Hours and hours, days and days, without sleep or food, until he collapsed. He had his first breakdown when you were a little tyke.

"I thought, *Well now, that's a good thing. He'll get help finally.* But the more time he spent with the doctors and on the medicine, the worse he seemed to get. A group of us men fasted and prayed and laid our hands on him, but he kept getting worse and worse. I thought—and I'm no psychiatrist—but I thought, *Why doesn't he go home?* Tell that crazy family that God made him brilliant for a reason, and if they were any kind of sane, they ought to be supporting him. Maybe if he'd tell them what's what, he'd get rid of the manic studying and guilt. But he just bottled it up inside."

He paused. "But then maybe that's just my thinking. The doctors said it was a matter of brain chemistry. So likely it was more complicated than the problem with his folks."

"You were my dad's friend."

"I was. We were pals from our freshman year at Rice."

"Did he ... Was he ever okay?"

"Sure. He was always serious, but he was a normal guy. He went out for pizza, made jokes, was fun to hang out with. You could always see them in his eyes though, those ghosts."

Sierra looked up at the towering pines by the fence. "I try to see him—in my memories, I mean. But there's nothing."

"Maybe it will be easier now that you know."

"Maybe."

Joe leaned forward and turned her face with his hand so that she had to look straight at him. "Gary had his failings, but he loved you."

He dropped his hand. "I remember lots of times seeing him with you cuddled up on his lap like a kitten. That's what he called you. Kitten. Had pictures galore of you on his wall. I swear, according to Gary, you were the smartest, most beautiful, and sweetest-tempered child on earth." Joe winked at her. "But looking at you now, I guess he was right. He loved your mama, too."

"But it wasn't enough." She dug her fingernails into her palms.

"No, I guess not. Sometimes, there isn't enough to make something right, not the kind of right we think God ought to give us. But I happen to think you and April are the reason he hung on as long as he did."

She closed her eyes. She'd worried when Mom hadn't wanted to talk about Dad. And when the professor had grown cool at Dad's

name, and when Carlos had suggested there might have been something wrong with him, the worry had turned into a hard lump of
panic. But he hadn't been anything horrible. Just sad.

She thought of the closed door to her parents' bedroom, one
of the few images she could remember. She remembered now. The
light in the study would be on all night. She'd find him in there
sometimes, working feverishly over something, when she woke in
the middle of the night. And then during the day, the door to the
bedroom would be closed, and Mom told her to whisper so they
wouldn't disturb him. Her mother treated Dad's sleep like gold. Was
there anything that would have made him join the waking?

Joe touched her arm. "Why don't we go back inside and look at
some old photos."

Sierra stood. "I feel as if I should remember you."

Joe smiled. "Understandable why you wouldn't. I was around a
lot when you were a baby. But after grad school, your folks moved to
Virginia, and I only saw you once in a blue moon."

They walked back into the house, and Joe began digging
among stacks of books until he found a photo album. He showed
her pictures of Dad hanging out with his friends. Joe had been
the best man at her parents' wedding. Dad looked happy enough.
But then Joe pulled out some photos of the time he visited them
in Virginia. Mom must have taken one of them—the two men
stood side by side, leaning against a wood rail fence. Dad's eyes
looked puffy, and while Joe had filled out, Dad had put on a serious
amount of weight.

"It was the medicine," Joe said. "Made him gain thirty pounds
in a month. When that round didn't work, they tried another. Some
medicines worked for a little bit. Some made him worse than ever.

But it was my feeling no medicine could undo what his folks did to him."

There was something eerie about the photos. In one photo, she could look at it and think, *Here's a man who's got his life ahead of him.* And in the next, she could see, *This is a man who might not make it.*

He patted her knee. "It's about time for you to head home, isn't it?"

"No, I don't think so." Sierra looked away, but from the corner of her eye, she could see him looking at her, weighing his words.

"I guess she doesn't know you're here."

Sierra inspected her feet.

"There ain't such a thing as running away, little girl. Your daddy tried that one, and it didn't do him one bit of good. If you want some kind of life, you're going to have to go home first. Face your mama. Face the memories of your daddy. Once you face the things you don't like, you can decide what to do."

Sierra looked out at the lawn, the horses, the country road, all so far away from the cobbled paths of a university. She jutted out her chin. "But you ran away. You have a doctorate, and you're out in the country with no one but horses to teach."

He chuckled. "Maybe I did run away and maybe I didn't. After your dad … And then my wife left me. It seemed time to come home to where it all started. I don't call going home running away myself. I call it a sabbatical. But I'm sure there's some who disagree."

"I'm sorry, Joe," she whispered.

He put his giant hand on her cheek. "Hit me with your best. I can take it. I'd rather see you duking it out over trying to be brave any day. You feel what you feel. And pretending you don't will only take you to a darker place."

"I can't go back." She balled her hands into fists, as if she could make it true. "My mom lied to me, Joe." She ducked her head. She'd have to go home. Where else would she go?

"Your mama can't take any more loss. Go home and tell her what's on your mind."

Sierra didn't answer.

"You're not going home alone. I want you to know that." She looked up to see him studying her. "The more sin-scarred the world is around you, the deeper God's compassion. He never leaves the side of the brokenhearted. Do you hear what I'm saying?"

He didn't let go of her gaze until she gave him a brief nod.

Sierra didn't take the bus back. Joe wouldn't hear of it. He set her in his Jeep Cherokee and drove her to Houston himself. Dusk was settling by the time the freeway widened to ten lanes.

Rain must have fallen during the day. Car lights shone and tires swooshed and hissed against the slick pavement. By the time she directed him to their exit, night was pressing in.

He gave her an uncertain look when he pulled onto their street, and Sierra pulled into her own corner of the seat. What must he think of their choice of apartments? He parked inside the gates under a yellow streetlight and sat behind the wheel, staring at the complex.

A couple of teenage boys dressed in low-riding jeans and oversize jackets meandered by at a measured pace, bumping into the Jeep on purpose. Joe's eyes flashed murder. "April," he muttered under his breath, "why didn't you tell me?"

He started to get out, but Sierra put her hand out to stop him. "If you don't mind, I'd rather talk to my mom alone."

He took out a pen and wrote a phone number on her hand. "You tell her to call me. There's no reason for you all to be living in a place like this."

"I'll tell her."

"God bless, kitten."

Joe didn't drive away until she waved at him from inside the apartment. She breathed a sigh of relief the place was empty. The answering machine flashed. Mom wouldn't get home until nine. Carlos wanted her to call. She deleted both messages.

Standing in front of the wall of art she'd made with Mom and that crazy picture of the woman and child in the center, she remembered Joe's question: Why didn't Mom tell him they were living like this? Mom was good at keeping secrets, wasn't she? With her smiles and cheery voice, she never once let on that Dad's accident wasn't so accidental.

Sierra felt light-headed looking at the painting. Where was Dad in the center tile? Where was the truth?

She put her head into her hands. Where was anything at all?

She took a hot shower, and by the time Mom got home, Sierra had pulled on her sweats and burrowed under her covers with the lights turned out. Mom looked in, and Sierra closed her eyes, playing the role of sleeping daughter.

CHAPTER THIRTY-ONE

Sierra woke, sensing something was wrong. Sunlight dappled her bed, and Mom moved in the kitchen. She could smell biscuits and sausages. The alarm clock said 9:03 a.m. She should be getting ready for church.

Then it came to her. The day in Tonkawa Creek.

She lay in bed for a long time, not moving, not able to think about doing anything. All she could think of was Dad planning his own death. Thoughts of his last day, of what he must have been feeling, trapped her beneath a lead blanket of exhaustion.

She raised her fingers and began counting as she whispered, "One foot and the next / he steps into speeding cars / and embraces death."

Seventeen syllables, Mr. Prodan. How's that for a haiku? Not very poetic, but it was true. With his last breath, her father hadn't chosen her or Mom. How could he have said he was doing it for them?

Eventually, the idea of lying in bed, letting the misery win, pricked at her. That's what Mom was so afraid of—that she was like Dad. It's why Mom grimaced when she found her teaching herself Romanian or reading a book late into the night. And Sierra *had* been like him.

But not anymore.

She slid out of bed and dressed in a yellow sundress Mom had bought for her, a dress she'd never worn. She brushed her hair till it shone and came into the living room.

Mom sat in a chair by the window, working on a sketch.

Sierra gripped the doorknob. "I'm not like him."

Mom looked at her, perplexed.

"I'm not going to hurt myself. You can stop worrying about me. You can stop protecting me from the truth."

Mom blanched. "Sierra ..."

She stood and edged toward her, but Sierra backed away. She wasn't going to let Mom finish. It would be too painful to listen to her apologize, to explain, to tell her it would all work out.

"It's all right. You were worried I was like Dad, but I'm not."

Sierra could see Mom trying to work it out, what Sierra knew, what she could say.

Sierra patted her mom's arm and quickly drew it back. "It's okay, Mom. Really."

She could still feel her mom groping for something to say as she slipped out the front door and began walking nowhere in particular. What was the point in going to church today? What was the point in staying behind to talk? Words were useless now. Mom had been right about that all along. The only useful thing was to be strong, be happy, and leave the darkness behind.

Monday afternoon, after Mom had gone to work, Sierra stood in the bathroom looking in the mirror. *Comb your hair out of your eyes, Sierra. Stop hiding your lovely face behind your hair, Sierra.* She didn't like the girl she saw in the mirror. She was timid. Insipid. The grieving girl Dad left behind. It was time for a change.

With her left hand, she pulled her hair back, letting her whole face show. The scissors lay on the counter. Mom often trimmed a bit of her own hair, making sure her short strands of hair stayed feathered just right. Sierra let go of her hair and picked up the scissors, holding them up in the light, considering. Then, with one snip, she sent a long chunk of hair to the bath mat below. And then another.

Her neck shone white and free in the mirror, and then her whole face. Until there was nothing but a cap of dark hair from her hairline to the nape of her neck. She clipped at the top and teased bits of hair, rubbing gel in until her scalp burned. But she'd got the look she'd wanted, more or less.

She felt naked, looking in the mirror, with her face for anyone to see. But she wasn't hiding anymore. She would look people straight in the eye.

After sweeping the hair up, she stood in front of the mirror and practiced looking herself in the eye. But she wasn't suddenly stylish and interesting. She only looked shorn.

In her room, Sierra pulled out a few copy-paper boxes. She piled the books and photos from her bottom drawer into one. Dad's Bible. The paper he'd been working on when he died. His Greek dictionary and Latin grammar book. Pictures of him.

She laid her hand on them, a final good-bye. On top, she laid clothes that wouldn't do anymore. Her oversize jackets and darker clothes. Those belonged to the Sierra who had been hiding from the world. They belonged in the back of her closet.

———◆◆❖◆◆———

When Mom saw her at the kitchen bar the next morning, she made a little moan. She put her hand up to her mouth, her eyes big, but she didn't say anything.

Sierra patted her hair. "It's okay, isn't it? It's even?"

Mom didn't answer.

Sierra had seen it in the mirror. It was short, but it wasn't lop-sided or patchy. She looked her mom in the eye. "I wasn't trying to hurt myself. I just wanted a change."

That's what Mom needed to hear. She gave Sierra a weak smile. "It's nice, really. Makes you look like a pixie." She headed into the bathroom. "Let me even up the back for you." Her voice wobbled, and Sierra began to worry she'd made a mess of it. She peeked in the glass on the hutch in the dining area for her reflection before she followed Mom into the bathroom.

Mom edged the scissors against the nape of Sierra's neck. "I had a call from Joe Wheeler today."

The scissors scraped metallically as Mom began to cut.

"I had to know, Mom."

"Sierra, I'm so sorry. I never intended not to tell you. At first, I thought you'd be strong enough to hear it in an hour, then a few days, a few weeks, and then it had been so long—"

Sierra put up a hand to the mirror. "I guess I gave you reason to worry about telling me the truth. But you don't need to worry about me anymore."

Mom put the scissors down and leaned back against the sink. It was the posture of a long conversation. But Sierra couldn't do it. She had to get to school. She needed to be able to smile and look people in the eye. "I don't want to be late."

She walked out of the bathroom, picked up her backpack, and raced for the door.

At school, people she didn't even know complimented her. They thought the new look suited her. Carlos caught up with her at lunch. He slid onto the bench next to her, the smell of hot grease rising off the pizza on his tray.

He rubbed her hair with his knuckles. "Hey, Brown Eyes. Nice cut."

She smiled brightly. "Think so?"

"I miss the long hair. But it's nice. Modern, you know."

Sierra felt better. People liked her look. Maybe the new Sierra had a future.

"I got the afternoon off." He leaned close to be heard over the roar of students in the cafeteria. "What are you doing with yourself?"

"Homework."

"Maybe I can help."

Brief images flickered across her mind—Mom helping Dad with the work he'd been too tired to complete, arranging his doctor's appointments. There were days she had even had to help him get dressed. It had been an unspoken arrangement. He'd be the weak one; Mom the strong one. Carlos was perfectly willing to step into Mom's role.

Poor Sierra, who couldn't get her act straight. Poor Sierra, who needed to be found when she didn't come home at night, who needed to be protected from Emilio, who needed to be reminded of her homework, who needed and needed and needed.

"Thanks, Carlos." She stood with her lunch tray. "But I think I can handle homework on my own. See you 'round."

She refused to look back, to see the flash of confusion on his face as she walked away. She smiled. Oh, she smiled until she thought her face would crack.

Carlos met her as she left the school steps the next day. "Hey, Brown Eyes."

"Hey."

"You weren't planning on walking home alone, were you?" he asked.

"It's not far."

He put his hand on her arm. "I'll walk you home."

"If you want."

It was a tense ten minutes. The red hand was up at the crosswalk. Cars sped by, oblivious to the school zone. How fast were they going? Forty-five, fifty-five miles per hour? Just inches from her feet. She couldn't catch her breath all of a sudden, and she could feel Carlos looking at her.

The light changed, and they crossed the street. Carlos said nothing. She said nothing. As they turned the corner, the sound of a bus dieseling nearby sounded the only refrain above the noise of the traffic.

Carlos punched in the security code at the apartment gate and opened it for her, following her inside.

At the foot of her stairs, he stopped. His face was drawn tight, and she knew that was her fault.

"Did I do something wrong?" he asked.

She smiled. "Of course not."

He leaned on the iron banister. "Then what, Sierra? What's with all the smiles-but-don't-get-too-close stuff?"

She met his gaze, trying to look sure of herself. "You're not too close, Carlos. I'm just changing. I don't need help at every turn."

"I never thought you needed help walking home, Sierra."

Smile, she told herself. *Look sure of yourself.* "No, of course not."

His face was hard when he looked at her, but she could see the hurt in his eyes. "You know, the one thing I thought I could always count on with you is that you were for real. What's with the empty words that don't mean what they say and the smiles that aren't really smiles? You've turned all plastic."

Her smile faltered. "I don't have to listen to that, Carlos. If you're going to be rude, I'll go inside."

"No, you don't have to listen to me." He shoved his hands in his pockets. "I've been by your side almost since school started last fall. I took you places when you needed to go. I helped you find your dad's friends. I listened when you wanted to talk and kept quiet when you didn't. But you don't have to listen to me."

"That's just it. Don't you see?"

"See what, Sierra?"

"You don't have to rescue me. I'm not weak."

His mouth dropped. "I get that. But could you maybe talk to me instead of cutting me out?"

"I thought it was time for a new start, you know?"

"A new start?" He looked at her so hard she had to turn away. "A new start without me? Is that what you're saying?"

She took a deep breath, trying to keep herself calm. Even in the courtyard, she could still hear the cars rushing by on the road. They were going so fast. And they sounded so close.

"You're so special to me, Carlos. I won't ever forget you."

He gripped the banister, and his whole body tensed. He shook his head. "Don't."

She swallowed.

"Don't, Sierra." The words that came out of his mouth sounded hoarse. "You want to be strong, I get that. But what you're doing, that's not strong."

She sat down heavily on the steps. "I think you should go now."

His eyes were liquid. He didn't go at first. He stood there, staring down at her, as if he could make her change her mind if he looked at her long enough.

"Sierra." That's all he said. Just her name.

Finally, he turned and walked back toward the gate. With each of his steps, it got harder for her to breathe. When he reached the gate, she stood, as if her legs had a mind of their own.

He turned back, not moving toward her, waiting, looking. She tried to mouth words that would make sense, words that would change things. But she couldn't find them, and he swung through the gate.

CHAPTER THIRTY-TWO

Nick did a double take when he saw Sierra in the hallway. At first lost in the press of students heading for class, she stopped to pick up some loose change she'd dropped. When she stood, she met his eyes and then gave him a confident smile that didn't belong to the girl he knew. The Caribbean-blue T-shirt with a wide belt that hung at an angle was out of character too. It was all very fashionable, and Sierra was a pretty enough kid to carry off the look. But as she walked away, the moment of hope he'd had seeing Sierra fashionable and confident just as quickly died.

Without the sheath of hair, those eyes were large and luminous. But the soul he'd seen there before was missing. And the smile she'd given him? He knew that smile—it was April's, and it masked a world of grief.

Later he asked Cindy Velasco if she'd seen any change in Sierra's schoolwork.

Cindy beamed at him. "She's turned in all her missing assignments. Complete. All A's."

He asked if she minded his taking a look at an assignment or two. Cindy gave him an annoyed glance but led him into her classroom. As Nick looked at the work under the fluorescent lights, he wanted to throw the papers in the trash. She'd turned in review questions for

Twelve Angry Men. Complete and accurate, true enough, but something any sophomore could have written.

Her persuasive essay argued for expanding cafeteria choices. When he thought of the kind of creativity she put into her haikus or of the picture she'd sketched of his old man, it was as if a different kid had written these.

Nick grimaced. "Was this topic assigned?"

Cindy shook her head. "They could write on any topic they wanted as long as they argued for one side or the other. We used the example of cafeteria choices in class, so I had a lot of those."

Nick set the paper carefully back on Cindy's desk. *Oh, Sierra, why this bland imitation of yourself?*

———✦✦✦———

He stopped Sierra in the hallway before classes began the next day. She pulled out of the current of surging students and gave him a bright smile.

"Sierra, talk to me."

"Talk to you about what, Mr. Foster?"

He didn't return the smile. "The haircut, the new style, it's very nice. And I'm glad you're turning in your homework. But there's something wrong, isn't there, Sierra?"

She looked him in the eye. "You don't have to worry about me, Mr. Foster. I'm okay. No one needs to prop me up."

"Who's propping you up, Sierra?"

"No one. No one's propping me up now."

She shrugged him off and headed for first period. Nick watched her disappear down the hall. Her usual slow step, as if each footfall needed to be negotiated, had been replaced by a quick, purposeful stride.

On the last day before spring break, she appeared in the doorway of his classroom at the end of the day. Everyone had cleared out as soon as the bell rang, and the hallways were deserted.

He spoke first. "You can't fool me with a smile, Sierra."

She kept to the doorway, holding the joyless smile steady. "You did a lot for me. You and your dad. I just wanted to come by and say thank-you."

He leaned back in his chair, crossed his arms. "That sounds too much like a good-bye for my ears."

She looked at her feet. "I'm sure we'll see each other, but I'll be able to take care of things on my own now."

Nick stood. She looked up. Her eyes held uncertainty in them as he joined her at the door, but she didn't look away. Those big brown eyes staring out of that small white face. The sheared hair made him think of a war survivor. A survivor, but not a victor.

"Sierra," he said softly, "you're scaring me. I want to see the real Sierra, even if she comes with a little sadness."

"I'm fine, Mr. Foster. I'll see you around after spring break, okay?" She ducked out the door, and that was it. She was gone, leaving Nick looking down the empty hallway after her.

———◆·◆·◆———

Nick's agenda required a couple of stops before going home. How could he encourage Sierra to be vulnerable with anyone when he kept his defenses up with his old man? Not that he hadn't tried to make peace with Dad before. He first made an effort to reconcile with Dad after he'd gotten out of the army. Back then he'd been hesitant to face Dad on his own and hoped a woman's presence would act as a buffer, so he'd brought Caroline with him.

Ten minutes into the visit, Dad said, with Caroline still in the room, "I hope you do not intend to marry her. She will always be taking from you and never giving."

Dad was right of course, but the memory of Caroline, shocked and hurt in Dad's living room, still stung. Every attempt at reconciliation with Dad had been rebuffed since, with only an occasional thaw.

But if nothing else, maybe Dad would have some insight about what was going on with Sierra. Dad had softened since last fall. Sierra and April were good for him.

Nick closed the door to his classroom. April. What was it about April? In the years after Caroline died, he'd carried out a frenzy of dating that left him exhausted and emptier than ever. When he finally got his act together, he dedicated himself to his career and kept to casual dating. He'd told himself that if a woman got to him, really got to him—a strong, stable woman, of course—he would consider settling down again.

But a woman never *had* gotten under his skin. Not until now. Okay, April was a long way from strong and stable right now. Maybe she was grieving for her husband or lost in some ache he didn't understand. She was worried about Sierra. But even underneath that, she had some inner joy, some light that shone through her. Not to mention, she was one of the few women Dad had allowed into his house since Mom died.

He'd get some groceries for Dad first and then head over there.

———◆◆◆◆◆———

Nick didn't bother knocking at his old man's house. He never did. Praying for a good day, he carried in the groceries he'd brought. Dad stood in the kitchen, mixing something. He peered into the bowl, stirring with a slow hand. Nick knew that look. Dad was in pain. It would not be a good day.

But Dad said agreeably enough, "Nicu, I did not expect you today."

Nick set the groceries down on the table, stacked a few cans in the pantry, and set a jug of milk in the fridge before taking a seat in the living room. He took more pleasure in the room now, what with the red wall and the pictures.

Dad came in from the kitchen with the bowl in his hands and narrowed his eyes. "You wanted something in particular?"

"Of course not. I just came to bring a few groceries and see how you were doing. As always."

"As always, I do not need anything. You think I do not know how to buy my own groceries?" It was going to be one of those days. Nick humored him. "Of course you can. I'm just helping out."

Sweat broke out above Dad's lip.

"Have you taken your meds?"

Dad started whipping the contents of the bowl with his spoon. "Yes, I have taken my medication. I have taken care of myself all my life. Do you think I do not know how?"

"Of course you do." All the same, Nick poured a cup of water and brought him a couple of Tylenol.

His old man glared at the pills and shoved them over the kitchen counter into the trash. "I spent five years in prison. Seven years in Bucharest after, and not once did you bring me my groceries. You did not tell me to take my medicines. And I survived."

Nick spread his hands. "Of course, Dad. You're the king of independence."

It was useless to point out the times Nick had been called to pick him up at the grocery store because something—a security guard, a wailing baby, or malfunctioning theft alarm—left him distraught and helpless.

"Look. Just sit down. Relax."

Dad gripped his sides, which he did when his oxygen levels were low.

Nick thought he knew all the snide things Dad could say when he was in one of his states, but he was unprepared for what came out of Dad's mouth next. "You were dead, Nicu. And I survived even then."

"I was dead?" A slow heat worked its way down Nick's arms.

His first thought was dementia. But the one thing his old man had was his mind. "I'm not dead, Dad. I'm right here, speaking to you."

"Of course you are not dead," Dad said in raspy voice. "I was speaking of the years I was in prison. You were dead then."

Nick looked at him, as if the words would form into some kind of logical coherence, but Dad only repeated himself. "You were dead. Dead, do you hear?"

Dad's breathing came in shallow bursts. His old man was allowed to say he was dead, and Nick had to take whatever meaning he could from that. He wasn't allowed to probe, because it would send Dad into a downward spiral.

Nick pushed the mixing bowl to the side. "Sit down."

Dad complied, and Nick brought the cup of water to the table. But once Nick sat down across from him, he couldn't just let the words stand. It rankled to hear Dad say he was dead.

"You know, I gave up a long time ago trying to make peace between us. But tonight I had the idea I might try again. Do you know why?"

Dad's only response was stiff attention.

Nick moved his chair around the table and close to his old man. "Because there's a girl who's alone. She's aloof from her mother. And she's trying to figure out her wretched life on her own. I know too well what that's like. I know what it's like for your life to spin out of your control at sixteen, seventeen, and not have a parent you can turn to."

Dad blinked, and his mouth formed a hard line.

"Sierra won't talk to me, but I thought to myself, hey, if I make peace with my old man after all these years, maybe she'll pay attention. So I come over here. I even think I might get you talking. You've been talking with April. But before I even start speaking, you push me away and tell me I'm dead to you."

Nick stood and paced, but it reminded him too much of Dad pacing, especially those first years when he'd arrived from Romania. He leaned back against the wall, forcing himself to be still.

"No. That is not it, Nicu." Dad opened his mouth to speak again, sighed, and gave up.

Nick came close again, but his old man only retreated, closing his eyes, his shoulders falling.

"No? It's not what?"

Dad just shook his head.

Nick dropped his hands. "For Sierra's sake, just once, can't you come up with something that doesn't make me wish I were anyone else's son?"

Nick went still again, willing his anger back down. *Help me to forgive.*

If Nick was still, Dad was a statue. "I did not come home to you, Nicu. Twenty years of anger we have between us. Thirty." He paused for breath. "What can I say now? What would make you wish to be my son?"

Did his old man not remember being a son himself? Did he not remember what the words of a father could mean?

"Really, Dad? Don't you honestly know? I'm too old to hold a grudge. All it would take is a few simple sentences to make a fresh start. Right now I'd settle for 'I'm glad you're not dead.'"

His father didn't move, and his voice was a monotone. "I am glad you are not dead."

"That's it? That's the best you can do?"

Dad groaned. "What I say will never be enough."

Dad was ashen. Nick strode to the table and returned with another couple of Tylenol and the inhaler. He waited while Dad swallowed the pills and puffed on the inhaler.

Dad had begun shaking. "You should go now."

"Sure. I'll go."

Before he left, he moved the phone near Dad. He left his inhaler within arm's reach. Dad looked at him, his eyes pleading. Nick was almost sure he'd try to apologize. But he only said, "How could I be a father to a son who is dead?"

Nick waited at the kitchen doorway. There was nothing he could say to that.

"Go. Go, Nicu." He flicked his hand at him, a feudal lord dismissing his serfs.

Nick closed the front door behind him. In the driveway, he balled his hands into fists and sucked in a sharp breath through his teeth, trying to remind himself *he* hadn't endured five years of torture. He didn't know how it would have broken him. The least he could do was accept what Dad dished out when the pain and memories took him some dark place Nick didn't understand.

CHAPTER THIRTY-THREE

Liza sat in Nick's classroom, taking notes at the speed of light. The English team had scheduled a unit on rhetoric. Nick didn't have a problem with the exercise, but he handled it with a couple of speeches, Sojourner Truth's "Ain't I a Woman" and Lou Gehrig's "Farewell to Baseball," something his students might actually take some interest in, not the dry worksheets the district assigned.

After school, he had a note in his staff mailbox:

Mr. Foster: You were off the curriculum schedule again. You are on notice. No more departures from school policies will be tolerated.

L. Grambling

The week went downhill from there. Friday morning, as he taught his fourth period he heard a voice coming from the stairwell outside his classroom. He thought it was her voice, though he'd rarely heard Sierra speak above a whisper. And her voice was clearly raised.

There had been a buzz of conversation a minute before, but his class hushed as all eyes turned to him, alive to his sense of alarm as he looked out the door. Raised voices in the hallway weren't unusual during the middle of the day when a half dozen lunch periods followed each other. To an observer who knew nothing of Sierra, the voice in the stairwell wouldn't signal any distress. But he did know her.

Nick set his book on the desk and turned to the door. "Javier," he said, "you're in charge until I get back."

And for the first time in his career, he walked out of a class in session.

He sprinted to the open double doors and swung down the stairs. It only took seconds to piece the situation together. Emilio rested his hands against the bricks, keeping Sierra trapped inside the wall of his arms.

She blocked her face. "Get off me. I'm not interested! Not even a little bit."

Nick was impressed by Sierra's confidence, but the words didn't faze Emilio. The boy's face flushed with anger. He flexed his arms. "Oh, you'll be interested in what I got to give, sweetheart. And some day, when you're alone, I'm going to give it to you."

Rage flashed through Nick, but he made himself stand still until somewhere deep inside he found a measured voice. "I don't think so, Emilio."

Nick walked down the stairs at a deliberate pace. If he counted his steps, he might keep himself from breaking every bone in the boy's body. "The only thing you're going to give Sierra is ten feet of breathing room."

The fury in Emilio's face was something else. He pulled back, but his hands circled Sierra's arms. Nick stepped behind him and put his hands on the boy's shoulders. He kept his voice deadly calm. "I'm telling you once, Emilio. Let go. Get to class. I don't want you within shouting distance of Sierra Wright again."

The friendly Emilio from seventh period was gone. He seemed to be working on adrenaline. He threw off Nick's hands and turned to face Nick. "You and me, Mr. F. I'll take you any day."

"I'm not looking for a fight, Emilio. But I've got to tell you, you're this close to facing assault charges."

"Whatever!" Emilio strutted up the stairs and out the door on the second floor.

As the door clanged shut, Sierra slid to a sitting position on the stairs. Nick came to her in cautious steps, afraid of startling her. He sat beside her. "Sierra?"

"I'm fine, Mr. Foster." Her words were silky quiet, and small tremors worked through her.

He couldn't take his eyes off the red handprints on her arms. He spoke softly to erase the anger coursing through him. "I'm proud of you. You stood up for yourself."

She looked as if she might cry, but he had to say what came next. "Sierra, what Emilio said ... he's a real danger to you. And not just at school. I need to report it to the principal's office. And to the police."

She shook her head with a vengeance, squeezing her eyes shut. "They'll make me come in. They'll ask me all kinds of questions."

Nick inched a fraction closer. "It's the law. And it's for your protection. Emilio could make things much worse for you than any set of questions."

She looked up to the doors. "Please, Mr. Foster."

"I'll be there at your side. But I have to report it."

"Not today. Please." Her voice was so small, so broken.

He thought about Sierra's haircut, her pitiful schoolwork, how she'd alienated herself from April, from him. He imagined her trembling and crying while being questioned, Liza hounding her, a roomful of other administrators behind her. Knowing Liza, she would probably make Sierra face Emilio again.

How could he refuse her this one request? He drummed his fingers on his knees. She could prepare herself over the weekend. And on Monday, she would have April by her side.

"Okay. Provided I let your mom know, and if she can't give you a ride home today, I do. But on Monday morning, before school starts, we'll need to talk to someone—the principal or the campus police."

She hiccupped and nodded her agreement.

Come Monday, he'd have to pay for the time-lapse. Liza would be furious. But if the weekend would give Sierra time to process the coming inquisition, it would be worth it.

———◆◆◆◆———

He texted April as soon as the bell rang, but just as he pressed Send, his room phone rang. The secretary told him to report to the office during his conference period.

When he got there, Liza sat perched on the corner of her desk. Officer Wilkins sat in a chair and Veronica, the sophomore counselor, sat in a second. Witnesses? Not a good sign.

"Take a seat, Mr. Foster." Liza pointed him to the remaining chair.

Nick seated himself, looking at the faces in the room for a clue of what this was about.

"I'll get right to the point," Liza said. "A student reported that you left your fourth-period class unsupervised for almost fifteen minutes."

"That's correct."

Liza gave a dramatic pause, looking from Veronica to Wilkins as if to verify the absurdity of his nonanswer. "Would you like to elaborate?"

He hadn't promised Sierra, but they had an agreement. "There was an incident in the stairwell that needed my attention."

"For fifteen minutes?"

Nick nodded.

"Did it occur to you to phone for help?"

No, it had not occurred to him. Not at first. He'd heard Sierra's voice and knew he had to get to her. And then later he hadn't wanted to spill Sierra's story. "It wasn't possible at the time."

She tapped her fingernails on the desk, as if considering, though Nick knew better. "I don't believe you referred any students to the office. What kind of incident was this exactly?"

She'd find out Monday it was a verbal threat, sexual harassment, probably assault, and he hadn't reported it. But what could he say now without betraying Sierra? She had enough on her thin shoulders. "A couple of students had a conflict. They needed a few minutes of coaching."

"Who were the students, Mr. Foster?"

He looked out the window. A bank of clouds drifted across the sky, dimming the light. This wasn't going to get any better. "I'm sorry. I'm not at liberty to say."

She laughed, and it wasn't a pleasant sound. "You're not helping your case, Mr. Foster. Leaving a class of thirty-eight students unattended for fifteen minutes is serious business."

Nick looked at Veronica, who frowned. Wilkins made big eyes at him, urging him to get his act together.

"Mr. Foster, I'm going to leave the room for a few moments. When I return, I expect details about the 'coaching session' this morning." She slid off the desk and tapped her way out.

Nick stood at the window, looking out at the staff parking lot, as Veronica and Wilkins kept silent. Was there some way out of this he was missing? There was only one right thing to do. Sierra was ready to crack. He'd told her he'd give her the weekend before reporting Emilio's threat, and he would.

A memory came back to him. His mom shaking her head at Nick, who, at fourteen, refused to give in on some scuffle at school that landed him a week of detentions. He'd felt sure it was a matter of right and wrong, though he couldn't remember what it had been about now. "Nicolae," his mother had said, "it is a grace to give in. Must you always be so stubborn?"

Liza returned with his file in her hand. She flipped through its pink notes. "I'm asking you one last time, Mr. Foster. Explain your absence from class today."

The file, the pink notes. He knew what they spelled. Quietly, he said, "I've explained all I can."

He could ask Liza to wait until Monday. But it would be pointless. Today Liza had him on the carpet for leaving his class. On Monday, he'd be in trouble for failing to report an act of violence in a timely manner.

She laid the folder down on her desk and turned to face him. "You give me no choice, Mr. Foster. I've given you repeated warnings. You're suspended until further notice."

The word *suspension* knocked into him. He'd seen it coming. He'd weighed his answers with it in mind. Still, he felt as if some vital thing had been kicked out of him.

He looked to Wilkins and Veronica, expecting at least a word in his defense. They knew him. They knew his character and his ability to bring kids up a level or two. But their faces only registered bewilderment.

"You have the rest of the period to gather your personal effects and leave your classroom. Officer Wilkins will accompany you."

Gather your personal effects. Leave your classroom. The words registered at some primitive level, but they sounded too much like a faraway echo to be real.

His classroom felt miles away as he walked with Wilkins. The bell had rung during their meeting, and his sixth period sat at their desks, pretending to write out review questions from the textbook under the lazy eye of the substitute.

Nick hesitated, trying to think what he might say to his kids. He couldn't think of a thing that wouldn't make the situation worse. It was evident Wilkins was Nick's police escort; as if Nick were a criminal, he stood at attention in the doorway. One last send-off from Liza.

His students stared as he pulled his briefcase out of the closet. As if Nick didn't feel like he'd been punched in the gut, he straightened to his full height and made eye contact with his kids—Jazzy and Selena, David and Cesar—all the way through the classroom. He gave the class a firm nod, then he turned, and for the second time in his career, walked out on a class in session.

CHAPTER THIRTY-FOUR

April tucked the folded paper in her purse as she entered the school office with Sierra Monday morning. The glass door swung shut behind her, closing them in a room of artificial light and clicking computer keys. Nick's email told her what he had witnessed in the stairwell, and that she should feel free to share the email with the principal and the police.

The odd part was Nick's statement that it would be in everyone's interest if he didn't attend the meeting. It wasn't like Nick to make a statement like that without explaining, and she hadn't been able to get in touch with him by phone.

The first bell buzzed, and the secretary escorted April and Sierra into the principal's office. April and Sierra sat quietly across the desk while Principal Grambling scanned the email.

The oddness of the situation only grew as the principal began to grill Sierra. "Mr. Foster intervened in the conflict? During fourth period?"

Sierra nodded.

"Did you ask Mr. Foster to help?"

"No," Sierra said.

"Did Mr. Foster tell you he was required to report the incident?"

Sierra nodded.

April edged forward in her chair. What was with the third degree on Nick? "Ms. Grambling, I think we've gone off track. I need some assurance you will protect my daughter while she's on campus."

The principal stared passively at April. "Of course. We're a zero tolerance school, Ms. Wright. We'll start the process immediately to have Emilio transferred to an alternative school with a more structured environment."

It was almost too easy. The principal only expected a short statement from them. She called the police in. Her daughter spoke in a clear voice as she described how the boy had cornered her and as she repeated his threat.

The principal stood and stiletto-tapped around her desk to see the bruises on Sierra's arms. Without hesitation, Sierra pulled up her sleeves. A lump caught in April's throat. Sierra had stayed strong.

But despite her apparent self-confidence, April couldn't help but feel some invisible core in Sierra had been shaken. As she sat with her back arched, staring straight ahead, something was missing in Sierra's eyes, some innocence that had endured even through these last dark years.

As April left the school, she fretted about Sierra's safety. There was no way she could pick up Sierra every day. Her varied work hours wouldn't allow it. How was she supposed to keep Sierra safe in the afternoons? She assumed the structured environment at the boy's new school still wouldn't keep him off the streets then. And he'd threatened to find Sierra alone.

When April reached their apartment, she shut the door behind her and leaned into the wall, wishing she had the heart to pray, wishing she had the faith to believe God would answer her if she did. What did she want? Safety for her little girl, but it was far too small a request. She wanted the scars washed from her daughter's soul. She wanted to see a smile on her daughter's face, a real one. But every time she prayed for Sierra, one more blow always fell.

April inspected the living room, as if some miracle lay in wait for the taking. But as always, the living room was tidy, nothing out of place. Chairs, sofa, end tables, a magazine rack. Burgundy leather under a stack of magazines caught her interest—her Bible. She had moved it here with a promise to herself to read it more often, but it had only gathered dust for the last few months.

April sat on the floor and flipped it open. The pages fell open to Isaiah, a passage she'd memorized and highlighted in more hopeful days. "Instead of the thornbush will grow the pine tree, and instead of briers the myrtle will grow."

Through Gary's earlier illnesses, she'd drunk in those words like a parched woman at a mountain spring. "It was a phase," she'd told herself. "God will strengthen us as He strengthened Israel in her tribulation."

The verses only seemed to mock her now. It was all briers. Years and years of briers. God was not going to grant her anything as green and sweet smelling as juniper.

———◆◆◆◆◆———

April took that day off so she could pick up Sierra when school got out. While it was still morning, she drove to Luca's. The smell of strong coffee and pastries wafted out the door, reminding her of her first visit. He invited her in, and as they had last fall, they sat at the table near his kitchen window.

April drank her coffee, looking through to the doorway at the family photos in the living room.

He set down the pastries and sat across from her. "There is something on your mind, April?"

"You always see through me, don't you, Luca?"

He rewarded her with a small smile. "Through you? No, no, but I do see your worry."

She pulled Nick's email from her purse and handed it to him. He looked concerned as he read it, and then confused as he reached the end, turning back to read it again. "Perhaps Nicu had other duties at work."

But she could see he no more believed this than she did. Nick was always there for his kids. Why wasn't he at the meeting for Sierra?

"At any rate, Luca, I don't know what I'm going to do. The boy's been transferred to another school, but that threat he made …"

Her first thought was to ask Carlos to walk Sierra home, but she hadn't seen Carlos with Sierra the last couple of weeks. Nick might be able to help, but he'd been out of touch since Friday.

"I work more afternoons than not, Luca; a number of evenings too. How am I going to keep her safe?"

Luca rested his chin on his hand. "It is simple, of course. I will meet Sierra at school, and she can remain with me until you finish your work duties."

April glanced at the inhalers and medicine bottles on the table. The school was only a mile from here, but a mile-long walk to the school, and another back almost every day in all sorts of weather?

"Luca, you are so good. But I can't ask that of you."

"You did not ask. Do you suppose I could rest with Sierra in danger?"

"No, I don't suppose you could. Thank you, Luca."

April took his hand across the table. His scars felt like smooth cord against her palms. She exhaled a pent-up breath. How far they'd come. Last fall, she'd believed Sierra needed to be protected from Luca. Now, there was no one she would trust more to look after her child.

As they ate the salty pastries, April's mind turned to the material on her desk at home—transcribed notes from Luca's story, retouched photos, her sketches—sitting in an unorganized stack. She hadn't put them together in a book yet. Sierra had been too much on her mind. Besides, Luca owed her one last chapter.

April leaned forward. "I was thinking of the story you've been telling me, the story of your time in Romania."

"You are waiting for the last words."

April put down her fork. "There you go again, reading my mind."

"Ah. Like any lover of stories, you wish to know how it ends."

"I'm a little curious, I have to admit."

Luca studied her. "But in your case, I believe you are more than curious. You wish to hear what happened to Luca Prodan and his son, because you have fallen in love with the son and, for an inexplicable reason, have grown fond of the old man in the story as well."

April gazed across the table at Luca. He couldn't buy his own groceries on a regular basis and didn't have a job, but he zoomed in on the truth with his ever-watchful eye. It shook her to hear him speak words she hadn't been able to say to herself. It was true. She'd fallen in love with Nick and had found solace with his father. "You'd only see through me if I denied it," she said quietly. "I love you both, each of you in a different way."

Luca looked steadily at her, and April couldn't help but think of Nick's straightforward gaze. "But you have not told my son you love him in any sort of way."

She pretended to take another sip of coffee, though her cup was empty. There was no point in telling Nick how she felt about him. Loving a man and having something to offer him were two different things.

Luca let the subject drop, turning instead to his appreciation of the photos and new odds and ends April had put in his home. He refilled her cup. There was a comfortable silence as the house settled.

Finally, April spoke again. "Will you tell me the rest of the story, Luca?"

The direct gaze gone, Luca stared down at the table.

How would she feel if she were in Luca's place, if she hadn't returned to Sierra when she'd been free to? April sat back in her chair, finding the frame that bordered Luca's relationship with his son. Luca felt he'd failed Nick. And they both knew Nick believed it too. She didn't want to push him, but they'd come this far.

"It's the piece of the story Nick needs the most," she said softly.

He stabbed his fork into his pastry and drowned it in gravy. Finally he shoved his plate away. "There is little enough to tell."

His eyes grew round and he swallowed. "For almost five years, I believed Tatia and Nicu were dead. My friend, Andrei, told me the truth after I was released from prison. He was a ranking member of the communist party. He had learned of our situation and had arranged emigration for my wife and son and promised them that I would follow when I was freed. Like a small boy, I cried that day. Tatia was alive. Nicu was nine years old. Andrei had to hold me up, because I could not even stand."

Luca put his hands on the table and looked out the window. "I packed a small suitcase and prepared to join them in America. I looked in a mirror. I had only just turned thirty, but I was stooped and gray. I would never again be the man Tatia married, never again be the father who carried Nicu on his shoulders."

Luca turned back to her. "Anything set my heart racing—a shout, a slamming door, the sight of a man in uniform. It was worse then, those first months out of prison. I survived each day only through the prayers I learned in prison.

"I carried my suitcase to the street where Andrei was to meet me. When I saw him next to his car, I felt suddenly hollow. Instead of walking toward him, I walked back to my building. How could I go to my family a broken man, hardly able to work? Tatia was so beautiful and strong and brave. Nicu was just a boy. I would be a burden to them. An embarrassment."

April closed her eyes. A burden. It sent a chill through her. There was no doubt in her mind it was the reason Gary had killed himself. But death didn't solve anything. Absence didn't. Oh, she understood that hard look in Nick's eyes. How dare they walk out of their families' lives and leave their wives and children to face the consequences?

Luca went on. "Tatia raised Nicu alone. She did well enough, as you see, and was able to provide for them both on her wages as a legal secretary. She tutored new immigrants in English in her spare time. I sent her help as I could, but of course, Romanian lei were all but useless in America. I only came to them when Tatia wrote to me that she was ill. Nicu was almost seventeen then, and angry. It would have been better for him if I had remained in Romania."

April reached for his hand. "You're wrong, Luca. Even if your relationship with Nick is tense, it's something. He needed you then, and he needs you now."

Luca shook his head. "I tried to speak to Nicu when I first came. But I could not speak of prison or of what happened before. Tatia never told him the reason I was imprisoned. Perhaps she did not know herself. At any rate, Nicu would not listen to me. When Tatia died, rage filled him. He got low marks in school. Some nights he did not come home or he came home drunk. He left the room if I spoke in Romanian, and my English was very poor at first.

"He thought I had abandoned him, and I did not have the will to explain to him. So instead, I lectured him about his homework and his behavior.

"I thought when he returned from the army, we would find a way to talk. But our way of speaking to each other only echoed those bitter words we spoke to each other after Tatia's death. He took care of me when I should be the one he found strength in. It made me angry, so very angry, and I fear I said things to him I should not have. At last, it was easier to accept that the possibility of my ever being a father to him had died when I went to prison."

Luca settled into his chair like a man returning to the present. He looked at the stove clock and blinked. "It will be time for school to end soon."

April nodded. She needed to be at the school when the bell rang, but it didn't feel right to leave. She stood. "I know a lot of time has passed, Luca. But you can still be a father to Nick."

"Perhaps." But his face denied the half-hopeful word.

Luca saw her to the door, and they made plans for him to meet Sierra after school the rest of the week. She walked through the blustering wind to her car with Luca watching her from the door. Neither of them seemed able to say the words that would make a difference to their children. Somehow she would find those words though, words full of strength and clarity and hope for Sierra. She'd find the words for Luca, too, if need be.

CHAPTER THIRTY-FIVE

April worked early hours Thursday. As she drove home, the unanswered phone calls to Nick came to mind, and she took the freeway exit to his place. Sierra was with Luca, and she needed to find out why Nick had been out of contact.

She walked up his steps, hoping he was home by now. School had only ended an hour ago. His windows were raised s the townhouse could take in the mild breezes. He didn't answer the door right away. Only after she waited a few seconds did she see him standing beside an open window upstairs looking down at her.

He was home and already in jeans and a T-shirt. When he met her at the door moments later, he looked downright rumpled, unshaven, and not as pleased to see her as she would have liked.

She almost turned away. What was she doing here? But that morning-disheveled look drew her. "I didn't come at a bad time?"

He had to think too hard about that one. "No."

He looked behind him. His living room had stacks of Coke cans and pizza boxes. Nick waved at the mess. "Sorry. The maid's day off."

The joke fell flat with only a straight face to accent it. He inclined his head outside. "It's less cluttered out back."

He stepped outside, closed his front door, and led her behind the row of townhouses. He glanced at his deck, but it was wet from a recent shower. He nodded at her to follow, and they trekked side by side down a path to the piney creek.

"The situation with Emilio?" he asked as they walked.

It bothered her that he had to ask. Sierra wasn't his obligation, but he'd taken an interest in her, and he worked at the school after all. "Emilio's been sent to an alternative school for the rest of the year."

"Sierra's okay?"

"As well as can be expected."

He cast a sidelong glance at her but didn't ask for more, just thrust a hand through his rumpled hair. He was so good. So strong. So Nick.

And she didn't have room for thoughts like these.

April strengthened her voice. "I was starting to worry about you."

"Were you?" His words carried a heavy dose of skepticism that left her suddenly cold.

"The last part of the email you sent me was a bit cryptic. And then you weren't answering your phone. Even your dad says he's hardly seen you."

He didn't reply. It wasn't her business. Why did she keep investing in Nick's life and his dad's? So they were vulnerable and bruised. But since when did she have answers to offer anyone?

"Nick," she said softly, "what's going on?"

"Life gets hectic sometimes. That's all."

They reached a scattering of pine trees. Nick dropped onto a fallen log that stretched across the creek, a thin rivulet of still water, and April took a seat beside him. In a place like this, she couldn't help but think of being a girl, childhood sweethearts. April let her feet swing over the stream.

She shook her head to clear it and bring her back to reality. A light breeze blew over them, settling her nerves. "Nick, did something happen at school? Your principal seemed more interested in you than in the fact that Sierra was assaulted and threatened."

"I'll just bet she did." He removed his glasses, tucking them into the pocket of his T-shirt, and rubbed under his eyes with his thumb and forefinger. When he looked at her, his eyes brought one word to mind—*haunted.*

April drew back. He was too decent for whatever distressed him like this. "Nick, talk to me."

"'Talk to me,' says the lady with the golden smile. When have you ever talked to me, April?"

Her head swung up.

He shook his head. "I'm sorry. I shouldn't have said that."

April covered her eyes with her hand, wishing, oh, wishing so much she could handle this differently, wishing she could give him a reason to confide in her. Not in a romantic way. Goodness knows, not that. But he needed a friend, a confidante.

He was watching her, and his eyes darkened to midnight blue. "I'm sorry, April. I am." He let out a guttural sigh. "I lost my job last week. Well, I'm suspended indefinitely. Close enough."

"Your job?" Nick's job defined him. But the timing sent a dark suspicion nipping into her thoughts. "The situation with Sierra—did it have something to do with it?"

He didn't answer at first. "I don't want Sierra to know about this."

She felt sick. He *had* been looking out for them.

"What happened?"

"I left a class unattended for fifteen minutes. It's what Liza Grambling was looking for, any excuse to let me go. She already had a stack of documentation against me. Every time I veered from the curriculum guide. Every time I didn't cross a *T* or dot an *I*. If it hadn't been Sierra, it would have been something else."

Nick scraped the heel of his shoe over the mud. "Add to that that my old man saw fit to tell me I was dead to him last week."

April looked down for a moment. "Your dad did believe you were dead, you know."

Nick looked askance at her.

"One of his prison guards told him you died. It was all part of the psychological torture. But he's made it so very clear to me that he doesn't wish you were dead. With all his heart, he wishes he'd done better by you."

"Well, he has a great way of showing it."

"I'm almost done putting his story together. When I'm done, read it. You'll see how much he loves—"

"It's the last thing I want to do." Something hard and angry streaked across his face. "I'd rather eat dirt than read some cute little book with words my old man refused to share with me time and again. Call me small-minded if you want, but if my dad loves me, he can say it." He gave her a hard look. "That's what people who love you do, you know. They say it."

"It's not always so simple," she said quietly.

He looked at the creek, and the silence settling around them was anything but comfortable.

He sat straighter, and his eyes cleared. "You know what, April, I'm tired of this thing we do where we talk around each other." He rubbed his neck. "Humor me. How about a game? I'll tell you something. If it's true, you repeat it. If it's not, just shake your head."

She gave a thin laugh. "We're a little old for what sounds like a version of Truth or Dare."

"Maybe." He held her gaze. "Maybe we're a little old to play the game we've been playing. We're not a couple of kids who need to keep everything under our hats, are we?"

April shook her head.

"Number one. You think of me as a brother."

She looked up at the trees, thinking desperately. It was what she wanted the truth to be. But it wasn't. It never had been. "I ... Nick ..." She gave in and shook her head.

He gave her a dark smile. "You don't owe me an explanation. I just wanted to know it wasn't true."

"The truth, Nick? This day isn't going at all the way I planned."

He laughed, and it was the first true pleasure she'd seen in him for a long time now. "No, I guess not."

He just sat on the log, watching her, making her feel breathless. He shifted closer, close enough for her heart to beat double-time. He looked hesitantly at her, and as much as she knew she shouldn't, she prayed for him to move closer still.

Nick slid his palm down the curve of her cheek. "Next question." The smile disappeared, replaced by an infinite sadness. "It will never work between us."

April concentrated on the touch of his hand against her skin, wishing the question would go away.

"It will never work between us," Nick repeated quietly, withdrawing his hand. "That's what you said. Yes or no, April?"

She held on to the log, wishing she could give him a better answer. It was too hard. Not even for Nick could the answer be yes. His face closed, and she knew he saw the regret written in hers.

"It will never work between us," she repeated quietly.

He waited, compelling her to go on.

"Our lives, Nick. They're so complicated."

He gazed at her until she thought she would wilt. "That's it?"

"Sierra needs me. I have to be a mother first."

"Haven't you noticed, April? Sierra isn't just another student at the school to me."

"I can't get involved with anyone. Not now." *Not ever,* a small voice whispered.

He went quiet for a few minutes, and he inspected her face as if he were reading a map. April looked away and then back. At last, he gave her a crooked, uneasy smile. "You're handling this all better than I did, you know. The loss of your husband and the problems with Sierra. After Caroline … after my wife died, I got into all kinds of trouble. I ran ten miles a day until my ribs showed. I punched a hole in my apartment wall. I punched a friend—or a guy who used to be my friend, I should say—and spent the night in jail. Youth was my only excuse, I guess, but my grieving wasn't graceful at all."

"Oh, Nick." She started to reach for him and then thought better of it.

He gave a bemused glance at her hand. "Look. I understand if you're not ready to move on with your life just yet. But it would mean a lot to me if you'd be open about your reasons. This isn't about Sierra. It's about you."

How could he say that? How could she *date,* for goodness' sake, when her daughter was lost in some sea of grief? Couldn't he see the frivolousness in the idea—candlelit dinners, kisses, and longing for more while her daughter sat at home alone?

He didn't say anything, as if he were waiting for something from her. But what was there to say? He knew about Sierra's state of mind, more or less. He didn't need to know her whole sob story. It wouldn't fix anything. So she only said, "You might be right, Nick. Maybe it is about me. But sometimes it's hard to know where to draw the line between being a mom and being a woman."

"Okay, April." He spread his hands. He sat staring at the stream again. Finally, he stood and offered her a hand up. Some bleak finality took hold in his face. "I'll walk you to your car."

He put his glasses back on and pushed them up the bridge of his nose.

It was a much longer path up than it had been coming down. She pushed herself up the way, trying to pull herself together. They stopped at the sidewalk next to her car.

"Here's another bit of truth, April. Mine. I can't be your brother, and it's too hard working out where I fit with you. If you need me for Sierra, I'm here. But I don't think you should come around anymore."

He was saying good-bye? She'd counted on his steady presence. His strength. His friendship. Him.

"Okay." She spoke in the quietest of voices. Nick stood only feet away from her, but already she felt the emptiness, knowing it was a void she had asked for.

When she didn't move, he stepped onto the pavement and opened her car door for her.

———————◆◆◆◆◆———————

She worked long hours the next two days. It was a relief ringing up sales, chatting with customers, lining up orders. There were no underlying emotions ready to erupt, no lives falling apart that needed to be patched together Humpty-Dumpty style. All she had to do was go through the motions. And because of her commissions, soon she and Sierra would be able to move to a better neighborhood and put this school year behind them.

As she leafed through her papers before she went home, Ms. Baines stopped her.

"What have you got there?"

April lifted the stack in her hand, and Ms. Baines slid out a photo. It was the picture she had taken last fall of the little boy on the swings. She had decided to print a few of her pictures after Nick encouraged her.

Ms. Baines held it out at arm's length and studied it. "Who took this?"

"I did."

That might just be the first smile she'd seen on the woman. "I thought you had an artistic eye. Do you have more?"

April shrugged. "A few."

Did a bulging portfolio that had been sitting in the closet for five years count?

"Bring them in some time. If you've got anything I can use, we'll blow one or two up and put them on the wall." She aimed her chin at the corner where the photographic art for sale hung.

April agreed, but selling her photographs was hardly at the top of her priority list right now.

———◆◆◆◆◆———

Sunday, after they returned from church, Sierra closed herself in her room, music on. After a burst of Samuel Barber's "Adagio," there was a lull, and then pop music April didn't recognize came on. What was that about? Sierra never listened to pop music. She didn't even like it.

Stifled by the loneliness in the living room, April found the stack of pages for Luca's book on her desk. She spread them over the coffee table. Maybe they wouldn't do any good for Luca and Nick, but it was something she could finish.

At first, she'd typed Luca's words from the tapes, but the printout looked so impersonal. In the end, she picked out a topaz-colored scrapbook with thick cream pages and began writing the words of the story in her best handwriting. Nick said he'd rather eat dirt than read Luca's words, that people needed to say they loved one another. Well, these words might not be spoken, but they were written in a human hand, the best she could do for the two men she loved.

On each page, she placed a photo, retouched to heighten the colors, or a pencil sketch to bring imagery to Luca's story.

It gave her something to do in the dark moments with Sierra. Her daughter wouldn't talk to her, but she could build a bridge for Nick to talk with Luca.

She hadn't admitted why she'd begun the project at first. Not really. But as she looked at Luca's story, scattered in thirty-five pages on the coffee table, she knew. She did it, as Luca said, because she loved his son. She couldn't give that love to Nick, and he wouldn't accept anything less. But she could give him something that might heal the rift with his father one day.

Sierra walked into the living room and thumped some books on an end table.

"Is everything all right, sweetheart?"

"Sure, Mom. I'm going to sit on the steps." She flashed a smile April's way and breezed through the front door.

April couldn't get used to Sierra's new haircut or those flashy smiles. She wanted her spirits to lift, but this wasn't even the real Sierra. She thumbed through Sierra's books as if they might hold a clue to what was going on. A geometry book and a couple of teen fashion magazines. Fashion magazines?

April smoothed an unruly curl of hair back into place. She tried to convince herself Sierra was happy, but she couldn't do it. Sierra had learned only weeks ago of her father's suicide. And that had been followed last week by the boy's threat. Sierra's attitude didn't sit right. There had been no outburst of grief, no anger. There had been no processing at all.

April slid against the wall, sitting on the living room floor, burying her head in her arms. Nick was gone. Sierra had put up higher walls. Even sweet Carlos had disappeared. She felt the strands that had been holding them all together, almost like a second family, fraying and tearing.

Now standing, watching Sierra through the front window, April felt a thousand years old. She had worried at Sierra's similarity to Gary, but this was so much worse.

Finally, April did the unthinkable. She picked up the phone and called her sister.

"Hey, Hill." April sank onto the sofa and tugged an embroidered throw around her.

"I know that tone. What's wrong?"

April let out a dry laugh. Just when she thought Hill didn't understand her. "It's Sierra. She found out about Gary."

"Found out about his suicide. Meaning you didn't tell her?"

April nodded as if Hill could see her through the phone.

Hill's voice took on an edge. "That's not good. What's her reaction?"

"I don't know. Everything looks right on the outside, better even. She cut her hair, has taken an interest in what she wears. She smiles. She turns her work in at school. But ..."

"Oh. She's pulling an April on you."

"What?"

"Come on, April. You know how it was way back when. Mom having one of her so-called spells. That guy, what's-his-name, Christopher? He'd broken your heart. But you gave that thousand-watt smile to everyone, kept talking about cheer club and prom dresses, like you'd never been happier."

Had she really been that see-through? But Hill had lived in the same house and dealt with her own blows, not nearly as peacefully as April. She'd stomped and thrown things. She'd screamed at Mom for not being a real mom and at Dad for living a lie. Strangely enough, it was Hill Mom seemed closest to later on. April was the peacekeeper, the one who drew imaginary sunny days in the sky for everyone to believe in. Like Dad.

Is that what she'd taught Sierra? Paint on a smile and bury your grief?

"Oh, Hill. Was I that unconvincing?"

Hill laughed. "Only to me. I spent my whole life watching Dad act like it was all good."

"I miss him. I miss his optimism."

"Yeah. Me, too." Hill sighed. "Throw a good fit, April. It always works for me. Everyone pays attention when Mom's not happy."

April tapped her feet against the coffee table. "Yeah, but Sierra's so sensitive I don't know what she would do with a fit."

"Good. Throw her off balance. You need to get her talking."

Funny, whenever April thought of Hill, she thought of how abrasive she was. She'd forgotten the late-night chats, the jokes. Hill had a keen eye.

"There's something else, isn't there, April?"

"Why do I always think you don't understand me?"

Hill gave a long, rambling laugh. "It's got to be money trouble or man trouble. I vote man trouble."

"How do you do that?"

"I'm a therapist. I've learned to read between the lines."

"Man trouble," April admitted.

"I just hope he's not another Gary—some poor guy who needs you to carry his load for him."

Did she really want to share her feelings about Nick? "No, he's so not like Gary."

"But?"

"But I pushed him away for long enough, and he said his good-byes. Only I don't want him to say good-bye. I'm just not ready for hello exactly."

She could hear Hillary clicking something, maybe a pen. "You've got to forgive yourself sometime."

April sucked in a breath. "What?"

"It's not your fault Gary killed himself, sweetie. He was sick, and there was nothing—absolutely nothing—you could do to save him."

April drew in a sharp breath. "What does that have to do with anything?"

"Gary didn't want you or Sierra to stop living. How is she supposed to learn it's okay to find pleasure in life when you can't allow yourself to take joy in anything?"

"Do you think I *want* to be unhappy?"

"When was the last time you did something for the sheer pleasure of it? Have you spent a whole afternoon taking pictures? Have you gone on a date? Gone to see a movie for you, not Sierra? Have you done anything at all just because it made your day a little brighter?"

When April didn't answer, Hill said, "Not since Gary died, right?"

April buried her head in the cushions. She gave her sister a muffled, "No."

"It was only your efforts that kept him clinging to life as long as he did." Something creaked over the line, like Hill had stood up. "Gary wanted you to be happy. You and Sierra both."

"I wish it was all as crystal clear to me as it is to you, Hill."

Hillary laughed. "Oh, it's only clear because it's someone else's life. Other people are so much easier to fix than yourself."

April told Hill good-bye and paced to the window, where she could see Sierra sitting in the same position on the steps as she had been half an hour ago.

She rested her hand against the window. Was Hill right? Was she punishing herself for Gary's death? She'd been so sure she was only keeping her little girl safe under her wings.

Chapter Thirty-Six

Sierra stood at the window in Mr. Prodan's library after school. A soft rain soaked up the sounds of traffic on the main road half a block away. Ribbons of water ran down the glass, blurring the plants outside into patches of greens and purples and reds, like a Monet painting.

Mr. Prodan came in, a book in his hand. "I have found an old reader in Romanian from my school days. I thought you might enjoy it."

Sierra forced a thank-you smile and took the book.

"If you do not want the book, you may say so."

Sierra flipped it open. "It's great, Mr. Prodan. Really."

He took a seat. "Then it is not the book."

"I don't know what you're talking about."

"Ah, but I think you do. I am comfortable with your sadness, Sierra. You do not need to smile for me."

Sierra felt the shakes start inside. She didn't need this. "I'm not sad. You don't have to worry about me."

"I do not worry about you because I have to. To my mind, we are friends, and I count it a privilege to share the burden of your sadness. Or your anger."

"I'm not angry."

She turned back to the window so she could get away from his all-too-knowing eyes. They were what had drawn her to him last fall—those eyes that looked like they'd seen it all, understood it all. But how could it be a privilege to share someone else's sadness? There was already too much sadness. No one wanted to borrow another person's.

She kept her back to him, hoping he would go into the kitchen and do what he always did—cook. But he didn't. She stayed at the window, looking out at the gray mist and splotches of wet flowers until her legs got tired and her back ached.

The quiet inside, the quiet outside, weighed on her. It was almost five when she turned to see him asleep with a book in his hand. She took the book and placed it back on the shelf. He held his injured hands at an odd angle in his sleep, his thumbs perpendicular to his other fingers, his palms impossibly flat.

The next day Sierra fought her way against the tide of students on her way to fourth period. Carlos hurried through the double doors and stopped in front of her.

"Hey, Sierra." He shifted his books, and he looked so sad and gentle she thought she might break into a hundred thousand pieces.

She gave him a quiet hello and pushed past, trying to pretend he was just some guy in the hall. At her locker, she swiveled her combination lock open. People shouted to each other, locker doors banged. She could pretend, but Carlos wasn't some guy.

Before she even got the locker door half open Jazzy leaned against it, causing it to slam shut. "How does it feel to be on top of the gossip food chain?"

Sierra gave Jazzy an even look. Eye contact. Make eye contact—it was something she had to remind herself of constantly. And gossip? She and Carlos were hardly worth talking about.

"You don't even know, huh?"

Sierra shook her head. "Know what?"

"No one told you about Mr. Foster?"

"What about him?"

"He's gone."

"Yeah? Gone where?"

"Girl, you don't keep your ears open, do you? He got himself fired over a week ago. Got himself fired over *you*."

"Jazzy, what are you talking about?"

"He left his class to hang by themselves, no teacher or anything, and they fired him. He's gone, girl."

Every muscle froze in place. Jazzy had to be wrong. Mr. Foster was the best teacher at the school. Everyone knew that. "They wouldn't fire him for protecting a student."

"Ya-huh. Bella de la Cruz works in the office fifth period, and she heard it all, even if the door was closed. Word is, the principal asked why he left in the middle of his class, and he said he 'wasn't at liberty to say.'" She used finger quotes. "But everyone knows why he left. He left 'cause he heard you fighting off Loose-Hands Emilio."

A terrible buzzing went off in her head. Sierra had asked Mr. Foster—begged him—not to tell anyone right away. Her stomach dropped. He hadn't told the principal what happened that day. Which meant one thing: she got him fired.

Sierra forced open her locker, pulled out her history book, and slammed the door shut. "See you, Jazzy."

She strode down the hall with her book under her arm. Jazzy trailed behind, probably wanting to know the scoop on Sierra's reaction.

Sierra rolled her shoulders. Well, she didn't have one. She scrubbed the heel of her hand across her face, erasing the strain. She flashed a smile Jazzy's way and kept walking. She kept walking right past her fourth-period class, losing Jazzy, down the stairs, past Officer Wilkins, who was talking sports with a couple of boys, and then out the front doors, into the misting rain.

She passed her apartment complex and kept walking. She wasn't going home. No matter what she did, she was a burden to people. Mr. Foster, Carlos, Mom, Mr. Prodan—all of them were doing everything they could so fragile Sierra didn't have to face anything bad.

A car sped by, splattering her jeans, and she moved farther from the road.

"Por qué te abates, alma mía, y te turbas dentro de mí," she whispered. *Why are you so downcast, my soul? Why so disturbed within me?*

She knew the psalm in English, French, Spanish, Romanian, and Hebrew. Just for fun, she'd taught herself to say it in a few languages she didn't even know. But in any language, it was the same. Downcast was downcast.

She let her stupid smile go. It wasn't hers anyway.

She lifted her face to the rain, so soft and cool. She didn't know where she was going. All she knew was she would scream if she had to spend another afternoon at Mr. Prodan's with him watching her, worrying over her.

April paced the living room. Sierra was out there somewhere. It was drawing close to midnight, and she was out there. The drumming rain beat the refrain for her. The drizzle had turned into pattering drops and then into sheets of driving rain a couple of hours ago.

Yes, Sierra had done this before, but it didn't make it any easier. It made it worse. Luca sat on her sofa, drinking cold coffee. She'd drunk several cups herself when she got home, but couldn't stomach the thought of another sip.

Please be somewhere inside. Please be dry and safe.

If only she could be out there searching for Sierra herself, but the police insisted that she should be at home in case Sierra returned. At the knock, she flew to the door.

"It will be Nicu," Luca reminded her. "He said he would come after he checked for Sierra in the streets around the school and the neighborhood."

It was Nick.

She had so prayed it would be Sierra, but of course, Sierra wouldn't knock. As Nick filled the doorway, she knew he was the next best thing. Just seeing him before her sliced her fear in half.

He shrugged off his slicker and hung it on a chair.

Nick glanced at the wall of Hebrew and Greek tiles, the lamps April brightened the apartment with, then at his father. She started to warm him a cup of coffee, but he cut her off. "I don't need anything, April. I'm going right back out."

He waited for her attention. "I've looked everywhere I can think of. I need to know, April: did anything happen to upset her recently? Emilio again?"

April looked back at Luca, then to the slip of paper on the

kitchen counter with Joe Wheeler's number on it. Nick followed her gaze, frowning.

April linked her hands. Why were the words so hard to say?

Across the room, Luca opened his hands and inspected them. With a matter-of-fact voice, he said, "Sierra learned only a few weeks ago that her father's death was not an accident, but a suicide."

April wrapped her arms around herself. Luca looked at her, asking her permission after the fact. It was only right. She'd made him spill his secrets. But it wasn't so easy when the truth exposed was your own.

Nick's eyes darkened, not with condemnation, but with pity. And maybe a dash of disappointment. For all the stark honesty they'd shared last week, she'd failed to share that detail with him.

Nick took a deep breath. "Okay. What places have you looked already?"

April looked to the ceiling, as if it would provide answers.

Luca filled in for her. "Carlos is searching for her. But the places she most likely would go—bookstores and museums—will be closed for the night."

"What about places she might associate with her dad?" Nick said softly.

April shook her head. "Carlos asked around the Rice campus. I can't think of other places she would associate with him. Gary wasn't from Houston. Sierra never lived here with him."

"Where was he from?"

"Near Wichita. I called the bus stations and airlines. Nothing. And she wouldn't have enough money to go far anyway."

April dropped her arms only to wrap them around her again. She looked from Luca to Nick. No one mentioned that the temperature had dropped with nightfall or that if the rain continued, the bayous would almost certainly flood. *Please, please, let her be inside some-where safe.* But the dark idea blipped on the edges of her thoughts that if she prayed it, God would certainly ignore it. Whatever Joe said, whatever her pastor said, a decade and more of heartfelt prayers that had gone unheeded led her to the only conclusion: God might perform miracles for other people, but He didn't answer *her* prayers.

Nick hesitated. "What about Emilio? Has anyone checked to see where he is?"

"The police visited him. He was home playing video games."

"The police are looking?" Nick asked.

"They're looking. Everyone's looking." April tried to bring a smile to her mouth. If she believed enough, if she hoped enough, if she even looked like she hoped enough, maybe her little girl would come home.

"Don't, April." He came close, reached out toward her face, but then dropped his hand. "Don't smile for me tonight. I don't need it."

"I need it!" Her voice broke, and she turned away. "I need to believe she's coming home."

He came behind her, putting his hands on her shoulders. She let his strong hands give her comfort. But when the tears started, she ran for the bathroom.

After a while, she braced herself with her hands on the bathroom sink. She washed her face with cold water and, with a shaking hand, ran a brush through her hair. For Sierra's sake, she had to be strong.

When she came out, Nick stood at the window, pulling the curtains back to look at the courtyard. He focused on something in the middle, or on something that wasn't there at all. Seeing Nick with such concentration on his face gave her a small notch of hope.

He dropped the curtains and rapped his knuckles on the wall, as if some decision had been made. Striding to her, he took her hands in his. "Sierra's upset and confused, but she wants life, April. I see that desire in her." He stopped for her to take that in.

April gripped his hands for dear life. She glanced at Luca for confirmation. He nodded. Was it true? Sierra seemed to have such a tenuous hold on life. That's why the secret had persisted, because April was afraid to believe Sierra would hold on when she could hardly force herself to go through the motions of her days as it was.

Nick gave her hands a final squeeze. "I'm going to look for her. I'll call you."

The door swung shut with a gust, and he was gone. She looked down at her hands. He'd squeezed them so hard they ached to the bone.

All night she paced, going from her bedroom to the kitchen, the living room to Sierra's room. She smoothed Sierra's blanket, set up her stuffed kangaroo, and arranged her books on her desk, as if she could ensure Sierra's return by keeping the room in order. Nick and Carlos called in from time to time, but neither had anything to report.

Luca found her standing in front of the muted TV in the wee hours watching the news. She was terrified of what she might see, but it soon became apparent it was a replay from the ten o'clock hour. The only current news scrolled across the bottom—temperatures dropping below forty and a rising count of rainfall.

"Come, April. Sit with me," Luca said.

They sat on the sofa. There was nothing to say, but he held her hand, and that was something. Soon enough, though, she couldn't help herself. She got up and began to pace again.

With the heavy cloud cover, it was almost eight before any light made it to the window. April's eyes burned. Her neck throbbed. And Sierra was still missing.

She turned around to see Luca on the sofa, eyes closed. She thought he'd fallen asleep and leaned to cover him with an afghan. But he opened his eyes, and she saw his folded hands. He wasn't sleeping. He was praying.

Grateful someone had the faith to pray, she went to splash more cold water on her face and check the TV again. The rain count showed over ten inches in twelve hours. An image popped up of I-10 with more water flowing down its lanes than the Brazos River.

She dropped to her knees to follow Luca's example. She folded her hands, closed her eyes, and tried one more time. *O Lord, hear my prayer. If you never hear another prayer from me again, hear this one.*

On TV, an eighteen-wheeler careened on the water like a drunken ship. Then the camera feed switched to Buffalo Bayou, swollen past its banks and lapping over the bridge.

CHAPTER THIRTY-SEVEN

A night of driving through every corner of Sierra's neighborhood, of questioning every street person, prostitute, and night guard hardy enough to be out in the storm turned up nothing. Nick even visited Emilio. Groggy with sleep, Emilio was furious he was suspected of foul play. He swore he hadn't seen Sierra since the day in the stairwell. His dad had stood behind him and said he'd had him under house arrest since Emilio had been transferred and that Emilio had been home since the bus dropped him off.

Nick checked Dad's house, but there was no sign of her. Somehow he knew she wouldn't go to the expected places anyway. She was more desperate now.

At first light, Nick pulled into McDonalds. In the parking lot, he wolfed down a bagel sandwich. He took a deep swallow of coffee and said his hundredth prayer. Where would she go? *Guide my thoughts, O Lord.*

He put his hands on the steering wheel and stilled his mind and body. Where would he go if he were sixteen and grieving and felt he had no one to turn to? Nick couldn't help the laugh that escaped him. He *had* been sixteen and grieving with no one to turn to.

At seventeen, he'd spent a few nights on the bayou, half a mile from home, the same bayou Sierra had to cross to reach Dad's. He'd

RACHEL PHIFER

been certain his father wouldn't find him under the bridge, and with the running battle in their home, he'd wanted to go where the only sounds were rushing water and tires rolling overhead.

It was one of the few places he hadn't been this past night. It was his last shot.

But as Nick backed out of his parking space, he prayed she wasn't there. After who knew how many inches of rain, it just wasn't a place for her to be.

He drove to the bridge between April's apartment and his old man's street. If Sierra had gone to this bayou, this was surely where she would climb down. He parked his truck on the street and jumped out. The water had turned into rapids, exploding past the concrete banks and working its way up the grassy hill on both sides. But Nick began making his way down the cement steps that hadn't been submerged yet just in case.

He reached the waterline, scanning as far as he could see. The rushing current carried a rancid smell, as if it had collected gallons of trash and sewage on its race to the sea. He zipped his jacket. There was no way Sierra was here. The only grass left was wet and steep. Surely she had more sense than that.

He'd found nothing of her whereabouts, not a hint. He had no scrap of hope to give April. He turned woodenly to go back up the steps.

A faint sound stopped him. He didn't see anything at first, but as he searched the water and hill for a second time, he spotted her. A wet, disheveled Sierra huddled under the bridge. The rapids were a yard beneath her feet. At first, he wondered why she hadn't climbed up the embankment—there was still grass left—but a more focused inspection showed the churned-up mud slicks where she'd obviously tried to make her way up. The hill was a difficult climb in good conditions. Saturated and slick, it had to be impossible. The story was all too clear. She'd spent the night here and, in the dark, hadn't realized how fast the water was rising. In the daylight, she'd found she was trapped.

He began dialing 9–1–1, but realized he wasn't even getting a dial tone. The heavy rain must have affected coverage. Even as he stood there, he could see the water rising toward her feet. She shivered and shook and had her heart in her eyes when she looked at him.

"I'm coming, Sierra!" he yelled.

He raced back up to his truck. He still had a rope from towing a friend's car last year. He secured the rope to the railing above the bridge and dropped it over the side, then he lowered himself, hand over hand, down the grassy decline, using the rope to steady himself. His hands burned. Every muscle quivered. His feet got stuck in the mud. But he worked his way down, inch by inch, staying close to the cement arch of the bridge.

His leg caught on something, and he couldn't move. He twisted to see what had a hold on him. A bolt, embedded in the cement, was snagged on his jeans. Nick groaned. He kicked and heaved until the jeans ripped free of the bolt, gritting his teeth as the bolt scythed across the back of his knee, shredding skin.

Keep going, he told himself. *Keep going.* Just as he almost reached her, his feet slid past, and he touched the rush of water. The icy bayou sucked and pulled at his feet like a riptide, and even though he was only knee deep, for a split second, he was terrified it was going to pull him under. He clung to the rope. Searching for every ounce of strength he could find, he gave a hard thrust of his feet and freed them from the impossible current.

Nick released a sigh and crawled back up the concrete under the bridge. In the harsh gray light, Sierra's face was white, her lips blue. He grabbed her hands and massaged warmth into them. "You're colder than the North Pole, Sierra."

She opened her mouth to answer, but nothing came out. How was he going to get her out of here? It had taken all his strength to hang on to the rope coming down. She would have to be a mega-athlete to climb up.

He closed his eyes. Could he carry her somehow? She was on the small side, but carrying a hundred-plus pounds up a slippery hill? He'd get them both killed. His best shot was to climb behind her in case she lost her grip.

"Sierra?"

He waited until her eyes cleared and he had her attention. He had to shout to be heard over the water. "This is important. I know you're tired. But you've got to use the rope to climb up the hill for me. I'm going to be behind you. You're going to feel like you have to let go of the rope, but you *can't* let go. No matter what. You have to use every scrap of strength you've got. If you lose your grip, we could both end up in the floodwaters. Do you understand?"

Her eyes large, she nodded. "I understand, Mr. Foster."

He rubbed her hands with a vengeance, trying to warm them. "Stand up and move. Get your blood flowing before we climb."

She stomped her feet and did a couple of lunges. Closing her eyes, she held out her arms and took in a deep breath, as if she could visualize oxygen moving through her limbs.

"Are you ready?"

She gave him a solemn nod.

Nick said a silent prayer and put the rope in her hands. He hoped he'd been right when he'd told April her daughter wanted life. Sierra had to want it with an unyielding will right now.

They grasped the rope and began to climb up. Her fingers turned white, and her shoulders strained as they made progress one step at a time.

They'd made it about a quarter of the way up the hill when her feet slid backward in the muddy tracks. She cried out as they both slammed into the concrete. The impact knocked the wind out of Nick, and he struggled to find air. Flecks of rust shook loose from the bridge.

He dug his boots into the mud, trying to keep them from sliding any farther. He knew the concrete must have bruised her. And the rope stung his hands, so the slip had certainly burned her tender palms, but she didn't let go.

"We can do this, Sierra," he said softly in her ear. "We *will* do this."

Her breathing was labored, and a groan tore out of her, as if she were finding strength somewhere deep inside of her. She stood stock still long enough for a cold sweat to break out on Nick's neck. But then she began moving again, hand over hand, edging her way up the grass, and Nick followed. It was agonizing and slow as they slid back and pressed forward, moved back and farther forward. But at last, the street was right above them.

Sierra crawled off the grass on her hands and knees to the sidewalk, and Nick collapsed beside her. He couldn't help but glance down. The place where they'd taken cover under the bridge only a few minutes ago was a raging river now. He lifted his eyes in thanks, shrugged off his jacket, and wrapped Sierra in it. At least the inside was still dry.

Sierra leaned her head against the truck's window. She felt so unreal, so cold and lost. Mr. Foster drove them out of the blocks of concrete and onto a wooded road. She tried to make sense of where she was, but her brain felt like it was filled with cobwebs. It had been such a crazy night and a crazier morning. She'd thought she was going to drown in the pounding bayou. A sob found its way into her throat, but she swallowed it.

She closed her eyes and only looked up when they drew to a stop at a row of townhouses she didn't recognize. Why were they here? She looked around, trying to make sense of the place. Light blue buildings with dark trim stood tucked between pine tree-lined sidewalks. The rain had stopped, but the black clouds and soaked tarmac remained.

She started to get out of the truck, but her legs didn't remember how to move. She stared ahead, trying to think what she was supposed to do. But she was floating, floating away.

Mr. Foster picked her up and carried her into the townhouse on the end, setting her down next to fireplace, and began building a fire. "Your mom will be here soon, Sierra."

A woman of about forty with long, platinum hair came in and cooed over her. She patted her skin, checking her temperature, Sierra realized. She could hardly feel her touch.

"Don't worry about a thing," the woman said. "You just rest."

She could hear Mr. Foster in another room telling someone he'd brought her to his house so his neighbor could give her a checkup. Exposure, he said. Is that what she had? Exposure?

"I'm Dr. Allen, Nick's neighbor. We'll get you in some dry clothes and warmed up by the fire, and you're going to be A-OK."

Sierra let the woman dress her. The doctor toweled her hair, tucked a quilt around her, and then slipped a hot water bottle under her feet.

She massaged some kind of gel into her hands and wrapped them up in bandages.

"That's good, baby. Cry it out."

Was she crying? Her eyes felt too frozen to cry.

The woman brought in a steaming mug that smelled like it had more sugar in it than coffee. Sierra swallowed it robotically, and then she was left alone by the fire. The flames flickered and licked orange and blue until she began to fade.

When she woke, she found herself in a big bed covered by a thick cotton burgundy comforter. Honey-colored light streamed onto a beige wall. Outside the window, a huge pine tree dripped with the remains of last night's storm. Cufflinks and combs sat on a corner of a big oak dresser, but mostly stacks of books littered the top.

Where was she? Sierra stretched, trying to make sense of her presence in the strange bed. Her whole body protested. Her hands burned. *The night on the bayou, getting trapped by the water, climbing up from under the bridge.* She shook her head, as if she could make the odd memory go away. He'd brought her to his house, he'd said. This must be Mr. Foster's home.

She eased out of the bed. The sweats she was wearing were too loose, and she had to hold the waist to keep the pants up. Her arms and legs wobbled like she'd run miles. But she couldn't help but inspect the books—thick military thrillers, science fiction in hardback, *A Tale of Two Cities* in threadbare paperback with yellow sticky notes poking out.

You could always tell a lot about a person by what they read. Mr. Foster must read it all. She liked that. The thought almost startled her.

She was warm, almost too warm. She still felt odd—heavy and vague and lost—but she couldn't seem to mind. She lay back down and let the world drift away for a long time until she heard voices. She couldn't make out what they said, but she recognized them well enough.

Mom and Mr. Prodan. Her mother had come to take her home.

Finally, she gathered herself.

She tiptoed out to a hallway, each muscle crying out as she opened a door to peek into the only other room upstairs. It was a study with even more shelves of books than Mr. Prodan had. She breathed in the scent of paper but forced herself to close the study door and climb down the flight of carpeted stairs. Rounding a corner into the kitchen, she found the three of them whispering.

They stopped when they saw her. Sierra had no idea what to say, so she just looked through the kitchen window. A wood deck perched over a gorge and a bulging creek below. It was still gray outside, but the storm had passed.

She could feel her mom's worry, but *sorry* wouldn't cut it this time.

"Sierra." Mom stepped close, her face fragile, as if the slightest movement would cause her to break. She reached out to Sierra but let her hand drop. "As soon as you're ready, we can go home."

"I'd like to stay here." Her raspy voice surprised her.

She stared at a wall, trying not to feel her mother's presence. It was so light here, so full of books and nature and life.

"Sierra ..."

Sierra walked back up the stairs, holding the sweatpants close. She slipped under the covers again, her back to the door. Maybe she wouldn't have to discuss it if she looked sick.

In seconds, the bed dipped when Mom sat down. There was a long silence before Mom said, "I've made my mistakes, Sierra.

Big mistakes. But no matter how I've failed you, I want you to know"—her voice cracked—"if something happened to you ..." Mom drew in a long breath. "You know what it's like to be left behind. Don't run away again. Okay, Sierra?" Mom let the question hang in the air.

Sierra couldn't turn around. She knew she should say something, anything. But her mind was a mass of garbled thoughts and feelings. She hadn't been trying to run away exactly. She just wanted to be alone for a little bit, in a place where everybody didn't look at her with worried eyes. And it was so beautiful on the bayou with the wind whipping under the bridge and the water splashing against the banks. She'd stayed until it became impossible to go home without making a scene.

It was so quiet she could hear Mom's breathing. Sierra studied the pictures on the wall. The minutes dragged, and it was a long time before she realized she was alone again.

An old-fashioned clock ticked on the wall. Her stomach began to rumble, but she didn't want to go downstairs again. Sierra tiptoed to the doorway. She could hear them talking again, and she moved to the top step, resting her head against her knees, listening.

Someone settled in a chair, and she heard an exchange of whispered voices. Then Mr. Foster spoke. "Do you trust me, April?"

"Of course," Mom said.

"Then I want you to go home and rest."

Sierra sat up, suddenly interested in what he was saying.

"Nick, I can't leave her. You know I can't."

She heard a rustling sound, like someone was shifting. "I'm sure you want to make certain Sierra's all right. You probably have important things to say to her."

Mom didn't answer, and Mr. Foster went on. "Let her rest. Give her some space. Just a few hours."

"Nick." Sierra shrank at the pain in Mom's voice. "I can't leave her. She needs to know I'm here for her."

"I know what I'm asking is hard, April. But I'm telling you this as someone who was in Sierra's position once. Someone who had his reasons to run away from home at almost the same age as Sierra."

Sierra eased forward. Mr. Foster running away? He seemed so together.

"You'll do Sierra more good by giving her some space. My dad and I are here. We won't let anything happen to her."

A few minutes passed and finally her mother spoke in a supersoft voice. "Okay, Nick. I trust you with Sierra. You know I do."

The front door opened and then clicked shut. Sierra breathed a sigh of relief. She listened to the voices of the men speaking, and the sounds of someone moving around in the kitchen.

"She is gone, Sierra," Mr. Prodan called out. "You do not need to hide on the stairs any longer."

Sierra let out a quiet laugh. Had he known she was there the whole time? She negotiated her way down the stairs, holding up the waistband of the pants she was wearing.

Only Mr. Prodan sat in the kitchen, a book in his hand. She looked around for Mr. Foster, spotting him in the living room shoveling ashes from the fireplace into a dustpan. The sun shone outside now.

"Your mother will come for you this evening," Mr. Prodan said.

He put his book down, made his way to the stove and ladled out a bowl of chicken soup for her and then another for himself. They ate in silence on bar stools in the kitchen until he laid his spoon down.

"You will forgive her sooner than you think. You and your mother are not bitter old men like Nicu and myself."

Mr. Foster gave his dad a guarded inspection from the living room.

"I'm not angry at my mom," she said.

"Ah. My mistake then." Mr. Prodan picked his spoon up and began eating again.

After lunch, Sierra climbed back upstairs with her own clothes, now dry. Mr. Foster said she could have the afternoon to herself, right? After she changed her clothes, she didn't stay in the bedroom but stole into the room with the books. Bookshelves filled two walls. A desk and a filing cabinet stood on the other side of the room beneath nature photos. Sierra browsed through the volumes. Dark hardcovers stood at attention, while weathered paperbacks flopped against them.

But the window was the best part. The deep sill, large enough to sit in, drew her. Mr. Foster must sit here sometimes, too, because a thick Bible with a worn leather cover sat on the ledge. She curled up in the corner of the sill, felt the sun-warmed glass on her arm, and thumbed through the Bible.

She ran her hand across a page with penciled notes and underlining. A soft sigh went through her. Mom had a marked-up Bible like this, but it mostly stayed hidden under the magazines now. She began reading John, and before she knew it, she'd made her way halfway through the epistles.

The daylight dimmed, and she knew Mom would be back soon. Her afternoon had gone by so fast.

The door opened. Mr. Foster put his head in. "I thought I might find you in this room. May I come in?"

Sierra put the Bible down as if he'd caught her snooping in his diary.

He drew up a desk chair. He remained silent so long Sierra began to fidget.

"How are you feeling?" he asked.

She looked down at her bandaged hands. "I have a sore throat. That's all."

"Sierra," he said, and stopped. Quietly he started again. "You should know if something happened to you, there are people who would feel your loss." He rolled forward on the chair. "*I* would feel your loss."

"I wasn't trying to kill myself," she mumbled.

His eyes glinted. "I know you weren't. You've got too much life in you for that. You showed that getting out of the bayou."

Sierra looked up in surprise.

"But you're too smart not to know you were exposing yourself to the elements and to criminals. You took a risk."

She drew back against the glass.

"Look," he said. "I'm not going to push you. But when someone spends the night outside in a near-freezing rainstorm, I think they're looking for help."

Looking for help? How could he say that? His help was half the reason she'd been at the bayou in the first place.

"Sierra, I'm not afraid of anything you have to say."

"You shouldn't have done it, Mr. Foster. You should have told the principal about Emilio. I wasn't looking for help. I especially wasn't looking for someone to lose their job for me. I'm sick of people treating me like I'm going to break."

Mr. Foster let out a rattled sigh. "Losing my job was more complicated than you think."

Sierra played with her fingers. She tried to say the words, but it was hard to push them out. Finally she knocked her head back against the window. "The worst part is you're all right. I *am* weak. I *am* about to break. I was born that way."

Mr. Foster gave her a big, unbelieving smile. "Sierra, you are *not* weak. A weak girl wouldn't have taught herself a handful of languages. She wouldn't have insisted on keeping in touch with an old man everyone insisted was dangerous. She wouldn't have had the will to make it out of a flood exhausted and half frozen. Don't let anyone convince you you're weak. You've got a core of steel inside you."

Steel? She looked for signs he was lying to her. No one had ever said anything close. "I'm not strong." Even her voice was small. "I think I'm like my Dad."

Mr. Foster sighed. "I never knew your dad, so I can't respond to that. All I can do is talk about the girl I see in front of me. Ever heard 'still waters run deep'? That's you. Your feelings, your senses, your thoughts, even your words run deep. And it's not easy staying true to yourself when you're different from those around you. It takes a special kind of strength."

She stared at him, trying to decide if she loved or hated the ring of truth to his words.

Mr. Foster held out his hand for his Bible. When she gave it to him, he flipped it open, but he didn't read anything to her. He just kept talking. "But if God made your river deeper and darker, He has plans for you. It may be hard. But I saw you climbing up the hill with the floodwaters ready to pull you down. God's already given you what you need, Sierra."

As she thought about what Mr. Foster had said, she couldn't get the image of the river out of her mind. A river running deep and

dark. She thought of the water she could have drowned in this morning. It had been deep and dark and wild. Nothing could contain it.

Chapter Thirty-Eight

April unlocked the door to their apartment, and Sierra headed straight to her room. April called after her, but the bedroom door closed and the lock clicked. April knew from experience she wouldn't be coaxed out.

The night was long and fitful with little rest. At dawn, she heard Sierra's feet padding down the hallway, and April made her way into the living room.

Sierra stood staring at the wall of tiles. She just stood there, her fists at her sides, until she leaned her forehead against one of the Hebrew squares. In the hazy light, her daughter looked weary and old.

"How could you have done it, Mom?" Sierra turned to April.

At last. April ought to be relieved Sierra was talking to her. But a knot in her stomach stubbornly refused to go away.

"How could you keep his suicide a secret? Dad was mine, too, you know."

April swallowed. "You're right. He was. I had no right to keep it from you."

"Don't. Don't do that."

April shook her head. "Don't do what?"

"Act all smooth. You stole him from me. You wouldn't talk about him, and I couldn't even remember him—the things he said and did. You can't just say you had no right to do it and expect it to be okay."

April inched toward Sierra, which earned her nothing but a glare. She wanted to tell Sierra how numb Gary's death left her, how scared she'd been Sierra would hurt herself, too.

She let her hands drop to her sides. "I failed you. I failed you when you needed me most. I could tell you all the things that went through my head, the reasons I didn't tell you the truth. But really, what I did was still wrong. What is there to say but sorry? And you're right. Sorry is a pitiful little word against the lie I let you believe."

Sierra looked away and began to pace. It was a frantic pace. She clung to her pajamas, then wiped her hands through her hair, sending it into short spikes. Her face was pinched. April wished she would let her hold her. But they were beyond the days when a hug and a kiss could make it all better.

Sierra marched back to the wall, stood rigid, staring at the tiles with a ferocity April had never seen in her.

"I think I knew," Sierra said.

"Knew what?"

"I think I knew he killed himself. A pedestrian accident. How likely is that? And I knew what he was like." Sierra let out a pained whimper and turned to April. "I think I made sure it was too hard for you to tell me. Because if you didn't tell me, it wouldn't be true."

Sierra looked up at a crack in the ceiling. "Crazy me, huh?"

April moved closer. "Not so crazy."

Sierra backed away from the wall, narrowed her eyes. And then, with a fast reach of her hand, she pulled a tile off the wall and threw it at the floor in the middle of the room. And another. And another. The tiles flew, one after the other, making a dull thunk as they hit each other.

"Mah tish-to-cha-chee nafshi? Va'the'heh-mee a-la-ee?" The strange guttural chant coming out of her daughter's mouth sounded like a curse. A chill raced down April's spine.

Sierra turned to face her, her arms spread wide. "It's Hebrew. 'Why are you downcast, O my soul? Why so disturbed within me?' Dad would have liked that one, wouldn't he?"

Sierra crouched and punched her fist into the pile until something cracked, either tile or bone. April wasn't sure. She held back a sob. She wanted Sierra to express herself. She did, but this?

"How could he have done it, Mom? How could he just walk away from me like he was crossing the street to heaven? He didn't even say good-bye."

April stood and came close, not close enough to touch, just close enough for Sierra to feel her presence. "He wasn't …"

He wasn't thinking straight, she wanted to say. Sierra waited for her to finish, but she couldn't. She was through making excuses, through with imaginary rainbows. Gary *had* been thinking straight. He'd had enough. Enough despair, enough of being a burden to his family. He'd simply given up. But there was no way she was going to say that to Sierra.

When April didn't finish, Sierra buried her head in her hands. Finally, she lifted her head.

"He didn't just take himself when he died. He took the biggest part of me. How could he not know that?"

Sierra huddled into herself. She clearly wouldn't accept April's touch, but without reaching out to her, what else could April do?

April yanked a tile from the wall and found some satisfaction in the crash it made as it hit the others.

Sierra looked up and their gazes locked.

April took a step toward her. "I want it down too. There's a lie in here, isn't there? And I'm so very tired of lies."

April pulled a second tile off. "We can't make it all better with a beautiful wall of art. And we can't bring him back with the words he loved."

Sierra pulled the next one off. Together, they pulled them all down, hurling them into the pile, pausing for each clunk until their arms ached. By the time they were done, the wall was bare except for the nails and center tile. The stack of cracked tiles in the middle of the floor created a small mountain.

Sierra leaned down, hands on her knees as if she'd been running.

April had to catch her breath and, half hysterical, started to laugh until tears ran down her face.

Sierra sank to the floor and pulled a broken tile to her. She sat staring into space before she whispered something unintelligible.

"What?" April said.

A little louder, Sierra repeated herself. "By day the Lord directs His love, at night His song is with me—a prayer to the God of my life."

April shot her a quizzical look.

Sierra looked away and then back. "That's what the rest of the psalm says. My soul is disturbed within me. Deep calls to deep. But His song is with me."

April nodded and started stacking the broken tiles, not sure what to make of the words.

"He *was* with us, wasn't He, Mom?"

April swallowed. "Yes, baby. God was with us."

She looked around the room for the song. Not a sound. And yet. As she took in the mound of tiles, she could *feel* the song playing, not with musical chords, but in the chords of the dawn. As if He were filling the room with Himself. She'd grown so used to feeling that God must be absent.

———◆◆◆———

It was past noon when April straggled into the kitchen. She searched the pantry for something to cook. Was it breakfast or lunch? Oatmeal or grilled cheese? She rolled her shoulders, working out the kinks, still trying to think through what happened. It was so surreal. She'd never wantonly destroyed anything in her life. But it had been cathartic. All the throwing and cracking left her feeling lighter. She thought it had done Sierra good too. And that psalm at the end.

A movement in the living room startled her. Sierra lay curled on the sofa with something wrapped inside her hands. She ought to be at school, but April had let her go back to sleep after their talk.

"What have you got?" April slid onto the sofa next to Sierra's feet.

Sierra slid farther into the corner of the sofa and opened her hands. It was April's Nikon. "I found it in your boxes with the photo albums."

April didn't say anything, just inspected the camera from afar like an exotic animal that wandered into her apartment. She studied her little girl, who didn't look so little anymore. Sierra handed it to her, and April took it, holding it lightly. She moved it into the sunlight, inspecting its solid form.

"Why did you stop taking pictures?"

Nick's version of Truth or Dare came to mind. She was so used to protecting Sierra from dark thoughts. "I was afraid of what I would see. The camera always picked up things the way they were. Light or dark. Shades of gray. Dad's hurt. But even with people I didn't know, I could see all their insecurities and regrets so much clearer when I was behind the camera."

Sierra opened and closed her fist. "You didn't like taking pictures?"

"I did like taking them, strangely enough." It was Gary who'd commented on the dark emotions in her pictures. And she'd felt the need to keep the light streaming in for him. Only happy thoughts and optimistic images allowed. But she couldn't blame Gary. He never asked her to stop taking pictures. Or to be his source of sunshine.

April ran her hand along the controls on the back of the camera. Her daughter hadn't taken an interest in what April did for a long time. Not since Gary's death.

Sierra pulled her arms around her knees. "Mr. Foster said even deep, dark rivers have a place to flow. I guess there's a place for sad pictures too."

April looked down, gratitude welling up in her for Nick. He knew what to say to Sierra. Not an impossible *be happy*. Just *there's a place for you*.

CHAPTER THIRTY-NINE

Nick stepped through the school doors halfway through second period. The hallways were deserted.

He took it as a positive sign that Liza had called him. If he gave a warm enough apology, maybe she'd let him back into his classroom with a reprimand.

The glass doors to the office closed behind him, and Gloria, the secretary, told him to take a seat. He waited. The bell rang. Kids poured out and filtered back into classes. Only ten minutes later did Gloria tell him to go in.

He found Liza sitting at her desk, pushing a form into a file and letting a pair of reading glasses slide down her nose.

"Mr. Foster."

Nick inclined his head and took a seat.

She laid her hands on the desk in front of her. "It gives me no pleasure suspending a teacher, particularly one with a long-standing reputation." She stopped, inspecting him, probably to see if he bought her line. He didn't. "Would you like to say anything for the record?"

For the record? What did that mean? "As you know by now, Ms. Grambling, I left my class to protect a student. If it had been anyone else, I would have followed ordinary procedures. But I was worried about how fragile Sierra Wright was. She was unable to face the police and school authorities at the time. I agreed to give her a few days to prepare herself, but I informed her mother immediately."

Liza stared at him, unmoved.

He dug deep, trying to find an apology that would reach even her. "I'm sorry. I violated procedures. I left a mess on your hands. For that, I'm truly sorry."

She tapped her fingernails on the desk. "I appreciate your candor. Unfortunately, you left more than a mess. You broke the law."

He stared at Liza. He'd been accused of acting without thinking through the consequences a time or two, but he had never broken the law. "I didn't intend for the assault to go unreported. I delayed the report until Monday for the girl's mental health. That's all."

"Yes, and that delay was a serious lapse. If the Cantu boy had carried out his threat against Sierra Wright in the intervening seventy-two hours and the authorities hadn't been notified, our school would have been liable, not to mention skewered in the media."

He hated that what she said made sense. But there was no way for him to make Liza understand that something more important than the school's name had been at risk—Sierra herself.

Liza's face remained a stone mask, and Nick wondered why he was here. She didn't want an apology. She showed no inclination of putting him back to work.

She pulled out another file, this one with his name on the label. "At the board meeting next week, I'll be recommending termination of your contract for ethical misconduct."

Nick saw white heat. Ethical misconduct? That term was reserved for teachers who hit a student. Or who slept with one.

If the district accepted her recommendation, not only would he never be able to work at this school, he wouldn't be able to teach anywhere. A long, empty future stretched out before him. He wouldn't be able to work with youth in any capacity.

"Would you like to make any other comment for the record, Mr. Foster?"

She was a superb actress. She didn't let a hint of her victory show. He'd never once realized who he was up against. Up until this moment, he'd thought her clueless, maybe a little power hungry. It never occurred to him she was this full of venom. If she simply wanted him gone, she could have him transferred next year. There were only nine weeks of school left.

He looked at her until she finally had the grace to look away. "For the record, I'll be in touch, Liza."

As he strode out, he heard her heels tapping into the office behind him. That was a sound he could happily live the rest of his life without hearing again.

<hr />

The next morning, Nick sat on the windowsill with his Bible.

It was 8:00 a.m. The tardy bell would be ringing. This was how Nick defined his days now: by what he wasn't doing. He wasn't teaching first period. He wasn't leading his classes through the last novel of the year, *The Contender*. And he wasn't helping his kids set goals for next year. Someone else was pushing his classes through practice tests for the state evaluation next week.

It was a poor way to live, measuring himself by what he wasn't doing.

He pulled out Jason's business card. His old army friend was now a partner in a law firm downtown. Jason told him if he'd really violated the code of conduct, Liza was probably within her rights. "But don't give up hope, Nick," he said over the phone. "Just because she's technically within her rights doesn't mean we can't make a good fight."

A good fight, but not a sure fight. The district cared more about the black and white of the code than about a kid who'd already faced one trauma too many.

What would he do with himself if he weren't teaching? The thought of pushing papers in an office gave him hives. He'd prayed for Liza to be softened. He'd prayed for his job to be restored. But he'd learned long ago that wanting something so much it hurt didn't earn an answered prayer. Sometimes all it earned was a sacrifice on God's altar.

"Our Father who art in Heaven," he began to pray.

Not as I will, but Thy will be done. Nick shook his head, as if he could make the intruding words go away. There was nothing he wanted to pray less than the Gethsemane prayer. But if Christ had needed to take the harder path for some better purpose, who was he to ask for an easier route?

He moved from the windowsill to the carpeted floor. Nick closed his eyes, feeling an ache so deep he didn't know where it ended. Sacrifice his job? He didn't know if he could do it. Crouching on his knees, he tried to let go of the career that had been the focus of his life for a decade and a half.

"I don't know how to be anything else, Lord, but you can have my job. You can have it. My hands are empty."

He reached out his hands as if Christ needed to see how empty his hands were. But he came up with closed fists. He'd lost his job.

And he'd lost April. Beautiful, artsy April who'd somehow charmed his old man into telling his story but didn't seem able to tell her own.

He forced his hands open. "I don't know how to let go," he groaned. "I only ask this one thing, Father: if I'm losing my calling, let it stand for something."

His fingers uncurled. He touched his forehead to the floor, and he would stay there, in the position of submission, until he knew he could leave his job in heaven's power.

"Not my will. Yours," he said in a grated whisper. "I will submit. By Your grace, I put it all in Your hands." His words submitted, but his body said otherwise. The muscles in his arms clenched and shuddered in protest.

In his mind's eye, he imagined putting his classes in God's palms, hands capable of marking off the heavens and weighing the mountains. For good measure, he imagined putting his old man in God's hands. And last, he put April there.

"I submit to Your will. By Your grace, I submit to You," he prayed over and over again.

He collapsed onto the floor facedown and spread his arms like a cross. He didn't move until every thought belonged to God and every muscle released its tension.

It had been a long time since Nick had prayed body and soul like this. It had been a long time since he'd had the time or felt the need to. Noon passed and the afternoon light had dimmed when, exhausted and spent, he lifted himself from the floor.

He sucked in a deep breath and let God's calm work its way through him. As he made his way downstairs, his prayer still whispered the refrain in the back of his mind. I submit to Your will. By Your grace, I submit.

Chapter Forty

Sierra sat on the stairs with her notebook. The world still lay in wetness, though sunlight filled the courtyard and shimmered off the puddles. The willow's branches hung low with the weight of rain. She closed her eyes, letting the smell of sweet wet wood drift up to her.

"Hey, Brown Eyes."

She thought she might cry. She'd missed Carlos so much. She opened her eyes to see him on the sidewalk below. He wore galoshes and held an industrial broom.

"Hey," she tried to say, but her voice came out wrong and broken.

"I'm glad you're safe. I was worried about you out in the storm."

"I'm fine. Thanks for thinking of me."

"No problem." He looked up to her, waiting for something from her, but she couldn't think of what to say.

"Got to get back to work."

She watched as he swept the courtyard dry. The sounds of the wiry bristles scraping against concrete, and swishing water filled the air. He pulled the giant broom in and pushed it out in circular motions, until he'd worked all the standing water into the grass. He was so strong, and not just physically. What would it be like to feel that nothing scared you, not even when living on the streets?

She was still on the stairs, pretending to write in her journal when Carlos carried the broom to the utility room. He made one last pass by the stairs. "I've got to be on my way. See you, Sierra."

He looked at her a few seconds and turned to go. She clung to the banister for support. She watched him walk to the security gate. He was giving her another chance, and she was letting him leave all over again. She could be strong too. It's what Mr. Foster had said.

As he tapped in the security code, she stood and made herself walk to the bottom of the stairs. Carlos turned and waited.

She searched for words that would make sense. In the end, she just said, "My dad killed himself, Carlos."

He started to walk toward her, ever so slowly. "Yeah, your mom told me the other night."

She knotted her hands. "I can't be like him. I've got to be strong, you see?"

"Okay," he said, both sadness and laughter in his eyes. "Don't be like your dad."

She gave a short laugh. "That's what I was trying to do."

"By breaking up with me? How is that going to keep you from being like him?"

"I didn't want to lean on you the way he leaned on my mom." She looked up the stairs toward their door. "I know she loved him. But I think maybe, just a little, my mom hated him for being weak. I didn't want you to hate me, not even a little."

He reached her. "So you decided to make me mad at you so I wouldn't be mad at you." He tapped her forehead. "You're too smart for me, Einstein."

He slid his arms around her uncertainly. She leaned into his shoulder, taking in his smell of sun and skin, staying in his arms a long time. It was warm and safe. But here they were again. He was sheltering her weakness.

He curled a lock of hair at the nape of her neck in his fingers and murmured, "I'm sorry about your dad."

"Me, too."

He pulled her in for another hug. They clung together until Carlos buried his face in her hair, laughing. "Your mom's watching us."

Sierra looked up. Mom stood in the window, watching, but she didn't seem to mind them together. In fact, she smiled.

———◆◆◆◆◆———

When Sierra left school Tuesday, Mr. Prodan was waiting for her at the curb. He asked if he could walk her to her apartment rather than taking her to his house. "Your mother is tired, and I would like for her to come home to a hot meal."

It was a nice day, but the walk left him flushed. When they went inside, she asked him if she could get him something.

"A glass of water, if you do not mind."

Sierra hurried into the kitchen and poured ice and water into a glass. He eyed the ice suspiciously as he picked his way to the sofa.

Sierra sat across from him in the armchair. He glanced at the tiles, now stacked against the wall. It was odd being with him here. He seemed out of place in this cramped, dark room. And so much had happened. Things were different between them, awkward.

She searched for something to say, breaking the silence at last with the question she hadn't been able to put to rest. "Mr. Foster said he didn't lose his job because of me," she blurted. "He said it was complicated. But at school, they think it was because of me."

His brow creased as he placed his glass on a coaster on the side table. "I do not know exactly why he lost his position. But I have no reason to think it was because of you. I suspect it is because he is good at what he does."

"For being good? Why would they fire him for that?"

Mr. Prodan rested his hands on his knees. "People are threatened by greatness. Especially if one's greatness does not look at all like the mediocrity they had planned."

Being fired for being great? Sierra linked her fingers, trying to make sense of it.

"In Romania, the communists were threatened by great minds. In America, it is different, but not always. Not always." He sighed. "My son is the best of teachers. I have seen letters among his papers from young men and women who were once his students. They credit him for much in their lives. It is not the normal way in America to write such letters?"

She shook her head. "I would never think of writing a letter like that."

Sierra tipped her head. Jazzy was in Mr. Foster's class. She loved it, and she wasn't someone who even liked school. He had a lot of students like her—kids who hated school but who tried harder because of whatever went on in his class.

Mr. Prodan gave her a curious glance. "You have a look about you."

"Mr. Foster's students do really love him. I bet they'd do a lot for him."

"They might."

Sierra sat a little straighter. Her feet started to tap, but she stilled them. "He's been teaching for a long time, right? I bet he has students who are grown now, maybe even some who have pretty important jobs, too."

Mr. Prodan eased back into the sofa, a small smile playing on his face. "True. But they do not know that his job is at risk. Someone would need to let them know that he needs their help."

Sierra sent him an answering smile. Someone could do that.

CHAPTER FORTY-ONE

When April walked in the door, the table was set for four, with a tablecloth, no less. A salad bowl sat in the middle of the table, and the smell of beef and onions drifted out of the kitchen. She stepped inside, tentatively.

"Did elves invade my apartment?" she asked, though she knew the smell of those spices. They were Luca's.

"Hey, Mom."

Sierra sat cross-legged on the floor in the living room with her laptop. Luca sat in the recliner in the corner, while Carlos jotted something in a notebook on the sofa.

Sierra looked up at her, and April forgot to breathe. There was excitement in Sierra's eyes.

April took in the scene.

"We're going to save Mr. Foster's job," Sierra said with a genuine certainty that had been missing from her daughter's voice for too long. Sierra looked to Luca.

"We are going to try," he corrected.

"We," Sierra said. "You, too, Mom." She hunched her shoulders. "Right?"

April sat down on the couch behind Sierra, scanning the web page on Sierra's computer over her shoulder, some kind of online policy book.

Luca stood. "At this point, we are only making a list. Students who know Nicolae. Perhaps some teachers."

Luca seemed a little cooler about the plan than Sierra, and April felt a twinge of doubt. She would hate to see Sierra face any kind of failure. Not right now.

"There's only one thing in our way," Carlos said.

"Only one?" April said with a smile.

Carlos looked as happy as Sierra. "Mr. Foster has the information we need. Luca says he's got hundreds of letters from his former students. And he's got his class roster."

"So? Ask him."

Luca looked away.

"What? He's not allowed to know his family and friends want to help him get his job back?"

Silence filled the room. Nick was a proud man, true, but it wouldn't hurt to ask.

"Mom, maybe you could distract him?"

April coughed. "What? So you can break in and steal his personal correspondence?"

Carlos grinned, and Sierra looked down at her computer again. That was exactly what they planned to do. Even if she were willing to allow her sixteen-year-old daughter to commit a misdemeanor, there was a hitch. So much more than a hitch. Nick had asked her to keep her distance.

"Mom?"

April gave a firm shake of her head. "I'm sorry, Sierra. I'm not going to allow you to break into Nick's house."

"It's not breaking in. Mr. Prodan has a key, and it's his son's house. And we're only doing it to help Mr. Foster."

"No."

"It's no different than you and Uncle Wes sneaking Aunt Hillary's address book so you could plan a surprise party for her that time."

She could never win at logic with Sierra. She'd have to try another tactic. Sierra deserved the truth, no matter how hard the truth. "I'm not welcome at Nick's house, sweetie. Things are a bit complicated, but he asked me not to visit."

Sierra looked at her, her eyes large and confused.

Luca wasn't bothered at all. "You would not be visiting him, so this is good. He would be visiting you."

"He told me he doesn't want to see me, Luca."

"Hmm. I do not think you understood what he said."

"He was quite clear."

"Nicu said he did not wish to see you? But people do not always mean what they say." There was a mischievous gleam in Luca's eye. "Perhaps he meant he wished for a reason to look forward to your visit."

April threw up her hands. "I can't believe this." She stood and gave Sierra an even glance. "You're not breaking into Nick's home."

She strode into the kitchen. She stirred the pot of simmering beef and onions and clanged the lid on it. What they were suggesting was ludicrous. Every bit of it.

When Luca came into the kitchen, she pointed the spoon at him. "You're wiser than that." She looked at the kids out in the living room, but they were busy whispering about their plan. Quietly, she said, "Luca, if you think I'm going to lure him to meet me with a lie, with a suggestion of offering something I can't ... Nick would never forgive me. Not even for his job."

"I did not suggest you lie."

"What *did* you suggest exactly?"

He took the spoon from her, opened the pot, and sprinkled crushed parsley from a bowl, then began to stir. "I suggested you tell him the truth."

"The truth?"

He put the spoon on the cutting board and stepped close, looking her straight in the eye. "We have shared enough, April. We can be honest with each other. You love my son. My son loves you. I only ask that you tell him so."

Luca was clever. Did he think he could kill two birds with one stone? But telling Nick she loved him would lead nowhere. Nick already had a good idea of her feelings for him.

He rested his hand on the counter, all mischief gone now. "Your daughter's plan, I cannot say if it will succeed. What is more important is that you and Nicu speak honestly with each other. You once asked me to do a very hard thing—to tell my own story. It was difficult, but I did it for my son. Yet, I think perhaps it was more important that I tell the story than it was for my son to hear it. So I feel I can return your favor." He dropped his gaze. "It is a hard thing after your husband's illness and death for you to think of building a life with another man, yes?"

"Yes," April said quietly.

"You do not have to build a life with my Nicu. But if you do this hard thing, if you tell him the truth of how you feel, of your love and your fear, you will be a stronger woman."

"You know it could just as well be you who talked to Nick. He has some things he'd like to hear from you."

"Yes, April, it could be me." But there was a challenge in his eyes.

———◆◆◆◆◆———

April paced her bedroom that night.

How could she? How could she just come out and tell Nick how she felt now? What good would it do to tell him she loved him but that she was paralyzed with fear and guilt and so many other emotions that would destroy anything good between them? She didn't even know how to talk to Nick.

———•◦⋈◦•———

The next night April tried, unsuccessfully, to distract herself with a novel in bed. Sierra wandered in and sat on the floor, a blanket wrapped around her shoulders. She didn't say anything for the longest time, just rested her chin on her knees. It didn't take a mind reader to know what was coming next.

"Why did Mr. Foster tell you he didn't want to see you?"

"It wasn't a rude thing. We didn't have a fight."

Sierra waited, and April knew she'd have to tell her. "Nick loves me. And I care for him too. But romance … It's too soon for me. After Dad. Nick asked for distance. His heart needs space to mend."

Sierra got a faraway look. She grieved for Gary too. But she'd no doubt been looking for a father figure. Wasn't that why she formed the connection to Luca in the first place? And Nick was quite a friend to her.

The light in Sierra's eyes sent a shiver through April. She'd been so sure getting involved would be too hard for Sierra.

"It's no good, Sierra," April said. "I'm not getting married again. I'm not sure I'll even be dating again."

"Okay." But Sierra stared into the air as if there were some image only she could see.

How had April not seen it? Nick as Sierra's stepfather. Luca as Sierra's grandfather. They were so special to her already. To bring them in closer, for Sierra to have two men she could count on as she put the pieces of her life together …

April closed her eyes. It was no good. It would destroy Sierra for April to start a romance with Nick she didn't think she could follow through on.

Sierra pulled the blanket close. "Funny, Mom. I never thought of Mr. Foster like that. I don't know. If you liked him, I think I could get used to the idea." She shook off her bewildered gaze. "But what Mr. Prodan and Carlos and I want to do, it's about Mr. Foster's job. If you don't want me to take his letters, I won't. But I've got a plan."

"What kind of plan?"

Sierra just shook her head. "I won't break into anyone's home or anything. You'll see."

Sierra's eyes blazed, and her whole face filled with determination. This was the girl, the one who could not only survive the heartbreak life threw her way but who could take the pain and mold it into something else. April wasn't going to ruin the moment by crying or getting syrupy. She just said, "I guess I will see. Let me know if I can help."

Chapter Forty-Two

April sat on the park bench. The park was quiet. An elderly couple strolled hand in hand on the jogging trail, and a mother helped her daughter down the slides.

"April."

Nick stood in the sunlight. Just the sound of his voice warmed her. She'd gone too many days without hearing it.

He took a seat at the other end of the bench. He was thinner, and dark circles under his eyes gave evidence of lost sleep. But the haunted look she'd seen in his eyes last time was gone, replaced by stillness.

What was Luca thinking? Nick was a man without a job, and his job had fueled his passion for life. This was no time to discuss her feelings for him.

She looked off to a wide patch of grass, wondering if he remembered meeting her here last fall. She'd been unable to take the picture of the men performing Tai Chi, and he'd taken her to his friend's to look at the photos in the back of the carpet shop.

"How's Sierra?" Nick asked.

"She's doing well. I know she's still got some dark days ahead, but I think she's turned a corner." The memory of talking with Sierra last night still left her in awe.

That snippet of news pleased him, but he let the conversation drop. He was here at her invitation, so he waited.

"It's Truth or Dare time again," April said softly. "Are you up for it?"

"I'll take truth for a thousand, Alex." He was quick on the uptake, references to Jeopardy and all, but despite the dry humor, his face remained guarded.

"How did I know you'd pick truth?"

Nick smiled. "In love and war …"

"I was really hoping for a dare. I'm not much with the truth." She let out a nervous laugh. Did he read the pain in her eyes, because his was spilling out for anyone to see.

A crow landed at their feet and began to peck at the grass. A runner sprinted by. She'd rehearsed what she would say to Nick, had alternate backup versions even, but her mind drew a blank. All she could think of was the space between them.

"I'm so sorry, Nick. The truth is hard for me." She slowed her breathing. "I don't know why I asked you to come here. You've already got so much stress. You don't need mine."

He reached his arm along the back of the bench. "It's okay, April. If you want to talk, I want to listen."

She took a deep breath. "I don't do truth. Painting rainbows over rainstorms. That's been the rule of my life. Fourteen years of my husband going in and out of hospitals and trying one drug cocktail after another, fighting a life-sucking, mind-altering depression I didn't even know existed. And I smiled and I said, 'It's going to get better' like a never-changing chorus, and I acted as if I believed God would make sense of our pain."

Her voice trembled and Nick slid close, taking her hand, enveloping it in both of his.

"I never once said, 'There's no hope left.' I wouldn't even allow myself to think the words. The only time I let my guard down was to encourage Gary to go to the history conference in Italy. He was doing better. I didn't say I needed him to leave me and Sierra alone for a couple of weeks because I was suffocating waiting for the latest treatment to stop working as they always did. But I guess Gary had learned to decode my words by then, because he went to the conference even though he knew he wasn't ready for it. He went to the conference. And he came home in a casket."

A muscle twitched in Nick's cheek, and his hands around hers grew tight. She looked out at the pond, gathering herself.

"So that night you kissed me last winter," April went on, her voice growing thick. "You were so alive with strength and goodness, and I just wanted you to hold me. But I told myself with all our family issues, we'd break each other's hearts and Sierra's and your dad's in the mix. I told you it would never work between us. I tried to find something sweet to soften my rejection of you and what was happening between us, so I said you were like family. I couldn't even tell myself the truth."

She looked up at the sky. "I can't let you love me, Nick. And I can't love you back. How can I? My husband is dead because of me."

He put his arms around her and rested his face against the top of her head. He didn't need to speak. His presence was enough. For now she let Nick's arms surround her and savored his comfort, the way a drunk must relish his last drink before going sober.

Nick kissed her temple, kissed her lips so briefly she ached for more, but he drew back. "April, you couldn't have stopped him. If your husband had stayed in town with you, and you kept painting rainbows for him and giving him that golden smile of yours, eventually, he would still have killed himself. You know that."

She looked into Nick's eyes, trying to hold on to that thought.

"You couldn't give him what the medicine and the doctors couldn't."

She drew a ragged breath.

"Some things aren't in your power. Your husband's condition was one of them."

April nodded, numb. It was true, but it didn't feel any more real.

Nick took her face in his hands. "I'll tell you one more thing that's not in your power. Me. You can't tell me I can't love you, because I do." He leaned in to kiss her forehead. "April, sweet April. You were right all along. Our lives are complicated." His voice grew rough. "We each have our own grief. Maybe we would add more rips to each other's lives. Maybe we'd hurt each other and Sierra and my dad."

He raised her hand and kissed her fingers. "But it's too late to worry about breaking my heart. You've broken it already."

CHAPTER FORTY-THREE

Two days later, April got out of the car with her camera, taking each step into the park carefully, as if she carried a bomb that would explode if she took a wrong step. If a person wanted to live in the light, they needed to get in the light, so she came to the park and, on an impulse, had brought her Nikon. It was early still, cool, and the park appeared empty.

Sierra and Carlos had been busy this week setting their plan into motion. Tomorrow would tell whether it would succeed or fail.

She found the bench, hers and Nick's now, and sank onto the seat. She was in the light, but she didn't feel the light.

Sierra was making progress.

Luca had told his story and appeared stronger, physically and mentally.

Ms. Baines had already put one of her photos on the gallery wall, and several customers had shown interest.

But April had felt so bruised since her talk with Nick. Talking about Gary hadn't brought healing. It had brought a terrible, soul-deep ache. Maybe it had been there the whole time and she'd been smiling too hard to notice.

She closed her eyes. A soft whisper seemed to carry on the breeze. *There is a time to tear and a time to mend.*

The Bible verse didn't bring much comfort. She'd been waiting for mending for so long, and every time she hoped, the fault line in her life only seemed to tear deeper into the surface.

The breeze continued to sift around her, ruffling through the grass, tattering the flags at the park entrance. A profusion of Indian paintbrush grew on the levee, and rushes lined the banks of the pond. Meadow green and petal scarlet and sky blue. How long had it been since she'd seen the colors around her—really seen them? The world had browned like a sixty-year-old photo the day Joe called to say Gary had killed himself.

The colors practically bathed over her now. It was so beautiful, so incredibly easy. She looked up into the cloudless sky as if she might catch the hand that had painted it all still at work.

A woman jogged on the trail with her dog. She stopped and kneeled down to untangle a knot in the leash, looping her arms around the husky's neck, burying her face into his fur, the way someone might give an affectionate hug to a young child. April couldn't help herself. She raised the camera, zoomed, and clicked. The woman stood and was gone.

April tilted the screen to avoid the glare. It was all there on the camera: the woman's patent loneliness, how she poured her life into a simple dog because almost certainly he was the only one to love her back. It was an image of loneliness and love, sorrow and affection. The pixels told the truth.

She aimed once more, taking a picture of the rushes on the pond, bowed in the wind, and the water rippling to the center.

A bit of poison drained from her. The ache wasn't gone, but it was a moment—His promise that life would not be filled with thorns forever. One day there would be pine tree instead of brier.

Color would replace dullness. Moment by moment, she would lay Gary to rest and life would return.

CHAPTER FORTY-FOUR

It was 8:00 a.m. again, and the first tardy bell would be ringing. Nick went to his knees at the windowsill. "If not this, then what, Lord?"

He couldn't imagine a future without students strutting into his class, masking the fact that they were only kids who needed somebody to care.

The doorbell rang and he sighed, wondering if he should let the visitor move on. But he gathered himself and descended the stairs. He didn't bother to comb his hair, and he was re-wearing yesterday's T-shirt.

Downstairs, Nick closed and opened his eyes, as if the sight outside might go away like the bizarre dream it appeared to be. Outside his window, a crowd of kids had gathered, and more wound down the driveway. Cars lined the curb. He smoothed a hand through his hair and opened the door. Ryan Brannigan stood in front of him, but there were more than a hundred kids behind him. At least half, maybe more, of all his students.

Ryan stepped forward. "Mr. F., the sub isn't teaching us anything. We decided if you couldn't come to the mountain, we'd bring the mountain to you."

Nick stepped onto the porch. His students. The greater part of his classes somehow had transported themselves ten miles down the road. For him. They'd come for him. But he had to say the practical thing. "Look, guys," he said loudly enough for them all to hear, "I can't tell you how much this means to me. But I can't let you do this."

They turned belligerent faces toward him.

"If what I taught you means anything, then you know you have to stay in school. You have to get your diploma, and you can't do it by skipping class."

Behind Ryan, Teresa Muñoz stepped forward. "We're not skipping class, Mr. Foster. We're having a walkout."

"It amounts to the same thing."

"That ain't true," she protested. "You said sometimes you got to stand up for something. Like Atticus Finch in the mockingbird book, right? Well, we say it ain't right for them to take your job away for protecting someone. And we're going to stand up and take the consequences."

How could he argue with that? He'd be arguing with himself. He pushed open the door and stood out of the way. Students crammed into his living room, onto the stairs, into his kitchen, and still there wasn't enough room. The rest crowded onto the porch and the sidewalk.

Elena called from the stairs. "So what are we going to learn today, Mr. F?"

He opened his palms. "I don't have a lesson prepped."

They laughed, because they all knew he never followed the lesson anyway. He looked toward the books on his coffee table to scan them for ideas, when he noticed some of the kids weren't current students. Some of them were too old.

First, he recognized Jade Miller who left his class, what—four, five years ago? She grinned when his gaze landed on her. "I thought you might have more to say than my professors at Georgetown, Mr. F."

He looked out the open door. Amy Romero, who provided him with boxes of books from the bookstore she managed now, waved from the sidewalk. Robert Balderas, who was a reporter on the local news, spoke to someone in the doorway. Some of the students went back fourteen years, to the beginning of his teaching career. His kids had grown up. They'd rallied for him, even flown in from other parts of the country for him. He raked a hand across his jaw. He couldn't take it in.

And then someone walked through the crowd who was too old to have ever attended his class. Students stepped aside and made way for him to take the stool at Nick's feet. "I thought also I might learn from you today, Nicu. I would make a better student than a father, it seems."

Something caught in Nick's throat. Was that an apology from his father?

"And I have heard, of course, that you are an excellent teacher."

And a compliment?

He looked into the kitchen where Sierra and Carlos huddled in a corner. He looked around, hoping for another who'd never attended his class, but April was nowhere to be seen.

"I don't know what to say," he said in a choked voice.

"That's a first," someone called from the kitchen, and everyone laughed.

"You guys are the best. You're ready to teach the lesson yourselves." He looked over the crowd. "Who set this up?"

Dad nodded toward Sierra. "It was her idea. She has been on the telephone constantly this week."

Sierra withdrew into the corner as all eyes turned to her. He thought of the determination, the conversations it must have taken to get all these people here. And for a girl like Sierra. "Turned a corner," April had said. "A core of steel," Nick had said. She'd proven them right.

"Thank you, guys." He gave them a rueful smile. "A few days ago I told God I'd walk away from teaching if that was His will, and I meant it. But I won't say it doesn't burn. Teaching … it's a grueling job, but it's who I am. I can't picture myself doing anything else."

He let his gaze sweep the crowd. "I wouldn't change a thing. Seeing every one of you guys here, knowing what you've made of your lives, or will …"—he looked at Sierra—"and seeing her safe. I'd do it ten times over."

He said nothing about what a tough lady Liza was. Having a school walkout would hardly sway her in his favor. But they'd taken a risk for him, and he wanted them to feel their power, if just for a day.

He gave his kids the floor. The lesson of the day turned out to be what his kids had learned in his class. Some touched on a favorite novel or how they learned to appreciate the power of putting their thoughts on paper. Others talked about sticking it out when life got tough.

Katie Stelling stood up and told how, at fifteen, pregnant and ready to drop out of school, she'd found herself in his classroom. She was a second-grade teacher now.

Marc Hernandez, an IT student in college, thanked Nick for helping him get diagnosed with dyslexia. He'd been lost in a sea of underachieving students, and, before Nick, all of his teachers assumed he was just one more kid who didn't see the value in school.

Still others spoke of lessons he didn't realize he'd taught.

Jesse spoke through the open window. "Mr. F. taught me you got to know people. You got to look them in the eye and let them know you see who they are before they'll listen to you."

All day long students came and went, keeping the downstairs full and the sidewalks jammed. Early on, pizzas were delivered, and a few people showed up with takeout, but when word got out about the gathering, the family of one of his students drove up with a catering van and set up a makeshift buffet outside his window. There were tacos, quesadillas, and sopapillas. No one went hungry.

It was after four when Robert Balderas stepped into the living room. "Mr. F., you'll be on television tonight. We've recorded a special. It's airing just before prime time."

Nick took a step back, alarm creeping up his spine. "Robert, I appreciate what you're trying to do, but I can't let you do it. This isn't about going head-to-head with my school. It wouldn't help anybody—not the school, and not me."

Robert blinked, but he stayed where he was. "The special's taped and set to air, Mr. F. It would be impossible to pull it at the last second like this. Besides, it's about time Houston knows what you do for the kids who come through your classes."

Robert inclined his head toward the doorway, and a cameraman walked in. "We left a thirty-second spot open for your comment."

Nick put his hands behind his back. He needed to make this good. He cleared his throat.

The cameraman put up his fingers, going from three to two to one, and Robert spoke into Robert's microphone. "Mr. Foster, what is your response to your suspension and possible termination?"

Nick ignored the camera and looked at Robert. "I'm not going to hide the fact that I violated the school rules. I put the school at risk for legal action and loss of reputation. I didn't keep the principal informed. She was entirely within her rights to suspend me. My only complaint is facing termination on ethical grounds. I believe it *was* ethical to leave my class in order to protect a student from an assault and to keep her identity private so that her mother could be with her when she informed the authorities." He turned to the camera. "That's all I have to say."

Robert and his cameraman left, and over the next hour, Nick's townhouse emptied until only the instigators were left: his old man, Sierra, and Carlos. Nick collapsed onto the sofa. The joy and strain of the day almost made him feel as if he were back in the classroom.

He leaned back against the cushions, ready to relax, until Sierra stood and silently crossed to him with several papers in her hand.

He unfolded them. The first page was an email from the editor of the local newspaper to Sierra. The short note stated that her submission would run in the personal interest section tomorrow.

The second page, written in Sierra's clear, poetic style, told how a teacher she didn't know had pulled her into his classroom and told her she was capable of more and then gave her a second chance to turn in her homework to her teacher. She told how Nick got her talking about what interested her when she flunked her finals, how he protected her from a boy who was threatening her in a stairwell, and last, how he rescued her from a flooding bayou and convinced her that she had the strength to live the life she'd been given.

She wrote it as a story, full of images and dialogue. And she made him out to be the hero of this story. Sierra Wright had found her voice.

He found his own voice surprisingly steady when he spoke. "I expect to see more writing like this from you, Sierra. This is only the first time I'll see your name in print."

———◆▸✕◂◆———

April's absence grated on him. She should be here. As it neared six, he couldn't stand it anymore. He leaned against the kitchen counter and called her at work. "April. Your daughter pulled off quite a show today."

"So I hear," she said softly. "I've been dying to know how it went all day."

His throat was parched. He took the cap off a water bottle and took a sip. "Why don't you come over and find out. There's going to be a special on TV. We'd like you to be here with us when it comes on." He let the line go quiet. "I would like you to be here."

It took her a few beats to answer. "I'll be there."

The special was just beginning when she walked in. Some of the tension drained from him as April found a seat next to his dad. The room was complete. Excitement brightened Sierra's face and April's lit up in response. It was only his old man whose face was drawn as he flexed and unflexed his fingers.

On TV, Robert interviewed his students and colleagues. Former gang members-turned-graduate students and failing students-turned-entrepreneurs told of what Nick's classes meant to them. Teresa, Ryan, and Jesse talked about what a typical day in his classroom was like. Robert included a few video clips of him teaching and working with students. Nick recognized a few segments—one had been taken during student presentations last year; another had been filmed by the school when he'd been nominated for teacher of the year. Interspersed with the classroom segments were views of crowded hallways and the run-down streets outside.

A short segment at the end discussed Nick's suspension, concluding with a clip of Nick's students crowding into his townhouse that morning to support him. In a voice-over, Robert told how, as a student, he sat at the back of his classes unnoticed—until Nick. "Nobody disappeared in Mr. Foster's class. He knew who we were, every one of us."

◆◆◆◆◆

Nick flicked the TV off with the remote. It was Nick and almost two hundred students a year. He put his heart into his work, but he didn't think he was the superteacher portrayed on the show.

No doubt the segment would have Liza breathing dragon's fire. He tried to focus on Liza's fury. He tried to stamp down the thin ray of hope lighting up inside him, but it was all too possible the news segment could have an effect higher up the district chain, and he knew it.

Nick leaned back, looking at the small gathering. A light came to April's eyes as she focused on her daughter. Sierra held Carlos's hand. Her gaze was still locked on the darkened TV, as if the story still played out to its ultimate conclusion on the screen.

April leaned forward. "So do you think you'll get your job back?"

"It's hard to say. The TV special might strike the right note with someone in the district."

"At the very least, all of Houston knows you lost your job for a good cause, and you're the best teacher in town. You'll have job offers from nearby districts."

"Mr. Foster," Carlos said, "all those kids lining up for you and that show on TV—there aren't so many great teachers like that. The school has to pay attention."

Sierra took his hand between both of hers, a smile on her face. Even Dad nodded.

"Maybe," Nick said, trying to keep his expectations from running past reality

"You're not just a good teacher, Nick. You're a gifted one. You will have a job come fall."

Golden words from the lady with the golden smile. Even the sun seemed to shine brighter at her words.

April picked up her purse, and Nick couldn't shake off a wave of disappointment. He wanted her here. It was right to be surrounded by the four people in his living room. But Dad looked bone weary.

"I'll drop you off at your house, Luca," April said.

Dad didn't respond.

Nick shot his father a worried glance. "Thanks for coming, Dad, and for your words. They meant a lot to me."

Energy came over Dad's face then, but it was a raw energy that set Nick back. "It was not enough. The words I said to you, Nicu, they were not enough."

Nick moved to the ottoman across from Dad. "It's all I ever asked."

April motioned to Sierra and Carlos and started to ease toward the door, away from the private moment. But Dad called her back. "Please do not leave, April. I am only able to say what I say now because of you. You will help me if I go astray."

April came closer and put her hand on Dad's shoulder. Dad raised his hand to keep it there.

He turned to Nick. "I am not good at speaking. I want you to listen."

"I'm listening."

Dad's eyes cleared. "I am very proud of the man you have become. You are a fine son, a fine teacher, and much more. But instead of telling you, I have driven you to anger. I am like the sparrows that live in my yard. They can sing only one song. I could only sing the song of death I learned as a young man. Even for my own son, whom I loved, I could not learn another song. I have sinned against you, Nicu, and I ask for your forgiveness."

Nick drew in a sharp breath. He thought he was too old and sure of himself to need his father to say he believed in him. But the words rocked through him like a gale-force wind.

"*Tată.*" The Romanian word slipped out. He had never called his father *Tată*. As a child he would have called him *Tati—Daddy.*

Dad looked up at him, stunned.

Nick forced the words out. "*Tată, binențeles că te iert.*"

Sierra translated quietly for April and Carlos. "He said, 'Dad, of course, I forgive you.'"

Dad looked at April. "My son," he said. "My son has not spoken to me in Romanian since he was four years old. It is the only forgiveness I need."

CHAPTER FORTY-FIVE

April watched father and son together. Their blue eyes blazed at each other, a matching severity on their faces. To a stranger, it might seem they were locked in an argument. To April, it looked like love. She imagined capturing the image of anguish and forgiveness sorting themselves out with her camera. It would be a picture to be proud of.

She thought of her topaz book sitting at home with Luca's story. She'd give it to Nick soon. He was ready to read it. And when he was done, she'd give it to Sierra. It would do so much for her to see what Luca went through. And here he was, right beside them, getting stronger every day.

Next to her, Carlos leaned down to Sierra with a heartbreaking smile. "You hungry, Brown Eyes?"

April felt a twinge of worry, just the normal thoughts of a mother with a teenage daughter—broken hearts and teenage hormones.

"Hey, Mom." Sierra came to her side. "Can Carlos and I get something to eat?"

April put her arm around Sierra's shoulder. "You did great, Sierra. You were brilliant, really. I'm so proud of you."

This time, Sierra didn't pull away. She put her arm around April briefly before slipping off to join Carlos.

"Have her home by ten, Carlos," April said.

He smiled at April as though he guessed what she was thinking. "I'll have her home on time, Mrs. Wright, safe and sound."

———————◆◆◆◆◆———————

The sun was setting, sending amber flames across the sky. April stood on the deck, letting father and son have a moment to themselves. After a few minutes, the door opened and closed behind her. She didn't turn to see who it was. She knew by his step.

"Hey," she said, as Nick joined her.

"Hey, yourself." He leaned his hands on the railing.

She turned to look at him. He was still too thin, but that lost look in his eyes had been replaced by a gleam, a gleam that lit some place within her that had been dark for too long.

"How are you feeling about everything?" she asked.

"Those kids really came through for me. It's the most hope I've had in weeks."

April looked off into the pine trees. "There's a lot of that going around lately. Hope's a seductive thing."

"I know what you mean." He looked at her with a steady, searching gaze.

"Oh?" she said weakly.

"I laid some of my deepest wishes on God's altar earlier this week. And when it looked as if He might be returning two of them to me—my job and my dad—it occurred to me He might just bless me with the third as well."

Warmth crept up April's neck and into her face.

He had a boy's earnestness in his eyes when he looked at her. It felt as though the years were stripped from her and she was a girl again. For a fleeting moment they were two kids without decades of hurt and doubt behind them.

"April, am I wrong to hope?"

A pulse beat in her throat as two different answers fought it out. "Nick. It would break my heart if I brought ugliness into your life. It's tempting to think I can open my hands and let Gary's death flutter off like a bird in flight." Her voice seemed to fade away into the evening air. "I've tried that though. It doesn't work."

He moved his hand beside hers on the railing, a finger's width away. "I'm not asking you to put your grief aside, April. It's too real to put behind you. I'm asking you if I can be part of your life while you heal." He paused, and a remnant of his emptiness called out to hers. "I'm asking if you'll be a part of mine while I put things back together with my dad and my job. Because I want you beside me, in good times and bad."

She closed her eyes, wanting to believe, wanting so much to be whole enough to have something to give Nick in return.

Nick stroked the back of her hand. "I wonder how many years my father lost because no one coaxed his story out of him. He lost decades waiting for someone like you to help him face his past."

She opened her eyes, finding Nick's blue eyes focused on her, willing her to have faith in them.

"How long are you willing to spend swallowing your pain, alone, April?"

She had waited and waited for God to heal Sierra's wounds and hers with a quick wash of His Spirit. She'd been so sure that places of pain and suffering were devoid of God's blessings. But God had been with them right in the midst of their pain. Deep calling them into His depths. Today. These last months.

The sky softened to champagne clouds and the pine trees dimmed to silhouettes. How could she not believe? She opened her mouth to speak but could hardly find the words. It had been so long since she had said yes to anything. Nick stood before her, and that gave her the strength she needed.

"Truth or dare," April said, steadying the tremor in her voice.

Nick tipped his head to her, his glasses slipping, and April pushed them back up for him.

"We've had enough truth for today," he said. "How about a dare?"

He leaned down to her, and his arms, solid and strong, drew her to him. As his lips touched hers, the scent of sweet pine drifted up to meet them.

CPSIA information can be obtained at www.ICGtesting.com
Printed in the USA
LVOW05s1842130813

347707LV00004B/834/P